David Kettlehake

Other Books by David Kettlehake

Fever
Strawman
Gray (Book One of The Firebrand Trilogy)
Black (Book Two of The Firebrand Trilogy)
White (Book Three of The Firebrand Trilogy)

Copyright ©2024 by David Kettlehake
All rights reserved

This is a work of fiction. Names, characters, businesses, places, events, locales, and incidents are either the products of the author's imagination or used in a fictitious manner. Any resemblance to actual persons, living or dead, or actual events is purely coincidental.

Library of Congress Control Number: 2024947838

Cover Design by: Alexios Saskalidis
www.facebook.com/187designz

No part of this book may be reproduced or transmitted in any form or by any means without written permission from the publisher.

For information please contact:
Brother Mockingbird, LLC
www.brothermockingbird.org
ISBN: 978-1-960226-18-1 Paperback
ISBN: 978-1-960226-23-5 EBook

For Dick Francis,
British steeplechase jockey and mystery writer,
whose books have given me so much joy and inspiration.

1

Boon Dohir woke to a blistering band of pain coursing through his head, as if the space between his ears were being vigorously flossed with barbed wire.

He cracked open an eye and studied the view overhead. Above him were perforated acoustic tiles, roughly the same type and size he remembered seeing in every classroom from kindergarten through high school. These particular tiles, however, were stained a foul yellow he associated with age and decades of committed smoking. He considered the view a little longer, eventually convinced he'd never seen this exact ceiling before. Unfortunately for him, this wasn't nearly the surprise it should have been.

He was naked except for a sheet draped sloppily across his midsection. Boon glanced around, observing the lamp with the crooked shade, the dingy walls, and a closed door. Morning light slanted in from a window on the far side of the room. To his right lay a naked girl, their shared sheet barely covering her shapely ass and legs. She was turned away so he couldn't see her face, but he was pretty sure it wouldn't matter. He hadn't the foggiest idea who she was, and there was little hope that a good look would enlighten him. The girl had very short, blond hair and a tattoo of a dove on the back of her neck. The dove held something in its beak, a green twig or leaf. He couldn't tell which in the dim light.

Aspirin, he thought darkly, the pain behind his eyes now throbbing in harmony with the hammering of his heart. *I need aspirin. And coffee. Gallons of coffee.*

With extreme care, he crept from the bed, planted his feet on the matted carpet, then stood and willed himself not to puke. Several waves of hot nausea nearly turned an already sketchy morning into an epically terrible one, but the threat passed after a minute of intense concentration. Now coated in a full-body sweat, he padded softly around the small space and tried to locate his clothes. Without too much trouble he managed to recover everything but his left shoe, which he finally found lodged behind a chair in the corner. Dohir bundled his belongings up in his arms and silently slid through the door into the next room, which turned out to be a small kitchen. Dirty dishes were piled in the sink, and a dusty, wilted blue flower in a University of Cincinnati mug was on the windowsill. If the naked girl had any roommates, they weren't up yet, which suited him just fine. That part *never* stopped being awkward as hell. Boon dressed and let himself out the front door and into the cool June morning.

The houses up and down the street were old two-story frame structures from the early 30s and in various states of upkeep, mostly shabby, with a scant few newly painted and nicely landscaped. Through the morning haze, the downtown Cincinnati skyline was visible a few miles away, which helped orient him. He fumbled his phone from his pocket and saw it was only a few minutes after six in the morning. He clicked on his map app, and through the magic of GPS found his exact location, pleasantly surprised to see how close he was to home. His apartment was in Over-the-Rhine, one of the more ethnically diverse parts of the city. OTR was an eclectic patchwork of neighborhoods and a mélange of economic levels and ethnicities. He considered Ubering home, but in the end figured the exercise and fresh air might work some of the alcohol toxins out of his system. There were several other people already out and about on this Sunday morning, some with leashed dogs and armed with the requisite plastic bags, a few with travel cups of coffee. If any of them could tell he was doing the walk of shame, they didn't let on. Thankfully, the queasiness in his stomach was beginning to fade.

Within a few blocks, the area began to look familiar. After he'd walked another five minutes, he was right around the corner from his apartment. He stopped at a local coffee shop, one tucked between a trendy diner and a mom-and-pop hardware store. He ordered the largest to-go cup possible, black, which he paid for in cash. He always paid in cash. The young girl who checked him out smiled warmly and thanked him, mercifully not commenting on his appearance, which had to be frightful considering how he felt. He didn't say anything, just over-tipped her a few bucks, and continued towards his apartment. Boon sipped the scalding coffee and felt himself edging towards humanity again, albeit only in tiny increments.

He turned into an alley next to a small bread store called Loafers. This particular section of town had already been partially gentrified. It was a mixture of run-down and gated pawn shops, check-cashing stores, and fresh new restaurants and bistros. In the evenings, he was as likely to step over a homeless guy passed out in his own piss as he was to see a well-dressed couple out on the town. Shiny new Mercedes and BMWs vied for parking spaces with rusty pickups and tricked out Subarus. He passed by the bakery and the smell of fresh bread enveloped him in its homey, old-fashioned aroma. Boon stopped and breathed deeply, the warm scent giving him a welcome flashback to his youth. His mother used to bake bread on weekends, fluffy white loaves with thick crusts that always burned his fingers when he cut away a slice too soon, which he inevitably did. The bakery was one of the reasons he'd chosen this place.

He walked down the narrow alley to a door in the side of the brick building, the smell of bread clinging to his clothes in a yeasty cologne. The black door appeared ordinary but was actually heavily fortified and would hold up to anything shy of a battering ram and grim determination. He should know, since he'd installed it himself. He entered a series of numbers on a keypad before pressing his thumb against a sensor. He felt several clunks, and the door swung inward. Boon ascended a flight of steps that creaked and muttered with age and his two hundred pounds. When he arrived at the top, he flipped a light switch and fluorescents flickered into life. He entered his apartment.

It was a single large, plain room partitioned by furniture and structural support poles, the walls and ceiling painted a noncommittal gray. For all the personality the room exuded, it could have been cut and pasted directly from an Ikea catalog. His low, neatly made bed was directly in front of him and a small kitchenette was tucked off to the right. Contrary to the house he'd just left, there wasn't a dirty dish in sight. A sleek black leather couch was parked precisely in front of a flat-screen TV. There was no other furniture and no sign that anyone else ever frequented the flat, which, in fact, no one ever did. A tiny bathroom was tucked out of sight behind the kitchen. To anyone's eye, it was an external display of a highly organized and tidy mind.

He sighed and headed to the bathroom where he downed three aspirins, hardly noticing how their bitter taste lingered on his tongue. After stripping off his clothes, he spent the next fifteen minutes in the shower, scrubbing himself vigorously until his skin was nearly stop-sign red. He spent an inordinate amount of time and attention cleaning his crotch and groin. He forced himself to remain there with his head down until the hot water ran out. Shivering, he finally stepped out and toweled himself off.

With forced care and precision, he shaved, brushed back his black hair, and dressed in fresh jeans and a T-shirt. Barefoot, he switched off the light and made the short trip back into the main living area.

Boon sat in silence for a time before retrieving an expensive acoustic guitar from a closet. He strummed a few chords, then attempted several songs, some Ed Sheeran, a few Beatles classics, and something from REM he'd been wrestling with, but his head was still aching and he wasn't much in the mood. Besides that, he wasn't very good, which irked him to no end since he was good at pretty much everything else. It pained him to know that he had music in his heart, but very little in his hands. With a frown, he placed the instrument next to the TV and sat back down, wondering how he was going to fill the rest of the day. Contrary to most people, he hated weekends. They were filled with too many empty minutes that allowed painful memories to chisel through his carefully constructed defenses.

He stared out the window at the rows of buildings across from his apartment and wished for the day to be over, even though it had barely begun. Finally, he got up and went to the kitchen where he mixed himself a tall gin and tonic.

What the hell, he thought. It was five o'clock somewhere.

2

It was Monday, and Dohir arrived at his office at six o'clock in the morning, long before any of his employees. He parked his black BMW outside an aging factory on Cincinnati's near west side, then walked to the door and killed the central alarm. The huge space inside was dark and reeked of machine oil and burnt steel. It was a particular stink that seemed to stick like grease to the inside of his nose. He followed the walkway to the center of the building until he came to a metal staircase hugging the wall. Boon held on to the handrail to steady himself as he went, his head still pounding from yesterday's all-day binge. He spent some time keying in the code to the heavy door since, like his apartment, it was much more substantial than it first appeared. Once inside, lights buzzed and clicked into life with the hum of a tranquil beehive.

The office was not much of an office, not in a traditional sense. It was roughly forty-by-forty feet and outfitted with little more than chairs and old Steelcase desks. A massive electrical panel on the back wall was filled with switches, each labeled with names like *Conveyor–Paint Station*, or *Main Belt–Oven*. There were no computers to be seen, but on every desk squatted expansive monitors. Boon peered down through a window at the dark shop floor a story below him. Nothing moved down there. The huge old lathes and presses were silent, and the meandering conveyor belts were as still as snakes on a frosty morning. He knew that dust would continue to cling and gather upon everything, until decades from now the hulks might become one with the earth, forgotten dinosaurs of a proud industrial past. He went to the control panel and flicked a few switches. Overhead lights blinked on and illuminated a path from the main door to the office.

In another corner near the door were a dozen small TV screens. Half of them were showing multiple views outside, while the rest were dormant. He watched the live ones with detached interest as vehicles of all types drove past the factory, the expected mix of cars, SUVs, along with the occasional pickup truck or van. A green and white Metro bus trundled by, thick diesel smoke belching from its exhaust stack as it motored away. None piqued his attention until a white police car eased up to the four-way stop. Boon kept an eye on the cruiser until it pulled away. He saw it pass through three different monitors, eventually exiting his field of vision completely. He pursed his lips for just a moment, then prepped an old-fashioned Bunn coffee maker for duty, emptying old grounds before rinsing and filling two pots from the small sink. There was a fogged mirror above the sink, and his reflection stared dispassionately back at him, the dark eyes and black hair in stark contrast to his light complexion. The surname Dohir had its roots in the Middle East, more specifically northern Syria, he knew. But with his straight nose and pale skin he appeared much more Western than a descendant of the lands once ruled by the Ottoman Empire. He slid the glass coffee pots onto the burners and flipped the switch. Red lights dutifully came on. Comforting hisses issued from the guts of the reliable old machine.

As Boon waited for it to finish, he took a moment and checked out the exterior monitors again. While he watched, a bright red Mini Cooper embellished with a Union Jack on its roof wheeled in and parked smartly by his car. Next to his large German sedan, the hatchback was diminutive, more like a Hot Wheels toy than an actual vehicle. The driver's door swung open and a girl in her mid-twenties hopped out. She was tall and moved easily, possessed of a smooth and natural athleticism that was inherited, not learned. She wasn't bulky or overly muscled, but finely toned and visibly comfortable in her own well-defined skin. She wore a tight magenta-colored top, with spaghetti straps and black capris. Even in the monitors, he could see the flow of muscles move beneath the bare skin of her arms and legs. She was quite stunning and was sure to turn heads wherever she went. She slammed the door with enough authority that her tiny car shuddered, then strode briskly toward the factory. Her black hair was thick but short and smooth and was cut in a harsh diagonal slash where it touched her neck. She flipped her hair out of her eyes with an unconscious twist of her head. Boon always expected a girl like her to be adorned with tattoos and piercings, but that wasn't the case at all. He knew her as Sasha, although he doubted that was her real name. If he had to describe her in one word, it would be *intense*. He saw her slide a clear container of some thick liquid the color of pond water from her backpack and sip on it through a straw. The office walls trembled as the heavy door boomed shut behind her.

Before Sasha had ascended the steps another car pulled into the lot, this one a gray convertible Mustang, its black top snugged up tight against the chill of the morning. A trim Black man with very short hair eased out. Unlike Sasha, he walked slowly and with purpose, each movement thoughtful and calculated, nothing rushed or done in haste. His mouth was puckered up in a whistle as he gathered up a slim leather briefcase from the back seat, smoothed his silky silver shirt, and ambled toward the building. He went by the name of Miles, a name Boon always figured was a tribute to Miles Davis, but that was just a guess. He didn't know if Miles played music, but the man could generally be found humming some tune under his breath or tapping his fingers in an even cadence on his desk. He was almost always in good spirits, too, which Dohir found both endearing and a little annoying.

As Sasha and Miles entered the office, several more cars arrived, their drivers grabbing briefcases or backpacks as they headed inside. Boon saw the people he knew as Clem, Patrice, and a vastly overweight and bearded man who went by Sir Jim. In no time Clem and Patrice were in the office with their laptops out, plugged into the monitors and fired up, but several minutes ticked by before Sir Jim's impressive bulk heaved into the doorway. He was huffing and puffing, his triple chin quivering, the trip up the stairs clearly not to his liking. Sweat beaded his broad forehead like condensation on the inside windows of a sauna, and he grasped the doorjamb for support. The skin around his eyes and mouth was an unhealthy pink tinged with the green of new grass.

"Boon, my dear lad," he said after he'd had a moment to catch his breath. His voice was a rich, deep baritone, and his diction was precise, each letter and vowel spoken with intent. With a voice like that he could be doing movie trailers, and Boon wondered for the hundredth time if he'd ever done any professional voice work. "I'll never understand why in heaven's name you picked such a locale. No elevator? The second floor? You'll be the death of me."

Dohir smiled lightly. "Sorry, Sir Jim," he replied, but there was no apology in his voice. "It fits the bill better than anything else. And the price was right."

Sasha didn't look up from where she was plugging her laptop into the monitor. "It's good for you, old man. If you don't take better care of yourself you're going to go tits up any day."

The big man perched on the edge of a desk. The floor underneath him creaked, and something structural may have popped. "My dear, just because you prefer to flagellate yourself on those devilish weight machines day and night doesn't mean the rest of us should. I prefer a more sedate pace to life, thank you."

Sasha still didn't look up. Her fingers were performing a blurred dance on the keyboard as she logged in and booted up multiple programs. Screens blinked open and closed so quickly that anyone susceptible certainly would have suffered a seizure. "Whatever. It's your funeral, big fella."

During this back-and-forth banter, the other three were hanging out by the coffee machine waiting for it to finish its time-honored task. Patrice was a slightly heavy woman with a round, doughy face and very curly brown hair. Boon knew little about her past except that she was originally from out east, but had lived in Ohio so long that all traces of an accent were gone. She was watching the interaction between Sasha and Sir Jim silently, her plain mouth pursed in disapproval of the younger woman. Boon was never sure what the source of the friction was between them, but the two had very little to do with each other. On the plus side, Patrice was phenomenal with numbers and numeric sequences, a talent bordering on the savant. She was a living, breathing calculator, and was able to accurately quantify the value of whatever complex task Boon could toss in her generous lap. She was invaluable and more than worth whatever friction she generated. Most of the time.

Boon waited with controlled patience while the Monday morning routine wrapped up. Once they were all seated and staring at him, he stepped towards the center of the room.

"Okay, let's get down to business. I was reviewing the pipeline, and it's starting to look a little too thin for my liking. There aren't nearly enough deals in the Discover or Assess phases. I know we've closed some pretty decent ones lately, which is great, but we need to keep that pipeline full."

Sir Jim cleared his throat, a deep rumble that bordered on the palpable. "I've got quite a few leads to start on. They're only cold calls at this point, which is why I've not moved them into Discover yet. Give me a few days and I'll see where we stand. I'm sure a few of them will come to fruition."

Boon thanked him. "I realize yours are typically smaller dollar amounts, but every bit counts toward the whole. Who else has something for me?"

Sasha took a sip from the foul-looking green drink in her container, her cheeks collapsing as she sucked hard on the straw. Her smooth black hair was parted on the side and she had to brush it behind her right ear to keep it from falling into her face, which it did anyway. "I'm still working on that coding lead. The one Clem was telling you about. Remember?"

"This is the one from last week?" Boon asked.

"Yeah."

"Good. One of you give me an update, please."

The tall man cleared his throat. When Clem spoke, his Southern drawl was thick and easy, a voice certain to put the wary at ease and the unwary to sleep. He had an infectious, lopsided grin that rarely left his face. He was a warm blue to Sasha's bright red.

"Like the pretty lady said," he began, "we've been doing research into some home banking apps popular with a whole boatload of banks and credit unions around the country. I got some intel from a few underground listservs I like to frequent, bless them. The chatter I've heard is that there's a small flaw in the coding that we can manipulate. We may be able to do something with that. It's a long shot, but y'all know that sometimes long shots can pay off handsomely."

Boon agreed. "They certainly can. Okay, keep digging into that and let me know. I don't want to spend too much time on that unless we've got some proof it'll pay off. Good work. Miles, what about you?"

Miles smoothed his shirt and sat up. His voice was soft but strong, confident without being arrogant. Family history had predetermined that he was going to be short in stature but had also blessed him with the ability to command respect from others, including everyone gathered here. It wasn't at all unnatural for people to stop whatever they were doing when he spoke. "I'm still working on that credit card deal we talked about last week, but I'm not sure it's going to amount to anything. There's been so much in the news lately about plastic card fraud that this may be a bust. I'll know more later this week."

"If it works, it's worth a lot," Patrice interjected. "According to my math, it could be a huge deal."

Boon nodded. "Thanks. Keep working on that, Miles, and we'll check back later. And just to bring everyone up to speed, I've got the Marsden deal I'm going to try and close today or tomorrow. I'll know more soon. If I can wrap it up, it'll do enough to keep the lights on and the creditors at bay for a while. We might all get vacations, too. Any questions?"

Most of them smiled or chuckled at his reference to keeping the creditors at bay. He waited a few seconds, but no one had anything else to add.

"Excellent. It's a new week, people, so let's get busy. Good luck, and let me know if you need anything. Happy hunting, everyone."

The morning wore on. This group had been together, off and on, for about a year, so for the most part they knew what to expect from each other. Which is not to say that they got along every minute. Boon sat at his desk near the door and quietly worked on the Marsden deal, all while keeping a watchful eye on Sasha and Clem. She was not always easy to work with, and at times could be a downright pain in the ass, as he knew from experience. But if anyone could handle her, it would be the laid-back Southerner. By her own admission, she was a tech geek, more comfortable interfacing with computers than people, and with a tendency to hammer through problems that sometimes needed a gentler touch. Clem's easy-going ways were a good yin to her yang as he eased her through interactions that were outside of her comfort zone. She was a "guy's girl" who tended to get along better with men than women. She was in good hands with Clem.

At lunchtime, Sir Jim happily pronounced that he'd unexpectedly closed three deals already. The total was about twenty thousand dollars, which buoyed everyone's spirits considerably. It wasn't much in the grand scheme of things, Boon understood, but small victories were victories nonetheless, so he sprung for pizza for the office: gluten-free veggie for Sasha, meat lovers for Sir Jim, and a smattering of everything else for the rest. Having them delivered was out of the question, so he picked them up himself and hustled back to the office while they were still hot. His Bimmer reeked of pepperoni and would for days, but the morale boost was well worth it. Sometimes small gestures paid big dividends, even if they were gluten-free and covered in cooked pineapple, a combination he found more disgusting than appetizing.

He worked on the Marsden deal all afternoon, gathering more personal information and digging deeply into the man's past. The stars were aligning nicely so far and he had high hopes for success. He already had everything he needed for the phone company and had laid the groundwork at the bank up in Dayton, which was more than half the battle. Others in his position might have rushed through and tried to slam the deal home, but that wasn't his way. He was methodical and thoughtful and never did anything in haste. Well, not in business anyway. He was a planner, and for him, the devil wasn't just in the details; the details were everything.

When he next looked up it was after five o'clock. He couldn't believe the day had flown by so quickly, but sometimes that happened. He leaned back in his chair and intertwined his fingers, flexing and cracking his knuckles loudly. Sasha glanced at him and began powering down her computer, picking up on his nonverbal cues. The others stood and talked amongst themselves for a moment while they gathered up their gear.

"Not a bad day today, people," he announced to the room. "No big closings, but that happens. Let's all be here tomorrow nice and early so we can get a jump on it. And everyone be thinking about how we can close a few more deals before the end of the week, okay?"

Sasha gathered up her computer and flipped her hair out of her face with a sideways look at him. She hoisted her backpack over a shoulder and nearly bolted out the door without a word to the others, same as always. Patrice and Clem chatted quietly and said goodnight to him as they passed. With a loud groan, Sir Jim forced his bulk from his beleaguered chair and patted Boon's shoulder heavily as he ambled by, murmuring that he'd see him in the morning, cursed steps notwithstanding. Miles was the only one left as Boon moved around the office and powered down the monitors.

"Got any plans for tonight?" the trim man asked.

Dohir didn't answer immediately. He continued prowling around the room, pushing in chairs, turning off the coffee maker, and tossing out a few stained paper cups. It was part of his daily routine, and routines like this were very comforting to him.

"Nothing. I might go work out. Why?"

Miles shrugged. "I'm headed to a little club near downtown. It's amateur jazz night. Most of the acts will certainly suck, but some aren't too hateful. Thought you might want to join me."

Boon smiled at him before he continued tidying the office. "Thanks, but no."

"You sure? It might be fun. And we can heckle the acts that aren't any good. It's expected, and that alone is worth the price of admission."

"I'm sure. Thanks, anyway."

Miles raised an eyebrow as if debating saying something more. Instead, he gently placed his laptop inside his briefcase. He decisively snapped the latches home, the two clicks loud in the quiet office.

"I know we're not supposed to fraternize after hours, Boon. But damn, I don't think one night out on the town in a dark club is going to hurt anything. In all the time I've known you, I swear I've never seen you have any fun or do anything outside the office. That's just not healthy, man."

Dohir went to the door and killed the lights, a clear indication that the conversation was over. Miles sighed and walked out. He began whistling a tune, a song Boon recognized but couldn't immediately place. Something from the sixties or early seventies? It would bug him until he figured it out, which was probably what Miles had intended. The earworm was already boring into his head and he glared at Miles, who just winked at him playfully while his precise whistling never missed a beat. Boon shut and locked the door behind them and together they exited the factory. Each man got into his own car and drove away without another word. The inside of Boon's still reeked of pizza.

Twenty minutes later, he was back at his apartment. The quiet, sterile place elicited no emotional response from him, it was simply a few hundred square feet where he slept and spent time away from work. He purposefully bypassed the cabinet where he stored his liquor and changed into gym shorts, a T-shirt, and sneakers. In no time he was behind the wheel again and navigating the narrow streets of Over-the-Rhine. He merged onto the interstate and drove south across the Ohio River into Kentucky. A short while later he parked outside a small, privately owned gym not far from the Newport Aquarium. The facility was more geared to boxing and fighting than to the casual workout crowd, as evidenced by its two elevated rings and dozens of speed bags dangling like rows of obsidian tears along the walls. But there were also free weights galore, plenty of treadmills, a score of heavy bags, plus a few climbing machines. He didn't have to show a membership card at the door, and there was no one sitting at a desk checking if you belonged or not. It was that kind of place. Boon simply walked in and tossed his keys and phone in a cubby by the door. He was hit with a mix of sweat and high humidity, with hints of leather and cleaning products. It didn't look like much and was definitely not one of the pricey chains, but it was tidy and clean. Best of all no one felt the need to strike up a conversation. Boon liked it.

Standing outside the nearest ring and staring into it was the owner, a middle-aged Black man named Duke. He had been a boxer in his day, as anyone could see by the unnatural angle of his nose and a pair of lumpy, misshapen ears. Duke had a voice as raspy and harsh as a lifelong smoker, but he somehow made himself heard above the fighters going toe-to-toe on the canvas. Boon checked out the two in the ring and wasn't surprised one of them was Sasha. After all, she was the one who'd recommended this place to him.

"No, no, turn your body to the side, Sasha. You're showing too much. Be a smaller target!" Duke yelled. "Don't open yourself up like that!"

Sasha had on headgear and thin, lightweight training gloves. She was also wearing pads that strapped to her bare feet and laced up above her ankles to protect her shins. The tight top with the thin straps she'd worn at the office was gone, replaced by a bulky T-shirt and oversized silky shorts. A mouth guard puffed out her lips and cheeks. Her opponent was a young man who easily topped her by six inches and slid around the ring with an easy, sublime grace, almost as if on ice. His long brown hair trailed down his back in a loose ponytail. Even above all the noise, Boon could hear their heavy, liquid breathing around their mouthguards.

As he watched, Sasha took a step back, then shot forward and landed a punch on the side of Ponytail's head. Before he could counter, she jumped backward and had her hands up, shielding her face. Her elbows were tucked in to protect her midsection.

"Sasha!" Duke admonished with a bark. "Go for the combination! Always go for the combination. Punch, and then follow up another strike. Boom, boom! Another jab. A kick. You know better!"

Sasha refocused. She tried a similar move, but this time landed the punch with her left then spun completely around and connected with a powerful backhand that momentarily staggered her taller opponent. He blinked once and shook his head before stepping in with a spinning kick that sliced dangerously through the humid air, just clipping the side of Sasha's headgear. She stumbled, seemingly stunned. Ponytail grinned and pounced, his gloved hands up and ready to deliver a knockout blow. He was about to bring his fist down when she turned and landed a thumping side snap-kick against his midsection with her left foot. He stumbled backward into the ropes. Sasha may have smiled through the mouth guard. Dohir couldn't be sure.

"Crafty, Sasha!" Duke said, laughing and clapping slowly. "Very crafty. I like it."

Boon watched the sparring for another minute before heading to the machines lining the far wall. If Sasha had seen him, she'd given no indication of it, which was just how it was supposed to be. He was wary of even being around her outside of the office.

He stood on the platform at the base of the climbing machine and carefully attached the safety strap. For the next 30 minutes, he blanked his mind to any and all outside distractions and concentrated on placing his hands and feet carefully on the steps as he climbed in place. There was no finesse involved, just a monotonous period of never-ending rungs that soon had him dripping with sweat that quickly became one with the thick atmosphere around him. When his time was up, he wiped off with a towel and cleaned up the machine. His legs were pleasantly sore and heavy. Then he put in five miles on the treadmill at a brisk seven-minute-per-mile pace before spending an hour on the free weights. He kept the weight light but did a high number of reps; he wasn't going for bulk but was more concerned with keeping toned.

When his workout was complete, he cooled down by walking on the treadmill again. Sasha was nowhere to be seen. Duke was busy gently scolding a young man in the weight area for doing squats incorrectly. When his heart rate had returned to normal and he was done sweating buckets, Boon wiped down the machine and gathered up his belongings. He was back in his car a short while later and on the highway towards Cincinnati. The night was clear and the skyline of the city gleamed before him, the Reds' and Bengals' stadiums off to his left. Below him was the dark ribbon of the Ohio River, a black swath separating Ohio from Kentucky.

It fascinated him that the river, while impressive, was still a rather narrow boundary between two such different cultural areas: Cincinnati was the democratic, more liberal North, where people spoke with a Midwest accent and used such phrases as "You guys", and a can of carbonated beverage was usually a "pop." Northern Kentucky, on the other hand, was the more conservative South, a place where a twang was commonplace and a greeting of "Y'all" was the norm. And while a can of northern pop was most assuredly a "soda" or simply a "Coke" on the Kentucky side, the division was even more pronounced when it came to race and religion. The two neighbors could be as divergent as Ireland and its Northern sibling. For years the differences there had been marred by death and destruction with The Troubles, something that for the most part hadn't happened here since the Civil Rights Era, but had begun rearing its ugly head again of late. Still pondering the inequities of life and the lottery of birth, he eased his BMW over into the right lane and took one of the downtown exits toward home.

And then it came to him, the name of the song that Miles had been whistling. It was *Alone* by the Four Seasons. He smiled, his eyes following suit and crinkling in unaccustomed pleasure. He was surprised it had taken him so long to recall the tune. He remembered listening to it as a kid while buckled up in the backseat of his mom and dad's minivan, Frankie Valli's falsetto crackling out of the tiny dashboard speakers. The back seat of their Chrysler had smelled of vinyl and mom's groceries, while his dad's cologne wafted to him on the manufactured breeze of the air conditioning. Warmth spread through his chest at the powerful auditory memory. Dohir was sure Miles had been going for a light-hearted musical jab at Boon's reclusive lifestyle and hadn't a clue how this might otherwise impact him. Regardless, it had been more effective than the man could've guessed, or that Dohir wanted to admit. Sometimes his self-imposed isolation was more than he could stand.

The sterile reality of the apartment did nothing to ease the chill in his soul, even with the strains of *Alone* still caressing the coolness of his heart. He showered with none of the vigor of the previous morning, then tossed on some clean shorts and a T-shirt. For an hour he flipped through channels on TV in the hopes of finding something to capture his attention. Nothing did. Comedies were silly laugh tracks and sensible resolutions, dramas dared him to think too deeply, and sporting events bored him with their fanaticism. A gin bottle hidden behind a closed cupboard door beckoned him silently, but powerfully, and in the end, he poured a sizable shot into a glass and filled the rest with ice and tonic, telling himself the always unconvincing lie that he'd have just the one. Hours later, the bottle was two-thirds gone and he was passed out on the couch. The TV and lights were still on. Ice in his otherwise empty glass surrounded a puddle of condensation that dripped down the side of the table and darkened the carpet.

3

Boon's head was once again pounding a funeral dirge a few inches behind his eyes, and the piercing morning sunshine had him scrambling for sunglasses the instant he left the apartment. It was six-thirty in the morning, but even at that early hour, the sun was bright and bothersome in his debilitated state. Once more berating himself for his stupidity and lack of self-control, he pulled the door of his apartment shut behind him. He stood there and blearily tried to recall where he'd parked his car the night before, annoyed at himself for forgetting. Before he had time to figure anything out, he saw red and blue flashing lights bouncing off the walls from up the alley, toward the bakery and the main drag. Curious and cautious at the same time, he tugged up his collar and made his way toward the commotion.

When he rounded the corner, he spotted three police cruisers parked in front of the bread store, their light bars pulsing. A small crowd had gathered just outside their perimeter behind yellow caution tape. Groups of people were talking in low tones to one another, everyone's eyes focused on the store. Or, more accurately, they were focused on the damage that had been done to it. With a start, he saw the main window was shattered, as was the antique leaded glass in the door. Inside he could see that equipment had been trashed, and one of the heavy ovens was toppled over. Worse yet were the swastikas and anti-Semitic slurs that had been spray-painted in bright red across the walls. Boon felt the skin across his face tighten and his back teeth clench. The hangover-induced fogginess in his mind evaporated under the onslaught of his suddenly inflamed emotions. Injustices in general infuriated him, but specific acts of hatred or prejudice pushed him over the edge. He felt his hands clenching at his sides like he was stepping into the ring at the gym.

As he watched, he noticed one of the policemen talking to the despondent owner inside the store. They walked around together, pointing and taking notes, and even from this distance Boon could hear broken glass crunching under their shoes. After a few minutes of this, the cop closed his notebook, handed a business card to the middle-aged owner, and shook his hand.

"We'll be back in touch soon, Mr. Price," the policeman said. "Call that number if you need anything."

Boon heard Mr. Price kindly thank him, saying he hoped they found something soon. As the police were finishing up, Dohir looked away from the store at the rest of the people gathered with him behind the police tape. At the back of the group, he spotted three guys in their early twenties who were trying to check out the commotion without being too obvious about it. He felt certain he'd seen them around the neighborhood before, perhaps at the coffee shop down the street. Two of them were Black, tall and lanky, their pants hanging low with their underwear hanging out. The other was a skinny white kid with a shaved head and bright neck tattoos. Boon threaded his way over to them. When they spied him coming, the white kid nudged his companions. The three stopped talking and stared at the intruder with flat eyes.

"You guys got a minute?" Dohir asked.

They closed ranks around each other protectively and said nothing, their faces a study in neutrality. Boon stood there, his question left hanging in the air. The white kid's mouth twitched a few times before he eventually answered. When he spoke, his upper lip curled in what had to be a perpetual, adolescent sneer of disdain, an expression that must have driven his parents and teachers crazy.

"Who wants to know?"

Dohir motioned toward the bread store. "I do. I don't like what happened here, that's all. You guys know who did it?"

"You a One Time?"

Boon wasn't certain what the hell a One Time was, but figured from the way the kid said it the term must have been slang for a policeman. "A cop? No, I'm not, I'm just a guy from the neighborhood, that's all."

One of the Black youths snapped his fingers and chimed in, "Yeah, man, I seen you around here before. You drive that big ass Bimmer, right?"

"Yeah, I do."

The other Black teen asked, "What's it to you? Why you care about some damn bread place?"

Boon tilted his head toward the store and Mr. Price, who was wandering around in a bit of a daze, hands jammed in his pockets and just coming to grips with his next steps: insurance companies to call, glass companies to line up, someone to fix his oven, painters to sand down and cover up the filth tattooed on the walls. The police were still taking notes and pictures, and a local news crew had just wheeled up in a big white satellite truck with an oversized number nine painted on the side. "I hate seeing innocent people getting screwed, that's all. And I like this place, you know?"

The taller of the two Black teens followed Boon's gaze. "Yeah, I get it. Mr. Price, he's a good dude. Let me use his phone once when mine was dead. Sucks someone did this."

"What's your name?" Dohir asked the kid who'd just spoken. He wasn't sure, but he got the impression he was the leader of their group.

The youth scrutinized him as if by sharing this information he was giving Boon some level of control over him. He looked to each of his companions before answering.

"Dante. Why you want to know anyways?"

His back to the police cars and the crowd, Dohir reached into his pocket. He pulled out his wallet and withdrew five one-hundred-dollar bills. He handed the cash to Dante, who looked at the wad in open amazement before making it vanish in his front pocket.

Boon said, "That's a down payment. I want to know who did this, and I bet you guys can find out. If you do, there's another five hundred bucks in it for you."

The white kid stepped forward, full of himself now. "Five big ones? What if we just walk away and do nothing? What then, man?"

Boon shrugged. "Then I'm out five hundred bucks and you guys throw a kick-ass party. But…if you find out who did this, then there's another five hundred in it, and you can throw an even bigger one. And no one will ever know where I got the information. You have my word on it. Anything you tell me stays between the four of us."

Dante threw his head back and laughed. A gold tooth gleamed. "You crazy, man!"

Boon wrote something on a scrap of paper he picked up from the street. "Yeah, maybe. But here's my phone number. Call me when you find something. Do we have a deal?"

The skinny white kid loudly echoed Dante's opinion. "You fuckin' crazy, man," he howled.

"Probably. But just let me know, okay?"

Dante laughed again. "Whatever, man. Whatever."

The trio started down the street, five hundred dollars richer, slapping each other on the back and shaking their heads at their good fortune and crazy white guys with money to burn. Boon stared after their retreating forms.

"Happy hunting," he called after them. Dante gave him half a wave over his shoulder, laughing all the way.

Even with the time spent outside Loafers, Dohir beat the others to the office. When everyone else arrived, he was showing no signs of his earlier hangover and seemed his normal, taciturn self. Among the rest, there was the standard morning milling around and greetings, along with casual questions about his or her prior evening, talk about some baseball game, and normal grumbling concerning the early start to the day. Sir Jim fulfilled everyone's expectations and was the last to arrive, and while he didn't vocalize his objections to the location of their office again, his nonverbal cues–the wheezing, his sweating brow, and the way he flopped dangerously into his chair–were more than enough to transmit his disapproval. Boon gave them all time to get settled before he stood up and addressed them.

"Good morning. I'd like to get updates on what we have in the pipeline. I didn't hear anything major happen yesterday, but I'm still interested in your progress, if any. Miles, you want to go first?"

Today Miles was dressed in a simple cream-colored polo shirt, coupled with dark slacks and expensive shoes that Boon thought were Italian. The cut of the shirt accentuated his slender frame. He turned to the group.

"Thanks, Boon, but I don't have much to report, I'm afraid. Not much progress on the credit card front."

"Are you recommending that we cut our losses and move on? Has it come to that?"

Miles puffed his cheeks and exhaled with a hiss of air not even strong enough to blow out a candle, tapping his index finger on the desk in time to a song only he heard. His dark brown eyes were liquid and thoughtful. "Maybe. Just give me a day or two and I'll let you know. It doesn't look all that good right now, however."

Dohir wasn't happy, but he also understood the landscape in which they worked. With huge credit card breaches recently in major banks and places like Home Depot and Target, he'd known all along that this could be a bust. Still, it was disappointing that Miles' efforts might have been wasted. He drummed his own fingers on the desk for a few seconds, then came to an executive decision.

"Okay, tie up any loose ends, cover your tracks, and shut it down. No need to expend any more energy, unless you can convince me otherwise."

Miles stood up straight and began to lift a hand to protest, but his objection wilted under Dohir's steady stare. His arm flopped back down to his side. The somber news was accepted by everyone as a normal outcome, but it was clear Miles was upset. The man cared about results and how they impacted the team.

The others took turns bringing the group up to date, but nobody had anything earth-shattering. That was normal as well; there could be a hundred dead-ends to a single success, and while that was universally understood, it still did little to lift their spirits.

"That's it for now? Thanks for the updates, and happy hunting, everyone."

Boon set to work himself. He donned his headset and began making phone calls and doing more legwork. He was going to close the Marsden deal today, even if it killed him.

Halfway through the morning, his cell phone rang. Boon saw the number and stared at it for a few seconds, still and unblinking. When he answered he spoke in low tones, so hushed no one else could hear him.

When the call was over, he pocketed the phone and announced that he was heading out and would be back in the afternoon. Clem gave him a wave and a soft smile, his good-natured face framed by the crazy mop of his hair. Sasha's eyes may have lingered on him for a second, but she gave no other indication she'd heard him. Her fingers never stopped their muted waltz across the keyboard as she plowed ahead on her project. It wasn't out of the ordinary that Boon came and went during the day. They were used to it and knew not to ask questions.

The day was warm and he gladly rolled down the car windows, especially since there was still a faint whiff of pizza lingering inside. The next time he picked up lunch, he reminded himself, the food would go in the trunk. He drove north until he was out of metro Cincinnati and into the suburbs, where he soon exited the highway. Ten minutes of meandering through an increasingly posh residential area he came to an ornate gate tucked in the middle of a long hedgerow. In wrought iron above the entrance was the name Cloverwell, the letters intertwined with vines and tiny white flowers. He turned in and drove down a narrow, winding drive bordered by an expanse of lawn so well-manicured it would have shamed most greens-keepers. A dozen or so workers in tan uniforms were tending to the property, mowing, trimming, and weeding. He pulled into the parking lot and found an open space between a Bentley and a Ferrari, his BMW appearing quite tame next to the other European exotics. He got out and walked toward the structure looming before him, a large Victorian expanse of white wood, red tile roofs, and ornate trim. Three towering spires reached upwards and seemed to pierce the blue morning sky. The entrance was at the terminus of a wide staircase, a large green "C" standing out prominently on the doors. He entered without hesitation and with an air of familiarity.

Inside it was much of the same, not a shout, but a constant murmur of prestige and multi-generational money. There were thick padded carpets, antique furniture along the walls arranged in sitting areas, and paintings of bucolic landscapes in heavy gilt frames. The hushed atmosphere was library quiet. The underlying and incongruous scent of rubbing alcohol and cleaning solutions were the only indicators he wasn't in a posh country club. Boon walked up to a uniformed man at an ornate desk that was devoid of anything but a computer.

"Good morning, sir," the man said pleasantly. "How may I help you?"

"My name's Boon Dohir. I'm here to see Hannah Collins. Dr. Rivera called me."

The man pulled up and consulted a list on his PC. "Yes, Mr. Dohir. Go right ahead. Room 1113. Do you know the way?"

"Yes, thanks."

"I'll let Dr. Rivera know you're here."

The hall was wide and silent with Boon the only person in sight. Shoulder-high oak wainscoting dressed up the hallway, and decorative wall sconces provided soft illumination. He walked down the hushed corridor and went left at an intersection and past several closed doors. He came to one with 1113 in brass numbers mounted next to it and paused for several moments, head down and unmoving. His breathing was much more rapid than it had any right to be. When Boon grasped the doorknob, he found his hand was trembling and slick with sweat. They were the same uncomfortable sensations he suffered each time he stood in front of this door, even after all these years. He doubted it would ever change or improve. He opened the heavy door and stepped inside.

The room was large and airy, with a huge picture window looking out over the great expanse of manicured lawn. There were plenty of comfortable chairs and couches scattered about, all unoccupied. Near the window was a modern hospital bed that was completely out of place in such a well-appointed room. Supine on the bed and hooked up to several monitoring devices was a young girl, blond, with a narrow face and slightly open mouth. She was thin and spare, her face so pale and porcelain smooth that her age was difficult to determine. She could have been as young as fourteen or as old as her mid-twenties. But Boon knew to the day how old she was.

He stood far away from the bed, unwilling or unable to move closer. Time dragged on as he listened to the muted beeping of the heartbeat monitor counting out the even, measured moments of her life. He couldn't bring himself to step a foot closer.

The door behind him eased open and a man with tight curly salt and pepper hair walked in. He was cursed with an exceptionally large nose that occupied far too much acreage on his face, but fortunately for him he was also possessed of stunning gray eyes that inevitably commanded everyone's attention instead. He was dressed in a more professional variation of the same uniform worn by the outside workers, but instead of garden tools he clutched a stethoscope in one hand and a computer tablet in the other. His shiny brass name tag said "Dr. Rivera." He smiled briefly at Boon, but it was shallow with little teeth and just as much warmth. He extended a soft, manicured hand, which Dohir accepted. Boon had always liked him, not for his personality, which the man sorely lacked, but for the unswerving dedication to his patients.

"Nice to see you again, Doctor."

"Thanks for coming."

Boon ducked his head toward the young girl. "How's Hannah? Has her condition changed?"

Rivera didn't answer immediately, but instead he moved toward her. He consulted his tablet and scrolled through several screens before he gently brushed a lock of blond hair away from her cheek. The doctor cared about her, that much was clear. He was a good man in a tough profession.

"She's fine and...unchanged, which is both good and bad, I'd say. But that's not the primary reason I called." He tapped on the tablet then handed the device to Dohir. "Here's her...ah, projected bill. I know you prefer paying a year in advance. It comes due next month, but I wanted to give you plenty of notice."

He had forgotten Rivera's somewhat annoying habit of pausing in the middle of sentences to think, or gather his thoughts, or whatever. Boon took the tablet and looked at the dollar amount. He'd seen estates sell for less.

"That's fine. I'll wire you the money tomorrow."

"Yes...that's all well and good," the doctor said as he accepted the device back. Then his tone and demeanor changed, turning more serious. Dohir had never seen this side of the man before, not like this, and it set alarm bells off in his head. "But it's not the only reason I called. Hannah's...um, been with us for a while now and her condition has never improved. She's been in a...PSV for years and the longer that continues, the less likely it is she'll ever recover."

PSV. *Persistent Vegetative State*. A chronic or long-term condition, one that differed from a coma in that patients in a vegetative state could open their eyelids, might even smile or grind their teeth. They could swallow or shed tears, or grunt or scream for no reason at all. The longer a person remained in a vegetative state, the less chance they had of regaining awareness. Boon had studied this condition thoroughly.

"What's your point?" he eventually asked, his voice suddenly cool.

Rivera pursed his lips and held the tablet across his chest like a shield. "Because there comes a time when care, no matter how, ah...comprehensive, is no longer enough. It's not about the money, it's not about the family, it's about the...patient and what's right for them. There comes a time when we have to consider that enough is enough."

Boon's stare turned so icy cold the doctor nearly took a step backwards. But he didn't.

"No," Dohir said. "She's here because Cloverwell is the best long-term care facility in the tri-state. I'll keep paying. You take care of her. That's how this works."

Rivera mentally regrouped. "I'm not saying it's something that needs to be decided now, it's just something we need to…ah, consider. Hannah has no other living relatives, and no legal guardian. The only person she has is you."

Boon was very aware of all this. He waited for more.

"Without you she'd…um, certainly be declared a ward of the State and would be in one of their facilities by now. And it wouldn't be unheard of by this time to have a judge declare her unrecoverable and permit… nature to take its course."

"That's not going to happen. I'll continue to pay, and you continue to care for her. Is that clear?"

Dr. Rivera stared at Boon for a full ten beeps on Hannah's heart monitor, the relative silence drawing out. Finally, he sighed, his stunning gray eyes blinking slowly. He reverted to his prior self, one not doling out grievous news to anxious relatives, but that of a man in step with his Hippocratic oath. "Of course, we'll take care of her. You know we will. I just wanted you to be aware of the circumstances and what Hannah's future could hold."

Boon looked away, back at the supine girl, and the ice thawed from his eyes. He didn't blame Rivera for following what he thought best for his patient. He walked up to Hannah, the closest he'd been to her so far.

"She looks thinner," he observed.

The doctor stepped next to him. "Yes. A feeding tube can only do so much. No exercise or solid food will eventually take its toll, no matter what we do. Physical therapy on PVS patients is a slow, losing battle."

Dohir stared at her. Hannah's skin was so thin and pale it was nearly translucent. Light blue veins showed through her cheeks and forehead.

The staff at Cloverwell did an excellent job of keeping her clean and comfortable, but at times she seemed no more than a wax figurine made up to look as human as possible.

"You'll keep taking care of her."

Rivera smiled lightly, still all lips and very little teeth. He placed a hand on Boon's shoulder, which for him was an extravagant, compassionate gesture. "Yes, of course."

"Good." He turned to go before grief consumed his face. When he was at the door the doctor cleared his throat.

"One question, Mr. Dohir."

"Yes?"

"You've been paying for her care all this time. May I ask what your relationship is to Hannah?"

"No, doctor, you may not."

He walked out of the room, the door clicking shut behind him.

4

Boon was in no mood to return to work, but the Marsden deal was coming to fruition and it was almost time to pull the trigger on it. He drove mechanically back to the yellow factory and went inside. It was well after lunch and everyone but Clem was at their desks and plugging away. Miles had been humming a tune, something upbeat and snappy, but stopped when he saw him.

"Hey, welcome back."

"Thanks. Any updates?"

Miles glanced around at the desks and people working on laptops or talking in low tones on their headsets. He shook his head. "Not really. Clem is at the courthouse downtown checking on real estate filings. You know, seeing who's filed recent home equity loans or refinanced their homes. Regular groundwork stuff. You going to finish up your deal today?"

"That's my plan." He didn't let on that work was the last thing on his mind. The trip to see Hannah was still weighing heavily on him. It always did.

Dohir sat at his desk and settled headphones on his head. He fired up the laptop and logged into one of his many offshore bank accounts, one with a substantial balance ending in a lot of zeros. In a few keystrokes he transferred enough funds to Cloverwell to take care of Hannah Collins for another year. Then he reviewed his notes around the Marsden deal.

He'd already spent considerable time building his relationship with Chet, the customer service rep at the bank in Dayton. Most importantly, he had all the information needed to convince the cell carrier to switch phone numbers at the proper moment. That was the crucial part of the entire enterprise, because if that failed this would all be over before it began. Boon felt some nervous energy begin to creep in, which was normal at this stage. From a cheap, pay-as-you-go burner phone he dialed the customer service number to one of the big cell phone providers. He carefully navigated through several options, finally landing with a real person.

"This is Suzy, how may I help you?" a pleasant female voice said.

"Hi, Suzy," he said. "This is Phillip Marsden. I'm going out of the country and need to forward all my calls from my cell to my work phone while I'm gone. Can you take care of that for me?" He gave her Marsden's mobile phone number, the one he wanted switched, and then the number of the inexpensive burner phone he was holding. That phone had a piece of masking tape with an M written on it.

"Certainly, Mr. Marsden. I'll just need to verify your identity and get some information."

For the next few minutes, they chatted amiably while Boon passed along any and all information Suzy requested, including personal information only the real Phillip Marsden should have known, and which Boon had acquired at some cost and effort over the last few weeks. When the representative was confident he was the real deal, she gave him the go ahead.

"That should take care of it, sir. How long will you need your calls forwarded?"

"Not long. Just a few days. I'll call back when I'm in the States again."

"Very good, sir. Have a nice trip."

"Thanks. I will."

Boon hung up. Without delay he dialed a Dayton number using the M phone. An automated voice came on the line, welcoming him to the Ohio Citizens National Bank and asking him to enter his party's extension. He did, and after two rings a male voice picked up.

"This is Chet, may I help you?"

"Hi, Chet, this is Phil Marsden. How are you?"

Boon could hear Chet's smile over the line. "Well, hello, sir. Nice to talk to you again. How may I help?"

"Well, Chet, I've decided to go ahead and purchase that retirement home in Florida, the one we've been talking about? I'm finally going to go for it."

"Good for you, Mr. Marsden. Good for you. How can I help?"

"I need you to wire $200,000 from my savings into my account at the Orlando People's Bank in Florida for the down payment. Can you take care of that for me?"

Chet said he would be happy to get that going for him. He asked for the routing and transit numbers of his account in Florida, along with some other more mundane information, which Boon supplied.

"And per bank policy, I'll need to call you back at the phone number we have on file, a number that hasn't been changed in at least 30 days."

"Of course. By all means. Always better safe than sorry."

The two of them hung up, and less than a minute later Boon's M phone rang. He thanked Suzy at the cell phone company under his breath and answered after the first ring.

"It's me, Chet."

"Thanks, Mr. Marsden. We just can't be too careful these days. Now, when would you like the transfer to take place?"

"Right now would be fine. I've got my closing set up for a few days and I'll be heading there soon."

"Very good, sir. With amounts this high I'll have to pass it along to my manager, Miss Harbaugh, to complete. It's too late to get it done today, I'm afraid, but she'll have the funds transferred before noon tomorrow."

They talked for a few more minutes about kids and family, warm and fuzzy tidbits that Boon had picked up over their prior conversations that served to lull the bank rep. They finally said their goodbyes, with Chet congratulating "Mr. Marsden" on his pending retirement home purchase.

"By the way, Chet, the number you have there on record is my home phone. But here's my work cell number." He gave the banker the actual number of the M phone. "If you need me, please call me here."

"Got it," Chet said.

Boon thought for a second, weighing his personal phone in his other hand. He needed to make sure Chet could get in touch with him, no matter what. "Come to think of it, that number I just gave you is my work cell. I'll give you my personal cell, too. I like to keep work and personal numbers separate. Cuts down on spam calls, you know?"

Chet muttered something under his breath about the evil of spammers, and accepted the information in stride. After another few pleasantries, they said their goodbyes.

Boon sat back in his chair and exhaled, his nerves still jangling but slowly calming. It was almost done. Almost, but not until the funds actually showed up in the Florida bank. But it was looking very, very promising indeed. He called the cell phone provider back and, thoroughly apologetic, reversed the phone number back to the real Phillip Marsden.

Sometimes being a professional thief was almost too easy.

Dohir waited until there was a break in the workday and announced the status of the Marsden deal. There were a few hoots of joy, mainly from Miles, and a warm smattering of applause from everyone else. They were all very aware what this might mean for them financially, and it made their collective day. It also made for a very festive remainder of the afternoon, which was just fine with Boon: after his visit with Hannah, he welcomed the dose of positive energy.

Even though Chet at the bank had assured him nothing would take place before noon tomorrow, he fired up the Orlando bank's website and logged into his account there. Currently the balance stood at an even thousand dollars, legitimate funds he'd deposited there months ago while this fraud was in its nascent stage. Every so often throughout the afternoon he refreshed the site just to see if the dollar amount changed, but it didn't. He had other work he could be doing, but he chose to monitor this watched pot to see if the water boiled.

When the clock ticked 5:00 he cracked his knuckles to release some tension, then began powering down his PC. Sasha as usual heard the telltale sound and bundled up her equipment and was up and out of her chair right away. As she passed him, she slowed as if to say something, but then turned away and was out the door with a flick of her hair. The others took their time and did the same, with Miles giving him a brotherly pat on the back as he exited. Soon Boon was the only person left in the office, and as was his habit he tidied the room before locking up. Finally, with the dirty factory squarely in his rearview mirror, he pulled out of the parking lot and headed north, up I-75 towards Dayton. The construction traffic was horrible and he spent more time doing ten miles per hour than the posted sixty-five. Since he was on no one's timeline but his own, he wasn't bothered by the phalanx of orange barrels, construction equipment, and agitated drivers that all served to slow him down. The big BMW eased along the rough highway and managed the potholes and sudden lane-shifts with Bavarian stoicism.

Soon, he was in the no-man's land between Dayton and Cincinnati, where farms and croplands were slowly being paved over for shopping malls and subdivisions filled with overpriced cookie-cutter homes on quarter-acre lots. It was predicted that the two cities would keep growing until they someday merged into one large metropolis. Boon thought it was a shame to lose the pleasant feel of the countryside to "progress", but he knew it was inevitable, like death and taxes. No, he corrected himself, just death—Boon himself never paid taxes.

Nearly an hour later, the Dayton skyline crept into view. He exited the highway, then spent some time cruising around the nearly deserted downtown area. Whereas Cincinnati was a bustling city with two professional sports franchises, the draw of the Ohio River, and some major corporate players like Proctor & Gamble, Dayton had suffered since the Great Recession. The streets at this time of day were nearly devoid of traffic except for police cars and RTA buses, and the wide sidewalks were empty of pedestrians save the homeless, the addicted, or the otherwise lost. Jobs and hope were rare treasures in a town where there had once been 20,000 good-paying General Motors jobs, but now there were none. "Generous Motors," as they had been known, had quit the town decades earlier, leaving not only vacant factories, but a pervading sense of loss that was becoming the new normal. Dayton's once proud industrial past was now an anchor dragging it down into the muddy depths of the Great Miami River, the brown waterway that snaked sluggishly through the city.

Boon sighed and turned left, passing under the highway and heading west, the sun almost directly in his eyes. He crossed over the river on a crumbling bridge and turned off 3rd street onto a side road, one that dead-ended after just a few hundred yards, not far from Wilbur and Orville Wright's original bicycle shop. There was an open field to his right bristling with construction equipment, backhoes, small bulldozers, and a few Bobcats shod with muddy treads. Even though it was early evening, a dozen men in yellow hard hats and vests were at work in the early stages of building what was immediately recognizable as a baseball complex. At this point it was not much more than a central cinderblock building the size of a three-car garage, but the four diamonds radiating out from that central hub were simple to discern. He got out of the car and leaned against it, surveying the site. A tall man in a white shirt and brown Dockers saw him and waved from where he was talking with several beefy workers. Boon waved back at the foreman, a man named Tom Fowler.

"Hi, Tom," he yelled, trying to be heard over the din of the equipment. "How's it going?"

Tom quickly finished up what he was doing and trotted over to him, rolled-up blueprints in his left hand. A conversation hissed unnoticed from a walkie-talkie at his hip.

"Good," he said, shaking Dohir's hand. Contrary to many foremen he'd had dealings with in the past, Tom's voice was quiet and low. Boon knew him as a man who used words sparingly, as if each one came at a cost. He was an outstanding boss who could get things done, which was the very reason he was here. Tom didn't seem at all surprised to see Boon. "We're putting in some OT, but we're right on schedule."

He rolled the prints out on the warm hood of the sedan and each man held down two corners. The paper was filled with precise black lines showing elevation, drainage, and the crisp outline of the four fields, complete with landscaping, lights, and signage. On the top was a bold heading that read "Third Street Fields." He pointed to the central structure.

"The bathroom and concession stand's almost done, as you can see, and we got the underground sprinkler system installed earlier this week. The ground itself is graded and we'll be bringing in the turf and crushed brick for the infields next week. Then come the fences and the stands. Kids will be playing here in a month. Month and a half, tops."

Boon perused the plans, pleased at the status. The Third Street Fields complex was funded by an "anonymous donor," with all necessary construction payments made through a trust account handled by a local attorney, a business associate of Boon's. There was also a hefty endowment designed to cover day-to-day operations, and that same attorney was tapping local businesses in order to bolster it. He was a heavy-hitting ex-political fundraising expert, proficient at twisting arms and prying open stubborn wallets. The anonymous donor had a lot of pull and even more connections, considering how quickly the project had come together, with the land purchased and the necessary permits issued in record time. When it was completed, the ball diamonds would provide a place for kids all over Dayton's impoverished West Side someplace to go and something to do. Even more, it would give them hope and a small shot at a normal life, something many sorely lacked. Satisfied that Boon had seen enough, Tom rolled up the plans and tucked them under his arm.

"I'll check back in a few days," Dohir told him. "Glad to see it's going well. How's the money situation?"

Under his hard hat Tom squinted one eye in thought. "We're coming in under budget right now. But you never know. The bids for the fencing came in a lot higher than we expected. That could be a problem."

Boon slowly surveyed the site, as if visualizing how it would look when finished. He could see kids in colorful uniforms playing, hear that particular crack of the bat as it connected, the umps barking out the count, and smell popcorn from the concession stand. He loved baseball, loved the complex strategy and the subtle tweaks that could determine the outcome of the game. Some people thought baseball was slow and ponderous and suffered from little action in this age of glitz and video games, but Boon knew they simply didn't grasp the beauty of it. He pitied them.

Boon himself had been a high school standout shortstop and could've played college ball, but had chosen to lay down his glove in order to focus on his studies. Now, he wanted the less fortunate kids from Dayton's West Side to share in some of the joys and opportunities that he'd benefited from as a kid. There was no way he was going to let some cost overruns spoil that vision. He knew the company installing the fencing and the backstops. In fact, the president was a friend who owed him a few favors. He told Tom he'd make a call and see what he could do.

His group at the factory office, especially Miles, kidded Dohir that he always "had a guy," no matter the circumstances. Need a special permit? Boon had a guy. Having a zoning problem? Boon had a guy. His phone, his modern day "black book," was replete with names and phone numbers that cut a wide swath across professions and economic classes. Dohir knew influential people everywhere and was not shy about tapping them when needed. After all, there was little sense in cultivating connections if you weren't going to use them. Boon was, if nothing else, a pragmatist.

Tom said a succinct goodbye and trotted back toward his crew. Boon watched serenely for another ten minutes before climbing back into his car and pointing the BMW's kidney-shaped grill toward Cincinnati.

Back on the highway, he dialed a Dayton number. Before he'd gone ten miles, he'd secured a lower bid for the fencing from the owner, Steve Kempler of Kempler Fencing, with assurances that all materials and labor would come in under their original estimate, along with an apology for the "confusion." The two chatted for a little bit longer with Boon finally asking about the man's teenage son.

"Jack's better, but not great. Thanks for asking," Steve said, his voice turning heavy. Kempler was a large, jovial man, thick through the middle but lean mentally, where it really counted. His joking nature concealed a serious and intense business acumen that had served him well. Much to their surprise and chagrin, more than one competitor had underestimated the man and had been blindsided, somehow losing a deal at the last minute to the laughing, boisterous businessman. But there was no joking or humor now, and his words came across flat and dull, as if machine-generated. "It's going to take a while. I don't know what I would've done if you hadn't helped get him into the treatment center. It's helping."

"It's going to be a tough road. I hope you're up for it. You and Jack."

Boon heard Kempler's long, drawn-out sigh over the phone, and could almost picture the man's faraway gaze. "You look back and think 'If only', you know? If only I hadn't been working all the time. If only I had paid more attention to the kids he was hanging around with. If only Julie was still around. I just want a normal life for him, you know?"

Boon didn't immediately answer. His own "if only" moment was never more than half a step outside his consciousness, lurking there and waiting to force its way back in. Sometimes it was the only thing he could think about. He found that his hands were sweaty on the leather steering wheel, and he was shaking, his heart abnormally loud in his ears. He blinked, and around him the familiar interior of his car was gone, replaced by another. In his mind, it was now pitch-black outside, and the pale emerald dashboard lights dimly illuminated the interior of a different car. Outside was a ferocious downpour, the rain hissing against the windshield with a sound of water being poured on a bonfire. The wipers were banging madly back and forth, with no hope of keeping up against the deluge. Suddenly, bright red taillights erupted in front of him. The dark shape of a vehicle was caught there for a split second, framed in the tight beams of his headlights. He mashed the brakes and swerved, but the taillights flew towards him like twin, deadly comets.

Then the vision was mercifully gone, and Boon was back in his car, still on the road to Cincinnati. Despite the excellent climate control there was sweat on his upper lip and beading across his forehead. The hair on his neck was damp. He desperately wished more than anything that he could hit life's rewind button, that he could go back and do one thing differently. Not for the first time, he felt that the weight of living was almost too much for him to bear.

"Anyway," Kempler continued, the silence beginning to draw out, "thanks again for getting Jack in. And don't worry, I'll send over the adjusted paperwork for the fencing." He paused for a moment. "And by the way, you owe me a rematch on the golf course, you son of a bitch. I'm still stinging from that round at the club last year. What'd you take me for, a few hundred bucks?"

Boon thought back, relieved at the change of subject. "Something like that, yeah."

"Okay, so what are you doing tomorrow afternoon? You've gotta give me a chance to win that back, man. My tender psyche can't handle such abuse. My treat."

Boon knew there was nothing tender about Steve Kempler, psyche or otherwise. He also knew a chance to augment their personal and business relationship was not something to pass up. Kempler's main line of work was fencing, but he owned a dozen subsidiary companies and had his hands in everything from construction to restaurants. Best of all, the man had contacts galore and loved parading them out like trophy wives. Dohir had nothing pressing that he couldn't put off. He would be more comfortable monitoring the Marsden deal from the office, but by then it should be wrapped up with a neat bow, assuming Ms. Harbaugh at the bank followed through on her part. Besides, Steve Kempler was as close to a real friend as Boon had, and he enjoyed spending time with him.

"Sure, I'm game, as long as it's later in the afternoon. Text me the address and time, and I'll be there."

"He said he was game, so I shot him," joked Kempler, his naturally cheery persona dialed back up to high. "Great. I'll have my admin set something up and send you the details. Been playing much this year?"

Dohir hadn't even swung a club yet. "No, not too much. I'm probably a little rusty."

"Your rusty is another man's best round, you cagey bastard. But at least that'll give me a chance. See you then."

They said their goodbyes and Boon hung up. The remainder of the drive home was a blur of asphalt and green highway signs, and he was so deeply entrenched in his own past and "what ifs" that he nearly missed his exit. Kempler's psyche may not have been bruised, but Boon's certainly was. The unsolicited flashback had had an almost physical impact on him, actually draining him of energy, just like it always did. There was only one surefire way to help dim the memories haunting him, and he suspected that once again it was going to be a bad night. Or, more accurately, that tomorrow would be a bad morning.

5

The bright light from the window lanced agony into his brain, a physical shock made no less acute by its ephemeral nature. His stomach heaved, and he had to swallow several times to make sure everything stayed where nature intended. After a few minutes of steadying himself, he sat up and was surprised and slightly heartened to see he was alone and in his own bed. That was a nice change, considering a few weeks earlier he'd woken up on the cold concrete next to his car in a parking garage in Kentucky with dried vomit crusted on his shirt. Boon was ashamed to admit this was his life now, but he felt powerless to change it.

He was still fully dressed from the night before, although his shirt was unbuttoned and twisted awkwardly around his midsection, and he only had one sock on. An empty bottle of whiskey was parked on his nightstand next to a half full water glass, the booze and water no longer perfectly mixed due to the differences in their specific densities. He dragged himself out of bed toward the bathroom, where he fumbled and nearly dropped the Costco-sized aspirin bottle as he wrestled it open. He washed down three tablets and stripped down for the shower.

Fifteen minutes later, he was dressed in khakis and a button-down shirt and ready for work. Sunglasses were not optional. He stopped at a gas station and paid cash for the largest coffee available. Food was a subject not to be considered until mid-afternoon, even more so since holding down the coffee was taking all his concentration. The day was not starting out well, but more and more often that seemed to be par for the course.

Thinking of par reminded him of golf with Steve Kempler that afternoon. His clubs and shoes were still tucked away in the trunk of his car where they had slumbered all winter. In this condition, he wasn't looking forward to the upcoming round but figured the fresh air might help clear his head. He hadn't received a text relaying the time and location of their round yet but was sure he would soon. Steve would make certain that was taken care of.

Even with the morning he was having, he arrived at the factory office before the rest of his team. The smell of the grease from the derelict machines made his gut flip-flop dangerously, but he clamped his teeth together and climbed the steps. Once in the office, he began his routine of powering up the monitors and getting the coffee maker in gear. Soon the others rolled in and were busy with their own morning rituals. Sir Jim was last, gasping like a man who'd just outrun a squad of Cincinnati's finest. His mottled skin was again that unhealthy green, and his face was coated in sweat.

"Jesus, old man, you going to die on the spot?" Sasha inquired, her mouth contorted like she'd just stepped in something. She was in her customary tights and workout clothing again. A pink top this time, with black yoga pants and eye-searing yellow shoes so bright they were like peering at the sun. "There's no fucking way I'm giving you CPR if you keel over, you know."

Sir Jim held up a hand to her. "I'm fine, my dear, thanks for your concern, real or manufactured," he wheezed, his breath rattling. "Just need a moment, that's all. Confounded steps."

Miles was dressed very smartly again, this time in dark slacks and a simple V-neck sweater. He checked out Boon and cocked his head to the side, appraising him. "You don't look so hot yourself, man. What'd you do last night? Go a few rounds with the champ?"

Dohir didn't deign to reply as he refilled his cup. "Okay, listen up, people. I know we've got the Marsden deal hopefully coming to a head today." There was a smattering of applause from the group and a happy yell from Miles. Once more he was reminded what a good group they were, and how lucky he was to have them around. When he first got into this business, he'd never envisioned this line of work could be so, well, *normal*, what with regular hours, a physical office, and events like celebratory pizza lunches. Almost the only things lacking were a group health plan and a 401k. And maybe it was so normal because he'd made it that way? Because this kind of stability was something they all hoped for, including himself? Maybe they all needed this sense of camaraderie? He knew he did, even if he was determined to keep them at arm's length.

"But that doesn't mean we can back off any existing deals," he continued. "We can't count on this until the money's in the bank. Let's go over what we've got going. Sir Jim, you first."

The big man checked his computer screen. "I've got four solid targets lined up, I'm happy to say. They all reside in the very posh Villages in Florida. Via the blessing that is social media, I've been doing some very detailed research into their families, and all have grandchildren who enjoy travel. I'll be tapping all four this morning as soon as I get their direct phone numbers."

Sir Jim's specialty was the Grandchild Scam. After researching the families through various social media platforms, he called wealthy grandparents and posed as one of their grandchildren. He then had to convince them "he" was out of the country, had gotten into trouble with the locals, and needed cash for bail or to pay fines. The key here was to convince the rich grandparents that under no circumstances could their "parents" find out or they'd get in even more trouble. He succeeded more often than not, usually to the tune of five to twenty grand. His voice skills were unmatched, were uncanny, really, especially when there was simulated static on the line designed to mimic a lousy international connection. Boon had heard him imitate a scared sixteen-year-old girl, a belligerent male in his twenties, and once, most impressively, a set of hysterical, adolescent sisters.

"Well done. Just keep me updated. Clem, how about you and Sasha? You two had that deal with the coding of the home banking app. How's that going?"

Sasha pulled herself away from the keyboard and screen and addressed them reluctantly, as if directly communicating with people were outside her skill set. "Fine. We're working on it."

Boon refrained from rolling his eyes. He should have known that if he wanted a thorough answer he should have asked Clem in the first place. Still, he pressed her. "That's it?"

"I'll take this, if that's okay with you, Sasha," Clem said, lifting a hand. "As y'all know, most people these days have a mobile banking app on their phones. Those apps have connectivity with the core data processing systems of banks and credit unions, the main database where all the customer info is housed. What that means is, the app talks to the core system like two youngsters chattin' between tin cans connected by a string. The two of them chit chat away and send information back and forth along the string so they're both up to date, second by second. The coding glitch we found is not in the app or in the core processing system, but in that tiny side program, that piece of string that lets these systems talk to each other."

"How does that help us?" Boon asked.

"We think we can attach a sliver of code to that tiny program and record the keystrokes of any folks logging into the system, making transactions, stuff like that. Easy as pie."

Miles sat up, intrigued. "So, you'll know their logins and passwords?"

"Bam! Give the man a cigar. Yeah, we won't be able to snitch funds directly from accounts, but we'll be able to record all their information, including social security numbers and passwords. This could be a gold mine, friends. Once we have the info we can log on and transfer out as much money as we like from their accounts."

There were murmurs of appreciation from everyone, even Boon.

"This could be huge," Patrice stated flatly, her eyes distant as she ran numbers through her head. "It's impossible to calculate the value of this without more data. Plus, depending on customer complaints and how often the system administrators perform penetration testing, we'd have limited time before they find out what we're doing and shut it down."

Boon felt a twinge of excitement. He'd never been too keen on Sir Jim's Grandchild Scam, but he let it continue since they only targeted the very wealthy, those people who probably had five or ten grand in the ashtrays of their Mercedes. On the practical side, those smaller amounts did wonders to keep the cash flowing, especially during lean times.

"Is this a standard Trojan, like Gh0st Rat or one of those cyber spying programs? Your malware won't enable you to take control of a system? It's just going to record keystrokes?"

"Just going to record keystrokes?" Sasha replied, her cheeks flaring red in a precursor to a volcanic eruption. "I've worked my ass off on this, you know. It's elegant and simple, and it's a pretty big damn deal."

"Yes, Boon, it's a pretty big deal," Clem agreed, jumping in to cap the eruption before the lava started to spew in earnest. "Companies are on guard surrounding all kinds of cyber threats these days. It's no small matter that Sasha was able to crack this and write the code so quickly. But like Patrice said, y'all need to work fast, before anyone else discovers the flaw. Good guys *or* bad guys. We should have it uploaded and ready in a few days. And yes, once we start transferring money we'll have to hit it hard, before anyone notices their balances have vanished. We've code-named our little baby S.A.S.H.A, for short," he said, spelling out the acronym with his trademark grin.

"SASHA?" Boon asked.

"Yes, our *Single Access Strong Hacking Attack* software. Slick, don't you think?"

"Yes, indeed. But please, don't waste any more time talking to me." He surveyed the rest of them. "Nothing else? Great, then happy hunting."

Boon checked his balance at the Orlando People's Bank. It remained an even thousand dollars, the same as yesterday. It was only 9:30 in the morning, still early, so he wasn't concerned yet. He would check again throughout the morning, and if nothing showed up by noon, he might have to reach back out to Chet at the bank.

Clem had been visiting courthouses around town yesterday, and had passed along his notes earlier that morning. Boon sat at his desk with the end of a chewed-up pencil in his mouth and perused the information. The quiet Southerner preferred using a spiral-bound notebook that he called Clem's Collections. He had filled it side to side with his impeccable handwriting, the print so tidy he may have been a draftsman in a prior life. Boon reviewed the entries, evaluating each one on its merits, moving quickly down the page and making notes in the margins. Next to each name he ranked them one through five, with five being his most likely next targets. There were quite a few fives.

Real estate filings were public knowledge, and they gave people like him invaluable information concerning balances, refinances, and selling prices. The filings also showed which financial institution held the mortgage. It was a fairly simple matter for him to determine who had equity, and how much they might have when he compared those numbers to home values easily combed online sites. It was also a fairly safe bet that if they had equity, they also had a home equity line of credit. New purchases were also targets, especially homeowners who had a low mortgage, but a high home value. These were his targets, just as Phillip Marsden had been. Boon had spotted the man's name on Clem's Collections a few months ago and had been working on it, bit by bit, ever since.

Boon was half way through Clem's list when his phone vibrated. It was a text from Steve Kempler's executive assistant, with the time and location of their golf outing, 1:30 at a private country club in a Dayton suburb. He'd have to leave by noon to be there on time.

He worked for a few more hours. As lunchtime approached and the status of his account in Florida remained unchanged, he tapped his pencil, concern gnawing at the edges of his confidence. He opened his desk drawer and pulled out the phone with the M taped to it. He dialed Chet's number at the bank and navigated the phone tree. He soon heard the banker pick up.

"This is Chet, may I help you?"

Boon's voice was calm and easy-going. He was very good at this. "Hi, Chet, this is Phil Marsden. How are you today?"

"Well, I'm fine, sir. I'm glad you called–honestly, I was just about to get in touch with you. I wanted to apologize for the delay, since you've probably noticed the transfer hasn't gone through yet."

Dohir forced a smile onto his face, making sure it could be heard, even if his gut was clenched into a tight knot. "As a matter of fact, I did. I talked to my banker in Florida a few minutes ago and he said it hadn't shown up yet. Is there a problem?"

Chet's voice lowered a few decibels, as if he had shifted in his seat or put his hand close to the mouthpiece. "Yes, well, no. Like I said yesterday, Ms. Harbaugh has to handle wire transfers of this size, and she's not here today. Well, she was here in the morning but something happened and she left suddenly. She just got back a little bit ago. I'm not really sure what's going on. I'll get to the bottom of it and let you know right away."

Dohir assured him it was fine and that he'd wait for his call, emphasizing his desire to get it wrapped up right away. He made sure Chet still had the number to Boon's "work" cell phone, the M phone, which he did.

The two hung up. Boon stared at his thousand-dollar balance glowing impersonally on the screen before him, his fingers drumming on the desk. The longer this stretched out, the more likely it was to blow up, but he was at the mercy of the Dayton bank now. There was nothing he could do. He placed the phone on his desk and waited for it to ring. No, he *willed* it to ring. The thought of a drink tugged at him, but he quashed the impulse as quickly as it had come; he purposefully didn't keep alcohol in the office for that very reason.

He reluctantly went back to Clem's Collections and made some additional notes, one eye always on the inert phone. The noon hour arrived, and talk around the office turned to lunch. No one mentioned the pending Marsden deal, and in fact no one talked to Boon at all. They treated him like a Big-League pitcher in the midst of a no-hitter, as if any mention or question of the status could jinx the deal completely. They tiptoed around him, then as a group filed out and left for lunch. He dimly heard them move down the steps, Sir Jim clumping along in their wake. Typically, he knew they wouldn't all go out and certainly not together, but in this case he understood. The factory door thudded shut and their voices were chopped off in mid-sentence. He was alone again. Only the occasional hiss and spit of the coffee maker broke the silence.

Ten minutes passed, ten minutes where the clock's second hand seemed almost locked in amber. With a huff of exasperation, he knew he couldn't wait any longer and had to head north. He locked the building up and was soon cruising toward Dayton. A little more than an hour later he pulled into the country club, where a nice young man in a crisp logo shirt and khaki shorts gathered up his clubs. Boon grabbed his gym bag of golf clothing and entered the air-conditioned clubhouse. He hurried downstairs into the locker room to change, aware he was running late. Steve Kempler was already there, dressed in loud plaid pants, a pink shirt, and a broad smile so bright it managed to eclipse his outlandish wardrobe. His booming voice greeted Dohir.

"There's my man! Cutting it a little close, aren't you? We tee off in ten minutes."

Boon forced his face into an easy grin that he didn't feel. "Sorry about that, Steve. Business. I've got a big deal I'm trying to close."

Kempler grunted. He understood the importance of work before pleasure. "Good. Maybe that'll distract you this afternoon. I need every advantage I can get! Come on, let's meet the guys."

Boon quickly changed and they headed to the first tee. When they stepped into the sunshine, they spotted two men waiting for them, one in his early sixties, and a much younger man standing behind him and off to the side. They were both dressed more conservatively than Kempler, but to outdo him in that department would've taken effort and intense online shopping. The older man was tall and in pretty good condition, Dohir noticed, except for a slight paunch and shoulders that gently sloped with age. He had striking white hair and eyebrows that almost seemed to shimmer in the sunlight. The younger man hung several paces behind him, as if in the presence of royalty. He kept crossing and uncrossing his arms, as if he didn't know what to do with them. As Boon stared at the older man, he felt he knew him from somewhere, but couldn't immediately place where. Kempler strolled up and placed his hand on the older man's arm.

"Boon, I'd like you to meet the Honorable Jeff Barton. And this is his clerk, Larry Block. You'll be paired up with his Honor, and I'll be with Larry. That okay with you two?"

Boon stood there in mild shock as the men agreed and shook hands all around, the judge passing normal pleasantries while Larry kept to himself. Kempler tossed a tee into the air. When it landed it was pointed at the judge, indicating that he'd tee off first. Boon's friend sidled up next to him and leaned close.

"In case you didn't recognize the name, Barton is a federal judge in the US District Court of Southern Ohio, based here in Dayton. He was appointed by the president about ten years ago. He's a founding partner of the law firm Barton, Putney, and Hammersmith. Ridiculously wealthy, and enjoys a lot of clout in the state of Ohio and beyond. A bit of a pretentious douche, but a good man to have on your side. Oh, and he also hates to lose, so don't fuck up."

"Don't fuck up. Got it."

Steve dipped his head towards the second man. "Larry's a late entry today. We were supposed to have the county prosecutor with us, but the judge said Georgie had to call off at the last minute. Larry is Barton's clerk, a few years out of law school, University of Chicago, I think. Smart, and a whiz at research, I'm told. His Honor is a decent golfer, but not great. I don't know anything about Larry. Either way, this should be fun."

Kempler hadn't let him down this time, and Boon mentally cataloged the names. He pulled out his driver and took a few swings to knock out the winter's cobwebs. The judge stepped into the tee box and, without a warm-up swing, drove his ball straight down the fairway. It landed just shy of a bunker on the left. He beamed in delight as the other three warmly congratulated him on the shot, especially Larry, who almost seemed to fawn over the man. The clerk walked up and wiped his hands on his pants, then swung and sliced it a little right, still in play but short of the first ball. Kempler gave the slight clerk a slap on the back hard enough to make him stumble, then stepped into the tee box. All humor vacated his being as he settled into his stance, his competitive nature rolling out from him in waves. He grunted as he swung and muscled the ball nearly 300 yards down the fairway, bouncing well past Judge Barton's shot. He turned to the others, beaming.

"That's what I'm talking about!" he shouted. He stared at Boon, pointing with his club. His grin was fierce and predatory. "Beat that one, Dohir!"

Boon hefted his driver. The smart thing to do was to lay up short and let Steve have his moment, but his own competitive streak wouldn't permit that. He set his ball on the tee and lined up. When he swung it appeared as if he'd put forth no effort at all. *It's all in the wrists and hips*, Dohir thought. *Just relax and let muscle memory take over.*

"Christ, he crushed it," Larry muttered from behind him, one of the only things he'd said all day. Admiration and a touch of envy were clear in the way he'd drawn out the *Christ*, turning it from one syllable into two. *Kee-riste.*

Boon's ball bounced cleanly over Steve's and landed in the middle of the fairway. It came to rest not far from the 150 flag, nicely lined up for a second shot at the green.

"Hey, Steve," the judge chided with a mischievous smile filled with white, even teeth, "you could build a fucking Wal-Mart between his ball and yours. Nice shot, Boon. And Larry, do yourself a fucking favor and take some notes. You could learn a lot from this guy."

Kempler stared daggers at him and slammed his driver into his bag. "Haven't played much so far this year my ass." Boon shrugged innocently.

The four climbed into their carts and moved out. Jeff Barton drove as they headed for his ball, and when they were out of earshot of the others he leaned over to Boon. "Seriously, that was a great shot. I love it when that SOB Kempler gets a beat-down. He's so fucking cocky. Keep that up and I'll owe you one."

Boon smiled and kept his eyes straight ahead. He was counting on it.

The rest of the round was much like the first hole. Kempler and Boon were clearly the two to beat, and the lead bounced back and forth between them throughout the front and back nines. The big difference was that Boon never had a truly bad shot or blow-up hole, even though he was distracted and repeatedly checked his M phone. He suffered through two bogeys, but the rest were all birdies or pars. Kempler stayed up with him until the 14th hole, a long par four where he chipped over the green into a staggeringly deep bunker. It took him two shots to escape before he angrily three-putted. Boon cleanly tapped in from five feet for another par. After that it was no contest. The big man looked ready to bite his putter in two.

"Goddam, Boon, do me a favor and fuck up, will you?"

But he never did. The round ended after three and a half hours and Dohir beat him by six strokes. Barton and Larry Block weren't even close, but the judge was visibly happy to see Kempler defeated so decisively. When it was over, they passed their bags to another young attendant who cleaned them up and transported them to their cars. The judge smiled and thanked them for the round, then tugged at Boon's sleeve and pulled him to one side.

"It was great meeting you," he said sincerely, beaming. "Top notch round. And I just took Steve to the cleaners, thank you very much. I had a good feeling about you." He flashed some bills at Boon with a grin, then dug around in his pocket for something, but his hand came out empty.

"Larry!" he barked in instant frustration, searching. "Where the hell is he?"

The young clerk hurried over. "Y-yes, sir?"

"Do you have one of my business cards with you? Mine are in the car."

Larry visibly blanched. "Sorry, sir, I don't. But I have one of mine." He pulled a card from his shirt pocket and handed it to the judge, who snatched it from his hand with an impatient frown. Using the scoring pencil, he scribbled his phone number on the back and passed it to Boon.

"Just give me a shout any time you want to play again. It'll be my pleasure." He looked Boon up and down as if he were assessing his potential value. An attendant pulled up in his car, an expensive Italian coupe. The judge got in, then rolled down the window and motioned Boon closer.

"Yes?" Dohir asked.

"By the way, you never said what you do for a living."

Boon smiled. "I'm in banking."

Barton smiled back at him in satisfaction, as if Boon's worth as a person had been validated by his career. With a wave, the coupe roared out of the parking lot.

Larry Block and Boon watched him as he left. When he was out of sight, the clerk seemed to relax for the first time that day, his shoulders dropping as pent-up tension escaped from his body. Boon raised an eyebrow at him.

"You like working for the judge?"

Larry didn't say anything for a moment, as if carefully sifting through words before letting them escape his mouth. "Yeah, sure, it's great experience. I'm learning a lot."

"You really didn't answer my question," Boon prodded.

The clerk stared at him, once again measuring his response. "He's okay, I guess. He can be kind of a bear to work for. I'm just doing it for the experience and to pay off my damn loans. Then I'll open my own practice and really start making bank."

"Good luck. I remember my student loans. They can be a bitch."

Larry studied him for a second, still being cautious. "Yeah, but I'm making great progress. It shouldn't be long now, then I won't have to deal with him any longer."

They chatted a little more while Boon waited for Steve to settle up in the clubhouse. As his friend was strolling towards them, Larry excused himself and hustled over to an old hatchback with fading paint and mismatched wheels. Boon studied the business card for a moment, then slid it into his pocket.

Kempler walked up and slapped Boon on the back fondly, one warrior to another. Now that the match was over and the scores tallied, he was back to his larger-than-life self. With his size, shape, and colorful clothing, he reminded Boon of a circus bear, genial enough on the outside, but with potential savagery hovering just below the surface. His laugh was deep and infectious, a friendly growl that rumbled up from his gut.

"Jesus, you were hot today. Haven't played much this year my ass!"

"Thanks for the round, and for pairing me with the Judge. Nice enough guy, and you're right–he's a good man to know."

"Yeah, I figured you'd appreciate that. I saw you sizing him up from the get-go."

"I hope I never have to come before him on the bench."

"Yeah, he's a real prick in court," he said somberly, then his face broke into a grin and he clapped Boon on the back again. "You took me again, you bastard. I'll get you next time!"

Boon couldn't help but mirror Kempler's honest exuberance, and was glad he'd played. That was what he liked about Steve; as much as the man hated losing, he loved the competition and spending time with people he considered friends. And when the fight was over, win or lose, he invariably bounced back to his back-slapping, jovial self. Boon quite liked him, and had from the first time they met. They said their goodbyes, got in their respective cars, and left.

Ten minutes into the trip home his M phone rang. He quickly picked it up and recognized the number as Chet's at the bank. He took a deep, calming breath and made his voice sound casual and friendly.

"Hello?"

"Hi, Mr. Marsden, I'm glad I caught you. This is Chet at the bank."

"Well, hi there, Chet. I hope you have good news for me. I'm getting ready to head down to Florida to seal the deal."

There was a momentary pause on the other end, and for a second Boon thought he'd dropped the call. He glanced at the display, but as far as he could tell, they were still connected.

"Um, yes, sir. Sorry for the delay, but I finally had a chance to run Ms. Harbaugh down, and she promised she'd get to it by the end of the day. I just…" His voice trailed off oddly, which set Boon's nerves jangling. *No! They were so close now!*

"What's wrong, Chet? Everything okay?"

"Uh, yes, things are just in a bit of an uproar here today, that's all."

"What do you mean?"

Chet paused, and Boon could almost visualize the man running responses through his head, just like Larry Block had. "Well, I'm not sure, but I think Ms. Harbaugh is leaving the bank. When I went into her office, she was tossing stuff into a box, and her face was all red. Like she'd been crying or something." He sounded concerned, and it was obvious he thought highly of her.

"That's too bad. I hope everything's okay. This won't affect my transfer, right?" Boon asked, trying to direct the conversation back to his problem.

When Chet spoke again, he was once more all business, albeit slightly apologetic. Boon could tell the customer service rep realized he'd crossed a line and shared more than he should have. "Of course, sir, of course. Here at the bank, we value service above all else. I probably said too much. Sorry about that. It's just upsetting, that's all. I'm sure the wire transfer will be made today."

They carried on with small talk for a few moments longer and then disconnected. Boon increased his speed to the maximum he felt comfortable doing without getting pulled over through the construction zones, eager to get back to the office and check his balances. He fervently hoped Ms. Harbaugh's issues, whatever they were, didn't bleed over into his business and screw everything up.

It was almost six o'clock when he wheeled into the factory parking lot, laying on the brakes hard enough that the tires chirped and his seatbelt locked up. There were no other cars there, which he'd expected at this hour. He parked just outside the door and jogged upstairs, taking the steps two at a time in his haste, then forced himself to calmly unlock the office door. He slid into his seat and logged into the account at the Orlando People's Bank on his PC. He checked out the new balance. The rare smile that broke across his face was huge and satisfied, a Vegas high-roller happily laying down the winning hand after going all-in. It was all there: $20,000,000. *Hot damn!*

Then he paused and tilted his head sideways, momentarily confused. The smile faltered and twitched. His eyebrows knotted as he leaned in to double-check the numbers on the monitor, for a second doubting his own eyes.

This wasn't right. There were too many zeros.

He continued staring at the screen in disbelief. Ms. Harbaugh hadn't transferred $200,000 as he'd requested. She'd deposited *$20 million!*

Holy shit...

Boon didn't know what had happened, but at that point he didn't care, either. Without thinking he opened a new browser window and accessed a secure server that Sasha had set up for him months ago. Fingers flying, he entered logins and passwords that only he knew, opening an encrypted file. On it were listed more than two-dozen financial institutions, complete with account numbers, passwords, and routing and transit numbers.

First, he transferred the entire $20 million to a bank in the Cayman Islands. That done, he rapidly began moving million-dollar chunks into different financial institutions around the globe, some still in the Caymans, others to Switzerland, a few in the Bahamas. Even then he wasn't finished. He moved each of those millions around several times, mixing up the amounts and bouncing the funds to different havens around the world, to the point where the convoluted money trail would be impossible for any outside entity, legal or otherwise, to follow. After an intense twenty minutes, the full $20 million was scattered across a score of countries and financial institutions, with no single entity holding more than half a million. Even then he wasn't finished. When he felt comfortable that his elaborate shell game was done, he split the sensitive information– the locations, account numbers, and dollar amounts - into several newly created, encrypted files and uploaded them into another off-shore server. Finally, he used a special program to completely wipe the history and any traces of his activity from his Internet browser, effectively erasing his digital tracks.

His hands were shaking as he sat back in his chair, and he was sweating like a defendant on trial. His heart was pounding so hard he was sure it was going to erupt through his shirt and splatter on his desk. He began shutting down the office for the night, locking all the doors behind him.

He'd never had a score like this before. Not even close.

This was huge.

6

The next morning Boon was in the office before everyone else, as usual. He was not hungover. He greeted each person normally as they entered. Dohir himself was seated at his desk, looking as if nothing out of the ordinary had happened. Miles was the first to approach him, sucking on a tall coffee concoction of some sort. He peered at him with an eyebrow raised and foam on his upper lip.

"So, how's it going? Any news?"

Boon grinned, secure that it looked natural. "I got it. The transfer's done and the money's already been moved. The full two-hundred grand."

Miles' face broke into a wide grin, his white teeth bright against his dark complexion. He turned to the office and proclaimed loudly, "The Marsden deal is done, people! We got it!"

The office erupted in applause and cheers. Miles high-fived Clem and gave a loud whoop. Sir Jim slowly clapped his hands, as if acknowledging an extraordinary Broadway performance. Patrice smiled, her face uncomfortable with the infrequent expression. Even Sasha was pleased. Her grin, when it manifested, was warm and almost petite.

The payout for a deal like this was simple: Boon kept twenty-five percent since he was the principal and shouldered the greatest liability. He was also in charge of recruiting, leasing the office, equipment, and everything else that went along with running a "business" such as this. The remaining seventy-five percent was doled out in equal shares, which equated to a tidy sum of thirty thousand for each of them. Tax-free, and completely under the table. The dollar amount for each person wasn't immense by any standards, but this was their eighth score of the year, plus all the smaller hits from Sir Jim. They added up to a pretty tidy sum per person.

"Not a bad payday, people," Miles stated happily, drumming a riff on his desk with both hands and spinning around in his chair like a kid.

Boon kept up his steady smile, never letting on about the actual amount of the transfer. He couldn't tell them the true amount, not yet. He still had no clue why that much money had been transferred to his Florida account, but a loss of this magnitude would ring alarm bells at every level of law enforcement, from the local boys all the way up to the Feds. Someone somewhere was going to be mightily pissed. No, he had to hold this one close to the vest for now. He had no choice. It was for their protection as well as his. At least, that was what he kept telling himself.

Beyond that, Dohir was no idiot. All along, his business model had been predicated on these illegal transactions flying under the radar of the law, and so far he'd managed to do just that. He'd always insisted on their scams staying under the $250,000 mark, enough to score the occasional big payout, but also small enough not to capture the attention of the FBI or other powerful Federal or state agencies. He'd never had to worry about local law enforcement, since for the most part they were ill-equipped and too busy with everyday crime to bother with him. Besides, amounts under $250,000 were usually paid by insurance companies or absorbed by the financial institutions themselves, and were written off as the cost of doing business. He knew very well how to thrive in this niche.

But $20 million? The temptation to jump on that had simply been too great. With that amount he could do so much. In fact, he might actually consider getting out of this line of work once and for all. A score of this magnitude was his golden ring, and he had snatched it without thinking.

"When's our payout hit?" Patrice asked Boon.

"A couple of days, just like normal. I need to make sure nobody can claw it back, not that they should be able to. I'll transfer your shares to your accounts then."

She nodded and continued with the day's work. The rest of the group talked and laughed a bit longer before following her lead. Everyone was back at it soon enough, and they were all decidedly upbeat. All except Boon: concern at the huge dollar amount gnawed at him, and he was worried he'd overreached this time. But beyond that he was suffering from guilt that he'd just lied to people who trusted and looked up to him, people that were as close to friends as he got outside of Steve Kempler. In essence, he had not only stolen from the Ohio Citizens National Bank, but from them as well.

Sometimes he didn't like this line of work at all.

When five o'clock struck, he leaned back and cracked his knuckles, sending Sasha out the door with a single backwards look at him. The others all left soon after. He tidied up and locked the doors and headed home. He cruised past the bread shop and saw that it was boarded up with a sign apologizing for the closure, but they planned on reopening soon "Bigger and *Breader* than before". He grinned at the pun, despite his current mood.

He parked behind his building and went upstairs. The sterile atmosphere greeted him as it always did, from his bed made with military precision to the dead eye of the television. On a whim he picked up the guitar and strummed a few chords, but music eluded him, as always. He tossed the instrument on the bed. The thought of another lonely evening there haunted him to the point where he changed into workout clothes and drove across the river to the gym, as much to stay in shape as to avoid the very real temptation to get hammered.

Two hours later, sweat still drying on his aching body from the strenuous activity, Dohir parked in the alley and walked to his door. As he was punching in the code, he sensed movement in the shadows nearby. Startled, he spun around, and a man eased slowly into the light. Boon guessed the newcomer was in his mid-thirties, with short, sandy blond hair just beginning to thin on top. He had a pleasant face and a calming smile, an expression he held so naturally that it had to be practiced. He was shorter than Boon, probably five-ten or so, but solidly built. He had on a light a tan jacket even though the night was warm, and Dohir was a little taken aback when he noticed a bulge under the man's left arm. He wore glasses, thin gold wireframes that hadn't been in style for years. As the newcomer stepped closer he plucked the glasses from his nose and cleaned them on his shirt, holding them up to the light for inspection afterwards. *Federal Agent* was the first thing that came to Boon's mind. The second was *Boy Scout*. The hair on the back of his neck sprang to attention and he resisted the urge to wipe his suddenly sweaty palms on his pants.

"Good evening. I hope I didn't startle you," the man said.

"No problem," Boon replied easily, his mind racing. "Although it's tough not to, especially in a dark alley in OTR. What can I do for you?"

The man held out a wallet. Inside was a white card with the letters FBI printed in a chunky blue font. "I'm Special Agent Hal Hollenbeck with the FBI. Do you have a minute? I'd like to ask you some questions."

The way the agent's two names flowed together, it sounded to Boon like they were a matched set, as if one couldn't be used without the other. Like Ronald Reagan, or Clark Kent. "The FBI? Really? Yeah, sure. What can I do for you?"

The agent smoothly pocketed the ID and gestured toward the front of the alley. "I'm asking around the neighborhood, looking into the incident at the bread store up the street. Loafers. Are you aware of what happened there?"

Boon was careful not to sigh out loud, and it was all he could do to mask his instant relief. "Well, I saw that the place got vandalized. Why's the FBI interested in that? Isn't that a little below your pay grade?"

"Sometimes. But due to the fact that it appears to be a hate crime, this is our jurisdiction." The agent's voice was soft, with no edge to it. Calming. Boon wasn't sure if he was tired, or if that was the way he always sounded.

"Oh, I see. I guess I didn't know that."

Hollenbeck pulled out his phone and tapped the screen a few times. "Your name is?"

"Dohir. Boon Dohir." He was half-tempted to give one of his numerous aliases, but decided against it. If he was asked to produce ID right now, this is what the fake driver's license in his wallet said.

The agent checked for spelling. "Dohir? Interesting last name. What is that? Middle Eastern?"

"Yes, good guess. Syrian, to be precise."

"Thanks. Address?"

Boon shared that as well, watching in interest as Hollenbeck took it all down. The man was quite adept at entering information on the tiny screen, his thumbs tapping away as smoothly as any Millennial. He asked how long Boon had lived here, whether anyone else resided at this address, and so on. It was all basic, routine stuff, the kind of information any law enforcement agent would ask. But it was information Dohir didn't like sharing with anyone, much less with the FBI. When asked, he gave the agent a fake phone number.

"Did you see or hear anything the night it happened?"

Boon shook his head. "No, I'm sorry to say, I didn't. I didn't know anything about it until the next morning when I was leaving for work. I saw the cops and the crowd there, that's all."

"Have you seen anyone out of the ordinary hanging around lately? Any strangers?"

Dohir chuckled once, gesturing around them. "Here, in Over-the-Rhine? That's all you see in this neighborhood. This place is pretty diverse, you know? We get all kinds of people in and out of here."

"Yeah, I'm familiar with it. I don't live too far away." Hollenbeck continued taking notes while Boon waited silently, his pulse beginning to flatten out. The agent plucked his glasses from his nose again and held them out to inspect for dirt or smudges. Not seeing anything, he fitted them back on his face, but not before Boon noticed the man's eyes for the first time; they may have exuded a practiced sense of calm, but there was some mileage hiding there below the surface, as if the agent had seen a lot during his time with the Bureau. Hollenbeck put away his phone, then held something out to Dohir.

"Okay, thanks for your help. Here's my card. Please let me know if you see or hear anything."

Boon accepted the business card and held it to the light. In the upper left-hand corner was the seal of the U.S. Department of Justice and the Federal Bureau of Investigation. To the right of that was Hollenbeck's name, his business address, office and cell phone, and a government email address. The card was of thick stock and heavy in his hand. He stared at it a moment before slipping it into his wallet.

The agent looked at him, his expression easy. "Thanks for your time, Mr. Dohir. Again, please contact me if you see or hear anything."

"Sure. You bet."

"I'd like to catch the guys that did this. It looks like a nice place, and probably makes great bread, too. Ever try it?"

"No, I haven't. Been meaning to."

Hal started walking away. When his body was half in and out of the shadows, he stopped and pointed towards Boon's door. Almost as an afterthought, he said, "That's quite a lock you have there. Expecting trouble?"

Dohir waved it away with a laugh. "No, not really. But better safe than sorry. I mean, look at the bread shop."

The agent tilted his head at the explanation. "Yeah, that makes sense. Thanks again."

"Sure. And I hope you get them. Happy hunting."

Hollenbeck turned and walked away, toward the main street. Boon could hear his shoes crunching on the grit of the alley as he vanished into the darkness.

Once upstairs, Dohir poured himself a gin and tonic and tried to relax, but that wasn't in the cards. He was concerned about being on the FBI's radar, even as peripherally as this. No, "concerned" wasn't a strong enough word — he was worried. In all the years he'd been in this business he'd managed to stay out of any databases of interest, either local, state, or Federal. He withdrew the business card from his wallet and toyed with it again. Now this Hal Hollenbeck character knew who he was, where he lived, and what he looked like. If for some reason the agent decided to do a deeper dive on him, the man would discover Boon's identity was less than legit, and that could throw up all kinds of red flags. He flicked the agent's business card between his fingers once more, the clicking loud in the sterile space. Boon had another apartment on the west side of Cincinnati that he never frequented, set up specifically for this type of circumstance. It was time to make a move.

But first, he needed a drink. Just one.

When he woke early the next morning, Boon was aware of two

things right away: one, he was suffering from another near-debilitating hangover; and two, he had a missed call from an unknown number, and whoever it was had left him a voicemail. Cursing his stupidity and weakness, he turned on his phone's speaker and after a few bleary, botched attempts, managed to hit the play button.

The first thing he heard was a muted rustling of clothes, followed by some breathing. He was about to hang up when a low voice began talking. He recognized it right away. It was Dante, the tall Black kid from outside Loafers bread store.

"Yo, Moneybags, this is Dante, from the bread store. You gave us a little incentive to find out what happened to Mr. Price's place, remember? Been asking around, and I think I found out the guys who done it. Well, one of them, anyways. Was some punk from the west side, kid named Muller, Jackson Muller. He's some kind of skinhead wannabe, or somethin'. It was an initiation thing he and a buddy had to do to join their fuckin' whites only gang. Some bullshit group called the American Patriots. They been braggin' about it all over town. And hey, if you don't mind, I might wanna have a chat with the dumbass, too. I'll expect payment next time I see you. Happy huntin' yourself, Moneybags. Don't be no stranger."

There was a chuckle, then a click, and that was it. Boon sat up and got a notepad from a drawer in his nightstand. He had a unique ability to remember numbers, especially phone numbers, but to be safe he wrote down Dante's, along with Jackson Muller's name and potential whereabouts. Then he put his head between his knees and for the next few minutes concentrated on not throwing up. Eventually, he got off the bed and went to shower and down some aspirin. It was time for work.

Once he was at the office and the rest of the group was assembled, he handed the slip of paper to Sasha. She took it and glanced at the information, then up at him, her eyebrows arching in a question.

"Do me a favor and find out where this Jackson Muller guy lives, okay?"

She put the paper next to her keyboard. "Sure. Work stuff?"

"No. Personal."

"Now?"

"Yeah. If you wouldn't mind."

"Okay, just give me a minute. Shouldn't be too hard, unless he's trying really hard not to be found."

"Yeah, thanks." Then he turned to address the rest of the group. He cleared his throat to get their attention. "Good morning, people. I've got some news I want to share with you." He waited while everyone spun in their chairs to face him.

"First, I should have your payouts to you tomorrow. I'll deposit the funds into your regular accounts, unless you tell me otherwise." There were some cheers at the news, and smiles all around. "Second, we've got a pretty full pipeline going, but we're going to have to put that on hold for a little while. The FBI paid me a visit last night."

That bombshell caused everyone to jerk upright, and the room suddenly got so quiet he could hear the ubiquitous HVAC system chugging away. Sir Jim cleared his throat and looked ready to bolt, although his ability to actually do so was certainly limited. Boon held up his hand, patting the air in front of him. His voice was therapist calm when he spoke again.

"Don't worry, it's nothing to be alarmed about. An agent stopped by asking about something that happened in my neighborhood, that's all. Nothing to do with us. But I had to give him my name, and he's got my address now, too. I think it'd be best if we bugged out, and if all of you went dark for a while. At least until all this blows over."

"Oh, damn, I don't like the sound of this," Sir Jim muttered.

"How long ya' think it'll be?" Clem asked, his normal grin absent.

Boon shrugged. "I don't know. I'm not taking any chances. I'll be moving out of my current apartment and into another one on this side of town."

Sir Jim tamped at his glistening forehead with a hanky. "Oh, damn," he repeated. "I do not like this at all."

"It's okay, Jim, it's nothing to worry about, but I'd rather be safe than sorry," he assured the huge man. "I'll contact all of you after I'm sure it's blown over. Okay? I want each of you to gather up your equipment and go. I'll clean up here. Now let's get busy."

This was not the first time they'd had to bug out on short notice, and they all knew the drill. There was minimal talking as they gathered up their laptops and removed anything personal from their desks. Boon went and stood by Sasha.

"Not you, Sasha. Not yet. Please find Jackson Muller first."

She glanced up at him, briefly frowned, but then her expression softened when she saw how serious he was. She opened up her laptop and got busy, her fingers clicking away on the keyboard. The others finished and made their way out one at a time. Clem gave him a warm pat on the shoulder as he passed by. Miles walked up to him.

"You sure we're okay? Should we be worried?"

Dohir smiled at him. "I wouldn't be concerned. This is just a precaution."

Miles raised a doubting eyebrow at him, but didn't argue the point. He collected his leather briefcase and was out the door. Boon could hear his rapid footsteps clanging down the metal stairs, followed by everyone but Sasha. She pressed a piece of paper into his hand and let it linger longer than necessary. She stared at him with an expression he couldn't read, as if she were about to say something, then packed up her own gear and was gone without a word.

Boon stared at her retreating back, wondering what that had been about. Then he studied the information she had shared with him. There were two possible addresses for Muller, both on the west side of town. He slipped the paper into his pocket, then spent an hour wiping down every surface in the office, from the desks to the coffee maker. When he was satisfied with his handiwork, he gathered up his own gear, plus the cell phones from his desk, then closed and locked the office door. He was sure to remove any fingerprints from the doorknobs and handrails. He locked the factory up tight, got into his car, and put the yellow building behind him.

Maybe this visit by the FBI wasn't entirely a bad thing, he mused. At least now he wouldn't have to feel everyone's eyes weighing on him all day long, while hiding the fact that he'd withheld such a huge payout from them. The chaotic guilt he was feeling would have less of a chance to surface.

But if that was so, he wondered, why did he feel like shit?

7

Boon moved into his west side apartment later that morning, which was a simple task since the only item he took with him was his guitar. Everything else he might need was already there, including clothes. The only moving van he required was the back seat of his car.

The next day he wired everyone's cuts to their accounts. The payout made a miniscule dent in the total take, which did nothing to ease his remorse–but not so much that he made any adjustments. He kept himself busy for the next few days by either going to the gym, running, or checking on his pet projects like the 3rd Street baseball diamond, the rehabbing of several houses in Cincinnati, and the gutting and replacement of playground equipment in a number of underprivileged areas. That said, the toughest task of all was forcing himself to steer clear of alcohol, but keeping himself and his mind busy helped.

On one of his trips up I-75 he stopped at a climbing facility located inside an old church near downtown Dayton where he spent the afternoon practicing his skills. The huge climbing walls began in the gutted church's basement and extended all the way into the bell tower. He was an excellent climber, and had already notched a number of challenging climbs under his belt in places like Yosemite and Arches National parks. He wasn't nearly skilled enough to tackle El Capitan, the mother of all climbs, but it was on his bucket list. Rock climbing, by its very nature, was a solitary endeavor, one that demanded tremendous concentration and planning–characteristics that were right up his alley. On the drive home at the end of the day his muscles ached so badly that he could barely lift his arms up to the steering wheel, which was exactly what he he'd been shooting for. But he hadn't lost his touch on the walls, and that pleased him.

His second apartment wasn't far from Union Terminal, west of the railroad tracks and I-75, and inside looked amazingly similar to his primary one in Over-the-Rhine. This section of Cincinnati was filled with more warehouses and industry than residential buildings, but it had the added bonus of a new microbrewery one block away.

On the fourth day there, he noticed his hands were trembling, coupled with a dull ache in the back of his head. The shakes had been getting worse over the last few days, but nothing like today. Boon didn't have to do an online search to know his body was craving alcohol. Desperate to take his mind off of the need to drink, he grabbed the scrap of paper with Muller's addresses from his nightstand. Next, he pulled Hollenbeck's business card from his wallet. Pursing his lips, he flipped the card between his trembling fingers. After a few seconds of staring into the void, he grabbed his phone and created a new and innocuous user name and email address. From there he sent the FBI agent a message. Under the subject line he put "Loafers Bread", and in the body typed "Please check this out," then added all the information he had on Jackson Muller. He hit "send". Immediately afterwards, he deactivated the account, then slipped the business card back into his wallet.

Content he'd done all he could reasonably do on that front, as a distraction he forced himself to concentrate on scrolling through local news online. Initially nothing much caught his attention. Then one headline from the Dayton Daily News grabbed his interest and his breath caught in his chest like he'd been punched. *"Local Man Murdered,"* the headline screamed at him. And underneath that, *"Businessman Phillip J. Marsden found dead in his home. Family distraught."*

The story was brief, only a few paragraphs, but by the time he got to the last line Boon was sitting bolt upright on the edge of the bed. He was shaking so badly he needed to grip the phone with both hands to keep from dropping it, but this shuddering had nothing to do with alcohol deprivation. According to the article, Marsden had been found duct-taped to a chair in his home, with damage to his face and body, and a bullet through the back of the head. Family and friends were devastated, and couldn't understand who could do this to such a fine man. An investigation had been opened.

He was not one to be easily stunned, but even so Boon spent the next half hour frantically scouring the Internet for additional information. Other news outlets had picked up the story, including some national ones, but none had anything more concrete to offer besides general biographical information: Marsden had been a model citizen, a member of the local Chamber of Commerce, a father of three, and a grandfather. One reporter had conjectured that the murder bore more than a passing resemblance to a mob hit, something that rarely if ever happened in Dayton. The police were of course confident that the killer or killers would soon be brought to justice.

Boon hopped out of bed and threw on some clothes. He flew down the steps and jumped into his BMW. With a squeal of tires, he shot from the parking lot and over to the highway toward Dayton. He violated his own rules and drove faster than he should have. Less than sixty tense minutes later he passed the exit for his baseball diamond near downtown, and continued into the northern suburbs. After crossing Interstate 70, he exited near the Dayton airport and headed west. On the corner up ahead was the Ohio Citizens National Bank branch where Chet worked. Boon slowed as he drove past, and the case of his Marsden-induced nerves spiked tenfold.

The windows of the bank were dark and lifeless. There was an imposing padlock on the front doors, a shiny red lump of steel that was incongruous against the black glass. A sign posted in the window stated that the branch was temporarily closed, but their Vandalia, Tipp City, and Troy offices were taking care of business as usual. They were very sorry for the inconvenience. He cruised slowly on past and didn't look back, his hands locked on to the steering wheel so tightly he could have been hanging over an abyss.

This was very bad for many reasons, and Boon knew it. Marsden was dead, murdered, and the bank branch where the wire transfer scheme had taken place was shuttered. The two events had to be related. In essence, he was sure he'd somehow had a direct hand in Marsden's death, even if he hadn't pulled the trigger himself.

He had never met the man before, not in person, but he'd researched him so thoroughly he felt a kinship with him. Now this stranger-not-a-stranger was dead, and it was directly attributable to Boon, the $20 million, and whatever had happened at the bank. Dohir had broken his own rule against going over his $250,000 limit, and now it looked like his greed had dragged him into some very deep shit. Deep and *violent* shit. Guilt gnawed at his soul as he kept his eyes riveted ahead of him, his ability to concentrate so impaired he was in danger of running his car off the road.

He arrived home and parked near the door of his back up apartment. As he got out of the car and slammed the door, he felt an urge to look over both shoulders before heading upstairs. He had no reason to be paranoid, and the fact that he was annoyed him. In reality, even if the people who had taken out Marsden were after him, Boon was convinced they had no idea who or where he was. As far as the killer or killers knew, he could be as close as next door, or sunning himself on some tropical beach. He was still berating himself for acting like a fool as he stepped inside, and, despite all his sensible arguments to the contrary, he couldn't resist making sure the door was securely locked behind him. He went upstairs into the living room.

As soon as he stepped inside, his phone rang. The M phone.

Boon pulled up short, his feet planted to the floor with roots seemingly sunk deeper than an ancient willow. The phone was over on the TV table, far enough away that he couldn't make out who was calling. He finally edged closer as it continued its jarring ringing. Four times. Five. The jangling seemed to get louder and louder, like police sirens rapidly approaching. When he'd finally inched close enough, he half-expected it to be Chet at the bank, but saw that the display simply said UNKNOWN NUMBER. With an unsteady hand he reached out and picked it up. A voice in his head screamed at him not to answer, that he was an idiot to even consider it, but there was no way he could stop himself. He felt like a curious child who knows he shouldn't touch a candle's flame, but does so anyway. Boon pressed the answer button and slowly put the phone to his ear.

At first, he didn't hear anything. Seconds passed while he hoped no one was there, then he caught the faint rhythmic sound of breathing. Nothing more, just breathing, heavy and even. Finally, a man's low voice spoke, his words colored by a thick Spanish accent.

"You have my money."

Boon said nothing. He peripherally noticed that he was holding his breath. He forced himself to exhale, but quietly, intent on minimizing the sound for some reason.

"You have my money. I want it back. Are you listening?" Those last three words were louder, more menacing. The speaker, whoever it was, was getting pissed off, his temper hovering a few degrees shy of a hard boil. When the man spoke again, he was nearly shouting.

"*Cabrón,* I am coming for you. I will have my money. And then I will make you pay for what you have done."

Because this was a cell phone, when the call ended there was no angry crashing of a receiver being slammed down, no sudden and ominous dial tone. Instead, the screen simply said "Call Over", and flashed the short duration of the call. Boon threw the device on the bed and rubbed his hands on the legs of his pants over and over, as if they were covered in a virus that stubbornly refused to be wiped away.

He stalked around the small space of the apartment for the next few minutes, nervous energy driving him from corner to corner. How the hell had the caller gotten his number, he wondered? The only person who had it was Chet at the bank. Was that why the branch was temporarily closed? Had the caller somehow coerced it out of Chet, along with Marsden's identity? Was Chet in trouble now, too? If so, why hadn't he read anything about the bank employee in the paper as well? This situation was completely and totally spiraling out of his control.

A drink, that was what he needed. He'd gamely resisted the temptation for days, but his tenuous willpower was suddenly overwhelmed. He rushed into the kitchen and rummaged around frantically, searching for booze, shoving glasses and bottles around in the cupboards in a panic. He had a little gin, but no tonic. There was also a splash of whiskey left over from some prior binge, but it was barely enough to wet the bottom of a glass. Then he remembered the brew-pub just down the street, and made a snap decision to head down there instead. He typically didn't go for beer since it took so much to get the job done, but he was out of options. He desperately needed to think, and he couldn't do that here since the walls of the apartment felt like they were collapsing in on him. The rational part of his mind still operating insisted this was a terrible idea, but the decision to drink had been made and now it was all he could think about.

It was still bright outside, but the sun was low in the west, lending the sky an almost pinkish hue. Boon got into his car and had it fired up before he realized how stupid it was to drive the short distance to the pub. He wasn't thinking straight, and that annoyed him, too. But he was already in and buckled up, so he quickly drove down the street and parked in one of the many open spaces available.

The pub was a converted warehouse, with two large open garage doors facing the street. The evening was warm, and small groups of people were sitting at round tables here and there, both inside and out, talking and laughing. The crowd was mainly younger and roughly evenly split between male and female, but here and there he spotted a graying or balding head. *Dream On* by *Aerosmith* was playing from speakers overhead, but in the background and not so loud to inhibit conversations. There was a short wrought-iron fence that bordered the outdoor porch on the sidewalk, a nominal barrier either mandated by local law or designed to partition off the sober from the sodden. He hurried inside.

The interior was open and airy, and dominated by a huge ceiling fan spinning lazily overhead. There was a long bar on the right where three female bartenders in tight T-shirts were expertly navigating around each other behind the bar, spinning and weaving in patterns that would've been the envy of a synchronized swim team. Boon stood in line behind several others, then in turn ordered a heavy stout from one of the bartenders. He paid her in cash, tipped her, and went back outside, in no state of mind to strike up a conversation. He sat alone at a small table near the black fence and took a long pull at his drink, polishing off nearly two-thirds of it in a single gulp. The thick ale tasted of chocolate and coffee. As easily as this one was going down, he wished he had ordered two. Or three. His frayed nerves were miles away from being calmed.

He barely had time to relive and rehash any of the recent events when three large black Cadillac SUVs roared past him, far exceeding the posted 35 mph speed limit. The vehicles' windows were so heavily tinted he couldn't see who or how many people were inside each one. Several drinkers sharing the outdoor porch noticed them tearing past, generating more than a few concerned murmurs and craned necks. The three blocky vehicles fairly flew past them and down the street, then squealed into the parking lot of his apartment building, where at least a dozen large men piled out of the same number of doors. Boon jerked upright in his chair and nearly spilled his beer. At this distance he couldn't make out fine details, but they all moved with speed and a shared purpose. And unless he was mistaken, unless his eyes were playing tricks on him, it looked like several of them had kicked down the sturdy door to his apartment and were flooding inside. He nearly shot out of his seat.

His first thought was *How the hell did they find me?* His second was to jump in his car and just get the hell out of there, to lay down some rubber and trust the road-handling prowess of German engineering to put as many miles as possible between him and them. This instinct to flee was primal and almost overpowering, and he could feel his feet twitching to just *go right now!* But he forced himself to settle down, and do the smart thing and observe what was happening from a block away. They may know where he lived, he insisted to himself, but there was no way they knew what he looked like. Whoever was storming his place shouldn't be able to pick him out of a lineup, much less spot him out from this distance. He was convinced he was safe here.

Or was he? If these guys were working for the man with the Spanish accent, and he had to assume that they were, and they were able to find him this fast, then why–and this realization chilled his blood–why wouldn't they also know what he looked like? All he could think about at that moment was Marsden. Marsden duct-taped to a chair. Marsden beaten. Marsden with a bullet hole in his head.

Shit, he thought. *Shit, shit, shit.*

Boon eased himself out of his seat and leaned against the wall near the garage door, where he could still watch without being seen, and without appearing too obviously ill at ease. He held the beer in his hand, but no longer felt any inclination to drink. He stared down the street toward his apartment, but there was no activity.

How the hell had the Spanish speaker been able to find him so quickly, he wondered? He'd left no trace of himself anywhere. He'd never come near Marsden, and had never gone into the bank. There was nothing connecting him to anyone involved with the wire transfer. The only connection was the M phone. Chet–and maybe others at the bank–would have had that phone number. There was nothing else linking him to this. Only the M phone. Suddenly he stood up straight.

Unless the Spanish speaker had been able to trace their call?

That shouldn't be possible, unless the man had connections to the phone company, or some law enforcement group. Or maybe he had some illicit, high-powered software that could do it? Dohir guessed that would be incredibly expensive and exclusive, but he doubted that cost would be an issue with this maniac. Even more terrifying was the realization that he had somehow locked onto Boon's phone, and potentially stayed locked on after they hung up. How else would he have been able to zero in the apartment so specifically? He repressed a shudder at how close he had come to disaster. What would have happened had he stayed home?

Several more minutes passed, and finally men began exiting his apartment. No, scratch that–they all looked like men, except one who might have been a woman. He could make out blond hair, and a build distinctive from the others. Plus, the way she walked was different. He watched from inside the pub as they got in their vehicles and drove toward him, slower and more law-abiding this time. Boon melted into the shadows as they passed by.

Once they had been gone for a comfortable amount of time, Dohir ordered another beer and sat back down at his table. He took a sip. He wasn't sure of his next step, but he knew going back to the apartment was out of the question. Boon couldn't be sure they hadn't left someone behind, or that they weren't somehow watching it. No, for now at least, his apartment was as welcome as Chernobyl.

The beer now no longer appealed to him, so he left it nearly untouched on the table and headed out. Once back in the BMW, he drove away from the apartment and into the fading light, comforted by the anonymity the increasing darkness afforded him. The car's headlights automatically came on as he hit the highway. Randomly he drove south on I-75, over the Brent-Spence Bridge and into northern Kentucky. He drove for over an hour, until the highway's hills and curves flattened out and he realized he was nearing Lexington. He exited north of the city, where he stopped to fill up his tank. Back in his car, he pulled out and merged onto the highway heading back toward Cincinnati. The world outside the comfortable, safe interior of the big sedan was dark and empty, the only lights being an occasional home or business well off the road. Other cars passed him, the glow of the dashboards eerily lighting up the faces of the drivers and turning them into ghostly apparitions.

Shit, none of this was supposed to happen! Not like this. Across all his schemes, in all the time he'd been doing this, he'd been so careful to make sure that the people he'd targeted were little more than inconvenienced. Any losses he'd caused were always indemnified by someone else, a bank or credit union, or faceless insurance companies with deep pockets and fraud departments that routinely dealt with this sort of thing. Or, like the grandparent scam, with amounts so trivial they could easily afford the money they lost. To them it was more of an embarrassment than a hardship.

And then the Marsden deal came along.

Hell, he'd been excited and anxious to close that one. The original $200,000 was near the upper threshold of his business model. But the expected amount had somehow morphed into $20 million, and despite his initial misgivings, he had plowed ahead. And because of that decision, Marsden was dead and his own life was on the line.

He drove on in silence, the muted hissing of his tires on pavement the only sound penetrating the inside of the luxury car. Almost before he knew it, he was winding down the section of interstate carved out of the huge hill south of the Ohio River the locals called the Cut in the Hill. The bright Cincinnati skyline was spread out before him, glittering in the night as if the horizon had been painted with stars. For just a moment, as he stared at the spectacle, he nearly forgot about Marsden and killers with Spanish accents, black SUVs, and the shitstorm he'd caused. He crossed back over the bridge into Ohio then exited the highway near downtown. Boon parked on the street close to Fountain Square, the car idling almost silently as he thought. He had hurt enough people, and he could not bear being the source of more. There was no way he could undo the past, but he could make sure he didn't make matters any worse. He knew what he had to do. It was time to shut down the entire operation.

Boon opened a secure messaging app on his phone and entered a pre-saved group name. On the message line he typed two simple words, "*Alas, Babylon,*" and without hesitation hit the send button. That phrase went out to all of the members of his team, informing them that their arrangement was over and that the operation was done, and to sever all existing ties with him and each other. They knew what this meant: they'd either been compromised, or were in very real danger. Maybe both. They might eventually understand what had happened if they caught the news about Marsden, or they might not. They might never put the two together, but it didn't matter. He sincerely hoped that they would simply move on with their lives, just as he had instructed.

Staring at the two words on his phone, he felt another wave of grief roll over him, one he hadn't expected. When he was younger, Boon had been outgoing and popular, friends with everyone. But events had changed him over the past few years. Now he was a loner, a solitary figure intent on keeping people at arm's length. Even so, and despite himself, he had become oddly close to his team. Cutting them out of his life so suddenly was more of a shock to him than he could have imagined. He sat in the idling car for a few more minutes, watching the world move on around him. Finally, he pulled back out into traffic.

He had never felt so alone as he did right then, and he didn't like it at all.

8

With both of his apartments likely compromised, but for different reasons — one by the Spanish speaker, and the other possibly by the FBI — Boon had few destinations left to him. He had no close friends where he could bunk down, and if he were being honest with himself, he didn't want to impose on anyone and potentially put them in danger. He briefly considered crashing in some seedy motel that didn't require ID or a credit card, but battling bed bugs and meth-heads sounded terrible. Instead, he decided to call in a favor, but one that wouldn't put anyone in harm's way. He texted Steve Kempler a simple question: *Got a minute? Boon.*

The answer *Sure* came back almost instantly. He dialed the man's number, and after a single ring Kempler picked up, his voice booming over the phone.

"Hey, Boon, what a surprise! To what do I owe this honor?"

"Sorry for bothering you this late at night, but I've got a favor to ask."

Dohir could hear a TV on in the background. It sounded like a sporting event complete with an excited announcer and crowd noise, but he couldn't tell for sure what it was. Kempler was a massive Reds baseball fan, so it was likely the game.

"Sure, no problem, big guy. What do you need? Happy to help."

"Anyone staying at your hunting cabin for the next few days? I could use a place to…lay low for a little bit."

The TV suddenly went silent. He had Kempler's full attention now. "No, there's no one there. It's empty. You're welcome to use it as long as you want. Deer season isn't for months."

"That's great, thanks."

A pause, then, "You okay? Everything okay?"

Boon forced a smile over the phone. "Yeah, it's fine. Everything's fine. I just need to get out of town for a few days. Personal stuff, you know?"

Another pause, and Boon was afraid Steve wasn't buying it and would want to dig deeper into unwanted territory. But when the man answered there was nothing except a twinge of concern in his strong voice. "No problem, no problem at all. As long as you're sure you're okay?"

"Yeah, I'm good, thanks for asking."

"Then go and enjoy yourself. You know where the key is, right? Under the brick on the back porch?"

Dohir did. He'd been to the cabin once before, back when his entire team had taken a week off and he'd had nothing else to do. He'd spent most of the five days there either drunk out of his mind or epically hungover. "Yep, you bet."

The two passed a few more pleasantries before saying their goodbyes. The turmoil in his head was mellowing now that he had somewhere to go that was very much off the grid. He could regroup and decide his next moves on his own schedule. He needed time to think and plan. The only other person who knew his location would be Kempler, and there was virtually no connection between the two of them — at least none that anyone knew about.

Feeling slightly better now that he had a destination in mind, Boon wound through the streets of downtown Cincinnati until he located State Route 50 east. He turned onto the busy road and followed the dark ribbon as it hugged the Ohio River, before it angled northeast and he passed through the small suburbs of Mariemont, Milford, and eventually crossed I-275. He kept going as the glow of the city dimmed behind him and the asphalt in his headlights grew narrow and more remote. He drove for over an hour until he got to Waynesboro, one of those burgs dotting the map that was little more than a Wal-Mart and an aging downtown filled with craft stores, pizza places, bars, and memories of better times. He navigated the twisting road through town and then back out the other side, still heading generally east. A few miles outside of Waynesboro he turned left onto a road only slightly wider than a single lane. With signs warning of Amish buggies, Boon continued more cautiously, until he came to a barely noticeable farm gate at the mouth of a rutted gravel driveway. There he parked and swung the gate open, pulled the car in, and shut it behind him. He continued up the tree-lined drive. Half a mile in, the lane opened up and he could just make out the cabin overlooking a large pond. Despite himself, he grinned.

Kempler's cabin was no more a cabin than Boon's BMW was a moped. The house before him stood three stories tall, with a wide, comfortable porch that ringed the entire structure. It was built into a hill, so the main floor was level with the driveway on one side, but was the second floor on the pond side. Outside lights ringed the porch and cast shimmers on the otherwise dark, still body of water. The fact that Kempler still referred to it as his "cabin" never failed to amuse him.

Boon pulled up to the garage, gravel crackling under his tires. He tested the big door and found it unlocked, and eased the car inside, the engine ticking and pinging as it cooled. He slid the door down, then walked around to the side of the cabin where he located a retaining wall made of large blocks. He slid one to the side, and spied a brass key on a ring exactly where it was supposed to be. He went to the door on the lowest level and let himself in.

Inside it was still and warm, the air conditioning either off or the temperature set high. A faint whiff of gun oil and bacon grease tickled his nose. For the next ten minutes he poked his head into each room until he was convinced he was alone. The cabin had eight bedrooms, two full kitchens, four bathrooms, and more mounted animal heads than a taxidermist's shop. Boon chose the bedroom on the top floor, a crow's nest of a room with windows on all four sides that gave him unencumbered views of the property. He kept the lights off as he got ready for bed. It was almost midnight when he crawled between the sheets. He was emotionally drained and exhausted, and was afraid he wouldn't be able to sleep, but he dozed off almost immediately. There was usually plenty of booze in the house, he knew, but this was one time he was too tired to fall prey to his vice.

Bright sunlight in his face woke him the next morning. Boon glanced at his watch and saw it was early, just before six o'clock. His head ached all over, like his brain had been bruised. He figured it was from an ongoing lack of alcohol in his system, and he almost laughed at the irony around that; it seemed no matter what he did, he woke up feeling like crap.

He stayed in bed a few minutes longer, then rubbed grit from his eyes and went to the windows, peering out each one. The pond, about the size of a city block, was tabletop still and shimmered in the sunshine. A light mist covered it from one end to the other. Two of the remaining three windows showed thick woods outside, and the fourth gave a good view of the gravel driveway winding back towards the main road. He hadn't expected to see anyone or anything besides perhaps some deer, but nevertheless was relieved when he didn't.

Boon went down to the main floor and one of the two kitchens. Kempler always kept the fridge stocked, and this time was no different. There were no perishables such as eggs or milk, but he found quite a stockpile of other staples. He cooked some bacon on the stove and relaxed at the table with a clear view of the pond. He waited patiently while the coffee brewed. It was the most relaxed and at peace he'd been in days.

When the coffee was done, he took his cup outside and sat in a rocker on the porch. He was thinking how pleasant this moment was, how easy life could be without worrying about a dozen scams and schemes, legal consequences, crazy people, and the well-being of his former staff. The downtime also allowed older memories to intrude, and he had no way of blocking them except with booze. But, as much as he craved it, drinking was not an option; he needed to figure out how to get out of this mess, and getting wasted wasn't going to help with that. A snapping turtle or carp splashed near the bank, sending ripples out into the pond, the tiny waves fading out as they traveled away from the shore. He slapped at an inquisitive mosquito hovering near his arm. The light mist hanging over the pond was an ephemeral blanket over the still waters. There was no breeze at all.

Then his phone rang.

He jerked involuntarily. This wasn't the M phone - that one was still at his second apartment and likely never to be seen again. This was his personal phone. He pulled it from his pocket and stared at the display, anxious that the words UNKNOWN CALLER might be there again. Instead, it simply read 513, the area code for Cincinnati and parts of southwest Ohio. He'd never seen a number displayed quite like that before.

Unlike last time, he successfully resisted the temptation to answer the call, instead letting it go to voicemail. He stared at the device until it chimed, letting him know he had a new message. Boon hesitated, then touched play.

"Mr. Dohir," said a man's voice. Boon thought hard, certain he'd heard it before. "Good morning, this is special agent Hal Hollenbeck of the FBI. I wanted to follow up on our earlier conversation, but haven't been able to catch you at your apartment in OTR."

Hal Hollenbeck. The FBI. How had he found him? *How had he gotten this number? What the fuck was happening?*

"You're a very difficult man to locate, Mr. Dohir. I'd like to talk to you about the incident at the bread store, and what you know. I think you've been less than forthcoming with me, sir. When you get this message, please call me back."

The agent left his phone number, which Boon still remembered from his business card, then said a polite goodbye. Boon scowled at the device, as if it had betrayed him. He set it down on a small table next to his chair and sat back, staring at it. Finally, unable to stand it any longer, he dialed the agent's number.

"Special Agent Hollenbeck here."

Dohir cleared his throat. "Uh, yes, this is Boon Dohir returning your call."

"Ah, excellent. Thanks for getting back with me so quickly. I appreciate it."

"Yeah, sure. What can I do for you?"

"Well as I said, Mr. Dohir, you're a difficult man to find. I've been waiting outside your apartment for days. Traveling?"

"Yes, you could say that. By the way, how did you get my number?"

There was a pause, and Boon could almost picture the agent cleaning his glasses. "The one you shared with me wasn't in service, oddly enough. But I ran across some acquaintances of yours while the local police were investigating some gang related activity, and during our discussion the vandalism at Loafer's came up. They mentioned something about a crazy white guy that matched your description who was looking into the same incident. I had a hunch they were talking about you, but wasn't positive until one of them mentioned the phrase 'happy hunting.' I seem to recall you using that exact term with me during our meeting."

Boon rubbed a hand across his forehead. Damnit, Dante and his group must have gotten busted for something.

"During the course of filling out the Bureau's FB-302 interview form," the agent continued, "I did my standard due diligence and checked a number of our federal and state databases, including the Ohio BMV and the credit bureaus. And, try as I might, I couldn't seem to find any official records for anyone named Boon Dohir. No Social Security number. No record of him at the BMV. No birth certificate or employment records. I find that odd, don't you?"

Boon didn't answer.

"And that got me thinking. I was making some notes and, I must admit, was doodling at my desk. I tend to do that while I'm thinking. I started rearranging the letters of your name, and discovered something very interesting. Imagine my surprise when I saw that the name 'Boon Dohir' is actually an anagram for someone else."

Boon grunted, a single syllable. Nothing else came out.

"When I rearrange the letters of your name, they spell 'Robin Hood.' Imagine my surprise."

He should have hung up the phone right then, but he didn't.

"So Boon Dohir is actually Robin Hood, the legendary fictional hero who steals from the rich and gives to the poor." Hollenbeck paused. "So, tell me, Mr. Dohir–why would someone conceal their actual identity and go by an anagram for Robin Hood? Do you, indeed, steal from the rich and give to the poor?"

"I don't know what you're talking about," Boon said with nominal conviction. No one had ever deduced his alias before. Not his coworkers, and not his business associates. Nobody.

"Which leads me to wonder," the agent said, "who you really are, and what you're up to. I think we need to meet face to face, Mr. Dohir. Or whatever your real name is."

Boon finally began shaking off the shock of the agent's discovery.

A light breeze began blowing over the pond, stirring the wispy blanket of mist. "No, I don't think so. That's not going to happen."

"Hm. I rather thought you'd say that. But if you'll indulge me, why did you pay a couple of locals for information about what happened at Loafers? And why did you make up a fake email account and send me said information? That really does sound rather 'Robin Hood-ish' of you."

Boon found his voice again. "Easy. I didn't like what happened to the bread store. I hate seeing innocent people harmed like that for no reason. I figured I could do something about it, and I did. Case closed."

"Very noble. And I'm very grateful, too. We found Jackson Muller, and he did confess to the crime, so thanks for your assistance. And by the way, your friends wanted me to remind you that you owe them another five hundred dollars. Only this time, tell them not to get arrested for assaulting Mr. Muller and his fellow gang members, much as they may have deserved it."

Boon rubbed his hand across his face. "I think we're done here. Goodbye, Mr. Hollenbeck."

"I'd still like to meet in person, Mr. Dohir."

"No, I don't think so. That's not going to happen."

"I disagree. I have a feeling our paths will cross again."

"No, they won't. Goodbye."

He hung up the phone and tossed the device on the table. He would have blocked Hollenbeck's number, but didn't think he could; how can you block a simple area code? Boon looked out over the pond. Gone was the peace he had felt just minutes earlier. It had blown away, like mist from the pond.

9

Boon nearly tore the cabin apart looking for something to drink, but contrary to what he thought, the place was bone dry. The irrational craving in his mind couldn't accept that fact, and was urging him into pulling a nonsensical stunt, including leaving the safety of the cabin and driving into town. In the end, the coherent sliver of his brain still operating knew that keeping his head down was the smart play. Besides, he kept reminding himself, there was nowhere else to go if he screwed this up.

Instead, he spent the remainder of the morning restlessly prowling around the cabin and property. Kempler owned over a hundred acres of the hilly, wooded land surrounding the house and garage, and he kept it as primitive and untouched as possible. There were a few trails wide enough for a four-wheeler to pass, but that was it. The idea was to attract deer, not scare them off. He spent some time hiking the trails around the property. Twice he noticed deer stands up in the trees, one of which was an oversized platform on the far side of the lake which gave a clear view of the house and yard. Boon took note of its location and wandered on.

He kept going, working up a sweat and covering several miles with nothing but the soothing sounds of birds and insects all around him. The day was warm, but it remained tolerable in the shadows of the trees. At one point he heard a crashing of branches in the near-distance and saw a brown flash and white tail, and knew he had disturbed a doe or a buck. Several hours later, he returned to the cabin and fixed lunch, which he ate on the porch. There was little else to do there, but he was okay with that. Kempler had a large screen TV in the family room, but the house was so far from civilization that no over-the-air channels came in: visitors lived on the several dozen DVDs that were stacked next to a player under the television. This downtime was just what he needed to help clear his head. Besides the absence of alcohol, he felt he could get used to this lifestyle quite easily. He kept his phone on him, terrified it would ring, but it didn't.

Evening came, and he cooked a TV dinner in the microwave, which he again enjoyed outside on the porch. It was overcast, with the sun invisible behind a shelf of dark clouds crawling in from the west. The air began to feel charged and heavy, and he could tell severe weather was not far off. That was fine with him. He had always enjoyed the technicolor wonder of a good thunderstorm.

He was cleaning up just as the first drops began striking the far side of the pond, skirting toward the house. Boon hustled inside as the rain began coming down in earnest. He made his way upstairs to the crow's nest bedroom where he could get a three hundred sixty-degree view of the storm. The rain was intense, heavy sheets of it slanting down across the pond and slamming against the windows. Lightning struck somewhere in the woods a short distance away, and thunder vibrated the entire house to its foundation. There was a creek off to the right feeding the pond, and he could see the water level was already rising from the deluge.

While he was busy watching the thunderstorm rolling towards him from the west, he almost missed the flash of light halfway up the lane leading to the house. Startled, he stared at that spot again, positive he had seen something but having no idea what it was. And then it came a second time. A brief on and off light, up the drive near where it exited from the woods toward the road. It was like a car door quickly opening and closing, or the errant beam of a flashlight. He suddenly wished for a pair of binoculars, but there weren't any at hand. He continued staring, but the light never manifested again.

Boon didn't wait. He couldn't be sure that what he'd seen wasn't something innocuous, like lightning reflected off a puddle, or a simple trick of his vision due to the storm. But he wasn't one to take chances, not after what had happened at his apartment. He hurried downstairs in the dark and made his way to the main kitchen. There, leaning up against the cabinet, was a 30/30 rifle that Kempler always kept handy, complete with a high-powered scope. In the light of the microwave clock, he checked and was relieved to see a shell already chambered. He released the magazine with a click, and saw that it held additional rounds as well. Quietly, he made his way to the cabin's lowest level, grabbed a camouflage poncho from a hook, and silently crept outside. Immediately the rain slammed against him and the wind threatened to knock him over. He scrambled over uneven terrain, once or twice tripping over unseen roots or rocks, and began circling behind the garage. The woods were thick here, filled with brush and thorns, and the going was so treacherous he slipped and nearly fell more than once. Fortunately, the driving rain and deepening night masked his movements and any sounds. Finally, thirty yards or so behind the house, he crouched down low and went silent, all his senses trained on the open area around the house.

Five minutes passed, then ten, and he neither heard nor saw anything strange. Water ran down his back and his shoes were soaked completely through. His nose itched. The rifle was heavy in his hands. He was considering standing up when he heard a sound. It wasn't much, perhaps no more than a foot scraping on wet gravel. Or a muffled cough. Regardless, it was enough to send adrenaline roaring through his system. He tensed up, his eyesight locked onto a dark shape that might or might not have just moved near the back door.

His first thought was that Hollenbeck had somehow tracked him down and decided to pay him a visit. After all, it was clear that the agent wanted to talk to him very badly. He'd said as much, and there had been ample time for him to drive here from Cincinnati. But Boon was fairly sure the man would simply come up the lane like anyone else and knock on the door like a normal person. He wouldn't be sneaking around, not like this. And besides, the longer Boon watched, the more convinced he became that there were several silhouettes inching around the house, not just one. Hollenbeck could have brought more men with him, but again, Boon just didn't figure he would operate like that.

No, the pragmatist in him was pretty damn sure the Spanish speaking lunatic had somehow tracked him here, and these men belonged to him. The man had managed to track his M phone before, and now Boon was convinced he had somehow located him through his regular phone. But how? Almost no one had the number.

Except Chet at the bank. *Damnit, Chet had it.* Boon had given it to him. If these crazy bastards had Chet, or somehow had access to his files at the bank, they probably had this number as well. Somehow, the Spanish speaker was able to track people by their phones, even if they weren't talking on them. He carefully reached into his pocket and turned his off. He wasn't positive that it would disrupt their ability to find him, but he prayed it would. His next task was to get the hell out of this mess.

Getting to his car was out of the question. It was in the garage behind a closed door and out of play. And besides, the narrow lane was probably blocked by whatever vehicle or vehicles these people were driving. He couldn't take that chance. Another way out would be for him to make his way up the drive and try to steal whatever they were driving, but he had no idea if the keys were there, or how many men were guarding it. No, that was out. Too risky. He might be able to make it to the road, but he was miles from anywhere and that option didn't hold much promise.

He was still deciding his next move when lights in the house suddenly started blinking on, one by one. Through the multiple windows he could see people in dark clothing moving from room to room. They were all armed. Apparently, they were done being stealthy and were trying a more direct approach. He counted six people, but there could have been more. And one of them was a woman. He watched as she pulled down her hood, revealing short curly blond hair, a round face, and tiny little eyes. Hot Rod red lipstick made her lips pop, even from this distance. She was quite clearly in charge, her pointed finger stabbing towards different rooms and upstairs as she directed the men.

Yes, there were six of them, including the woman. They must have been convinced he was no longer inside, since several of them were leaning against the kitchen counter, or otherwise relaxing in chairs. Their guns were no longer raised. The floor would be a wreck from their muddy feet, and the random thought popped into his head that he would owe Kempler an apology for the mess. One of them opened the fridge, rummaged around, finally emerging with a can of soda.

The woman was pissed. Her hands were gesturing everywhere, and she was barking at each of the men in turn. Every man at the receiving end of her ire ducked his head and avoided her eyes, actively working to deflect her fury. She lifted a small walkie-talkie to her mouth and snapped orders into it. Seconds later, headlights lit up the driveway and eased his way. He flattened himself to the soaked ground while a large SUV parked a few dozen feet away. The door opened, and a man emerged. He was gigantic, so large that the vehicle's suspension actually rebounded half a foot when his boots hit the ground. Boon's jaw dropped. He had never seen someone of such tremendous proportions before.

The giant lumbered toward the house. As his massive frame was outlined in the light from the door, he stopped. His head was the size of a bull's, and he swiveled it around towards Boon's hiding place, seemingly right at him. It was all Dohir could do not to bolt. There was something about the man, something primal, that froze Boon's blood and nearly loosened his bowels. He prayed he would never meet the man face-to-face. Finally, the giant grasped the doorknob with a hand the size of a catcher's mitt, opened it, and ducked low to enter. He had to turn partially sideways in order for his shoulders to fit through.

Boon desperately wanted to see the interaction between the huge man and the group, but his quaking legs flatly rejected his commands to move to a better spot. He couldn't see much else from his current location, but none of the men seemed to be talking, or even moving. Perhaps they were terrified of the newcomer as well? Even if that was the case, the blond lady didn't seem at all cowed, and was still gesturing this way and that, pointing in different directions. She finished dishing out orders or whatever she was going on about, and the men began moving towards the door. Boon, his feet finally obeying his instructions, took that as his cue to abandon his hiding place, and started easing deeper into the woods.

Keeping one eye on the house, he began edging toward the lake where he could move a little more freely. The rain continued pounding down hard, and the night was dark enough there was little chance he would be spotted. Still, he hugged the tree line, always keeping plenty of cover between him and the intruders. The ground under his feet was muddy and sucked at his shoes. With a start he realized he was leaving water-filled tracks, but there was nothing he could do about that.

Suddenly all of the lights outside the house burst on, to Boon's eyes as bright as an airport runway. Had he stayed where he was, he almost certainly would have been seen. Even so, the lights seemed to almost single him out. He froze behind a tree, as immobile as the trunk. Some of the men came outside on the porch. They were talking loudly, but were too far away for him to make out what they were saying. Boon wasn't even sure they were speaking English. When he was convinced he was still invisible to them, he figured he'd pressed his luck enough and it was time to get the hell out of there. He continued around the lake and eventually made it to the opposite shore, a trip that took at least half an hour. After a few minutes of searching, he located the large deer stand he had spotted during his afternoon walk. He awkwardly crawled up the narrow ladder with the rifle in one hand. The stand was the size of a child's tree fort, and gave him enough room to stretch out. Laying down like a sniper, he peered into the scope toward the house.

The wet lenses blurred the images, but he was finally able to get a better look inside. The only person he could see was the blond woman. She was pacing back and forth, and held something in her hand. At first he thought it might be her phone, but she kept moving in circles and staring at it, becoming more and more agitated. Finally, she threw it down on a nearby couch and stalked to the door. She almost seemed to be staring right at him, her body silhouetted in the lights of the house behind her. Eventually, she stormed back into the kitchen area, pacing anxiously once more.

Boon set the rifle down and tried to consider his options. In the end, the only plans that seemed to make any sense were to wait them out until they left, or strike out through the woods and away from the house, putting all this behind him. Frankly, neither one held much allure. He vowed that from now on, whatever happened, he would always have an escape plan in place before he hunkered down like this. He wasn't thinking straight, and that annoyed him.

He was still deciding what to do when he heard a branch snap below him. The sound wasn't loud, but it was sharp in the steady hiss of the rain. His blood froze again. He tried to convince himself it was the wind, or another deer. He waited, trying to steady his breathing, and kept himself as still as the night. Then the stand shuddered, a vibration as subtle as a guitar string being plucked. Someone's weight had been put on the lowest rung. *Shit!* They were in the woods looking for him, which was why he hadn't seen anyone else in the house. The stand twitched again. Gathered water on the leaves overhead rained down on him. Boon slowly turned around and held the rifle up.

The first thing he saw was a hand with a pistol. The hand holding it jittered and shook, since whoever was climbing the wobbly ladder was having trouble doing so with only one free hand. As he stared, a head began to crest the hole in the platform. When the man's eyes cleared the opening and he saw Boon, he tried to bring up the gun, but Boon was prepared and cracked him in the forehead with the butt of the rifle. The intruder's head snapped back and he let go, tumbling to the ground. Boon heard him crash into the ground with a wet thud.

Before the man could make a move, Boon jumped to the opening and dropped down feet first. He landed squarely on his attacker's chest. He felt something crunch under his boots, and the assailant barked in pain, then went still with his arms and legs splayed out. Dohir stared at the unconscious man for just a moment to make sure he was indeed out cold, then scrambled back up and ladder and retrieved the rifle. Panting and shaking, he knew he wasn't safe anywhere around here.

He struck out in the opposite direction, trying to penetrate the woods. But no matter what he tried, he couldn't make it through, not in the dark. Cursing under his breath, he realized he would have to make his way around the lake, up the hill a few hundred yards from the house, and down the lane towards the road. Boon didn't like that option one bit, but had no other choice.

He began creeping around the large pond. The going was tricky in the dark, and more than once he tripped over fallen logs or had to fight his way through thick brush. He didn't know how much time he had until they found the downed man, but he didn't want to be around when they did. Plus, the giant was still out here somewhere, and that thought urged him forward at a level just shy of total panic.

He cleared the deep brush on this side of the lake, hugging the trees. Up ahead the lights of the house blazed. He stopped every few feet and listened intently, making sure he wasn't walking into more trouble. Looking around he couldn't see anyone else out there, but he knew the remaining searchers were still after him. Carefully, he started off again, placing his steps carefully one at a time, intent on not making a sound.

As soon as he could, he angled right, up the hill and toward the lane. The big SUV was now visible in the lights of the house about fifty or sixty yards away. He stepped onto the lane and headed towards the road. If they were smart, he knew, they would have a man positioned somewhere along the lane, guarding against an easy exit. He once again stuck close to the trees lining the lane. He had only gone a few feet when the distinctive smell of cigarette smoke tickled his nose. Boon froze. There was someone close by, but where?

He waited. Then up ahead he spied an orange glow, visible for just a second while whoever it was held the cigarette up to their lips. Then the light vanished as they either cupped it or held it behind them. To make it to the main road, Boon had to somehow get by the smoker, but he had no idea how. The lane was narrow, and the woods on both sides were too thick to navigate. He was stuck again.

Then he heard a rumbling down the lane toward the main road, and saw headlights swing around in his direction. The lights bounced up and down as the vehicle slowly came towards him over the bumpy drive. The smoking guard detached himself from the trees and stood in the middle of the drive, blocking passage. Boon could see his rain-blurred outline in the oncoming beams. He couldn't tell if the guard was armed or not, but had to assume he was.

As he waited, Dohir expected the car coming towards him would be another SUV, just like the first. But as it neared, he could see that the headlights were low to the ground, and too close together. Plus, the engine emitted a loud, sporty burble, even going as slowly as it was. No way this was an SUV.

The car stopped when the driver spotted the smoker standing in the lane, and when the guard stepped in front of a headlight, Boon could make out the license plate. It was an Ohio plate that said KEMPLER1.

Oh, shit. Steve Kempler? What the hell was he doing here?

Boon moved without thinking. As the guard bent over to talk to Steve, Boon charged, the rifle gripped in his hands like a baseball bat. At the last second, the smoker heard him and stood up, alarmed. He quickly raised his hand with his mouth opening wide to sound a warning, but he was too late. Dohir swung the heavy rifle and connected on the side of the smoker's head. The man went down hard on his side. Unlike the assailant at the tree stand, this one didn't get back up. Boon stood there, panting, his hands shaking, hoping like hell he hadn't killed the guy. He looked and saw Steve staring up at him from the open window of the car, his shocked face drenched from the rain. Boon shoved down his hood so Kempler could see it was him.

"Boon? Jesus, what in the hell is going on here? Who the fuck was that?"

Dohir grabbed the window sill of the car. It was a black Corvette, a newer one that he knew Kempler was particularly fond of. He leaned down.

"Keep your voice down and turn your lights off," he ordered.

"Turn my lights off? Why? You need to tell me what's happening here." Kempler was used to being in charge, and wouldn't easily accept orders, even from a friend.

"Steve, you're going to have to trust me on this one, okay? I'll explain later. Please turn your lights off." The big man scowled, but acceded. "Good. Right now, I need to know one thing: how fast you can back this thing up."

"Back up? Pretty well. Why?"

"Good. Because you're going to need to be really good at it in about thirty seconds."

Without giving him a chance to ask anything else, Boon went to a nearby tree, one with a clear view of the SUV. He rested the barrel of the rifle against the trunk and lifted the scope to his eyes. He gently released the safety as he put the left rear tire of the SUV in his sights. He exhaled, didn't breathe, and gently squeezed the trigger. The report was thunder loud, and the result was exactly as he had hoped. He saw the left rear of the SUV jump as the tire exploded.

One down, he thought.

The 30/30 was a semi-automatic, so the next round was already chambered. Once more he raised the scope to his eye, but this time he placed the right rear tire in the crosshairs, intent on putting the big vehicle completely out of commission; a car may have one spare tire, he knew, but certainly not two. However, as he eased the trigger back, rain momentarily obscured his vision and threw off his aim. He should have stopped, but he didn't. The rifle bucked and bellowed a second time, but his shot went astray. The tremendous explosion as the gas tank of the SUV exploded dwarfed all other sounds, echoing across the pond and into the distance. The ass end of the SUV bucked and flew in the air as a roiling fireball climbed into the dark sky. Warm air smacked him in the face as the shockwave expanded outward.

Boon didn't wait to see what was going to happen next. He charged around Kempler's car and jumped into the low passenger seat. He threw the gun on the floor at his feet.

"We gotta go!" he shouted.

Kempler may have been more than a little confused, but he accurately interpreted the panic in Boon's voice. He slammed the car into reverse and floored it, flying backwards, spraying gravel and using the backup camera as his guide. Boon was afraid that he'd wreck, that he'd run off the lane and into a tree or a ditch, but he didn't. Steve soared out the lane and into the country road. He slammed the selector into drive.

"Punch it!" Boon yelled.

The fat tires spun under the tremendous torque of the engine as he mashed the accelerator, and Kempler had to back off a little before the car would actually move forward. Finally, rubber grabbed the asphalt, and the sports car jumped ahead.

Kempler didn't take his eyes off the road. "Where am I going?" he shouted.

"Anywhere. It doesn't matter right now. Just away from here!"

The narrow country road didn't leave any room for error, but Kempler handled the low-slung car like a pro. Rain slanted down and made the road even more treacherous than it already was, hills and blind curves coming up on them fast. Boon hoped no one was out in this weather, Amish or otherwise. They traveled in silence for several minutes while Kempler kept his eyes riveted on the dark Mobius strip of asphalt unwinding before them. A stop sign appeared at the intersection of a larger two-lane state highway. After several cars passed by, he pulled out and quickly accelerated up to the speed limit. Only then did Kempler spare a second to stare at Boon, his eyes flinty. When he spoke, his voice was tight with barely restrained fury.

"You mind telling me what the fuck happened back there?" he snapped. "Who was that guy that stopped me? And why the hell did you just blow up a god-damned Suburban in my driveway?"

Boon looked at Kempler's stony face glowing in the dim lights of the dashboard. He wasn't sure how much to tell his friend, and to be honest he wasn't even sure he could. Boon was so accustomed to living his life behind the walls he'd constructed that breaking through those barriers seemed nearly impossible. But in the end, he knew he owed the man an explanation. Maybe even the entire story. He stared straight ahead and watched the white lines on the highway flash past him.

"Okay. Short version, or long one?"

"What do you mean, short version or long one? Just tell me what the fuck is going on!"

"Yeah, okay. You've known me for, what, four or five years?"

Kempler grunted. "Yeah, something like that."

"In all that time, you've never asked me what I did for a living. In fact, how much do you really know about me?"

The windshield wipers clicked back and forth a dozen times before he answered. "Not much, really," he admitted. "But that's not important to me, not after you helped me with my son. Anyway, I'm a good judge of character, and my gut tells me you're okay." He stopped for a moment, then added, his tone a shade lighter, "Of course, I may have to reevaluate my opinion in light of what just happened back there."

Boon almost laughed out loud, and in the end he did actually smile, just a little. "Yeah, you might at that. That guy back there, the one in the driveway? He's part of a group of men that are either trying to capture or kill me. I'm not sure which yet."

Kempler glanced at him with one eye, the other still trained on the road. "You mind telling me why? And why you blew up that Suburban?"

"Blowing up the SUV was an accident. I was going for the other tire and missed. I was trying to flatten both back tires so they couldn't come after us. Bad shooting on my part, that's all."

"That doesn't explain shit."

"No, it really doesn't, does it?"

Kempler took both eyes off the road this time, and stared at Boon again. That hard stare may have only lasted a second, but it clearly conveyed what his friend was thinking: it was time for Boon to come clean. Looking at Kempler's outline in the darkened car, he reminded himself that this man had certainly just saved his life. And, as difficult as it was to share so much about himself, his friend deserved the truth. Boon sighed, and for the next few miles filled him in on the entire sequence of events, from the time he began the Marsden deal, to the wire transfer of the $20 million, to the Spanish speaker's men ransacking his apartment, all the way up to his hiding out at the hunting cabin. When he was finished, he felt smaller somehow, as if the confession of so many wrongs had somehow diminished him. Steve drove in silence for several minutes, and Boon wasn't sure what his friend was going to do next. He wouldn't blame him for kicking him out of the car and leaving him on the side of the road.

Finally, Steve said, "So you're telling me you're nothing more than a thief? A very good thief, but still just a thief?"

"Essentially, yes." He wanted to add that he only stole from people and companies that could afford it, or would barely notice the loss, but he didn't. To him, now, it sounded like a poor excuse.

"Until the $20 million fell into your lap?"

Boon stared at his hands. "Yes, until then."

"That was stupid. You had it all figured out, but you got greedy."

He didn't reply. He didn't feel he needed to.

"So, tell me more about these projects. The baseball diamond, the housing projects, all that. What's that all about?"

Boon squirmed in his seat. It was a time for confessions, yes, but he couldn't bring himself to explain everything. Some things, like the bed-ridden Hannah Collins, were too personal. He settled on a partial explanation instead. "My needs are pretty minimal, when it comes down to it. I like doing them. Call it guilt money, I guess. I like helping out where I can."

"What, like Robin Hood? Stealing from the rich and giving to the poor? Very noble."

Boon almost visibly jerked. This was the second time in a short window that someone had compared him to Robin Hood. It shocked him that two disparate men had figured him out when his motives had remained secret for so long.

"Yeah, like Robin Hood," he finally admitted.

Steve grunted and drove on in silence. They came upon a little burg in the middle of nowhere, a town not much more than a few houses and a gas station with a mom-and-pop pizzeria tacked onto the side. The place had a single traffic light, which turned red as they approached. Kempler eased to a halt. He tapped his finger on the steering wheel. Finally, he turned and stared hard at Boon.

"So now what?"

Dohir held out his phone, still powered off. "I'm convinced that somehow these guys can track my exact location by my phone. Some new tech I've never heard of and they shouldn't have. I can't turn it back on, that much I know." He tossed it in the cupholder between the seats.

"You'll figure something out, I'm sure. Look on the bright side–at least you're alive."

Boon smiled in the dark. "Yeah, there's that."

The light changed and Steve eased the Corvette down the road. They had only gone a short distance when Dohir asked, "By the way, what the hell were you doing there, anyway? What made you come out here?"

Kempler shrugged, a small motion nearly hidden in the dim interior of the car. "I wanted to check on you. Something wasn't right when we talked on the phone. I could tell. I figured I'd take a little drive and see for myself you were okay. Good thing I did."

"Very good thing. Thanks." Then a chilling thought struck him. "The cabin. They'll figure out you own the hunting cabin, and they'll come for you, too!"

Steve smiled. "I think not. The ownership of that place is run through so many LLCs and shell companies there's no way they'll be able to trace it. About five years ago I bought it when my wife and I were going through a rough patch, when Jack first started having problems. Things got pretty ugly, so I was hiding assets in case we ever got divorced. She never even knew it existed before she passed away." He grew silent. "She would have loved it out here, you know? I was so stupid…"

The admission was painful for him, Boon could tell. The fact that he had intentionally kept this from his wife would forever haunt the man. But it was done, Julie was gone, and Steve would have to live with this deceit for the rest of his life. It was a hard lesson for him, but one Boon understood very well. He lived with the demons of his past every day.

Kempler stared ahead. "So, what's next?"

Dohir didn't reply immediately, having wondered the same thing for quite a while now. Long term, he didn't have an answer. But he knew what he needed to do next.

"We need to go back to the cabin. Not right now, but soon."

Steve's head swiveled to stare at him, his eyes off the road longer than was safe. "Are you nuts? After what you've done? With them still after you?"

"Well, maybe. But I need to see if that woman left that phone tracker there. I saw her throw it on the couch in the living room. I'm hoping she lost it or forgot about it in all the commotion. If it's still there, I need to see it. It's important."

"We're not going back there now. No way."

"I know it sounds crazy," Boon said. "But if anyone knows a back way through the woods and to the cabin, it's you. You've spent more time there hunting than anyone. We can sneak in and they'll never know it."

Kempler pursed his lips, his expression clearly indicating he was unsure of Boon's mental state. Finally, "Yeah, I can get us there. There's an Amish farm that butts up against the property, and we can get there that way. But how do you know they'll be gone? I mean, you blew up their damn Suburban!"

"I think it was an Escalade. But yeah, I know. Either way, I have a feeling they won't want to stick around any longer than they have to. If I had to guess, I'd bet they're already gone, SUV and all."

Steve didn't seem convinced, but they didn't argue about it. The two of them drove another half hour, until they saw a glow in the distance that indicated a city, a bigger one this time. "That'll be Chillicothe," his friend said. "We can bed down there for the night."

They soon found an old motel on the outskirts of town, near the Scioto River. The Riverside Motel was made up of a tidy office building, with ten small, individual cabins, each no larger than an average family room. There was a pool out front, with a sign warning that swimmers did so at their own risk. The complex was old, but looked clean and neat. A neon Vacancy sign glowed on the outside of the office.

"This should do just fine," Boon said.

Kempler swung in and parked out of sight, his Corvette obscured by a dumpster. He went into the office and came back out a few minutes later, motioning Boon to follow. They went into cabin #2. Inside was a queen bed, a dresser, and mismatched nightstands. A modern flat-screen TV took up the entire top of the dresser. A small bathroom was tucked in the back behind a narrow door.

"No problems?" Boon asked.

Steve shook his head. "Nope. They were happy to take cash for the night. Nice people. I sleep on the left side, if you don't mind."

Both men took turns using the bathroom, then kicked off their shoes and got into bed. Dohir flicked off the light. The room smelled of age and

Pine-sol. Light came in through the window, but was filtered by the thin curtains. They laid there in silence for a minute.

"Steve."

"Yeah."

"Why are you doing this for me? You'd be completely within your rights to turn me in to the authorities. In fact, I don't understand why you haven't done it already."

His friend didn't answer right away. When he did, his voice was thoughtful. "I can't beat you in golf if you're behind bars, can I?"

Boon chuckled. "No, I guess not. But, really. Why?"

"Really? Okay. I value friendship, and how you helped me with my boy. I don't take any of that lightly. Sure, sounds like you fucked up royally, but that doesn't change everything else. I stick by my friends."

"I appreciate that, I do. But," he paused for a moment. "But I haven't told you everything. I can't. Some things I just can't talk about."

"Good. Sometimes too much talking is bad for a relationship. Let's keep it that way. Deal?"

"Yeah. Deal."

"Okay. Now get some sleep. We have to do something potentially really stupid tomorrow, and we need to get some rest. And no, I'm not going to kiss you goodnight or tuck you in. Friendship only goes so far."

He felt Steve's bulk roll over, and in moments the big man's breathing was heavy and even. Boon himself was wide awake, still charged up from the events of the evening. Eventually he drifted off, sure that he'd have wild dreams. He didn't.

10

They drove back towards the cabin the next morning. Boon was tense and sat low in his seat, on high alert for any ominous black SUVs sharing the country highway with them, but they never encountered anything suspicious. His head wasn't pounding this morning, which he counted as a win. However, in a new and annoying twist, his stomach had begun to ache and churn like he'd overindulged on junk food, and his hands were trembling so badly he kept them out of sight in his lap. Kempler was unaware of any of this, and drove the black Corvette with a level of indifference that Boon found highly annoying. Of course, if he were being honest with himself, that was likely due to how crappy he was feeling.

"How long you been doing this?" Steve asked him at one point.

"Years now," Boon answered.

"Years? Damn, you look like you could jump out of your skin any second. I don't know how you don't have an ulcer the size of Rhode Island by now."

"Yeah, well, I usually don't have guys out to kill me. Most of the jobs we do barely register with the authorities. Hell, the most threatening people I might run into are corporate insurance adjusters or irate senior citizens."

Kempler laughed and kept driving. Eventually he turned on the radio and picked up a classic rock station. With his free hand he tapped out a beat on his thigh, much like Miles would do. Boon tried to take his mind off how lousy he felt by wondering how his employees were doing. Thankfully, he knew, as long as they kept their heads down, there should be no way they could be implicated in any of this.

When they were nearing his cabin, Kempler turned right instead of left and jogged around a few narrow country roads. Minutes later he pulled up to a gravel driveway. A few hundred yards ahead of them was a white frame house, along with a small building next to it. A mailbox by the road had "Yoder" hand-painted on the side.

"You know anything about the Amish?" he asked.

Boon tilted his head thoughtfully. "I've seen that Harrison Ford movie *Witness* a few times. That's about it."

"That's it? Okay, follow my lead," he told Boon.

There were several other cars there already, as well as a handful of black buggies tethered to bored looking horses. People dressed in typical summer clothing were milling around the small building, and as they got closer Boon could see the place was a farmer's market. Steve parked in-between two vehicles and they got out. Together they walked to the small building. The day was warm, and the sun was hot on the back of his neck. Cicadas buzzed somewhere not far away.

The front of the building was open, and spread outside were bushels of corn, squash, apples, and pretty much any other local fruit or vegetable he could think of. Bearded men in straw hats and plain blue and black garb wandered around. A few Amish women in long dresses clustered together in small groups behind them, their white cotton bonnets bright in the sunlight. They talked and giggled quietly to each other, hands covering their mouths. Boon caught snatches of conversation in what he assumed was German. Some of the men glanced briefly at the two of them, and a few tipped their hats. Steve waved to them.

"Good morning! Is Caleb around?"

A clean-shaven young man pointed towards the house where several older men sat in rocking chairs in the shade, fanning themselves with their hats. Kempler said thanks and motioned for Boon to follow. When the seated men saw them coming, an older man with a white beard who Boon figured was in his early seventies waved at them. He had bright eyes, a shade of Caribbean blue that no colored contact lenses could equal.

"Steven, *guten morgen*. What brings you here?"

"*Guten morgen* to you, Caleb. I hope you're well?"

"As well as can be expected for a man of my years."

Steve stepped into the shade with Boon close behind him. "Do you mind if I leave my car here for a bit? I'd like to check out the back section of the woods and one of my deer stands. I have a feeling last night's storm may have knocked it down. It's easier to get to from here."

Caleb waved at him dismissively. "Of course. Please do so. Stay as long as you like."

Kempler smiled at him. "Thanks. We shouldn't be long."

As they turned away, Caleb cleared his throat. "Oh, Steven. Do you know anything about a loud noise we heard coming from your place last night? During the storm. A loud boom of some sort?"

Steve turned back. "Sorry, Caleb. I just got here. I'll check it out and let you know if I find anything."

The old man smiled back and waved again, then went back to chatting with his companions. When the two of them were far enough away, Kempler turned to Boon.

"Can you guess how old Caleb is?"

Boon shrugged. "I don't know. Early seventies, I'd guess."

"Ninety-three. And he still works the fields every day. And there's nothing wrong with his hearing, either. Follow me."

They rounded the small building and headed toward a tree line in the distance. Between tidy fields of corn and beans was a rutted path no wider than a cart. The sounds of the market behind them grew dim and then vanished as they put distance between them. Boon could see the path ahead stopped at the trees. Insects circled around their heads, and the buzzsaw drone of the cicadas grew louder. It was peaceful out here, and reminded Boon of hikes he had made in the past, when he was younger and before he had gotten involved in all this.

"I've had Caleb do some work on the cabin before," Kempler said, navigating around some puddles. "They do amazing stuff. The cabinets in the kitchen were made and installed by them. And all without power tools."

Dohir thought back to his recent stay there, but he'd been too concerned with his own mess to remember what they looked like.

"They're good people," his friend continued. "God-fearing and honest to a fault. Their work ethic is amazing. Guess that happens when you don't get distracted by TV or any of the modern conveniences that we take for granted. You know, things like cell phones."

Boon felt in his pocket for his. The thought of not having it was both alluring and a little unnerving at the same time. Over the years he had gotten so used to having one the thought of living without it seemed impossible.

"Not having a phone sounds pretty good to me right now," he eventually replied.

"I bet it does," Steve laughed, his voice loud in the relative silence.

They reached the woods. For the most part the trees were all old growth, with expansive trunks and branches so intertwined that cutting through without tools would have been impossible. Kempler followed the edge of the forest until he spied an opening, one so narrow it was nearly invisible. He pushed aside some low-hanging branches and stepped in. Boon was close behind.

The sunlight abruptly ended, and a second later they were enveloped in cool shade. The constant sounds of birds and insects stopped, and Boon couldn't help feeling that they had passed through a magical portal from one world into another. The path at their feet continued on between the trees, but it was so unused it was difficult to follow. Kempler forged ahead, shoving growth aside as he went. One branch whipped back and smacked Dohir in the face.

"Sorry about that," he said, although his chuckle didn't sound very sorry at all.

They continued on, turning this way and that, until even Boon's reliable sense of direction surrendered and he had to admit he'd be hopelessly lost without his friend leading the way. In fact, he was so turned around that finding his way back would have been impossible. Dohir kept his eyes locked on Kempler's broad back, and hoped he knew where he was going.

Ten minutes later Steve held up a hand, and they stopped. He crooked a finger at Boon to come close.

"See that ridge up ahead?" he whispered. "Once we cross over that we should be able to see the pond and the cabin. Stay quiet."

They bent down low and eased forward. In a tree ahead of them Dohir spotted an unnatural shape, and realized it was the deer stand. He tapped his friend's shoulder.

"Pretty sure that's where I landed on that first guy," he whispered. Kempler nodded but didn't move. Crouching, the two of them stared at that spot for what seemed like ages, until Boon's legs started aching from the uncomfortable position.

"What are we waiting for?" he asked quietly.

A flash of amused annoyance passed over Kempler's face. "You're not a hunter, are you?"

"Uh, no."

"Yeah, I can tell. Patience, Grasshopper."

Several more minutes ticked by before Kempler stood and crept forward, each foot placed carefully, soundlessly. When they reached the base of the deer stand, the big man cautiously crept up the ladder. Seconds later he came back down and inspected the ground. He held up a broken branch and twirled it in his fingers, then poked around at several more.

"See these?" he said softly, holding one up. "Probably snapped when your buddy landed here. I can't tell if he got up under his own power, or if someone helped him. But the important thing is that he's not here now."

Kempler climbed back up in the stand and stared at his house across the pond. Boon could see his head inch back and forth as he scouted out the area. Apparently satisfied they were safe, he climbed back down, jumping the last few rungs to the soft earth.

"Come on," he said.

With Steve still in the lead, they wound their way through the woods and around the pond towards the long driveway. While they were still concealed by the trees, Kempler pointed toward the lane.

"No sign of your blown to shit Escalade, except for that black spot and some burnt leaves high in the trees. They got that thing out of here fast. Whoever these guys are, they're efficient, I'll give them that."

Kempler took up a station where he could see up and down the driveway while still keeping the house in view. For the next half an hour they stood there, unmoving and silent. Dohir had never been deer hunting before, but if this is what it entailed, he was not interested. He preferred activities with more action. Even baseball was more exciting than this. After a while the boredom began to override his anxiety, and he tapped Steve on the arm.

"How much longer?" he whispered.

"Yeah, this is probably enough. Besides a buck nibbling on something close to the house, I haven't seen a thing. I think it's safe. Let's go."

Boon was shocked that he hadn't noticed the deer, but took his friend at his word. The two of them left the safety of the woods and slowly made their way towards the house, always keeping in the shadows. They passed the spot where the gravel was charred, and Dohir spotted some chunks of melted rubber and a section of a bumper. The stench of burnt rubber and plastic was all he could smell.

"They hauled away the car, but were in too much of a hurry to clean up," Kempler observed quietly. He bent down and picked up a scorched door handle, then tossed it into the woods.

When they got close enough, Steve furtively peered into several windows, then cautiously circled the house on the wrap-around porch. Boon wished they had brought the 30/30 with them, but that would have raised way too much suspicion with his Amish neighbors. He followed Kempler, keenly aware how visible they would be to anyone watching.

Finally, they got to the back door. Steve tossed it open and hugged the wall, ready for an attack that never came. He poked his head inside, then eased the rest of his bulk through.

"All clear," he called out after a few seconds.

Boon stepped through behind him and looked around, frowning. The place was a mess. Soda had been dumped on the floor, and furniture was overturned. The refrigerator door was open, and the contents were scattered across the hardwood floor. Pictures were smashed. The big screen TV had a hole in the center. To Dohir's eye it looked like they had trashed the place out of nothing more than petty spite.

"What a bunch of assholes," Steve muttered, shutting the refrigerator.

Boon stepped around some broken glass towards the living area. He flipped a chair back over, then went to the couch. He didn't see anything, but dug between the cushions until his hand brushed something hard and unyielding. He pulled the object out.

"What's that?" Steve asked as he began tossing trash into a garbage can.

Dohir inspected his find. It was a black box, bigger than a pack of cigarettes but smaller than a paperback book. There was a gray screen on the front above a keypad with numbers ranging from zero to nine. Three larger buttons ran along the bottom.

"I think it's what that blond lady had. I'm pretty sure it's the tracker."

11

Neither of them wanted to hang around the cabin any longer than they had to. Boon's car was still in the garage, so instead of hiking back through the dense forest, they drove to the Farmer's Market in comfort.

"This is a fine ride, Boon," Kempler acknowledged, running his hands over the soft leather dashboard and fiddling with the dials and switches. "And it's quick, too. I may need to get me one of these Krautmobiles."

Dohir had originally chosen the black BMW for its luxury and relative anonymity. Yes, it was big and expensive, but there were a lot of cars on the road just like it. He also enjoyed the attention to detail and excellent craftsmanship. Besides that, something as flashy as his friend's Corvette was out of the question. He liked to travel in comfort, but couldn't risk being noticed wherever he went.

Steve leaned back in his seat, wiggling his ample butt deeper into the cushion. He closed his eyes and they motored along in silence as Boon navigated the short drive back. When he pulled into the farmer's market a few minutes later, Kempler sat up, seemingly surprised they had arrived already. Boon eased up into an open slot.

"We're here," he said.

Kempler made no move to get out, but instead picked up the device Boon had located at the cabin. He inspected it for several moments, turning it this way and that.

"What are you going to do with this thing?" he finally asked.

Boon shrugged. "I don't know. I'll figure something out. First I need to see out how it works."

"Hmm. There's no serial number. No manufacturer's name, either. Nothing to show who made it or where it came from. Black market, I'm guessing."

Boon wasn't surprised. "Yeah, it's not something you can pick up at your local electronics store. I've never seen anything like it before. I'd like to say that in the wrong hands this could be an incredibly dangerous tool, but that's pretty obvious by now."

Boon slid the car into Park and waited while Kempler continued checking out the black box. The silence lengthened with neither of them making a move. Steve pushed some of the buttons and peered at it closely, turning it this way and that in his big hands.

"Steve," Boon finally said, "you don't have to stick around any longer. I can't thank you enough for what you've done. You certainly saved my life. For that, I'll be forever grateful."

Kempler grunted, still inspecting the device.

"But you should go now, before anything else happens. I can take care of myself from here on out."

"Oh, really? Is that so? Where are you going to go?"

To be fair, Dohir had no idea. Perhaps he'd just find the nearest highway and start driving. He had no destination in mind, but he couldn't stay anywhere around here. Interstate 70 wasn't that far away. He could take that west three quarters of the way across the country if he wanted to, and hopefully just disappear. It wasn't much of a plan, especially not for him, but it was all he had.

"I'll be fine. Trust me."

Kempler raised an eyebrow. "Really? You'll be fine? Let's recap, shall we? You've got some maniac and his posse after you, a guy who's already proven that he'll torture and kill to get what he wants. They might not know exactly who you are, but I'm betting they have a pretty good idea. And since you've got his $20 million, he's never going to give up. Oh, and I almost forgot, the FBI is on your tail, too. I don't call that 'fine' by any stretch of the imagination."

Boon's smile was thin and forced, an expression that stopped well short of his eyes. "Yeah, but I'll be fine. I've got some ideas."

Kempler blew a raspberry between his lips. "Ideas? Boon, like I said, I'm a pretty good judge of character, and I'm also pretty damn good at reading people. You've got squat. I can tell."

Dohir looked away, out the window and into the yard. Caleb and his friends were still chatting in the shade of the house, but the old man kept glancing at the BMW in curiosity. Boon was sure the old Amish farmer was wondering why the two of them had left on foot, and had arrived back in a car. A group of people with a cloth grocery bag overflowing with produce walked behind them, chatting loudly. They got into a car a few spaces away, their doors slamming and cutting off their conversation.

"It doesn't matter," he finally said. "You've done enough."

Kempler held up a finger. "How about this? Come back to my house with me. Wait, hear me out. Together we'll figure out how this thing works. Plus, that'll give you time to think about your next move."

As tempting as that offer was, Boon had no desire to put anyone else in danger. He shook his head. "No. I can't let you do that."

"Oh, come on. No one is going to connect the two of us. Jack's still at the treatment center, and I'm rattling around that big place all by myself. Two of us have a much better chance of figuring this out than you do alone, and you know it."

Boon sighed. He did know that, and the prospect of running forever sounded terrible. He was used to being a loner, but that didn't mean he enjoyed being alone. And Kempler was right — no one could connect the two of them, not even the crazy guy with the Spanish accent. He felt himself leaning toward agreeing with his friend, even though he didn't want to.

"But what if something happens? What if they find us?"

Kempler smiled. "How are they going to do that? Keep your phone off and lay low. At least for a few days. Hell, you'll be safer with me than you would be just driving around. I mean, who knows how many people he's got out there looking for you?"

Dohir couldn't argue with that either, even though he wanted to. The Spanish speaker may have resources he couldn't imagine, and just by being out in the open he might be putting himself and his team at risk. He felt his earlier resolve slipping, and, despite some serious misgivings, he knew it was what he needed to do. For now.

"Okay. Just for a few days, until I can figure out my next steps."

Kempler laughed and slapped Boon on the thigh hard enough that his leg stung. The car rocked with the impact.

"That's what I'm talking about! And don't look so worried. This'll be fun." He opened the door and got out, then stuck his head back in. "But first, let's get this car of yours hidden. For all we know they've got your license plate or something."

"Good idea. Where?"

Kempler pointed towards the woods. "We'll take it back to the cabin and leave it in the garage. We'll take mine home."

Boon tried to think of reasons why they shouldn't do that, but couldn't. There was no sense in taking a chance he could be spotted.

After a few seconds, he agreed. Steve eased his large frame into his Corvette, and they drove the two cars back to the cabin. Once there, Dohir pulled his car into the garage and shut the door, locking it behind him. He slid into Steve's car, being careful of the 30/30 still on the floor. Kempler turned the sporty coupe around, and they headed back out the lane.

As the Corvette's tail lights vanished over a slight rise, a huge figure detached itself from behind a tree from deep within the shadows of the woods. With fingers as large as sausages, the man dialed a number on his phone.

In Spanish he said, "Yes, it's me. I told you they'd be back. You should listen to me more often. Find the owner of the car with the license plate KEMPLER1. If you insist on worrying about this with whatever else you've got going on, this should help us find them all at one time." He ended the call and shook his head angrily. He stared daggers at his phone for a moment, then roughly stuffed it in his pocket. Under his breath the giant mumbled, "*Mierda*, I have to stop working for idiots like this."

It took a while to get from the cabin back to Dayton, even with the way Kempler was driving. His friend was, by his own admission, an "offensive driver" — meaning, he offended nearly everyone on the road. Now that they were away from immediate danger, he drove faster than Boon liked. And, while he had little patience for the majority of those sharing the road with him, Steve reserved most of his ire for anyone who lingered in the left lane of the highway too long. His curses for those people were long and loud, and typically consisted of some combination of the words *idiot*, *moron*, and *asshole*. More than once, Boon found himself holding on for dear life when Kempler made a drastic and unexpected lane change. He desperately hoped they didn't get pulled over, since he had no clue how to explain to Dayton's finest what they were doing with a recently fired rifle on the floor of the car. When they finally exited the highway in Centerville and headed north on Far Hills Avenue, he could barely pry his fingers from the death grip he had on his door's armrest.

After another ten minutes they crossed into the affluent suburb of Oakwood, past home to some of Dayton's more famous inhabitants like Charles Kettering, the inventor of the cash register, as well as Wilbur and Orville Wright. While some of the newer Dayton suburbs exuded a certain patina of wealth, Oakwood was synonymous with high taxes, superb city services, great schools, and old money. It was also the city most Dayton suburbs dreamt of being when they grew up, but deep down knew that goal was unattainable.

Kempler turned off of Far Hills and wound around several hilly, curving roads. Towering old trees lined the streets and provided a deep canopy of shade overhead. Huge brick and stucco houses drifted further and farther back from the road as the lots grew in size and stature. Long driveways grew longer, until many of the homes were lost behind the trees. Gates became more common, until they were the norm. At one of these, Kempler pulled up and pushed a button mounted on his visor. The gate swung open and the Corvette rumbled up a long, winding lane.

Dohir had never been to his friend's home before. He watched out the window as they drove, past a pond on the right and towards a flat-roofed brick house ahead. To Boon's untrained eye it bore some semblance to a Prairie Style home designed by the famous architect Frank Lloyd Wright. The rooflines were low and long, and windows stretched from one end of the house to the other. A round turret in the middle jutted several dozen feet above the rest of the structure. It was not what Boon expected to see tucked back here, imagining instead a more traditional two- or three-story mansion.

"Nice place, Steve."

"Thanks," he replied, staring at the house absently, as if he were looking inside himself instead. "Julie picked it out. She loved the lines of it, and all the windows looking out over the pond. The inside was beat up as hell when we got it, but she had a knack for decorating and we took it back to something like the original. I like it. It reminds me of her."

Boon watched as they pulled up to a four-car garage attached to the end of the house by a breezeway. Kempler pushed another button and the far-left door opened. They parked inside before standing and stretching from the long drive. The other three bays were occupied with a white Suburban, a Jeep of some kind, and a big motorcycle. The place was neat and clean, and smelled faintly of oil and soap.

Together they walked to the house. Boon spotted several small cameras with red lights glowing, each one focused on a different section of the driveway, house, or garage. He counted at least eight as they walked up the paver sidewalk to the front door. Steve tapped in a code on a keypad and they stepped inside.

The interior was just as beautiful as Dohir had expected, all dark wood, with no rounded edges anywhere. Right angles, squares, and rectangles were all he could see, even down to the light fixtures. Tan walls and beige ceilings complimented the thick wood trim. If he reached up, he could have touched the textured plaster of the ceiling with no problem.

"Come on," Steve said, pointing down a hallway flanked with windows. "The guest room is down here."

He followed him down a narrow hall, and together they entered a huge bedroom. The outside wall was nothing but a span of glass that peered out over the serene pond. A door tucked into the corner opened into a small bathroom, one with original fixtures like a claw and ball bathtub, and a white ceramic sink with old-fashioned silver handles. The single light fixture was over the sink and operated by a pull-chain.

"This is great, thanks," he told Steve.

"Good. Make yourself at home. I'll get us something to eat in a little bit."

Kempler left, and Boon went to stand by the window. The view really was incredible, he thought. The pond stretched a few hundred yards away, and ended at a tree line of old oaks that had to be a hundred feet tall. He knew there were other houses nearby, but the hills and woods made it feel like he could have been out in the country and far away from everyone, not in a posh neighborhood only fifteen minutes from downtown Dayton. He eased himself into a comfortable chair and relaxed, letting his mind wander as he stared at a handful of ducks that serenely paddled around the pond.

He admired the tranquil nature of the ducks and the calm way they went about their business. They had no worries except for their next meal, and perhaps keeping an eye on their young. There were no hunters out here trying to blast them out of the sky, no predators intent on devouring them without warning. Their biggest concern, he guessed, was how far south they needed to go in the winter. Yes, he envied them their simple, care-free lives. Although to be fair, most of his problems were of his own making.

He had brought the black box with him from the car, and he took a moment to inspect it. With a little trepidation, he pushed the red button on top, and the screen, about three inches square, flickered and came to life. In an easy-to-read font, it simply said NUMBER? He pushed a few of the numeric keys below that, and they filled in as he typed. There was a backspace key, and he pressed that and cleared them out. Intrigued now, he typed in a telephone number made up totally of fives. The display showed the ten digits, complete with hyphens right where they should be. A larger button below the numeric keypad said SEND, and he pressed that. The phone number blinked a few times, then came back with UNKNOWN across the screen. Boon cleared the entry. He wanted to try an actual number, and remembered the one from the bread store in OTR. He entered that. After hitting send, the screen blinked a few times and came back with LANDLINE.

"Hmm, so you know what a landline is. Interesting."

He didn't want to enter anyone's real cell number, not yet. That seemed too risky at this point. Later, he and Steve would experiment with an actual one. Maybe they could pick up a burner phone and run some tests with that.

He was still fiddling with the black box when Kempler called him for lunch. When he got there, Boon discovered that the kitchen was artfully built into the turret he had noticed from outside. Marble counters circled the room, interrupted here and there by modern cooktops, ovens, and a double-door refrigerator big enough to service a restaurant. A round island filled the center of the room. Above, windows ringed the turret, letting in so much light they could have been outside.

"Wow," Boon simply said, slowly spinning around to take it all in.

Kempler laughed. "Yeah, Julie loved the views from the rooms, but I fell for this kitchen right away. As you can tell," he said with a wink and a pat on his solid stomach, "I'm no stranger to a good meal."

The two sat down on tall stools at the island. Kempler had prepared fajitas for them, complete with slices of steak, chicken, and a steaming plate of green peppers and onions. A stack of tortilla shells was wrapped in a white towel to keep them warm.

"Did you just whip this up?" Boon asked, burning his fingertips on a deceptively hot tortilla.

"Yeah. Piece of cake. I like to cook. Dive in while everything's still hot."

They ate quietly. After three stuffed tortillas, Boon set the black box on the table. He explained what he had discovered so far.

Around a mouthful of fajita, Kempler said, "Sounds easy enough. Put my number in there and try it."

"Hmm. I'm not sure we should do that."

"Why not?"

Boon picked up the box. "I'm not sure. What if it's connected to some main system somewhere? What if I put your number in and someone else can see it? I'm not ready to take that chance. I recommend we go pick up a burner phone and try that instead."

Kempler wasn't convinced, but Boon insisted. They cleaned up their meal in a few minutes, the black box parked on the island between them. When the kitchen was in order once again, they made their way to the main room and relaxed in overstuffed chairs. The only things missing were snifters of brandy and some Cuban cigars.

"Okay, here's an idea," Steve suggested. "I'll go pick up one of those burner phones you were talking about. I'll leave mine with you. Once I've got the new one, I'll call you with the number. Then you can try it out."

"How am I going to know it's you calling?"

Kempler chuckled. "Wow, you really are paranoid, aren't you? Okay, when I call you, just the number will show up since it's not in my contacts. I'll let it ring once, then hang up. Then I'll call right back. Better?"

That was okay with Boon. He took Kempler's phone while his big friend grabbed some keys and left. Less than an hour later Steve's phone rang. A number with a Dayton area code showed for a second, then the phone went blank as the caller hung up. A few seconds later it rang again.

"Hello?"

"Yeah, it's me," Kempler said. "You got the number of this thing?"

"I do. Hang up, and I'll call you back as soon as I'm done."

Kempler did, and Boon entered the number in the black box. He finished, took a deep breath, and pushed SEND. He waited for a few seconds while the screen blinked. Then a full color map appeared, displaying all of Ohio and portions of the contiguous states. A cross in the center showed what Boon determined was his current location in Steve's house. The map blinked some more, then zoomed in around Dayton, then blinked again and a red dot appeared not too far away. The screen zipped in closer, until the dot ended up in a parking lot near a road in front of a large square, what Boon assumed was a stylized depiction of a store. A name and address appeared below the map. He called Steve back.

"You're at the WalMart in Moraine, on Dorothy Lane, aren't you?" Boon asked. "In the parking lot in front of the store? Three spaces from the entrance?"

There was dead silence on the other end for a moment. "Yeah, I am. That damn box told you exactly where I am just like that? Even when I wasn't using it? Wow."

"Yeah, just like that. Right down to the exact parking spot. Holy shit."

12

Boon directed him back to the house, but not before asking him to head into the store and make a few more purchases. He was waiting for Steve at the island in the kitchen when he got back, his friend's laptop open in front of him. Kempler sat down opposite him and set several shopping bags on the island.

"Here. Hope they're what you wanted. I had to go to a couple of stores to get everything. Kind of a pain in the ass."

Boon emptied the contents of the bags onto the island, four colorful boxes with pictures of mobile phones on the covers. He recognized all of the manufacturers, although Apple and Samsung were the most notable.

"Thanks, these are perfect," Boon said, then tilted his head at the laptop. "While you were gone I did some online research. When it comes to sales of phones here in the US, Apple and Samsung are the leaders by far. Motorola is a distant third. More importantly, for the most part these phones use either Apple's proprietary software or a version of Google's Android operating system. However, a few of the smaller manufacturers don't use either."

"Okay. What does that all mean?"

"Just this. Apple has a very useful Find My Phone feature built into their phones. You can set up your phone to be located using other Apple devices you own. It's also great for parents who want to track their kids and keep tabs on where they are. It can even find a phone that's been turned off for a while, usually up to twenty-four hours."

Kempler held up his own phone and stared at it. "I didn't know that. And if that's the case, I feel sorry for kids these days. There were lots of times as a teenager I didn't want my parents to know where I was."

"Yeah, me, too," Boon admitted. "But you have to intentionally and deliberately set this Find My Phone function up, and you need your password. It's not possible without it. Android software can do the same thing, but it's not as friendly or easy to use. However, the less popular cell phones don't have that feature at all, or its scope is very limited." He pointed at one of the boxes in front of them. "This Nokia, for example."

Steve frowned in thought. "Okay. But I still don't know what you're going for here."

"Well, the more I thought about it, the more I figured the bad guys had to be tapping into the systems of these major phone producers and hijacking this feature. I couldn't see any other way. But now I'm not so sure."

"What changed your mind?"

"When I was hiding in the woods at your cabin, I thought I figured out what was happening and turned my phone off. I have an Apple, and if they'd hacked into that system they should have been able to track me down even with my phone powered down. But they couldn't, clearly, or I wouldn't be here now."

"Ah, I get it," Kempler said, surveying the boxes in front of them. "How about using a phone's GPS system? That might work."

"Sure, but it still means our friendly neighborhood bad guys would have to hack their way into each operating system somehow. Even then, the cheaper burner phones don't always have GPS. I can't imagine that's how they're doing it."

"Good point," Steve said. "As far as I can tell, there's only one way to find out for sure. Let's fire all these bad boys up and see for ourselves what works and what doesn't."

"Yep. That was my plan."

After they set up all the phones, they tested them with the tracking device. In the end, they found that the tracker was able to quickly and accurately find every phone from every manufacturer when they were powered up, no matter if they were on a call or not. However, it couldn't detect them when they were turned off. None of them. The cursor just spun. When they finished, Boon turned them all off and arranged the quartet neatly in front of him. He held up the tracker.

"Okay, I'm not saying this is one-hundred percent conclusive, but I'm guessing our little friend here is not using the software from each company to locate them." Boon thought for a moment, tapping his fingers on the countertop. "While I was doing my online sleuthing, I also checked out the current methods of tracking phones. It turns out individual phones can be located by triangulating the pings from the towers, but it's not very exact. And the process can take time, and sometimes cooperation with different phone carriers. In fact, in densely populated areas, triangulating is pretty good and can narrow the location down to a few hundred feet. But in rural areas with limited towers, it might only get within a few miles. This thing nailed your location to the parking space in seconds, all by itself."

"I don't know how it does what it does, but it's pretty slick," Kempler said. "So, what do we do with it? Do we take it to the cops?" Steve asked. "Or how about that FBI guy who's looking for you. What about him?"

"Hollenbeck? I don't know. Maybe. I need to think first."

"Well, I'd recommend thinking fast. This is some high-tech shit here. I gotta think the guy who lost it isn't going to be very happy, you know, on top of the fact that you've also stolen $20 million from him."

Boon didn't answer. He was too busy trying to figure out how he could use this technology to their advantage. He needed to come up with a strategy that would extricate himself from this mess, while at the same time keeping his team and Steve safe. No matter what, he wasn't going to go off half-cocked, not again. He'd made that mistake when he grabbed the $20 million, and look what a terrible choice that was turning out to be.

"Tell you what," he said, pocketing the tracker. "Let's sleep on it tonight, and tomorrow we'll come up with our next steps. This is too big to rush. I need to think."

Kempler didn't have any issues with that. It was late afternoon, and they spent the rest of the day relaxing as well as they could. The house was equipped with a dedicated media room, complete with plush reclining chairs and a huge TV. The two of them watched a Reds game, and before he knew it he'd been sucked into Kempler's vortex of enthusiasm. They both jumped up and yelled like true fanatics when the home team won with a walk-off homer in the bottom of the ninth.

"That's what I'm talking about!" Steve shouted, pumping his fist in the air. "That's how winners win!"

The game had chewed up a good portion of the afternoon and part of the evening as well. They ate a light dinner of meats and cheeses from a charcuterie board Steve artfully prepared, then headed off to their respective rooms. When he got settled, Boon turned off the lights and sat in the easy chair, staring out at the pond that slowly grew darker and less distinct as time ticked by. The ducks became still as night fell, only flinching when a fish or a frog disturbed the water. Alone like this and with nothing to occupy him, it took Boon no time at all to realize how long he'd gone without a drink. His hands lightly trembling, he tried to ignore the strident urging of his mind to see what kind of booze Steve had in the house. Since Kempler liked a cocktail or three as much as the next guy, he knew his friend would have the place well-stocked. It took every shred of his willpower to remain where he was, even though he had a death grip on the arms of the chair and was sweating much more than he should have been considering the temperature in the room. He tried to relieve some tension by getting up and walking around, pacing in the limited space. He desperately wished he could go work out.

In the end, he stripped down to his shorts and substituted a round at the gym with pushups, sit ups, and running in place, anything physical he could do in the area between the bed and the bathroom. Sweating in earnest after an hour of this, he figured he'd done enough, and sat on the floor to cool down. Outside, the pond was a darker black space, nearly indiscernible from the rest of the yard. Landscape lights illuminated the long lane all the way down to the trees, where they eventually vanished between the trunks on the way to the street. He brushed his teeth with a new toothbrush he found in the medicine cabinet, then slid between the sheets in the darkness. The muted sounds of crickets barely penetrated the windows. Once in a while he heard a splash from the pond, but other than that it was quiet. He closed his eyes, hoping that sleep would come.

An hour later, however, he was still awake. He checked his watch and saw that it was nearly eleven O'clock. His body may have been ready for sleep, but his mind had different ideas. He couldn't get the image of Marsden out of his head. Marsden, tied to a chair and pleading for his life, as his eventual killers tortured him for information he didn't possess and couldn't share. Marsden's family and friends mourning a good man's horrible death. A closed casket, with his wife and children surrounding it, all asking why their husband or father had been murdered. Surely by now, the FBI and others were involved and had discovered the illicit money transfer, and were even now working to determine who was to blame and how they were connected. They would have talked at length to Leslie Harbaugh and Chet at the bank, and would know what had happened, or at least would have an idea. No law enforcement agency could connect Boon to any of this yet, but that did nothing to ease the torment gnawing at his soul. His heart preternaturally loud in his head, Boon rolled over and squeezed his eyes shut so tightly his cheeks hurt.

Eventually, though, he did go to sleep. But it was fitful and restless, and did nothing to dispel his guilt and exhaustion.

Sometime later he jerked awake with someone's hand over his mouth. He started to panic and sit up, but a strong arm gently pushed him back.

"Quiet," Steve hissed into his ear. "We've got company."

Now Boon did sit up. "What? How?"

"I don't know," Kempler whispered, his mouth so close Boon could smell his toothpaste. "The security cameras picked up some motion. I spotted at least four or five of them. Armed. Come on. We've got to get out of here."

Shaking, Dohir eased himself out of bed and slipped on his clothes and shoes. When he zipped up his pants, the noise hit his ears louder than a garbage disposal full of forks. He padded quietly after Kempler, who went out the bedroom door and turned left, toward the main room. They hugged the walls in the hallway, but because of all the windows, they couldn't do that in the main room. Kempler pushed Boon down, and the two of them army-crawled between the furniture to the other side.

They quickly made it to the kitchen. Steve stopped and peered out the doorway. After a few seconds he leaned close to Boon again.

"They're right outside. We'll take the breezeway to the garage. Follow me."

Boon nodded, even though it was dark and the motion was invisible.

Kempler moved ahead, but Boon urgently plucked at his friend's shirt.

"What?" Steve hissed.

He held up a finger, then backtracked into the kitchen. Feeling around in the near-dark, he located one of the burner phones they'd left on the island. He slipped it into his pocket along with the tracker and his own phone, then placed a hand on Kempler's broad back and they moved towards the other end. The big man eased the door open on soundless hinges, and they slipped through. He kept his hand on his friend's back as they navigated through the small space, until they came to another door.

"Breezeway," Kempler whispered. "The door at the other end opens into the garage. Be ready to move fast."

Boon didn't have to be told twice. Steve was just turning the doorknob when a loud crash and splintering of wood came from several rooms behind them.

"They broke down the front door! Go!" Steve yelled.

The two of them sprinted through the narrow breezeway, Boon just a few steps behind. Kempler didn't slow down, just lowered his shoulder and hit the door to the garage so hard it slammed open with a bang louder than a gunshot. Loud exclamations came from behind them in the house. Motion detectors inside the garage turned on several lights as they ran inside.

"Which car?" Boon shouted, staring at their choices.

"The Suburban!" Kempler yelled back.

Boon flew to the white Suburban and jumped in the passenger seat, slamming and reflexively locking the door behind him. Kempler ran around the front of the boxy SUV and leapt behind the wheel, breathing heavily.

"Buckle up," Steve commanded him. "This is going to get rough."

Boon fumbled nervously with the seat belt latch, finally feeling it click home. Steve pushed the ignition button and the big Chevy roared into life. Foot on the brake, he slammed it into reverse and revved the engine.

"What about the garage door?" Boon yelled over the din reverberating around the enclosed space.

"No time," his friend shouted back at him. "Don't worry. I own a garage door company, too. Hold on!"

Kempler released the brake and the garage door exploded as the back of the SUV slammed into it. Huge splintered sections spun into the driveway as the Suburban plowed through without slowing. Kempler didn't let off the gas until he was almost to the house, then jammed it into drive. The rear tires spun and smoked on the concrete driveway until they found traction, then the big vehicle jumped forward. When the headlights swung around, they caught two armed men right in the faces, and Dohir saw a flash of dark hair, and very surprised eyes. Both were raising ugly looking weapons towards the SUV but had to hastily abandon those plans as the Suburban rapidly picked up speed and shot toward them. Steve laughed as he clipped one of them with the front bumper.

"That'll teach you to mess with me, you sorry fuckers!" he shouted over his shoulder.

They roared down the long driveway. Kempler mashed the button on his visor and the gate at the entrance to the lane began to open. He slowed just enough to make sure they didn't crash into it, then whipped the wheel and they were off his property and onto the narrow road. Boon caught a glimpse of a black SUV parked on the berm. He looked back and saw tail lights burning red as the vehicle began to turn around.

"Here they come!" he shouted.

Steve grunted, never taking his eyes from the winding road that was coming at them fast. Boon saw they were doing almost eighty miles per hour on a road designed for a sedate twenty-five. In seconds, they blew through a stop sign and screeched onto Far Hills, the ass-end of the SUV kicking out sideways and nearly clipping a telephone pole.

Kempler floored the vehicle again, and the big V8 answered with a throaty roar of delight. They were quickly back up to eighty, the darkened storefronts and houses whizzing past them in a blur. Dohir held on tight as they made repeated lane changes without slowing, the few cars and trucks on the road blaring their horns at them as they swerved from lane to lane. Steve never looked their way, his eyes locked on the road as it unwound before them. The dotted lines on the road became a white blur.

Boon twisted around in his seat. Headlights a few hundred yards behind them were zig-zagging back and forth. He couldn't tell what the make and model was, but he didn't need to.

"I hate to sound like a TV cliché, but they're gaining on us!"

They were coming up on red light at a major intersection, and Steve slowed only enough to make sure he didn't T-bone someone crossing in front of them. Once through he floored it again and the big Chevy surged forward, throwing Boon back in his seat. The black SUV behind them didn't slow down and barreled through, gaining precious yardage.

They passed through three more major intersections, and each time Kempler's slightly more cautious driving allowed their pursuers to narrow the gap.

"Uh, Steve," Boon said, yelling to be heard above the roar of the engine and squealing tires. "What's your plan?"

His friend didn't answer, just increased speed. Boon held onto the handle above his head, but even that couldn't stop him from being slammed from side to side.

Just as they were coming up on another red light, a police cruiser passed them going the other direction. Boon's heart sank as he watched the cop car quickly turn around and come after them, its red and blue light bar flashing in their rear-view mirrors and reflecting on Steve's tense face.

"We've got cops now!" he yelled.

Kempler growled, "About damn time."

At the intersection he slowed enough to turn right, all four tires skidding on some loose gravel. Two other police cars had joined in the chase now, but Steve didn't slow down. He came up to a smaller street on the right, and whipped the SUV around the corner. A hundred yards up was an entrance to a parking lot, and he turned into it so fast he drifted off the driveway and onto the grass. In front of them was a tan brick building with lots of windows lit up, a surprising number considering how late at night it was. He mashed the brakes hard, jammed the Suburban into park, and killed the engine. In seconds, the three cop cars had him blocked in, the policemen in all three climbing out of their cars with hands hovering near their weapons. Two other officers charged out of the door in the brick building. Steve put his hands up where they could easily be seen. Boon caught a glimpse of the black SUV as it drove slowly behind them on the narrow street, before it disappeared into the darkness.

"Jesus, where the hell are we?" Boon whispered, staring at the cops inching warily toward them from all sides.

"This, my friend," Steve said with a grin, "is the Oakwood Police Station."

13

Boon knew the value of connections. After all, he had made good use of them throughout his career. Kempler, it seemed, also knew how valuable relationships could be. As it turned out, he was a friend to more than a few of the policemen on duty that night. He was also a significant contributor to the local Fraternal Order of Police, as well as several other prominent police-based charities. In less than five minutes, they were inside the police station breakroom, drinking bitter vending machine coffee and laughing with several of the officers on duty.

"Sorry, I just got spooked, that's all," Steve was saying, holding court and chuckling at his own false stupidity. "I swear, after I flipped them off for tailgating I thought those guys were coming after me. It was probably just some dumb kids trying to act tough. I'm sure I freaked the hell out of them when I pulled in here! Sorry to cause so much trouble, guys."

One of the cops, a stocky man with a mustache that made him look a little like an 80's porn star, shook his head. "Damn kids," he muttered, commiserating with Steve over the stupidity of today's youth.

Kempler laughed again and slapped him on the back. "I know, right?"

The two of them chatted a bit more before the stocky policeman waved them away. "Just take it easy, okay, Steve? No more high-speed chases, at least not until I'm off duty. Deal?"

Kempler laughed again, shaking his head. "You got it. Thanks, Roy. And hey, let's head out for a round of golf next week, if you've got time. My treat."

Roy ushered them out of the police station and into the night. "You're good to go. Unless you want an escort back to your place?"

Boon and Steve climbed back into the SUV. "Hell no, that's not necessary. Like I said, I'm sure it was just some stupid kids. We're fine."

Roy slapped the side of the SUV. Steve waved at him, and pulled out of the parking lot. When the police station was out of sight behind them, Dohir sighed and slid down in his seat, physically and emotionally spent.

"Jesus, let's not do that again, okay?"

Kempler's jovial manner was gone, replaced with a stony expression. "Agreed. That was too damn close. But right now, let's put some miles between us and this town."

They quickly got on I-675 south. Steve's driving was sedate and controlled this time, his speed hovering just above the limit. Even at this late hour there were plenty of cars and trucks sharing the road with them. Boon looked at the clock on the dashboard and saw it was almost two in the morning. In a few minutes, they merged onto 75 south toward Cincinnati. The highway was busier, which was fine with Boon since it provided additional cover. Steve got behind a semi-truck and set the cruise control.

"How the fuck did those assholes find out where I live?" he growled. "It doesn't make any sense."

Dohir shook his head. "I don't know, but I'm really sorry about what happened back there. Your garage door, the cops, the whole thing."

Kempler shot Boon a brief glance, his mouth tight. "What? No, I'm not worried about any of that shit. The garage door can be replaced. No, those sons of bitches invaded my home and came after both of us. This was all a little bit of fun and games before. But now they've gone and made it personal. Now, I'm pissed."

Boon wanted to say it hadn't been all fun and games for him, but this wasn't the time. He'd never seen his friend so furious, and he was more than a little relieved it wasn't directed at him. Kempler kept his eyes locked on the road in front of them, his jaw working hard around clenched teeth. Yes, he'd seen Steve mad before, but nothing like this.

They drove past a sign welcoming them to Warren County, and kept going south. Soon they were in the more rural area between Dayton and Cincinnati, the lights on either side of them thinning out.

"You asked me a little while ago what my plan was," Steve said eventually, his voice edging closer to normal. "Now I'm going to ask you the same thing. We can't go to either of the apartments you told me about. The cabin is out, and so is my place. So now it's my turn to ask you; what's your plan?"

That was a great question. The trouble was, at that moment, Boon had no answer. He was a planner by nature, always had been. Whether it was school, sports, or work, he'd always carefully plotted his next move, never acted in haste, and never took the first step unless he had the next ten figured out. Well, except this last time with Marsden, and look where that had gotten him. But these last few days hadn't given him the luxury of his normal, careful deliberation. He was out of his element, and he wasn't comfortable operating like this.

"I don't know," he admitted after a while.

Kempler grunted. "Well, we've gotta go somewhere. We can't just keep driving."

Boon looked out the window at the passing lights. "I know."

"Fucking awesome," Steve grunted again, shaking his head.

They drove for a few more miles in silence, with both of them peering ahead of them at the dark, featureless highway. With a deep sigh, Boon sat up straight and began digging in his pockets.

"What are you doing?" Kempler asked.

"Something I wish I didn't have to do," he said. "But I can't think of anything else." He pulled out the new burner phone and dialed a number. He heard it ring several times before it went to voicemail. He cursed under his breath when the default message came on.

"Miles, it's me. Boon. I...I could use some help. Please call me back at this number as soon as you can." He hung up and sat back in his seat.

"Hold on a minute," his friend said. "I thought you broke off contact with your people?"

"I did. For all I know Miles followed orders, tossed his phone in the trash, and will never get the message. But I had to try. We don't really have any other choice."

Kempler's eyes were still steely as he stared at the highway, his hands gripping the wheel. Dohir stared ahead at the few cars and trucks sharing the road with them, periodically glancing at the phone in his lap. He jumped in his seat when it rang.

"Miles, thanks for calling back," he said.

"Boon, hey. Sorry I didn't answer before. I didn't recognize the number. You okay?" Miles asked, his voice muffled and hard to understand. There was some loud music in the background, and crowd noises. Laughing. Tinkling of glasses. If history was any indication, Miles was clubbing it.

"Yeah, I'm fine. Got a minute?"

"Sure. Gimme a sec while I step outside. I can't hear a thing in here."

There was some rustling on the other end, and eventually the level of the music dropped. "Thank god you called, cause these guys suck. I've heard better bands in subways. What's up, my man? What happened to the *Alas, Babylon* you sent out?"

Boon paused. It was tearing him up to ask for help, especially because by doing so he might be endangering the lives of his co-workers. Could Boon put Miles' safety, perhaps his very life, at risk?

"No, forget it," he said, his voice thick with regret. "Forget I called. Sorry to bother you."

"Whoa, hold on a minute there," Miles shot back. "What's going on? What do you need? Talk to me, man."

Boon rubbed his forehead with his free hand. "No, I can't do this to you."

"Screw that, dammit. Just tell me what the hell's happening."

Out of the corner of his eye, he felt Steve's eyes on him. He had almost forgotten that Kempler was in this mess because of him now, too. Steve was just as screwed as he was. Doing nothing meant his life was in jeopardy, too.

"Okay. I could use a place to crash and lay low for a while. I know I said we're not supposed to do this and I gave the order, but I don't have any choice. And it's okay to say no. Believe me, I'd understand."

There wasn't even a second's delay before Miles said, "What the hell are you talking about? Man, of course you can come over and crash. I've got plenty of room. As long as you need."

Boon felt himself smile despite all that had been going on. "Careful. Don't agree too fast, not until you know what's going on."

This time Miles did pause. Then, "So, how much trouble are you in?"

"It's Marsden. There's a lot that I haven't told any of you before. People are after me. Very, very bad people."

Miles didn't say anything for a moment. "These bad people, are they the ones that killed him?"

So, he had seen the news stories. He closed his eyes before he answered. "Yes, they are."

"And they're after you? Damn, man, I knew something was wrong with all this! I just knew it! I could tell. You were acting weird. I just couldn't figure out why. What's going on?"

"I'll tell you all about it when I see you, okay? For now, we just need to hide our car and lay low for a while. Hopefully just for a few days."

"We? Who else is with you?"

Boon glanced at Kempler. "A friend who's been helping me out, and now he's stuck in this mess, too."

Miles sighed, and for a second Boon was afraid he'd changed his mind. "Yeah, okay. Come on over," he said, and shared his address in a suburb on the east side of the city. "Just pull up to the garage when you get here. I'll be waiting."

The GPS said it would take them about forty-five minutes to get to Miles' place. They took the bypass east around Cincinnati, and exited at Route 32. They continued past a darkened mall and some smaller shopping centers, eventually turning into a neighborhood of small, older bungalow homes. They drove slowly by a dozen or so before Boon spotted the address.

"Right here. Turn in," he instructed.

Steve did, then had to stop short when Miles stepped out of the shadows. He waved them down the driveway and into a small detached garage tucked behind the house. Kempler went slowly since the SUV was nearly too large to fit in the tight space. He killed the engine and they got out. Miles walked up to Boon and gave him a hug and a slap on the back, a bit of warmth that Boon wasn't expecting.

"You okay, man?" he asked, looking him in the eyes.

Boon tried to smile, but his slumped shoulders and slow nod belied any authenticity. "Yeah, just been a rough couple of days. I can't tell you how much this means to me."

Kempler rounded the vehicle, and Boon introduced the two of them. Miles appeared positively tiny next to the big man. The two shook hands before Miles motioned them out of the garage.

"Let's get this big ass Suburban hidden, okay?" he said.

Miles pulled down the garage door, then the three of them walked to the house, through the side door and into a small vestibule. When they stepped from there into the cramped kitchen, Boon stopped so fast Kempler bumped into him from behind with a grunt.

Beyond the kitchen was a tiny living room, complete with a beautiful black grand piano and an assortment of saxophones, trumpets, and a single trombone fitted into racks on the wall. But that was not what surprised Boon. Squeezed into the small space were all the members of Boon's team.

"Hey, boss," said Clem, leaning against a wall with a big lopsided grin on his face, his hair so messed up he'd certainly just gotten out of bed. Next to him was Sir Jim, who had somehow shoehorned his impressive bulk into a narrow easy chair, his feet propped up on an ottoman. Sasha, her athletic build hidden in a bulky sweatsuit, was perched on the edge of the piano bench. She had her hair held back by a thin headband. Patrice was sitting up straight on a kitchen chair with her arms crossed, a sour expression on her doughy face. He'd heard Sasha describe the woman's expression as "standing bitch face" before, and that certainly fit now.

"What the… I don't understand," Dohir stammered, so shocked he almost staggered backwards.

"Take it all in, ya'll," Clem laughed. "For once the boss is tongue-tied. Pretty sure this is a first!"

It took another few seconds for Boon to find his voice again. "What are you all doing here? I only called Miles because I had no choice."

"My good man," Sir Jim said in his deep baritone, stifling a yawn behind a meaty hand. "Miles told us you were in trouble. We're here to help."

"Yep," Sasha added, with a mischievous grin. "We're the fucking calvary, that's what we are."

Boon was still gathering his wits about him, albeit slowly. "Hey, guys, I appreciate it, I really do. But this is dangerous. You should not be here. I didn't even want to get Miles involved. Besides, I gave the Alas, Babylon, command. You're not supposed to be seeing each other. Ever again."

All of them smiled at this and shared knowing looks. Boon glanced at each of them in turn, but couldn't understand what was going on.

"Oh, hell, someone tell him," Sasha said, her eyes dancing as she fought to hold back a laugh. "Poor guy looks like he's about to stroke out."

"Fine. I will," Sir Jim rumbled. "My good man, despite your instructions to the contrary, we gather together on a rather regular basis. None of us have what you might call a significant number of friends due to the nature of our work. Too many questions we can't answer, you know."

"But it's not what you think," Clem interjected calmly as Boon's eyes widened. "We're very careful when we get together, usually just to watch a movie, play cards, or have dinner. We keep to ourselves and don't attract attention."

"Oh yes, and whatever you do," Sir Jim added, "do not play poker with Patrice, no matter what she says. She's a savant. She'll own your car before the third hand."

Clem took a few steps forward and clapped Boon on the shoulder. "It comes down to this," he said in his easy southern drawl. "Like Sir Jim said, Miles told us you were in trouble, and we wanted to help. You've been there for us. Now it's our turn."

Clem's words couldn't have hurt more if the soft-spoken southerner had hauled back and punched him in the face. They had no idea what Boon had done, not only surrounding the events leading up to Marsden's murder, but with the $20 million payout, too. They had trusted him, and he had betrayed that trust. He didn't deserve their help and loyalty.

"No, you don't understand. You don't owe me anything. Not now."

Sasha cocked her head at him, sitting up straighter, her bright eyes suddenly alert. "No? Why not?"

Dohir glanced over his shoulder at Kempler, who inclined his head at them. "Tell them, Boon," he urged. "You need to tell them everything."

He stared at each of them in turn. Admitting his betrayal was going to be one of the hardest things he had ever done, especially after this display of friendship. In fact, it was proving to be so difficult that, given the choice, he would have gladly turned himself over to the Spanish killer right then and there instead. He walked slowly into the living room and sat down hard on an open chair. *Just start,* he told himself. *They deserve that much. Just tell them the damn truth.*

So, he did. For the next ten minutes, he revealed everything that had transpired over the last few days, holding nothing back. Admitting to his deceit was painful at first, his words halting, almost pulled from him in a tug of war between honesty and regret. But once he got going, they tumbled out so fast he barely had time to take a breath. In fact, when he wrapped up, he was physically winded, as if he'd been running from something. Boon held out his hands and saw them shaking, and realized again how badly he needed a drink. Or wanted one, he wasn't sure which anymore. He kept his eyes down, still staring at his palms, afraid to look anyone in the eyes.

Clem finally broke the heavy silence. "Well, that's a whole bunch to take in."

"Yes, it is," Patrice added, the first words she had uttered so far. "Have you screwed us over before?"

"No. Never," he declared flatly. "I've always been above board with all of you."

She made a dismissive sound with her mouth. "Like we can believe you now."

Boon half-expected them to all get up and leave, but no one made a move. He glanced up and saw Sasha staring at him with an expression on her face he couldn't decipher. He noticed the tiniest warming of her eyes, perhaps a minute upturning of the corners of her mouth. It was something he never expected, especially not from someone as intense as she'd always been. He saw for the first time that her eyes were light blue, with some darker flecks in them. Why hadn't he ever noticed how pretty they were before?

Miles stepped into the middle of the room, instantly commanding everyone's attention. He held up his hands and gazed down at Boon. "Okay, my friend, you screwed up. Big."

"Yeah, he did," Patrice echoed to the room.

"But, that's done," Miles continued, giving her a fleeting look. "It's over. The question now is, what do we do?"

"How about we all get our share of the $20 million?" Patrice added. Sir Jim's head bobbed up and down in agreement. The rest of them didn't move. Boon couldn't tell what they were thinking.

"Yeah, I don't think that's a good idea, at least not yet," Clem offered, patting the air in front of him as if to tamp down the volatile atmosphere. "We may need all that if we want to get this crazy Spanish guy off Boon's back."

Dohir sat up in his chair and ran his fingers through his hair. He sighed. "First of all, you have no idea how much I appreciate that all of you are still here. I mean that. Second, I don't think just giving him back his money will take care of him. He doesn't seem to be the forgiving type. I've told you a little about what he can do, but you've never talked to him.

You haven't heard the hate and anger in his voice. He's not going to let this go. He won't stop until he's got me, and maybe all of you, too." He dug his phone and the tracker out of his pockets and put them on a small end table next to him.

"That's the tracker?" Sasha asked, her interest piqued. "May I?"

Dohir pushed it to her. She turned it on and watched as the screen came to life, flipping the small device this way and that, inspecting it as if it were a Rubik's Cube she felt compelled to solve.

Kempler stepped from the kitchen into the living room. He cleared his throat loudly, and all eyes swiveled to him, as if his inherent gravity was pulling them that way. "Listen, you people don't know me from Adam, but Boon's right. This guy won't stop coming after us, any of us. Trust me. His men broke into my house and would have killed both of us if we hadn't gotten away. He murdered this Marsden guy. Who knows what else he's done?"

"What are you proposing?" Miles asked warily, verbalizing what the others were certainly thinking.

"I'm saying," Steve continued, "that we need to do something about it. Any of you play football?"

Sir Jim raised his hand. "I did. Offensive line in college. A lifetime ago."

Sasha stopped inspecting the tracker. "You're shittin' me, right? You?"

Kempler inclined his head toward Sir Jim. "So, you know what I mean when I say that we can't play defense with this guy and hope he goes away. We need to go on the offensive. We have to go after him and take him out, on our own terms. Before he does it to us. It's the only way. Right, Boon?"

As one, every pair of eyes in the room shifted from Kempler to Dohir. Feeling the pressure of their stares, he stood and walked into the kitchen and opened the refrigerator. Inside was some orange juice, milk, and some other odds and ends, but not what he was craving. He couldn't believe Miles didn't even have a single beer or bottle of wine in there. His hands trembled as he closed the door.

"Yeah, I'm afraid he's right. I'm sorry, but at this point I think it's the only way. Get him before he gets us."

It took a few seconds, but then they all agreed, even Patrice, although she was a few seconds behind the rest. Sasha stood and flipped the hair out of her eyes.

"Screw it," she said. "I'm in. Let's get the son of a bitch."

14

Everyone hung around for a little bit afterwards, even Sir Jim, who could barely manage to string four words together without a jaw-cracking yawn. Not long after that, Clem was literally asleep on his feet and would have toppled over if Sasha hadn't caught him. Boon stood up, stretching.

"Okay, people," he said. "Let's call it a night. It's late, and we're all too tired to think straight. If it's okay with Miles, we can reconvene here tomorrow."

Miles agreed. They all said their good nights and began dribbling out the door one at a time. Boon felt a tap on the shoulder, and followed his host as he led him to a bedroom down a hallway. The room was small, with only enough space for a double bed, a narrow dresser, and a pair of matching nightstands. Keeping with the theme in the living room, artwork on the walls depicted musicians from all different genres. Boon thought he recognized a few.

"Thanks again, Miles," he said, realizing he had been saying thank you to quite a few people lately. "I'll never forget this. You got a place for Steve to crash?"

"Sure. Upstairs. Most of the space is taken up with more instruments, but there's another bed and a bathroom up there. Promise, I'll take good care of him." With a final smile, he left and closed the door behind him.

Boon sat on the edge of the bed and kicked off his shoes. With a deep sigh he leaned back on the inviting covers, closing his eyes. After a few seconds he realized if he didn't get his clothes off soon, he was going to fall asleep just as he was. He stood and stripped down to his boxers, then gratefully crawled between the sheets. As he was nodding off, he had enough sense to kill the light next to the bed. He rolled onto his stomach and closed his eyes, physically drained, sleep seconds away from claiming him. Just as he was about to drift off, he heard a slight noise, a gentle swishing sound, like the bedroom door had just opened and closed. He was about to sit up when he felt someone slide under the covers on the other side of the bed.

"What? Who?" he said, alarmed.

"Hush," Sasha whispered. "Pretend I'm not here. Um, too late to drive home now. Scooch over."

She didn't exactly press herself into him, but neither did she try to keep her distance. Her hair was so close to his face he could smell her shampoo, a fruity bouquet that reminded him of apples and strawberries. Her arm draped itself over him as she settled deeper into the covers. Within seconds her breathing slowed and became even.

After that shock, it took Dohir at least another half hour to fall asleep. As he finally began to doze off for good, Sasha now spooned up tight against him, he recalled the odd look she had given him earlier that evening. He wondered what the hell was happening right now, and, more disturbing, how little control he seemed to be having over his own life all of sudden.

When he woke up the next morning, he was all by himself in bed.

He glanced over to the other side to make sure he hadn't imagined the whole thing, but there was a visible dent in the pillow where Sasha's head had been. He got up, dressed, and made his way out to the living room. Miles was already up and seated at the piano, gently playing, his long fingers moving fluidly over the keys.

"I didn't wake you up, did I?" he asked, not stopping.

Boon stretched, working the night's sleep from his back. He shook his head. "No, I didn't hear a thing."

"Good. How'd you two kids sleep last night?" His melodic voice held more than a tinge of humor in it.

"Uh, fine. But what the hell was all that with Sasha?"

Miles stopped playing and gave him a sideways look, one of equal parts pity and amusement. "If you don't know, man, I'm not going to tell you."

"What are you talking about?"

Miles went back to his music, focusing once more on the keys before him. His fingers moved so gracefully they almost seemed boneless. "Okay. Think about it. Do you really think she works for you because she has to? A girl with her talents? Her looks? Man, she could have a legit tech job anywhere she wanted to. And for more money, too."

Questions suddenly flooded his head, but before he had a chance to formulate words, Steve thumped down the steps and entered the room.

"Is that really you playing?" he asked, staring at the slight man. "You're good."

"Thanks. It's how I relax."

There was a pot of coffee on the counter, and Dohir wandered over in a daze and poured himself a cup. He cradled it in his hands and sat down in the living room, enjoying the music. The tune itself wasn't anything he knew, but that didn't detract from its inherent beauty. Now that his guests were up, he played with a little more passion, louder and more defined. Boon envied him for his talent. His own lack of musical ability felt like a shadow eclipsing his soul.

Miles finished with a flourish, the final notes growing softer until they faded to nothing, like mist settling then dissipating over an open field. His eyes were closed and his head was lowered. He turned on the bench and faced them.

"Bravo," Steve said loudly. "Bravissimo."

"Thanks," the musician replied with a smile, dipping his head in a small bow. "Just a little ditty I've been working on in my spare time."

"I don't know much about this stuff," Kempler admitted. "But you sound good enough to do this for a living."

Miles' hand drifted back to the keys, but he didn't play a note. "Yeah, well, that's harder than you think. Making a good living in the music business is brutal. You can do okay, but without connections or a lucky break, you're just another handsome dude on a piano."

Kempler didn't snap his fingers, but the revelation was so clear he may as well have. "Now I get it. That's why you work with Boon."

"Yep. I play when I can. Some studio work, but mostly for myself these days, to be honest. The money I make working with him pays the bills. It's a good arrangement."

Dohir sat quietly with his coffee cooling, only partially listening. He'd always suspected Miles was musically inclined, sure, but he'd had no clue about this side of the man's life.

"Did you come up with any grand scheme yet?" Miles asked him.

Boon jerked back to the moment. "No, nothing yet. Working on it. Besides sleeping, I've been a little preoccupied with something else all of a sudden."

Miles laughed, his white teeth a sharp contrast to his dark skin. "I bet you have!"

Kempler shot an interested look between the two men. "What am I missing? What happened?"

"Ask Boon," Miles said, casting a knowing glance his way. "You gonna tell him, or should I?"

"It's nothing," he answered, studying his cup. "Just something with Sasha, that's all."

Steve paused for a moment, then laughed, a booming bellow that far exceeded the capacity of the room. "Oh, yeah, her. She's got the hots for you, I could tell."

"You could?"

"Sure. It was clear as day. This can't be news to you, can it?"

Dohir felt his face redden. "It is. Does everyone know but me?"

Miles shrugged. "I can't say, but probably. I can't believe you never noticed. The looks she gives you all the time? Hanging out at the same gym? This can't be news to you, man."

It was indeed news to him. He'd always thought she was physically very attractive, sure, and he'd always been blown away by her knowledge and skills. But his strict policy of keeping everyone at arm's length had never let him view her as anything but a co-worker.

Kempler laughed again, tapping the side of his head. "For someone as bright as you, Boon, sometimes you can be a little dim."

Dohir was torn between talking more about this new personal situation and his more pressing problems, but this choice was taken off the table when Clem sauntered through the front door with his big sloppy smile. He was loaded down with a box the size of a small suitcase.

"Breakfast is served, y'all," he announced proudly, whipping open the lid with a flourish. "Fried dough dipped in sugar. Just like God intended." As they munched on a variety of donuts, Sir Jim entered, followed by Sasha. She was back to her typical workout gear, with her hair pulled back. No one bothered to knock before entering, Dohir noticed, which went a long way to validate that these types of get-togethers were indeed a normal thing for them. Out of the corner of his eye he glanced toward her, but she was in a friendly conversation with Miles. He did notice that she refused any of Clem's donuts, and instead was working on one of her green breakfast drinks, like normal. He was suddenly unsure how to act around her.

Miles meticulously wiped some powder from his hands on a napkin, then surveyed the room. "We're all here except Patrice," he said. "Anyone talk to her today?"

"Not me," Clem said around a mouthful. "Not since last night. She said she'd be here."

None of the others had spoken to her, either. By mutual consent they agreed to wait a little longer. Fifteen minutes later, however, Miles stopped drumming his fingers on the chair and looked at his watch.

"Hold on, I'll call her," he said. Boon and the others watched while Miles waited for her to pick up. Eventually he lowered the phone. "No answer. It went right to voicemail."

"She's most likely on her way here," Sir Jim said while poking around the box, finally landing on a huge jelly filled.

"Yes, I'm sure that's it," Clem added. "She wouldn't answer while driving. She's too cautious. Let's give her a little more time."

They all agreed, Dohir included, although there was now an undercurrent of worry. The casual conversations they'd been having withered and died, and they sat there staring at the door or out the window, as if willing her to walk through. At one point Sasha got out her phone. When he saw that, something clicked in Boon's mind. He sat up straight and urgently patted his pockets.

"Where's my phone?" he asked, his voice laced with sudden concern. "And the tracker. Where's the tracker?"

Sasha quickly dug in her backpack and withdrew the device. "I've got it right here," she said, holding it up. "Sorry. I was looking it over last night and forgot to put it back."

Boon's anxiety eased, but only a fraction. "I put my phone on that table last night. That's the last time I had it. Did anyone pick it up?" He looked around the room, and to a person they were all shaking their heads or looking at each other. No one had seen it.

"I'm sure it's here somewhere," Miles assured him. "Come on, people. Let's do a search."

But after a few minutes of hunting between cushions and under furniture, it was evident that the phone wasn't there. Boon even looked underneath the bed and dresser in his bedroom. He walked back to the others empty-handed, a scowl on his face. Miles was standing with his arms crossed in the middle of the room.

"Hate to say this," he said, "but it's not here."

"And neither is Patrice," Sasha added, saying out loud what everyone was thinking. "Seems a little suspicious. Someone tell me I'm wrong."

Oh, shit, Boon thought, putting two and two together. "Everyone, right now, turn off your phones!" he ordered in a panic. "I mean it. Turn them off now!"

As they all powered down their devices, Dohir's legs were suddenly so weak he nearly fell into a chair. He leaned forward and cradled his head in his hands. His heart was racing, and the donut he'd just eaten suddenly soured in his stomach. For what had to be the hundredth time, he wished he had never pursued this Marsden scam.

"Boon, what's going on?" Kempler asked him.

He took a deep breath, trying to calm himself. He didn't know how much time they had, but he knew they had to get out of there. The only saving grace was that Miles' house was far outside of Cincinnati, and even farther from Dayton. He didn't know where the Spanish maniac was holed up, but he doubted he was close by. They probably had time, but not much.

"Gather up your stuff," he said, standing. "We've got to get out of here."

"Why?" Miles asked, grabbing his arm. "What's happening?"

"Patrice, that's what. She took my phone. I bet she was hoping to make a deal with whoever is after me. But she's way out of her depth here. If she turned it on, knowing he'd find her, then he's got her. We'll all be next."

Clem stood and shook his head. "Ah, now, she wouldn't sell us out. She wouldn't do that to us."

"Not to intentionally hurt you, no," Dohir agreed. "But to get her share of the $20 million? Or a reward from him? You bet she would. You heard her last night. She probably thinks she can strike a deal with this guy. But she doesn't know him. If he has her, none of us are safe."

Clem lifted a finger to disagree but lowered it when he had a chance to consider Boon's words. The soft-spoken southerner's head drooped.

"She has all your phone numbers, and knows where you all live, right?" Dohir asked the group. One by one they all said yes, looking at each other with wide eyes. "Then we need to go. Now. They could be here any second. And trust me, you do not want to be here when they show up."

15

Thirty minutes later, they met at a small diner in Kentucky, not too far from Sasha and Boon's gym. They congregated in a small back room, as far from the other diners as they could get. Their waitress brought them water and breakfast menus, promising in a pleasing southern twang to come back in a bit.

"First, has anyone ever been here before?" Boon asked, keeping his voice low enough not to be overheard. "Would Patrice know this place?"

They all shook their heads, and Miles said. "No, I usually stick to the other side of the river."

Dohir took a deep breath, trying to figure out where to begin. He looked at each one of them in turn, seeing a variety of expressions staring back at him, from Sir Jim's palpable fear to Steve's simmering anger. He was beginning to view them all in a new light, not just as fellow employees, but as friends — friends who were now in danger because of him. They had risked themselves on his behalf, even though he had never intended to get them involved. Now it was up to him to figure a way out of this, no matter what. This was his fault, and he was going to own up to it.

"I know I've said this before, but I mean it. I'm sorry for getting you all wrapped in this mess. It was a stupid, greedy thing to do, and I'm going to regret it for the rest of my life. I hope I can make it up to all of you. Somehow." There were murmurs from around the table, but no one was yelling at him, which he took as a win.

"But first, we need to figure out if Patrice did what I think she did. Sasha, can you access your phone or texts from your computer?"

She tilted her head with a pitying look as if to say "Really?" then pulled her laptop out and set it on the table. They all waited while her fingers danced over the keyboard, much like Miles' fingers had flown over the piano keys. It was as if she possessed the same skills, but with a different instrument.

"Boom. I'm logged in," Sasha announced. "I'll see if anyone calls or texts."

"Can you accept a phone call on that thing?" Boon asked.

"Yes. Phone calls, video calls, or texts. Everything can be routed through here."

Sir Jim lifted his hand. "Do you think that's wise? Would they be able to track us through her computer, even without her cell phone?"

She thought for a moment. "I don't know. But if you're worried, I can disable everything except texting. That part is internet-based and has nothing to do with an actual cell phone. It's an instant messenger service. People can text from PC to PC without using a phone at all."

Boon said, "Yeah, you'd better. We just don't know enough yet. Better safe than sorry."

"Okay," she replied, tapping a few keys. "Done. Everything but texting is disabled."

The waitress came back with a smile on her face and a notepad in her hands, asking what they'd like. Boon was in no mood for anything but coffee. The rest of them ordered the same, except for Sir Jim who got something called the Breakfast Bonanza, consisting of eggs, bacon, plus biscuits with gravy. When the waitress left to put in their order, Sasha turned to him and shook her head.

"Jesus, old man, you really are pushing for a coronary, aren't you?"

"No worries, my dear. Just trying to keep my strength up."

Miles cleared his throat. "Well, what do we do now, Boon? Wait?"

"That's exactly what we do. We need to treat this like a hostage situation. There's nothing we can do except wait for them to get in contact with us. We just have to sit tight."

Steve Kempler sat back in his chair, his face simmering red. "Jesus, that's it? We just have to sit here? What about cops? Do we get them involved?"

"I don't think that would be a good idea. Your nose is clean, Steve, but if we get the police involved, I'm pretty sure the rest of us would be spending a long time behind bars. But if Patrice did what I think she did, then I wouldn't worry about waiting long. I have a feeling we'll be contacted soon enough. They'll try all your numbers until someone answers."

"And if you're wrong?" Clem asked. "If Patrice just overslept and forgot to turn her phone on? What then?"

"I hope that's the case. If so, we regroup and figure out how we can go on the offensive, as Steve put it last night. Until then, please trust me. This is our best option."

"Jesus, I hope so," Kempler growled. "We're running out of places to hide. I don't even know where the hell we're going to crash tonight."

The waitress brought their drinks and Sir Jim's steaming platters of food. All of them watched in disbelief as he consumed every last scrap, mopping up the last dregs of gravy with a chunk of biscuit. When he was done, he patted his mouth with a napkin and belched quietly.

"The man eats like a damn Viking," Steve said in admiration.

Sasha stared at him in awe and wrinkled her nose in distaste. "That amount of food would feed an entire Vietnamese family."

"And they would have loved it," he commented. "It was quite enjoyable."

As the rest of them were discussing the number of calories he'd just consumed, there was a soft ding from the PC on the table. Their conversations stopped like they'd been slapped, and as one they turned and stared at Sasha. She bent over to read something on the screen.

"Well?" Miles asked.

"It's from her," she said. "Well, I think it's her. She's asking where everyone is. Says she's at Miles' house. What should I say?"

Boon said, "Has she ever called or texted you before?"

Sasha shook her head. "No, never. We're not exactly BFFs, as you've probably noticed."

Boon sat up straight. "Okay, we can pretty much rule out it's really her. Tell her I'll call and give her directions where we are."

Sasha's head jerked up from the screen, her eyes wide and round. "Call her? Are you crazy? The second you turn your phone on they'll know where we are!"

"No, they won't. Just send the message. I'll be right back."

Dohir watched her type, and as soon as she hit the return key, he got up and walked to the front of the diner. The place was filling up, with people chatting and enjoying themselves all around him. He walked up to the hostess station at the front and got the attention of the young lady there. She couldn't have been much older than sixteen.

"Hi, does the restaurant have a phone I can borrow?" he asked her.

The hostess smiled at him, a touch of confusion in her voice. "Sure, I guess. Don't you have one?"

"Yeah, but the battery died."

She furrowed her brow. "What about your friends back there? Don't they have one you could use?"

Boon gave her his most sincere smile. "Oddly enough, all their batteries are dead too. Strange, right? I'll only be a minute. Honest."

"Oh. Okay." She pulled a black landline phone from under the counter. "Here you go. Please keep it short. We take reservations on that."

"Thanks. I'll just be a minute."

She cast him an odd glance, as if the terrifying possibility of living without a phone had never occurred to her, then stepped away to help a group of people who had just walked in. Boon picked up the handset, and heard a dial tone. First, he dialed *67 to mask the diner's number, then he punched in Patrice's number. A second later it started to ring.

On the fourth ring, there was a click when someone answered, but whoever it was didn't say anything. Boon didn't speak either, just stood there with the receiver up to his ear while the sounds of the diner moved around him.

"You blocked your number," the Spanish speaker eventually said. "And you're not using your phone."

Boon pressed the receiver up to his ear and cupped his hand around his mouth. "You bet. Let's talk."

"There is nothing to talk about, *cabrón*," he hissed. "You have my money. I have the woman. *Comprende*?"

"You're right. It is that simple. I propose a trade; your $20 million for the woman. Even up. And your word that you'll leave us alone after that."

"You have no power to bargain!" the man snapped. "I am in charge and I make the rules. I will kill her and come for you. And because she annoys me, I will enjoy it!"

Boon had to suppress a smile. Yes, he certainly had Patrice.

"I have all your phone numbers and I know exactly where you all live. You will not survive the week!"

"Wait!" Boon said, his hand shielding the mouthpiece. "You don't have to do that. Let's just make a trade and be done with it. The woman for your money. It's easy. No one else has to get hurt. We can work this out."

There was heavy breathing on the other end of the line, then, "Why? Why should I agree to this? Tell me."

Dohir looked around, but no one was near him. "Because this was all an accident. I wasn't going after your money. Just Marsden's. But something happened at the bank. I saw the $20 million and acted without thinking. It was a stupid mistake. Don't make her pay for that. Please. Let's make the trade and be done with it. You'll get it all back. Every penny."

There was a pause on the other end, and some muffled talking that Boon couldn't hear. Finally, after what felt like an eternity, "*Bien.* Agreed. My money for the woman."

"And you'll back off and leave us alone, right?"

After several breaths, he said, "Sí. Yes."

Boon sighed with relief, although the man's response lacked conviction. Even so, the genesis of a plan was forming in his mind, but there was a hitch. This was where it got tricky.

"And I need your word you'll come in person. I'll transfer the entire amount to you, but to you alone. No one else. I want to see who I'm dealing with. And besides, are you going to trust this much money to anyone else? I mean," he said, emphasizing these last words, "you already lost it once. You don't want to take that chance again, do you?"

Dohir heard a rustling sound as if the man had covered the mouthpiece. There was an indistinct conversation going on, some voices raised, and finally a word that sounded like "basta."

"I do not appreciate being told what to do. But you have my word. I will come," he replied as if the words were being pulled from between his locked jaw. "But, if we see anything suspicious, we will kill the woman and then we will kill all of you as well. We will hunt you down, one by one. You have my word on that, too."

Boon couldn't help but think about Marsden and the man's ultimate fate. "I don't doubt that. We need to meet somewhere public. In the open. That's the only way I'll do this. Do you know where Fountain Square is in downtown Cincinnati?"

Some muffled talking again. "Yes."

"Good. How long until you can get there?"

More talking in the background. "An hour and a half, *mas o menos*."

Boon didn't understand that last bit, but he got the gist. "Good. I'll meet you there at noon. At the base of the Tyler Davidson statue. The big statue with the water coming out of its hands. You can't miss it."

The Spanish speaker said nothing, he just ended the call. Boon stood there for a moment, sweating, his knees so weak he had to hold on to the hostess station to keep from falling over. He hung up the phone, thanked the hostess, and made his way back to the table. The others were all staring at him in silence. Clem had his coffee cup halfway to his mouth, but it was suspended there as if he were paralyzed.

"Well?" Kempler asked, breaking the ice. "What happened?"

Dohir slid into his chair. He picked up his own coffee cup, but his hands were shaking so badly he couldn't drink it. He set it back down and exhaled, his cheeks puffed out. He imagined he was a few shades paler than usual.

"We have a deal. We're going to make the exchange at Fountain Square at noon today."

Each person in the group sat back and smiled, relieved, except for Steve. He squinted at Boon. "You're not going to tell me you trust this guy, are you?"

"No. Not as far as I can throw him. Which is why we've got to get there before him. He said it will take him 90 minutes to get there. My guess is he'll be there in less than an hour. We've got some work to do first."

"Work? What kind of work?" Miles asked.

Boon managed a small smile. "You'll see. Sasha, I'm going to need you most of all. Are you in?"

She grinned back at him, her blue eyes alive. She leaned forward and rubbed her hands together, as if a gauntlet had been thrown.

"Fuck yes," she said without hesitation.

16

The monument at Cincinnati's Fountain Square was an impressive sight. Originally dedicated in 1871, the landmark was named after Tyler Davidson, a businessman from the city's historic past. Originally meant to rival the great fountains of Europe, the granite and bronze statue was designed to glorify the blessings of water. Streams of it flowed from the palms of the nine-foot-tall Genius of Water, also known as The Lady. A large pool contained by a concrete lip encircled the entire fountain. That's where Boon was seated now, his back to the constant roar of splashing going on behind him. Every so often a light mist dusted his hair and eyebrows, taking his hair from black to gray and prematurely aging him.

The afternoon was warm and sunny, a day where spring had finally thrown in the towel once more and allowed Ohio's summer to flex its might. Humidity, a summer staple in any Midwestern town, was oppressive enough to soak snug clothing, especially collars, bra straps, and the elastic bands of underwear. The sun sizzled almost directly overhead and threw random rainbows in and around the thick mist rolling across the square. There were hundreds of people in their own little worlds moving every which way around Boon, all with phones in their hands, up to their ears, or held flat in front of them as they carried on loud conversations, seemingly oblivious to the masses surrounding them. The fact that Dohir wasn't brandishing one was almost enough to make him appear suspicious. He did his best to blend in while he waited and, although his head rarely moved, his eyes never stopped darting in all directions.

It was already after noon and no one had shown up yet. But he wasn't too worried. Not yet, at least. In fact, he'd suspected it might go down this way. Making someone wait was a typical power play. But that was okay, because he needed the Spanish speaker to see him out there, alone, no matter how long it took. Boon was asking the owner of the $20 million to reveal himself, and there was no way the man would until he was certain there was no danger. Dohir was also sure he wouldn't come alone, and that he would have men positioned all around Fountain Square prior to making an entrance. That was okay, too.

Boon glanced at his watch. His back was already damp from the fountain and his shirt was starting to stick to him. He was pretty sure the seat of his pants was soaked through from being perched on the edge, too. Even so, the mist wafting over him periodically served to keep some of the heat at bay, so he was content with that. While he waited, several hundred more people passed by him without a glance, treating him as simply another random body relaxing in the summer sun.

Another thirty minutes ticked by. It was almost one o'clock, and despite his enforced patience, Boon was starting to get concerned. The lunch crowd that had served to partially camouflage him was thinning out. Outdoor tables at restaurants ringing the Square were slowly emptying.

Where were they? he wondered. He found he was wringing his hands, and made himself stop. Then he spotted them.

A shiny black Cadillac Escalade with heavily tinted windows pulled up the one-way street just south of him. A rear door on the side away from Boon opened, and a good-looking man with black hair and a dark complexion stepped out and walked behind the SUV. He was sharply dressed in tan slacks and a button-down blue silk shirt, open at the collar. He was tall and thin, with an angular face behind mirrored aviator sunglasses. He moved easily, smoothly, a man in harmony with his body. He scoured the area, his gaze finally landing on Boon. The newcomer extended an arm and crooked a finger at him, beckoning him toward the SUV in what was most certainly an order, not a request.

Dohir stood and walked toward them. He hadn't been sure how this would go down, but he suspected it might be like this. He threaded his way through the remaining passersby, down some steps, and found himself looking up at the stranger. He stopped when he was a few feet away.

"Yes?" he asked, unsure how to start.

The man didn't speak. The rear door of the SUV opened, and the tall man moved aside so Boon could see inside. Seated there was a squat, heavyset older man in black pants and a white shirt. Gold chains were looped around a neck thick with excess flesh. His eyes were small and dark, like a doll's eyes in an otherwise human face. The nose between those eyes was a mangled mess, a likely sign of being on the business end of a fist too many times. But what caught Boon's attention was his long white hair. It was slicked back, curling slightly where it touched his collar, and was bright against his dark skin and the black leather upholstery. The man looked him up and down, his expression neutral.

"You have my money?" he said in an accented voice, one instantly recognizable to Boon. It seemed to be made up of equal parts rage and annoyance, and it caused a shiver to run up and down Boon's back.

Dohir pulled the burner phone from his pocket, the one he had taken from Steve's house. "I do. Right here. You have the woman?"

The white-haired man tilted his large head toward the rear, to the third-row seat. Boon leaned down and peered into the dark interior. He saw Patrice back there, a piece of silver tape across her mouth. Her eyes were huge and wide in her fleshy face. There was a bruise on her left cheek, and dried blood crusted around her nostrils. Her eyes were shiny with tears. She was shaking.

"You didn't have to hurt her," Boon said, his voice harder than he meant it to be.

The white-haired man dismissed him with a wave of his hand. "It was nothing. A few love taps from Señor Gonzalez to shut her up, that's all." He motioned toward the front of the Cadillac.

Dohir turned toward the driver, and his blood seemed to thicken and freeze in his veins. The man behind the wheel was certainly the same one he'd spied at the cabin, before Boon had blown up the SUV. Gonzalez was massive, so huge the steering wheel looked like a toy in his hands. The top of the giant's head brushed the roof of the SUV, and his long black hair hung down over the headrest. Boon caught a glimpse of his face in the rearview mirror, and saw a pair of shadowy eyes surrounded by scarred and pockmarked flesh. Dohir had to suppress another shiver.

"Still, you didn't have to hurt her. That wasn't necessary," he repeated, tearing his gaze away.

"Bah. It was nothing. *Basta*. Where is my money?"

Dohir held out the burner phone. "In here. I have the full $20 million in a single account, ready to transfer to you. Give me a routing and transit number and I'll send it to you. Every penny. Just let the woman go first."

The man stared at him with his tiny eyes narrowed almost to slits.

"Luis," he said, flicking a hand toward the back seat.

The tall man circled around to the back of the vehicle and opened the big hatch. There was some commotion for a few seconds, then he strolled back with Patrice next to him. There was a red rectangle of angry skin across her lips and cheeks where the tape had been ripped off.

Patrice was rubbing her wrists. She was still visibly shaking as Luis held tightly onto her arm so she couldn't bolt, which didn't seem likely at all. Boon was pretty sure it was all she could do to stay upright.

"Now you," the man in the SUV said. He started to recite a long string of numbers, but Boon fumbled around and couldn't seem to get them right. After several tries, and with mounting frustration, the man stabbed out his hand.

"Give me your phone. I'll do it myself!" he growled.

Dohir stepped back. "Oh no, you don't. You're not getting my phone. Just text them to me and I'll cut and paste them in. That way we'll both be sure to get it right."

The man growled again, but pulled a phone from his pocket. "Your number?"

Boon shared the burner phone's number and waited for a text. When it popped up, he carefully copied and pasted the information into the proper fields into the app of his bank, one based in Switzerland. He typed in the dollar amount, double-checked he had the right number of zeros, then hit the send and confirm buttons.

"It's done," he said. "Now I'll take the woman and you'll never see us again."

"Wait," the man barked, throwing up a hand. "No one moves until I am sure the funds are in my account."

Boon watched while the man entered information on his phone. They all waited in silence while traffic and people moved around them, everyone else oblivious to the tense scene playing out on the busy street. Finally, after what seemed like much longer than the minute it was, the man grunted and slid his phone back into his shirt pocket.

"It's there," he grunted to Luis. "Let her go. I have it all."

As soon as his grip was off her arm, Patrice sagged against Boon. She latched onto his shirt and began crying. Dohir patted her shoulder and told her in a low voice that it was going to be okay. He looked once more at the man in the SUV.

"We're done here. I hope we never see each other again."

The man's only answer was a slammed door. Luis smiled and got in the other side. With a deep roar and a chirping of tires, the big vehicle roared off down 5th Street, rounded a corner, and was gone. Boon watched it go, still holding Patrice up. After a few moments, they began walking back toward the fountain with his arm around her waist to keep her upright and aimed in the right direction. The two of them slowly crossed the Square, entered a parking garage, and made their way to Kempler's white SUV. He gently placed the sobbing woman into the front passenger seat. Kempler and Clem came and stood next to Boon.

"Clem and I spotted at least three of his men in other parts of the Square," Steve said. "They were trying to look casual, but were easy to pick out."

"They never made a move towards ya'll," Clem added. "Just watched. They left right after the Caddy did."

"I figured as much. Think they saw you guys?"

They both shook their heads. "I doubt it. I may be big," Steve said, "but I can be sneaky when I have to be."

Boon sighed. "Thanks. I'm just glad that part is over."

"That was almost too easy," the big man muttered, glancing back the way they had come. "Think he'll keep his end of the bargain?"

"No way in hell," Dohir replied. He took a second and turned off the burner phone. "I just had to make it sound like I believed he would. He didn't get where he is by leaving loose ends lying around. He'll be back for all of us sooner or later. None of us are safe while he's still free."

Steve grunted. "Damn, Boon, I sure hope you know what you're doing."

Sasha rounded the SUV and strolled up to them with a big grin on her pretty face, a pleasant expression Dohir wasn't used to seeing. He found himself smiling back at her. She brushed a lock of dark hair out of her eyes. Her computer was in a bag around her shoulder.

"Tell me you got what you needed," Boon said hopefully.

"You bet your ass I did."

Dohir felt like hugging her, but for some reason wasn't sure he should. The recent revelation of how she felt about him was throwing him for an emotional loop, and he was unsure how to act. After a second, however, he stepped close and did anyway. Without a moment's hesitation, she hugged him back, squeezing so hard it took his breath away.

"All of it?" he asked her, their cheeks close.

Sasha pulled back from him and their gazes locked. There was a satisfied, predatory glint in her eyes, like a lioness with cornered prey. Contrary to Boon, she was loving this.

"Yep. Every fucking bit of it."

17

Boon's head was spinning with everything that had happened in the last week, but even so, he knew one thing for certain: before they did anything else, he had to find them a safe place to lay low.

As big as Kempler's Suburban was, it was a snug fit for the seven of them. Boon and Patrice were in the front buckets and enjoyed an abundance of elbow room, but Steve and Sir Jim, both large men in their own rights, were wedged uncomfortably next to each other in the second-row bench. By default, that left Clem, Sasha, and Miles sardined shoulder to shoulder in the third row, with the tall southerner's hair smashed against the headliner. The AC in the vehicle was barely able to hold its own against the hot sun streaming through the expansive windows.

As they headed north on I-75, Boon took the powered-down burner phone and stored it in the center console. He had shared the number with the crazy Spanish speaker during their exchange, which meant the device was permanently tainted. With the tall buildings of downtown shrinking in his rearview mirror, Boon turned to Patrice. She was gently sobbing, her face a splotchy red mess. Her head was against the side window and she stared at the passing scenery with vacant eyes.

"You okay?" he asked, although it was clear she wasn't. He wasn't sure what else to say. He had never been good at this sort of thing.

She sniffed and wiped her nose on the back of her hand. Traces of dried blood dotted the skin there, and she stared at it as if confused where it had come from. From the back seat Sir Jim handed her a few tissues. She accepted them in a daze, and spent the next few minutes cleaning herself up.

"I could have gotten all of us killed," she eventually said, her voice low.

Boon turned to her. "Yeah, but you didn't. We're all okay."

"I got greedy," she admitted. "I thought I could strike a deal with him. That was so much money, and I was mad you weren't sharing it."

There wasn't much Dohir could say about that, because it was true. A sum that large was enough to make just about anyone crazy. Hell, it had corrupted him, too. It was difficult to admit, but he told her that. It would have been the height of hypocrisy not to.

Patrice didn't answer immediately. She continued staring blankly out the window at the passing scenery, once in a while wiping tears away with the crumpled tissue. Finally, she took a deep breath.

"Just drop me off somewhere," she said, sounding defeated.

Boon blinked a few times. "What? No, I'm not going to do that. I've screwed up, too. I'm not going to abandon you now." He stopped, then added, "Of course, I can't speak for everyone else."

In the rearview mirror, he saw the rest of his people sit up and look back and forth at each other, as if surprised they had a say in this. A few seconds passed and no one, it appeared, felt inclined to mete out judgment on her. Sasha finally spoke up.

"Ah, fuck it, girl. You messed up. But it wouldn't be the first time one of us has done something stupid. I say we keep her."

Boon checked Sasha out in the rearview mirror. In the second their eyes locked, she shrugged her shoulders, as if to say, "What the hell?" He couldn't believe she was the first one to forgive Patrice, especially considering how the two of them always butted heads. His perception of Sasha's character, already on the rise, leaped up several notches.

Now that the ice was broken, the rest of them began nodding in agreement. Sir Jim stretched out a meaty hand and patted Patrice tenderly on the shoulder. She sobbed a few more times, relieved. She grasped the comforting hand and squeezed it in appreciation.

"Thank you, everyone," Boon stated, bringing them back to the present. "That means a lot to me. To both of us."

"Yeah, a big hairy kumbaya moment for sure," Steve grunted from his seat behind Boon. "But that doesn't do us much good, does it? We still don't have anywhere to go. I for one don't intend to wander the highways like a damned gypsy for the rest of my life. I've got a business and a son to get back to."

Sir Jim cleared his throat with the rumble of a diesel motor turning over. Boon swiveled his head to glance at him.

"You got something for us, Jim?"

"Um, yes. I may have a place for us to go," he admitted.

Forty minutes later, having traded the Cincinnati skyline in their rear window with a smaller downtown Dayton version in their windshield, they exited I-75 and headed east. With Sir Jim directing from the rear seat, Boon eased through increasingly rough neighborhoods filled with broken down houses, abandoned cars, and empty sidewalks. Most of the homes were boarded up with yellow and black "No Trespassing" signs tacked to every window and door. To Boon, this looked like a place to avoid all of the time, not just at night.

"Hey, uh, cool neighborhood," Miles observed sarcastically from the far back seat.

Sir Jim directed him to turn left at an aging warehouse in view of the highway. Boon pulled up next to the building, which stretched an entire city block from east to west. The place was enormous, three stories tall, with the second and third floors almost completely constructed of windows, most of which had been broken out. Sir Jim told him to park before a set of four massive garage doors.

"What the hell are we doing here?" Steve asked, glancing cautiously outside.

"I'll explain in a minute," Sir Jim answered. "Hold on."

He lumbered out of the SUV and punched some numbers into a keypad mounted outside. The big garage door motored up, leaving an opening large enough for a full-sized semi-truck. Boon pulled in, and behind him saw the door close. They all piled out, Clem twisting his neck and back to get the kinks out of it.

They were in a surprisingly neat and tidy loading dock. They followed Sir Jim up a small flight of stairs and down a wide hallway with electrical wiring and HVAC ductwork running overhead. About fifty yards later, they were stopped by a windowless steel door. On the walls around them were faded black and white framed pictures of very old delivery trucks with the words *Sunshine Biscuit Company* painted on the sides. Other aging pictures showed women in white uniforms working an assembly line, with bulky and complex machinery all around them.

"Sunshine Biscuit Company?" Boon asked, moving from picture to picture.

Sir Jim rattled some keys in his hands, searching. With a satisfied grunt, he unlocked the hefty door and pushed it open, flicking on a light at the same time. Everyone filed past him into a large room, one complete with an old-fashioned linoleum floor, gray painted brick walls, and a sagging drop ceiling. A few ancient metal desks were pushed out of the way, and a large table was positioned in the center of the room. A row of windows lining the outside wall did a poor job of letting in light, since all but a few had been painted over with the same gray paint as the rest of the room. Tape and pieces of wood held some together that had been broken from outside.

"Okay," Sasha said, pointing. "What is that thing?"

Against the far wall was a square metal box about the size of a large walk-in closet. It was tan, with no breaks in its sides except for a single door. There was a tiny window set into the door, up high at eye height. Other than that, it was featureless.

"Yeah, I'm with Sasha. What the hell is that?" Kempler asked. "A panic room?"

"Not exactly. It's an audio production booth," Sir Jim said, smiling proudly.

Sasha stepped up and swung open the door, peering inside. She turned on a light, illuminating a control panel, a few computer screens, and a desk chair large enough to handle Sir Jim's ample mass. When she closed the door, it shut with a substantial thunk.

"Yeah, okay," she said. "What the hell do you do with it?"

"As far-fetched as it may seem," he told her, "I do have a life outside of our many hours together, my dear. In my free time I produce all manner of audio spots for a variety of companies. Voice-over work. Commercials. Some public service announcements. Even training videos for corporations. Lately, I've been working with a company in California on a series of anti-bullying campaigns for junior high youths."

Sasha had opened the door again and was inspecting the computer equipment in interest, running her fingers across the keyboard.

"And you do this when? You're with us all the time."

"My dear, I'm quite good at what I do, and I can typically get what I want in a single take. I have several evenings and most weekends free, which is plenty of time. In my prime, this is how I made my living. Only when I retired did I get connected with Boon."

"But why?" Miles asked.

Sir Jim spread out his hands. "When you're self-employed, there are no pensions or 401k programs. I earned a very good living in my day, but I found that wasn't going to be enough to keep me comfortable for the rest of my life. I needed something to augment my retirement. Between what I earn with us, and my occasional work here, I am very comfortable. Plus, I quite enjoy it."

Boon thought back to all the times he'd wondered if Sir Jim had had a side-hustle like this. Glancing at Miles and Sasha, he realized he'd learned more about them in a few days than he had in all the months before.

"That's great," he said, "but I don't see how that's going to help us now."

"What if I told you there were beds and a small kitchen in the room down the hall? Would that ease your mind?"

Boon stared at him, a smile forming at each corner of his mouth for the first time that afternoon. "As a matter of fact, it would."

Once they had checked the place out and claimed their beds, Boon asked them to gather back in the main room. Sir Jim had produced some snacks in a small spread, including cheese and crackers, chips, and a plastic container of surprisingly hot salsa. When everyone was comfortable around the table and had a chance to munch on something, Boon got their attention.

"Sir Jim, if you don't mind my asking, what the hell is this place?"

The large man smiled around a mouthful of crackers, then brushed a few stray crumbs out of his beard. "Just what you saw in those pictures. This used to be the Sunshine Biscuit Company. Have any of you ever enjoyed Cheez-It crackers before?" Most everyone admitted they had. "This is where they were first made, back before the company was bought out by Kellogg, or Nabisco, or one of those other soulless conglomerates. This was a commercial bakery. Up until a few years ago, there was another building next door just like it, and there are even tunnels underneath our feet that used to connect the two."

"Tunnels?" Sasha asked as she nibbled on a cracker. "Why would they have those?"

Sir Jim smiled. "They used them to transfer supplies from one building to the other, out of the weather. This old hulk is for sale, but it's been on the market for years. A friend of mine is the realtor, and he lets me use this section of it for a little side money."

"Aren't you worried someone might want to, you know, buy it? Or even look at it?" Miles asked, leaning back in his chair.

Sir Jim laughed long and loud, waving his arms around him. "This decrepit hulk? No, no one is interested, trust me. Hardly anyone cares about Dayton any longer, especially not something in this zip code."

"You couldn't find someplace else to set up that thing?" Clem asked, raising an eyebrow toward the metal booth. "You know, like a regular house or something?"

"Not really. As you might expect in our line of work, I tend to move around a lot. But no matter where I go, my little friend stays safe and sound right here."

Boon pushed away the bowl of chips he had been absently nibbling on. "Okay, that's all very well and good. Thanks for the history lesson, but we've got some decisions to make." The rest of them stopped talking and stared at him. Patrice no longer looked ready to collapse, but her face remained pale and her hands fluttered as if she couldn't figure out what to do with them. Miles and Clem were quiet and composed, as he would expect, while Kempler was leaning forward in anticipation. Sasha's face was alight with an almost ferocious delight that should have scared him, but didn't.

"We're safe for now, thanks to you all, and especially to Jim," Boon started. "Unfortunately, it's only temporary. The crazy dude who abducted Patrice has his money back, but I'm certain he'll come after us again. He's not the type to let this go."

Patrice's pale face blanched even further, now the color of skim milk. Miles leaned back in his chair and exhaled softly, his cheeks puffing out.

"But why would he bother?" Clem asked. "He's got his money."

"Because I stole from him, and in his world, an insult like that can't go unanswered. I've never worked for people like him, but I've worked with people who have worked with people like him. I bruised his pride, and he can't let that go unpunished."

Miles snapped his fingers. "You disrespected him."

Boon pointed at him. "I did, indeed. If word got out what happened, he'd be a laughingstock. If he doesn't get revenge, others might think they can do the same to him. A guy like that in his position can't live with that hanging over him."

Sir Jim dropped a handful of chips back into the bowl in front of him, his appetite apparently gone for once. "You're sure of this?"

"Yeah, pretty sure."

"What do we do now?" he asked.

"The way I see it, we have two choices. One, we can try to disappear forever. Take what money we have, and vanish. But if we do that, we'll be looking over our shoulders forever. None of us will ever feel safe again. It might work, but it's not something that appeals to me at all."

Miles pursed his lips. "Or? You got a second option, I hope?"

"Or, we can do what we discussed before. We can go on the offensive and take him out before he can do the same to us."

Each person at the table looked around at the rest of the group. No one made a sound, but their silence spoke volumes. Boon could see in their faces as they considered the prospect of forever being hunted and never again knowing a minute's peace. Unappealing didn't begin to describe it.

Kempler was the first to speak up. His hands were clasped together so tightly on the table in front of him the knuckles were the color of ice. "Going on the offensive, huh? What exactly would that look like?"

Boon tilted his head towards Sasha. "I don't know yet. But when I made the exchange with our Spanish speaker, I texted his phone number and bank information to our resident hacker here. Using her SASHA program, she was able to record all of his keystrokes as he accessed his bank, including his login information and password. We know where the money is, and how to get at it again."

Miles' eyes grew almost comically round in his dark face. "Are you telling me you can hack into his account and yank it all back?"

"Yep. Assuming he hasn't already transferred it somewhere else. If it's still there, we should be able to grab it."

Patrice squirmed like there were rats at her feet. "Oh my god, why would we do that? That's crazy!"

"Because if we do, he'll be so mad he'll come after us right away. We won't have to wait and wonder when. He'll come after us on our terms and our timeline, and we can use that to our advantage. People that pissed off act rashly and make mistakes, and we can use all that to our advantage."

Clem sat back in his chair and ran his hands through his messy hair. "You are playing with fire there, my friend."

Boon spread his hands out in front of him. "Yes, I am. There's no turning back if we take that route."

"But we can't make a decision now, not until we've got a plan worked out," Miles finally said, thoughtfully. "And whatever it is, it has to be bulletproof. No margin of error."

"He's right," Kempler added. "It's gotta end up with that son of a bitch locked up forever. Along with the rest of his goons."

Dohir agreed with them completely. It wasn't hard to see what course of action Steve and Sasha would prefer, but he wasn't as sure when it came to Miles and Clem. Patrice still had that caged animal look about her, which he supposed made sense considering what she had been through. As for himself, half his mind was leaning toward pulling up stakes and going dark forever. It was the easy way out, even if it meant looking over his shoulder for the rest of his life. If it had just been him, and his life was the only one on the line, that was certainly the way he'd go. But he wasn't alone. No, he had the lives of his friends to consider. He couldn't throw them to the wolves. He doubted anyone except Kempler had the financial resources to disappear forever, and he was sure none of them had his experience in vanishing off the grid. In the end, while no overt decision had been made, they sat around the table and started brainstorming ideas. However, after a few hours of going back and forth, and with everyone's nerves fraying, nothing they came up with seemed foolproof enough.

"I don't know about the rest of you," Sir Jim said, "but I could use a break. I'm famished."

Boon cracked his knuckles and leaned back in his chair. "Yeah, I could use something, too. You got anything here besides crackers?"

"No, but there's a place about ten minutes away that makes a great deep-dish pizza. I'd be happy to order a few pies. And before everyone panics, there's a land-line here we can use to order."

Everyone agreed, except Patrice, who said she wasn't in the mood for food. In fact, she looked about ready to vomit. Sir Jim ambled over to the phone and dialed a number, and, after a few pleasantries, ordered enough food to hold them for days.

"They'll be ready in twenty minutes. I told them we'd pick them up, since nobody delivers to this part of town."

When the time came, Kempler and Clem paired up and headed out, armed with the garage door code and clear-cut directions from their host how to find the pizzeria. Boon heard Steve's Suburban fire up and the big door roll open. After it backed out and the door was lowered, the roar of the engine grew faint as the two of them drove away. They had only been gone a few minutes when there was the soft clunk of a car door being shut outside their windows.

"Good lord, what are they doing back here already?" Sir Jim asked.

The hair on the back of Boon's neck sprang to attention as he shot to his feet and ran to the windows. His breath caught in his throat when he saw three black SUVs parked outside the loading dock doors. Armed men were piling out.

"Shit," he hissed, leaping away from the window. "They found us!"

18

Boon hadn't taken more than a few steps when the building shook as a terrible crash came from the direction of the loading docks. At first, his racing mind couldn't figure out what it was, then realized they must have used one of their SUVs as a battering ram to smash through the garage door. If that was the case, there were only seconds before they were discovered.

"Lock that!" he shouted. Moving with impressive speed, Miles flew to the steel door and slammed home the deadbolt.

"That should slow them down," he said, panting "But I don't know how long."

Boon's mind was working furiously, running through and dismissing scenarios nearly as quickly as they came to him. After a few seconds, while everyone stared at him with panic stamped across their faces, he came to a conclusion. He pointed to Sasha.

"Fire up your computer. Jim, please tell me you have wi-fi here."

"What? Oh, of course. The network is *Ghoulardi*, password ERNIE. But the signal is only good right here. The thick walls block it outside of this room."

That was a double-edged sword. They had internet access, which was essential, but it was limited. It boiled down to some of them being trapped here while there were barbarians at the gate.

"Got it!" Sasha yelled, throwing up her hands in victory.

Boon spun towards the big man. "Jim, you said something about tunnels, right? Do you know where they are and where they go? Can you get away from here?"

"Yes. They're down the hallway, away from the loading docks. They open up in the vacant lot across the street."

"Perfect. Take Miles and Patrice with you and get the hell out of here."

Sasha spared him a brief glance. He needed her here and hated what might be about to happen, but it was the only way to keep the others safe. Their eyes met, and she gave him the smallest of nods, as if she understood it, too.

"What about you two?" Miles cried out.

"Don't worry about us. We'll stall them. You have to get out of here. Now!"

Sir Jim moved for the door with better speed than Boon thought possible, but terror was always a great incentive. He was gone in an instant, with Miles right on his heels. Patrice, however, was rooted to the ancient linoleum. She had her arms locked across her chest, and her head was shaking back and forth like a metronome on high. Her eyes were huge in her round face.

"Patrice, what are you doing? Go with them!" he yelled, pointing at the doorway.

She shook her head and refused to budge. He wanted to grab her and force her after the two men, but there was no time. Cursing to himself, he hurried over to the landline phone Jim had used to order the pizza just minutes earlier. He lifted the receiver and dialed a number from memory, hoping like hell he had it right. When he heard it ringing, he dropped the receiver and ran to Sasha, placing his hand on her shoulder. Seconds later, they both jumped when someone began pounding on the locked door. She spared him a quick glance.

"Gee, sounds like someone wants in," she said. "Okay, I'm ready. Now what?"

"Get into his bank account and let me know when you're ready to make a transfer."

"Will do," she said, shockingly at ease considering their predicament. Her fingers flew across the keys while the pounding on the door increased in volume, sounding like additional fists and the occasional boot had joined in. He jerked again when there was a gunshot and a round dent the size of a golf ball popped into life next to the doorknob. He knew they couldn't wait any longer. He grabbed her arm and nearly lifted her off the chair.

"Come on! We're out of time."

"Where the hell are we going?" she asked, gathering up her computer and holding it to her chest.

Boon pointed at the sound booth. "In there. That should slow them down."

The two of them rushed over to the large metal box and dashed inside. "Patrice, come on!" he shouted, but she was still glued in place. Cursing under his breath again, he and Sasha jumped into the booth and slammed the door behind them. There was a lock on the door, but it looked terribly fragile considering the abuse it was about to suffer.

Sasha's fingers danced on the keyboard. More booms forced their way into the booth as additional shots were fired, but their refuge had acoustic panels lining the inside walls that muffled the noise. Boon was just beginning to hope the door to the loading docks would be able to withstand all this punishment when it slammed open. Through the tiny window he saw armed men pile into the room. Luis, the tall man from Fountain Square, was with them. They roughly shoved Patrice aside but otherwise ignored her.

"Let's hope his account doesn't require dual authentication," Sasha murmured, almost to herself.

"Hold on. You mean it might? We don't know that already?"

"Nope. It's meant to deter unauthorized access like this. It's usually outside of the normal login keystrokes. Fingers crossed."

They both held their breath as the first of the men outside realized where they were hiding. Muted pounding came from the door and the doorknob jiggled, but it stayed securely locked.

"I'm in!" Sasha shouted over her shoulder in victory. "Hot damn, the money's still there. The dumbass hasn't moved it yet."

Boon nearly pumped his fist in celebration. Without hesitating, he gave her the routing and transit numbers of an account in the Bahamas he'd used for years. He made sure she carefully repeated each number as she entered it. They wouldn't get a second chance at this.

"That's it. I hit the enter key, and boom, it's all gone."

"Do it," he ordered.

Her index finger came down on the button. The second that was done, he grabbed the PC and threw it on the floor as hard as he could. He jumped up and down on the remains, over and over, grinding the shards into dust with his heel, until there was nothing left but bits of plastic and glittering splinters of circuit boards.

"Damnit, Boon, that was new," she said, looking up at him, slightly annoyed.

He was panting a little, but he managed a smile at her. "I'll pick you up a new one when this is all over. Promise."

She opened her mouth to reply just as the door to the booth burst open. Boon barely had time to turn around before a dozen strong hands roughly grabbed at him, dragging him out into the middle of the room. He heard Sasha swearing loudly as she was yanked out right behind him. In seconds, they were both slammed down into chairs next to each other, while Luis and at least ten other pissed-off men stood over them with pistols drawn. Most had the darker skin tones of someone south of the border, except two or three who could have been locals. Luis stepped forward. Boon was sure the man would be raging or screaming and ready to rip their heads off after all the trouble they'd put him through, but he wasn't. In fact, Boon noticed, his heart pounding, the man's demeanor showed nothing but a serene tranquility, a fact that worried him more than anything.

"What brings you to the Sunshine Biscuit Company, Luis?" Boon asked, trying to keep the terror out of his voice. Considering the words came out a little jumpy and squeaky as if he were a teen going through puberty, he didn't think he'd been very successful.

Luis knelt down smoothly until they were eye-level with each other. "Where are the others?" he asked, ignoring the question.

Boon glanced around the room. Ten pairs of dark, smoldering eyes were staring down at him in a loose circle. In movies and TV shows, the hero always said something flip or cocky right now, but he didn't have that in him. "Yeah, they're gone."

Luis' lips thinned as he took a deep breath. "I can see that. Where are they?"

"I don't know."

Boon's head snapped sideways as Luis back-handed him across the face. It happened so fast he never saw it coming. White light flared in his head, followed by a ringing in his right ear. He felt something warm trickling down his chin and figured it must be blood.

"I will ask you again," Luis said, resuming his easy pose. "Where are the others?"

Boon blinked rapidly a few times, trying to clear his head. "I told you I don't know."

This time the slap came from the other side. He hadn't even seen Luis raise his hand.

"I'll ask you one last time, and then I'm going to start working on her," he said, tilting his head toward Sasha. "And I'll make you watch."

Boon's blood froze, but he didn't reply. With the sigh of a man who had been through this many times before, Luis motioned to one of his men. He was thick and husky with no neck and long, muscular arms. He stepped up to Sasha and raised his fist. He was just about to bring it down when Patrice jumped forward with her hands out.

"Stop! You don't have to hurt them," she blurted out, pointing. "They left. Two went for pizza. The others are hiding in some tunnels under the building. They ran when you got here."

Luis took her at her word and snapped his fingers. Several of his men broke away and dashed out the doorway in the direction she pointed. Although Boon's head was ringing like his head was filled with carillon bells, he focused on Patrice.

"Damn it, Patrice, what have you done?" he asked through thick lips.

Slowly, she reached into the pocket of her pants and pulled out a flip-phone, a model that hadn't been popular for years but was small and easy to conceal. She opened it and the display glowed blue. It trembled in her hand.

"I'm sorry," she said, starting to cry. "He said if I helped him, he'd let me go. I didn't know what to do!"

Boon's head dropped. Next to him, Sasha tried to leap up from her chair but was held back by Luis. She began cursing at Patrice, her screams bouncing off the hard walls. The men gathered around and grinned at the vitriol pouring from her mouth. When Sasha's string of expletives ran out, she slumped back in her chair, seething.

"We gave you a second chance, you bitch," she finally hissed at her.

Patrice clutched at her chest, tears flowing freely down her thick face. She couldn't bring herself to make eye contact with either Boon or Sasha. After a second's hesitation, she stepped up and gingerly placed the small phone on the table. She clasped her hands in front of her and looked at Luis. The outside corners of her eyes drooped in despair and fear.

"Can I go now?" she asked him meekly. "I did what you said."

Luis smiled at her with white, even teeth. With a magnanimous sweep of his arms, he motioned toward the steel door.

"Of course. You are free to go."

She caught Boon's eyes for just a second, then turned to leave. As she neared the exit, Luis snapped his fingers and one of the men lifted a pistol and shot her in the back of the head. Blood and hair splattered against the doorframe in a dark Rorschach blob, and Patrice fell face-first with a sickening thud onto the linoleum. Her feet twitched a few times, and then she was still. Blood pooled around her head, the red so dark it was almost black.

Boon jumped out of his chair, screaming, but Luis hit him so hard he was knocked to the ground. He sat on the cold floor, staring at Patrice's now still form, muttering under his breath and shaking his head back and forth, almost unable to comprehend what had just happened. Sasha's hands flew to her mouth, but no sound came out.

Luis pursed his lips. "Stupid, stupid woman," he said, almost sorrowfully. He glanced at the tiny phone on the table, and for the first time noticed the landline phone was off the hook. With a tilt of his head, he picked up the receiver and put it to his ear. After a few seconds, he carefully hung it up and stared at the two of them.

"You were calling someone?" he asked.

Boon's head felt as if it were filled with a thick fluid that was slowing down the neurons firing in his brain. A portion of him wondered if this was what a concussion felt like, and imagined it must be. In a groggy voice, he said, "Was going to call 911, but we never got a chance. We didn't have time."

Luis turned his attention to Sasha. His voice, when he spoke, was the same deadly calm as earlier. "Who were you calling?"

"I wasn't calling anyone, you fucker. I never touched it."

Luis grinned around the room. "I like this one. She's got fire in her belly." Several of his men smiled, and one licked his lips. He motioned in the direction of Patrice's body with his head, and two men grabbed her legs and pulled her away from the doorway. A trail of blood followed her in a smear across the floor. Just then the men Luis had sent to search for Sir Jim and Miles returned alone. Luis' lips compressed to thin lines when he saw them.

"Well? Where are they?"

"I don't know," one of the local men answered sheepishly, his voice surprisingly high for a man his size. He had a slight accent, pronouncing the O in "know" long and hard, like he was from somewhere way up north. His head was shaved, and he couldn't help running a nervous hand over his shiny scalp. "It's a freaking maze down there, eh? We almost got lost."

"Galo is not going to be happy, Alan," Luis growled. A moment later, he shrugged his shoulders. "No matter, perhaps he will forgive you since we have this one." He held out his hand and one of them passed a pistol to him. He leveled the barrel at Boon.

"I wouldn't do anything stupid," Boon cautioned him.

Luis cocked his head, smiling. "Really? Why not?"

"Your boss. You said his name is Galo, right?"

The gun dropped a fraction of an inch. "Why?"

"Because I've got his twenty million, and if you kill me, he'll never see it again. To be honest, I don't think he'd be very happy with any of you if that happens."

19

When Luis began working him over in earnest, the man did so methodically and without haste, almost like a surgeon performing a twisted operation. Boon, duct-taped to the chair, was helpless to protect himself. To keep his mind as occupied and detached from the beating as much as possible, he tried to count the number of times Luis hit him. Somewhere around the fifteenth punch he lost track, but the location of the money his abuser so desperately wanted remained tucked away in Boon's battered mind. To be fair, his brain was so mushy from the abuse he probably couldn't have recalled it anyway, no matter what Luis ended up doing to him. Torture, he remembered reading somewhere, was rarely effective in extracting accurate information from the victim. Luis had never seen that article.

Boon's head was throbbing and every inch of his face was already puffy and misshapen, like an over-cooked hard-boiled egg. One eye was crusted shut and had quit working a few punches ago. He made the mistake of coughing and nearly jerked out of his chair as pain lanced up and down his side. He was pretty sure he'd never hurt so much, until he thought back to the time as a kid when he'd wiped out on his go-kart going down a steep hill. That little stunt had put him in the hospital for a few days, wrapped head to toe in gauze like a cartoon mummy. On the plus side, at least then he had gotten ice cream each day. Luis didn't seem like the kind of person who would reward him with anything but more misery.

Once, during a break in the abuse, he dimly watched as Luis' men gathered up the shattered remains of Sasha's computer and spread them out on the table. The bald one, Alan, was nudging pieces around with his finger and muttering something to the others. In the end, they poured the shards into a plastic bag. Luis looked from the bag to Boon, his eyes turning into ugly gashes in his otherwise handsome face. A large vein in the man's temple pulsed where before there had been nothing.

"I am tired of asking, and you have to be tired of this abuse. How can we retrieve the money?" he demanded, smoothly kneeling down until he was eye level with Boon again.

"You can't," Dohir lied, his words slurred around swollen lips. "I told you. All the information was on that computer."

"I don't believe you. You have to have access somewhere else."

Boon shrugged, although the gesture was nearly lost, bound as he was to the chair. "Don't know what to tell you. Figured if I can't have it, no one can."

Luis dipped his head, his anger held in check by the thinnest of threads. He stood up and motioned to the others around him, barking out orders in a haphazard combination of Spanish and English. In his scrambled head, Boon called the mixed-up language "Spanglish." He chuckled at his own joke, his voice sounding weird and high-pitched in his ringing ears. Two men stepped up and started ripping the duct tape away from his chair.

"*Bien.* If that's how you want it. We'll take you back to Galo and let him deal with you. Or perhaps he'll give you to Señor Gonzalez for a while. You know who he is, right?"

They finished tearing off the rest of the tape, and Alan and another man hauled Boon to his feet. His knees buckled and nearly passed out, but they roughly grabbed his arms and held him up, shaking him to keep him awake. Others stripped the tape from Sasha, who was glowering at them with fire burning in her eyes. Boon couldn't understand why the hell she wasn't terrified. If anything, she looked more pissed off than scared. When they were done, she roughly shook off their hands and took a step back. A husky man with olive skin reached for her. She danced half a step forward and smartly struck him in the face with the heel of her palm. The man stumbled back and shook his head like a dog being smacked on the snout with a newspaper. The husky man touched a finger to his nose. It came away smeared in blood. Everyone else stopped what they were doing and burst into laughter. Sasha kept her hands up in a defensive posture.

"Keep your filthy hands off me, fucknuts," she ordered, grinning slyly at him.

Luis broke into a smile and chuckled. "*Oye*, Pablo, you going to let her get away with that? She's just a girl!"

Boon raised his head, even though he was convinced his skull had to weigh at least a ton. "Sasha! Stop it! What the hell are you doing?"

She ignored him as Pablo, his ego bruised as badly as his nose, growled and rushed her. She seemed to almost magically glide backward before striking him twice more, rocking the man's head back, each impact sounding like a book being dropped flat on the floor. Boon recognized the combination from her sparring sessions at the gym. The man took an urgent, undisciplined swing at her, but she had already danced well out of range. The laughter increased, which did nothing to alleviate Pablo's embarrassment. Blood was now running freely from his nose and into his mouth, coloring his teeth pink. He spit a red glob on the floor then lunged at her with a menacing snarl. Sasha shuffled aside this time, kicking out and connecting with the side of his knee. There was a crunching sound like two handfuls of uncooked spaghetti noodles breaking in half. The attacker screamed and spun almost gracefully to the floor. His bloody face was knotted in agony as he grabbed at his leg with both hands.

Luis' mercurial smile faded. He snapped his fingers and a second man advanced, the short, squat one with no neck. Rightfully wary of her after what he had witnessed, the man moved forward with much greater caution than Pablo had. Perhaps realizing he couldn't match her speed or skill, he opted for a brute-force approach. He charged at her with his thick arms out wide, meaning to bring her down. Boon lunged forward to help her, but the two men held him back.

Sasha didn't try to avoid her attacker, but instead jumped high in the air and kicked him in the face with her heel. The blow was so fierce that no-neck's head snapped back like he'd been clotheslined. He was already out cold when he crashed limply to the floor, skidding in a heap at her feet.

"That was fun," she told Boon, grinning widely.

Luis growled something under his breath and raised his pistol at her. His dark eyes smoldered. "That's enough. We're done playing games. Time to go."

Sasha relaxed but remained where she was, arms now held loosely at her sides. She cocked her head at him, a sneer marring her face. "Wow, a gun? Really? What are you, a pussy? Scared a girl might beat you up?"

One of the thugs restraining Boon sucked in a breath and took a small step backward in shock. The others around the room exchanged glances, eyebrows raised at the challenge and muttering under their breath. Luis' already narrow lips nearly vanished as he stared at her. He barked out an order and two men rushed forward to drag no-neck out of the way. Pablo hobbled off to the side and collapsed into a chair, his face still twisted in pain. His swollen knee was already tight in the leg of his pants, reminding

Boon of an overcooked sausage casing ready to burst. Luis gently set the pistol on the table, then slid off his expensive shoes and socks. He tucked each sock into a shoe, then set them aside. He shuffled his feet back and forth to test the traction on the hard floor. Satisfied, he straightened up and smoothed his shirt with care. His dark eyes never left her.

"This is not going to go well for you," he told her, edging closer.

Sasha raised her hands in a defensive posture again. "Blah, blah. You sure talk a lot."

Luis sprang at her. His fists blurred as he went for her face, moving so fast it was impossible to tell where one punch started and the next one ended. Sasha's arms and hands absorbed the majority of the blows, but she was forced backward, almost to the wall. Once the initial flurry was over, Luis calmly stepped back and spread his arms out wide. He wasn't even breathing hard. The smile had returned.

"Your turn," he told her.

Sasha advanced on him. Perhaps realizing her opponent had the greater reach, she went at him with her feet instead of fists. Her first attack was similar to the one that had taken out no-neck, a jumping kick that narrowly missed his head. She landed on one foot and immediately spun and clipped his shoulder with a second kick. Luis was forced to backpedal just as she dropped to the floor and tried to sweep his legs out from under him. He jumped over her outstretched leg before calmly stepping away. Sasha leaped to her feet, her defenses back up.

"I can take you," he said, stating this the same way someone would declare the sky was blue or water was wet. "And you know it."

"Most girls I know don't even talk this much," she replied, intentionally egging him on.

Luis huffed once and came at her again. She got her arms up, but this time he didn't relent as she was forced back. A dozen blows jackhammered her forearms, until he changed tactics and went for her gut instead.

Sasha was forced to lower her guard, which was the opening Luis had been waiting for. The blow, when it came, caught her in the cheek and sent her flying backward.

"Sasha!" Boon cried out, straining against his captors. "Stop this, dammit!"

She stumbled, dazed, but kept her feet. Luis quickly grabbed her and spun her around, his arms around her neck in a headlock. She tossed elbows at his face and gut, but there was little power behind them and they did no harm.

"You're too pretty to permanently damage," Luis hissed in her ear. "I think Galo will have other plans for you."

Her head drooped and she sagged as if in defeat. Still locked in his captors' arms, Boon's heart crumbled. Luis turned and smiled at his men in victory, and at the same moment, Sasha brought her heel down hard on the top of his bare foot. There was a sharp crack, followed by a howl from Luis. Sasha slipped under his weakened grasp and delivered a side snap-kick to his stomach, sending the man flying backward. Before anyone else could react, she dove for the gun on the table. She grabbed it with both hands and leveled it at Luis as he moaned and cradled his broken foot.

"Let him go!" she screamed, motioning at the men holding Boon. "Let him go or so help me I'll shoot your boss."

Boon felt his captors' hands fall away from him, and he staggered over to her. His head still felt like it was filled with damp cotton, but it was clearing a little more with every passing second.

"You okay?" he asked, a hand on her arm.

"I'm fine. I think it's time to go, don't you?"

"You scared the shit out of me, you know."

She was about to reply when a smoking canister the size of a spray can bounced through the open door, coming to rest against Patrice's body.

Boon wasn't exactly sure what it was, but he had a pretty good idea. He grabbed Sasha and yanked her through the doorway at the other end of the room, the one leading to the tunnels.

"Cover your eyes!" he screamed as they flew across the threshold, the gun flying from her hand. Half a second later there was a tremendous boom and a blinding flash of light as the concussion grenade exploded. Howls of pain and shock ripped through the room as Luis and his men screamed in agony and confusion. The explosion was so loud that, for a few seconds, Boon could hear nothing but a high-pitched whine and his own heart pounding at a sprinter's pace.

As they stumbled away into the darkened hallway, he looked back with his one good eye. Through the smoke, he could see heavily armed men in black gear storming the room. Behind them, he caught a glimpse of fair hair and the gleam of gold rim glasses behind a protective facemask. He turned away, and they lurched into the darkness.

Sasha was yelling something, and although Boon couldn't hear what she said through his damaged ears, he got the gist of it. With the muted sound of gunfire popping at their backs, they ran through a long corridor filled with more overhead pipes and old pictures on the walls, then skidded to a halt at an opening on their right. A faded sign above the door said *North Building*, with an arrow.

"This way," she hissed, and he realized his hearing was already returning. They ran down some steps to a dim corridor. The way ahead of them was narrow and poorly lit, with a few lonely bulbs mounted on the walls. Water was puddled here and there, throwing back rippled reflections of the lights. They quickly intersected another corridor, and Boon tripped and fell over something. As Sasha pulled him to his feet, he saw rusty steel rails heading off into the distance.

"That way," he said, pointing.

She took him at his word and they started off again. There were no more sounds behind them, or at least none they could hear. They followed the tracks as they ran straight and true. Several times they passed other darkened corridors leading elsewhere, but they stuck with the main line at their feet. A few minutes later, he tugged at her arm.

"Hold on," he mumbled. "I just need a second."

Sasha looked like she was going to snap at him, but her expression immediately softened when she got a good look at his condition. She reached out and gently touched a finger to his face while he tried to settle his breathing. After a minute they started off again, but slower this time. She held onto his arm to keep him from going down.

"How in the hell did the cops know we were there?" she asked.

Boon pointed backward. "Those weren't cops. They were FBI. That call I made just before Luis and his men got here was to Hollenbeck, the agent who talked to me the other day. He was back there. I saw him."

"The FBI? Are you crazy?"

"Probably. But I couldn't take a chance with the local cops. They're not experienced in this sort of thing and might have gotten us killed. And speaking of that, what the hell were you thinking back there? Why'd you pick a fight with those guys?"

Her eyes twinkled in the near dark. "I couldn't let them take us somewhere, could I? I knew if they did, no one would ever see us again. I needed to keep us there as long as I could. At the very least I figured Clem or your buddy would call the cops when they got back with the pizzas."

Boon paused, knowing she was right. If they had been hauled away, there was a very good chance they would have vanished forever. "Okay, just promise me you won't do anything that stupid again, okay? You could have been really hurt."

For a reply, she kissed him on the cheek. She took his arm again and the two of them kept walking. In a few hundred feet the track ended at a brick wall, but there was a damp stairway leading upwards next to them. With only one good eye, Boon's depth perception was out of kilter, so they carefully ascended the slick steps in the dark until they spotted a sliver of light above and ahead of them. They eased forward until the light became a manhole-sized opening large enough for them to crawl through. They were about to climb out when they heard the murmuring of hushed voices. Sasha pulled him back with a finger to her lips. They listened for a moment until Boon smiled and stuck his head out into the night air.

"I wondered where you guys might be," he said softly.

Parked near the opening was Kempler's white SUV. The hulking shadow of the Sunshine Biscuit Company building was a block or more away, a massive black rectangle with a kaleidoscope of blue and red police lights bouncing off of it. Boon figured the FBI must have called the cops for backup.

Waiting there with anxious looks on their faces were Kempler, Clem, Miles, and Sir Jim. Steve helped lead Boon to the vehicle.

"Jesus, Dohir, you look like three miles of bad road," he mumbled.

"Are you okay?" Clem asked, then looked around. "Where's Patrice?"

"I think we need to get him to the hospital," Sasha declared, ignoring his questions. "He's hurt pretty bad."

Boon held up a weak hand. "No. No hospitals. Too many questions."

Kempler surveyed the vacant lot and neighborhoods around them. He held out his hands. "Okay. Then where? I'm open to suggestions."

"Don't worry. I got a guy," Boon answered.

Despite the circumstances, his big friend laughed. "Christ, how'd I know you were going to say that?"

20

Boon flinched and sucked in a sharp breath when Dr. Rivera pressed on his left side.

"That hurts, I gather," the doctor said, keeping his head down as he worked.

"Yeah. Little bit."

"I bet it does. You've...ah, almost certainly got a few cracked ribs."

With his soft hands, the doctor continued checking his patient over, up and down, front to back, *tsk, tsking* to himself at the not-so-subtle bruising that had already started to manifest over Boon's face and body. He cleaned up Boon's injured eye and put an adhesive patch on it. With a small penlight, he shined the beam back and forth into Boon's good eye several times, flicking it this way and that. There was more pressing and probing around his neck. When the doctor finished a few minutes later, he straightened up. Concern twisted his thick eyebrows.

"You sure you don't want to tell me how this happened? It might help with my diagnosis."

"Why don't we just say I ran into a door?" Boon said.

"Uh, huh. Exactly how many doors did you run into?"

They were in an examination room at Cloverwell, in a wing of the complex far from Hannah Collins. Dohir was sitting on an exam table with his shirt off, and Sasha was leaning against the wall, her arms crossed. There was a bruise forming under her eye, and a dozen smaller ones on her forearms, but otherwise she seemed fine. At the moment her attention was on Rivera, her eyes narrowed as if she didn't completely trust him. The doctor sighed.

"If that's how you want it, fine," Rivera said. "From what I can tell, for starters you likely have a concussion and several cracked ribs. I don't think there's any internal bleeding, but without a more thorough examination, I can't be sure of that."

"It could be worse," Boon said.

"I'm not done. Your eye may have suffered permanent damage. You should see a specialist about that as soon as possible. All I did was clean it up. Your depth perception will be off with that patch, so be careful." He let his steady gaze travel up and down Boon's bruised body. "The rest seems to be…ah, soft tissue damage, which will heal in time. Nothing else broken that I can tell. For now, let's try not to run into any more doors, okay? Especially with that concussion. You'll need to take it easy for at least two weeks."

He grinned at the doctor. "I'll be more careful, thanks."

"In the meantime, you're going to be very sore. It'll be bad tomorrow, and even worse the next day. Take acetaminophen for the pain, not aspirin or ibuprofen, and use ice packs to keep the swelling down. There's nothing we can do about the ribs. They should heal on their own in five to six weeks."

They talked for a few more minutes, then shook hands and said their goodbyes. Rivera ushered them out through a side door, the same one they had come in earlier. The doctor looked him up and down one final time. He shook his head, the slightest of grins on his terminally stoic face.

"Let's not...ah, do this again, okay?"

"I hope we won't, believe me."

It was late at night and the Cloverwell parking lot was dark. Everyone else was waiting for them by Kempler's Suburban. In the lights from the few overhead lights scattered around, Boon could see that Clem's eyes were still red and swollen from crying. Miles was unusually quiet and withdrawn, but the big-hearted southerner had taken the news of Patrice's death harder than the rest of them. Kempler stepped up to Boon.

"What's the prognosis?" he asked, tilting his head at the eye patch with concern.

Dohir waved him away. "I'll be fine. Just banged up, that's all."

Steve went to instinctively clap him on the shoulder, then pulled up short. Boon leaned up against the SUV, grimacing quietly. He was exhausted, and felt he could pass out at any moment. His body desperately wanted sleep, but there wasn't time.

"Fine my ass," Steve said, surveying him up and down.

"Okay, I'll be fine soon enough. No permanent damage. Couple of cracked ribs, mainly."

The big man grimaced. "Ouch. That sucks. No golf for you."

Boon patted his friend on the shoulder, and looked at each of the people gathered there. He couldn't believe how badly all of this had spiraled out of his control. Just weeks ago, before Marsden, this group had been little more than acquaintances to him, employees who came into the office in the morning and left each night. They had had their own lives, separate from his and far removed from the death and deception they'd suffered since. And every bit of it was because of him. Yes, his own life these last few years had been a trainwreck, filled with self-destruction and seclusion, but at least his was the only one he'd been screwing up.

But that was all gone. Two people were dead, and they were on the run from a murderous, vindictive bastard who would stop at nothing to make sure they all ended up the same way. If there was any good from any of this, any at all, it was learning how Sasha felt about him, and how he was beginning to care for her in return. He took the opportunity to lean up against her then, and felt her press back into him, which lifted his spirits ever so slightly. He gave her arm a squeeze.

"I need a payphone," he announced.

As it turned out, that was easier said than done. With the advent of cell phones, payphones were no longer the ubiquitous ports of communication of the past. They eventually located one of the relics south of Dayton, not far from the highway at a BP gas station. When they got there, Boon dropped in a quarter and dialed a number. After a single ring, a familiar voice picked up.

"Special Agent Hollenbeck here."

"Ah, hello. This is Boon Dohir."

"Mr. Dohir, I was hoping you would call. I take it you're alright?"

"I am. Basically. Thanks for…responding so quickly to my call earlier tonight."

"My pleasure. Sorry it took so long, but I had to assemble a strike team out of the Dayton field office, which entailed some additional steps. And thanks for delivering those men to me, even if a few of them were the worse for wear." He paused for a moment. "They are some very nasty people, Mr. Dohir. You're lucky I figured out where you were. My guess is things were about to go very badly for you."

"You guessed correctly. Can we get together and talk? Tonight? Just the two of us?"

"Yes, I think we should. I've got a lot of questions, including some concerning a Jane Doe currently in the Montgomery County Morgue. Where and when?"

Boon's throat clenched at the mention of Patrice. He glanced down the street at an illuminated yellow sign he had spotted earlier. "There's a Waffle House near the Dayton Mall. They're open all night. Meet me there in half an hour? Alone."

"I know where it is. I'm still at the Dayton office. See you there in thirty. Stay out of trouble until then, okay?"

Boon moved slowly back to the SUV and climbed into the passenger seat with only a few grimaces. Any time he breathed deeply, or moved quickly at all, the pain from his cracked ribs stabbed like hot pokers into his side. Even taking a deep breath was a new adventure in pain. He was terrified to sneeze.

"Okay, the meeting is on," he told them. "Drop me off at the Waffle House up there. He'll be here in a little bit."

"Man, are you sure you know what you're doing?" Miles asked, leaning forward from the back seat. "I mean, this is the freaking FBI we're talking about here. Once they've got you, they've got you."

"Don't worry," Boon assured him. "I've got a plan."

Kempler pressed him on what he was going to do, but Dohir kept silent. To be fair, he couldn't share details with them, because, despite his assurances, there was no plan. Right now, all he could do was throw himself at the mercy of the feds and hope they could work all this out. He would take the hit and any punishment himself, but at least the rest of them would be safe. That was all that mattered now.

They were still complaining bitterly when Kempler pulled into the restaurant parking lot and Boon carefully slid out. Their protests continued, but he refused to be swayed no matter how much they objected. He stuck his head back inside the open door of the SUV and smiled at them as well as his battered face would permit.

"Okay, it's time for you to go. Park somewhere out of sight, but where you can keep an eye on me. Assuming he doesn't take me in when we're done, come back and get me. But if I'm arrested and go with him, don't follow. Got it?"

Steve frowned at him. "Yeah, we got it. I don't like it, but we got it."

The big vehicle rumbled away down the road. Boon watched it go, then shuffled through the door and into the brightly lit restaurant. There was no one else in there at this time of night, thankfully. He made his way to a corner booth facing the door and eased in, wary of his aching midsection. An older waitress with her blond hair up in a bun and a pencil tucked behind her ear strolled toward him. When she looked at his face, she nearly jumped back a step. Her hand fluttered up to her mouth.

"Oh my gosh, sweetie, you look awful. Are you okay?"

"I'm fine, thanks. Had a, uh, car accident earlier tonight. Can I get a coffee, please?"

What he really felt like ordering was a large gin and tonic, but he was pretty sure that wasn't on the menu here. As she headed back towards the kitchen and he was alone, he realized how many days had passed since he'd had a drink. Three? Maybe more? He'd lost track. He hadn't gone that long without getting hammered for months. Probably years, if he were being honest with himself. Actually, he knew precisely when he'd gone from being a regular, social drinker to what a professional would likely consider a hardcore alcoholic. The binges and blackouts. The forgotten nights and weekend benders. Connecting the dots to alcoholism was not hard at all.

But right now, at this moment, did he really want a drink that badly, or was he simply continuing with a terrible habit he'd perpetuated for so long? Alcoholism was a disease, a crippling, brutal, horrible disease that shattered the lives of people everywhere. Was that him? Was he craving a drink because he was addicted, or was his incessant boozing simply a way to help him block out events in his past? In the end, he wondered, did the difference even matter?

Sitting in the lonely booth late at night, every inch of his body either muttering or screaming at him in pain, he realized he'd avoided taking a hard look at himself like this in years. To be fair, he wasn't enjoying the self-reflection. He was still pondering the turbulent detour his life had taken when the door swung open and Hollenbeck strolled in. Considering the man had been hip-deep in an armed raid just hours ago, the guy appeared downright normal. He was sporting the tan jacket again, complete with the bulge under one arm–which, if Boon were being candid with himself, he rather appreciated this time. The agent gave the room a quick scan, saw it was empty, then came and joined Boon at the booth. He smoothly sat down on the bench seat across from him.

"Mr. Dohir, if you don't mind my saying so, you look like hell," he said, his eyes tracking up and down Boon's face. He plucked his glasses from his nose and polished them with a napkin from the table. "I could make light of it and say you should see the other guys, but I have, and most of them look better than you."

"Yeah, it's been kind of a rough night."

The two men fell silent, each waiting for the other to carry on the conversation. While the silence dragged out, the waitress brought Boon his coffee. Hollenbeck smiled at her and politely ordered a decaf. Boon thought he should eat something, but his head was still pounding and there was a high probability he'd puke if he tried. After a "Sure thing, sweetie," the waitress spun smartly on her heel and headed back to the kitchen.

"What would you like to know?" Boon finally asked, the drawn-out silence becoming uncomfortable. To mask his unease, he tried to take a sip of his coffee. His hand was shaking so badly he slopped most of it onto the table. A wave of exhaustion made him lean back in the booth. He closed his good eye.

Hollenbeck's expression softened as he replaced his gold-rimmed glasses. "Why don't we get you checked out first? You look like you're going to pass out."

Boon shook his head, then instantly regretted the sudden motion. "No, there's no time for that. He'll be coming for us, and I don't want to make it any easier for him than I have to."

"Fine. Let's talk about that. Who are the men we picked up? They aren't talking, no matter how persuasive we are. And we can be pretty persuasive."

For the next ten minutes, Boon told him everything, from the time he started working the Marsden deal until their escape from the Dayton warehouse. The only information he withheld was anything having to do with his friends. He used the aliases they'd always gone by, and offered nothing more. He kept Kempler out of it completely. To his credit, Hollenbeck never reacted to anything Boon told him but continued making notes on his phone while they talked. He only interrupted the flow of information when he needed clarification or additional details.

"We'll get back to your Robin Hood past later. But right now, tell me about this thing you took from them, the phone location device. You still have it in your possession?"

"I do, just not on me." He described as well as he could how the device worked, its accuracy, and its speed.

"I've never heard of anything like that before. I'm going to need that, you know."

Boon understood but wasn't ready to part with it just yet. "I figured as much. It's amazing and terrifying, especially considering how immediate and precise it is. In the wrong hands it's one of the most dangerous pieces of technology I've ever seen. I'm not sure I trust anyone with it. Not even you. It's way too 1984 for my liking."

Hollenbeck's smile was fleeting, as if deep down he agreed with Boon's concerns. "Still, I'm going to need that."

"I know."

Hollenbeck started taking notes again. "The body we found. Who is she?"

Boon rubbed a hand over his face. When he managed to speak, his voice sounded thin and distant, even to him. "Patrice. I don't know her last name, or if that's even her first name. She worked for me. She was taken and held until I gave the money back the first time, when I made the exchange downtown. He must have made a deal with her, promising she would be freed in exchange for tracking us and turning us in. The tall guy named Luis had her killed at the warehouse."

"You don't know anything else about her? How is that? You said she worked for you?"

"Honestly, I don't know anything. That's the arrangement I have with all of them. I intentionally keep them as distant from me as I can, so I can break everything off if I need to. It's safer if I don't know. That's the way I've always done it. I have no idea if she has any friends or family, where she lives, or anything else for that matter."

The agent sighed, as if this weren't the first time he'd gone through this. "Okay. We'll do what we can to locate next of kin, although if she doesn't have any prints or priors, it won't be easy." The agent sighed again and made some more notes. "Now, you keep referring to 'him.' Who exactly is that?"

Boon shrugged. "I don't know, except one of his men called him 'Galo' while we were at the warehouse."

At the mention of that name, the agent stiffened in his seat like he'd touched a hot wire. He was so startled he nearly dropped his phone. It was the first time Boon had ever seen the agent caught off guard. Hollenbeck peered at Boon, his glasses reflecting the white lines of the overhead lighting.

"What did you say his name was?"

"Galo. At least that's what it sounded like. You know him?"

Hollenbeck was quiet for a moment, then set his phone down and touched an app on the screen. Music began playing out of the tiny speaker, a classic rock tune Boon recognized but couldn't place. Maybe the *Doobie Brothers*? The agent ducked his head low and motioned for Boon to do the same. Leaning close like he was about to share state secrets, he said, "This is important. Everything I'm going to tell you from here on has to remain between the two of us. Do you understand?"

Boon said, "Yeah, sure."

The agent studied him, as if gauging his sincerity. "I'm serious, Boon."

"I get it. Why are you freaking out?"

Hollenbeck pursed his lips. "Fine. I don't think I have any choice. Tell me, how familiar are you with the workings of drug cartels?"

Boon shrugged. "Not at all, really. I've always steered clear of that business. Why? And what's with the music?"

Hollenbeck waved his question away. "Let me give you a little background. The Mexican state of Michoacán is west of Mexico City and butts up against the Pacific coast. It's home to some of the most ruthless drug gangs in all of Mexico, including some you've probably heard of before, like La Familia. The leadership of these cartels tends to fracture often, usually due to arrests, assassinations, or shifting alliances. However, within the last few years, a new coalition has formed, an unlikely one bringing several of these significant bodies together into a single massive entity. It goes by many names, but the one you've most likely heard is *El Grupo Nuevo*. The New Group. Now, who do you think the leader of this organization is reported to be?"

Boon felt the blood drain from his face. "Galo."

"Bingo. Galo, otherwise known to those of us in the business as El Blanco. The White One."

Thinking back to the only time he'd seen him in person, Boon said, "Yeah, with that crazy white hair, that sounds about right. You've had dealings with this guy?"

The agent's vision turned inward and he scowled, as if a spigot had opened and flooded his skull with unpleasant memories. "I have. I've been in some close calls with him more than a few times in the past. Every time we think we've got him and are ready to grab him, he vanishes. It's like he somehow knows we're coming. In fact, we were so close once last year there was still a burning cigarette in an ashtray when we broke into his hotel room. Somehow, and I don't know how, he keeps slipping away."

"What do you mean? How does that even happen?"

Hollenbeck didn't answer right away. His eyes behind the glasses slid left then right, as if verifying once more they were alone. Boon shifted in his seat, for some reason more uncomfortable now than at any other time since the agent had sat down. Hollenbeck removed his glasses and polished them on a napkin again, even though they were as clean as the day they were made. Boon waited.

"The amount of money El Grupo Nuevo has at its disposal is staggering. More than you can imagine. More than most small countries, as a matter of fact. This is what we've been afraid of for decades. In the past, these separate groups have used their money to buy influence and some level of safety in the US. But they were amateurs and rarely successful. We think Galo has changed all that."

"How?"

"We don't know for sure. We're just guessing, but we assume he's steering clear of the lower levels of law enforcement. You know, street cops, local sheriffs, people like that. Instead, we think he must be focusing El Grupo Nuevo's wealth and influence on assets with real power. Higher-ups in law enforcement. Maybe Federal judges or elected representatives. It's the only possible answer. We can only guess that with the immense financial power at his disposal, he may have infiltrated many different levels of law enforcement or the US Government." He paused. "To be brutally frank, almost everyone is suspect."

Something in Hollenbeck's words froze Boon's blood in his veins. His voice so low it barely registered above the music, he said, "Oh, shit, you think he might have compromised the FBI, don't you? You don't even trust your own people?"

The way the agent's head dipped confirmed Boon's suspicions. Hollenbeck drew a deep breath. For a few seconds, the question simply hung out there, heavy with dread. He kept his gaze locked on the top of the table.

"No, if I'm being honest, I don't."

21

The waitress strolled back with a pot of coffee in each hand, one with a brown band and the other with an orange one. She expertly splashed more in their cups and asked if they wanted to order any food. Both men declined, and she vanished back into the kitchen.

"Okay, let's shift gears," Hollenbeck said. "The money. Where is it now? The twenty million."

"It's safe and sound in one of my accounts. There's no way Galo can get at it."

The agent pursed his lips. "You really poked the bear with that one. He'll never stop coming for you until he gets it back, or he kills you, or both. Probably both. Trust me–I know this guy as well as anyone."

"I'm getting to know him, too. I was going to use it to lure him into the open so we could somehow take him out, although we could never agree or figure out how to do that. If we couldn't come up with a solution, at the very least I was going to distribute it to my team so they could vanish forever. Or at least try to."

Hollenbeck's expression was sad but sincere. Close up, the agent looked a little older than Boon had thought at first, perhaps closer to forty than thirty-five. Plus, the man seemed exhausted to the core, as if he'd already lived through an entire lifetime of battling dragons and tipping at windmills. "He'd find you eventually, you know. With the resources at his disposal, there's no place on earth you could hide forever."

Boon rubbed his hands over his face. "I know. But we were out of options and I didn't know what else to do. But you didn't answer my earlier question; what's with the music? I get that you're trying to mask our conversation, but from whom? There's no one here."

"Just not taking any chances. Now, who else besides Galo was involved with all this? Did you get any other names?

"The only other ones I heard were the guys you've got in custody already. The tall guy, Luis, Pablo, and some local muscle named Alan. Oh, yeah, there was also some monstrous guy named Gonzalez."

This time the agent did what could only be described as a comical double-take. He held up his index finger for emphasis. "Hold on. Did you say 'Gonzalez?'"

"Yeah, I did." Boon went into as much detail as he could regarding the giant, drawing on the few glimpses he'd had of the man in the dark at Kempler's cabin and in the SUV in Cincinnati. Halfway through, Hollenbeck stopped taking notes and stared into the distance.

"Okay, I get the feeling you know this guy," Boon said.

The agent pulled back a little. "I do. We have…history together. I ran into him during another operation in South America not long ago. Some of us helped get him out of a jam down there when his crazy employer turned on him. He's very expensive hired muscle. And brutally intelligent, despite his outward appearance. Only the richest and most powerful criminals can afford the guy. In fact, it's almost a status symbol of sorts to employ him."

Boon shivered in the booth. "He's freaking horrifying, that's all I know."

"He is at that." He tapped a finger on the tabletop, thinking to himself. "I always wondered what happened to that sneaky bastard. He'd probably still be down there if it weren't for us. Honestly, I figured he'd be dead by now. I would love to know how the hell he made it out of the Amazon by himself on foot…"

"Let's hope you never get a chance to ask him," Boon said.

The agent brought himself back to the present. Dohir shared the address of his factory office, along with the location of his second apartment. Hollenbeck had recovered from the earlier double shocks of Galo and Gonzalez, and was once again diligently taking notes. After some additional back and forth, they both realized there was little more outstanding. The agent carefully wrote something on a napkin and slid it and a single key over to Boon. On the paper was an address in a suburb north of the city.

"What's this for?"

The agent tapped the napkin. "Do you guys have anywhere to go tonight?"

"No," he admitted. "Not really."

"I thought so. It's a safe house," he said, collecting his phone and standing up. "I'm assuming your friends are waiting somewhere to see if I arrest you or not. After I'm gone and they pick you up, go there and lay low while I figure out our next move. It's not safe for you anywhere else."

"So, you're not going to arrest me?"

Hollenbeck said, "No, I'm not. At least not now."

"That's only marginally comforting, but I'll take it." Boon pointed to the key. "But you said you don't even trust your own people. How is this safe?"

"Don't worry. Thanks to governmental sleight of hand and the wonder of red tape, no one else in the Bureau who matters even knows this place exists. It's not on our books, not as a house, anyway. I keep it handy for special circumstances just like this."

Boon accepted both items and stuffed them in his pocket. The slight movement caused his ribs to twitch, and he flinched involuntarily. If Hollenbeck noticed his fleeting grimace, he didn't comment on it. The agent left some money on the table for the coffee and a tip, and the two of them left. The night air outside was cool and felt wonderful on Boon's face.

"I'll come over tomorrow morning. Until then, don't leave. And whatever you do, don't turn your phones on. There's plenty of food there to tide you over for now. Oh, and stay off the highways and use surface roads. It'll take longer, but it's safer."

"And what then?" Boon asked.

"Then we figure out what we're going to do. Just get some rest tonight, okay?" He looked Boon up and down, a small, sympathetic smile on his face. "You and your merry men need it, Robin Hood."

The agent said goodbye, then got into a sedan and drove off. Boon leaned against a light pole for several minutes until Kempler pulled up. He rolled down the window.

"That's it? He just let you go? How the hell did you manage that?"

"Long story." He handed the napkin to him. "Here's our destination for tonight. You know where this is?"

Steve took it. "Don't need to. The nav system will find it."

"It's a safe place to lay low. I'll explain on the way."

Boon walked gingerly around the vehicle and got in. Buckling his seatbelt was such an uncomfortable chore he almost skipped it. Once they were underway, staying off the highway as Hollenbeck suggested, he filled them in on his conversation in the restaurant.

"That's some heavy shit," Miles said from the middle row when Boon was done. "I mean, if he can't even trust his own people at the damn FBI, how are we supposed to know who we can trust?"

"Right now, I'd say the only person we can rely on is Hollenbeck," Boon answered. "He could have arrested me on the spot, and he didn't. I don't have any reason to doubt him or his story. Not after all this."

Forty-five minutes later they pulled into the driveway of a blue two-story set far off a country lane in rural West Chester, north of Cincinnati. The driveway next to the house was long and narrow, curving around behind the darkened structure. Kempler eased the Suburban around to the back until he was out of sight from the main drag.

"Just give me a minute to check the place out," Boon told them. "I'm sure it's fine, but no harm being careful."

Boon unlocked the door and stepped inside. The air was warm and stale, as if the place had been shut up for a very long time. For some reason that made him feel marginally better. He fumbled around for a light switch. When it clicked on, he found he was standing in a modest-sized kitchen covered in old-fashioned wallpaper, with dated cupboards and linoleum countertops. There was a large rectangular table surrounded by mismatched chairs. A rusting pot-belly stove was tucked into a corner. He reached out and touched the dark metal, which felt marginally colder than the air.

Boon walked around and flicked on more lights as he went, first into a small living area with an ancient tube TV, then a dining room, and finally into a tiny half-bath. Up the creaking steps, he found four fully outfitted bedrooms and a bathroom with lime green fixtures. Everywhere he looked there was a fine patina of dust covering all horizontal surfaces. No one had been there for a very long time, which also made him feel a little more secure. Satisfied he was alone he made his way downstairs and motioned everyone in.

"Yikes. Could use some redecorating," Sasha commented with an exaggerated grimace. She peered closely at the walls. "I think my grandma had this same wallpaper in her house, and she's been dead for decades."

Clem noticed the pot-belly stove and smiled for the first time that night. "I don't know. Feels kind of homey to me."

"Beggars can't be choosers, my dear," Sir Jim said to Sasha. "Anyway, I'm exhausted and need to catch a few winks before I fall over."

Boon said, "Agreed. I think we're all pretty whipped. There are four bedrooms upstairs, and plenty of beds. Go pick one, and we'll meet back down here in the morning. Sound good?"

As a group, they trudged up the steps and one by one vanished into the bedrooms. Sir Jim, huffing and puffing, asserted he snored louder than a freight train and took the first one on the right. Clem and Miles claimed another, while Kempler called dibs on the third. That left the last one for him and Sasha. She closed the door behind them and quickly stripped down to her underwear and flimsy top, then slid under the covers, stretching like a satisfied cat. Boon crawled in after her, careful of his ribs, and more than a little aware of her next to him. She reached out and turned off the lamp next to the bed.

"How are you doing?" she asked softly, her face now only inches from his.

Boon considered how to respond. He didn't know if she was asking about his physical condition, his mental shape, or about their sleeping arrangements. In the end, he opted for the first choice.

"I've been better, but I'll heal. Sore all over, and my eye itches like hell under this patch."

She reached out a hand and placed it tenderly on his cheek. Her fingertips were warm. "I'm sorry about that. I wish I could have done something to stop them, but I couldn't. It was killing me to see you get the shit beat out of you like that. I could kill that fucker Luis."

He took her hand in his and she clasped it tightly. "I know. I would have told them anything they wanted if they had tried to do anything to you. I almost did."

She leaned in and kissed him gently, her lips lingering for a few seconds. "You taste like coffee."

Boon smiled in the dark. "Sorry."

"No, it's okay. I like coffee. I don't drink it, but I like it."

He pulled back a little. It was pitch black in the bedroom, but even so he could sense her proximity. "Sasha, help me understand all this."

"Understand what?"

He sighed. "Why you're interested in me. I mean, I'm a freaking train wreck. I've got more issues than you could know. I drink way too much. Like, a lot. And I've…done things I can't talk about. Worse yet, I got us into this mess, and we may never get out of it. You could do so much better than me."

"Yeah, probably," she answered, laughing softly. "Okay, definitely."

He frowned in the dark. "Hey, wait a minute."

She snickered and nudged him with her elbow. "But seriously, from the first time we met, I knew there was something about you I liked. Here we are in this shitty business, doing shitty things to generally decent people. But through all that, you never got shitty yourself. And you never let us get that way, either. We could have done so much worse to so many, but you kept us focused and, well, grounded. Plus, you made it all seem so…normal, I guess. I've never had that before. I had a feeling right away you were a good man, at heart at least." Sasha put her hand on his chest. "And, I don't know, but I felt like you needed someone to help take care of you, to keep you safe from everything we were doing. I've dated a lot of meatheads from the gym in my time, and then you came along. You're smart, funny, and caring. Our past shouldn't define us. Not mine, and not yours."

He swallowed, touched by her words. "Thanks."

"And you're pretty easy on the eyes, too. Well, not at this moment, but usually."

He laughed out loud at that, his mood improving, then grew quiet when he remembered the others were trying to sleep in the adjacent rooms. He snuggled into her and felt her press against him. Their bare skin, where they touched, was so warm they could have been sharing a sunburn.

"I never wanted to get involved with any of you," Boon said softly. "I mean, my intentions were good. I knew if the shit hit the fan, I needed to be able to cut everyone loose without hesitation. But now, looking back, that isolation feels pretty ignorant. And anyway, you were always so, I don't know, wound so tight. I didn't think you liked anyone, me included."

She sighed, the sound loud in the hushed room. "Yeah, well, you had that stupid rule about not being friends, you know? Plus, I was always pissed at myself for not having the guts to make a move. Every day I would show up, ready to tell you how I felt, and every day I chickened out. So yeah, I was mad, you know. At myself."

He propped himself up on one elbow. "What changed?"

She drew a lazy circle on his bare chest. It tickled, but he did his best to not show it. "That first night at Miles' house, when you and Steve came over, I saw how easily this could all go wrong, and it dawned on me that if I didn't do something I might never see you again. You could vanish out of my life, poof, just like that. I didn't want that to happen. I saw my chance, and I took it."

He kissed her again. "I'm glad you did."

"Yeah, well, too bad you've got those busted up ribs," she whispered into his ear, giving it a playful nibble. "Otherwise, I'd let you thank me for real."

The same thought had crossed his mind, numerous times, actually, but sudden movement of any kind was sadly out of the question. Instead, he kissed her long and hard before pulling away, surprised to find they were both a little out of breath. His rapid pulse pounded in his ears.

"We'll have to save that for later. Let's talk about it again in, say, five weeks."

She chuckled once more. "Deal."

Sasha and Boon were the first ones up the next morning. He was stiff and sore, and tottered about like an eighty-year-old the day after a fall. Together they explored what the kitchen had to offer, poking around the cabinets and refrigerator. In the end, they found frozen English muffins, along with a tub of butter in the fridge. There was also a pound of bacon, but the expiration date on that was long passed and they decided to skip it–which was okay with Sasha since she didn't eat meat. Much to Boon's relief, they also stumbled onto a bottle of acetaminophen. Boon washed three down and waited for them to take the edge off. Together they munched quietly on muffins fresh out of the toaster. Even the simple act of chewing was painful.

While they waited on the arrival of Hollenbeck, one by one the others drifted down and joined them. Steve was first, and after he joked about Boon's assortment of bruises, he examined the bacon and debated cooking some up until he tore it open and gave it a sniff. There was a coffee machine that Miles prepped and got going, and while it brewed, he set out Styrofoam cups for everyone. Soon the comforting smells of breakfast and the low murmur of chatter filled the old kitchen. Boon noticed with interest that no one was talking about their predicament, instead, perhaps, content to hold out until the FBI agent showed. He didn't blame them, since he was happy not to have to do the thinking for the group for once.

They didn't have to wait long. Several minutes later everyone sat up straight when they heard car tires on the gravel outside. Motioning them all to silence, Boon peeked between the curtains. When he saw it was Hollenbeck's sedan, he exhaled in relief.

"Isn't this a homey bunch," the agent said with a small smile once he was inside, seeing them all gathered around the table or leaning on counters. "I hope everyone had a nice night."

There were general murmurs of agreement, punctuated by a huge yawn from Sir Jim. For the next few minutes, they went around the room and introduced themselves to the agent. When that was done, Miles offered Hal a cup of coffee, which he gratefully accepted. It was black and fresh out of the pot, but Hollenbeck tossed it down like a shot of tequila. Boon peered closely at the man's face, and noted how red and tired the agent's eyes were behind the glasses. The rest of them may have enjoyed a solid night's sleep, but he guessed the FBI man hadn't had that luxury.

"It's been a busy twelve hours," he began, rubbing hands across his face. "The men we arrested at the factory still aren't talking. There's no sign of Galo or Gonzalez, either, not that I expected anything different. I'm sure they've gone to ground somewhere."

Clem looked around, then half raised his hand. In his easy southern drawl, he asked, "What does that mean for us? I mean, they're still out there. According to you and Boon, we'll never get a minute's peace until they're caught."

Hollenbeck agreed. "Sadly, yes. As long as Galo is free, I can't see how any of you will ever be out of harm's way. You may have noticed already, but he's not exactly the forgiving type."

"Well, Mr. FBI guy, that's fucking great," Steve growled. "I don't know about the rest of you, but I'm done running from these sons of bitches. I've got a son to take care of, and businesses to run."

The agent plucked the glasses off his nose and polished the already sparkling lenses on the sleeve of his jacket. Boon was beginning to understand the man did that when he needed time to read the room or wanted a few extra seconds to gather his thoughts. Afterwards, Hollenbeck looked at each of them in turn, as if sizing them up.

"What I'm about to tell you can never leave this room," he started, his earlier levity gone. "Is that understood?"

One by one, they nodded. The agent surveyed each person individually, purposefully not moving on until everyone in the kitchen had complied.

"Good. I don't know how much Boon has told you," the agent continued, "but I can't afford to get the Bureau involved because I'm not entirely certain who I can trust. I'm guessing Galo has been using his resources to build and buy influence everywhere he does business, including here in Ohio. I have no way of knowing who's on the take. The way he's able to elude capture would make sense if he's got people on the payroll in the justice system and peppered through all levels of law enforcement. But in the end, I can't be sure who has and hasn't been compromised."

"This just gets better and better," Sasha said, her voice thick with sarcasm.

"Also," he went on, not paying attention to her, "if I do get the Bureau involved, that means all of you will certainly be arrested and charged with any number of federal crimes. Theft. Fraud. Probably money laundering. Possibly accessory to murder. I can't see how any of you come away from this without significant jail time."

Everyone but Boon physically blanched at the agent's blatant, matter-of-fact statement. The threat of arrest for people in their line of work was always hovering somewhere in the back seats of their minds, but it never occupied the front row nearly as poignantly as it did just then. Boon, on the other hand, had pieced together the potential ramifications the second he'd found out Marsden had been murdered. For the rest of them, however, this had just gotten very real.

Miles set his coffee down on the counter slowly, thoughtfully, as if the Styrofoam cup were a priceless piece of China. His eyes were wide and bright against his dark skin. He pointed at the agent.

"Okay, but I'm still not a hundred percent sure why you haven't arrested us yet," he said. "I don't get it. Help me understand that."

Hollenbeck slipped his glasses back on, where the lenses magnified the severe expression currently baked into his eyes. "Because doing so isn't going to help me get Galo, that's why. And honestly, you're the only ones I can trust."

Boon raised his eyebrows, not sure he had heard correctly. "Wait a minute. What are you saying?"

"I'm saying," Hollenbeck replied, his voice haunted by past failures, "that I'm going to nail that son of a bitch once and for all. But to do that, I'm going to need your help."

22

Sasha was the first to speak. "Count me in. I'm tired of running from these fuckers."

Boon grabbed her shoulder as if trying to restrain her from her own impetuous nature. Even that slight movement made his ribs scream their displeasure. "Sasha, hold on. You've seen how these guys operate. If we do this and it goes south, we're dead. You know that, right? Look what happened to poor Patrice."

"Yeah, and if we don't, it's just a matter of time until they find us and the same thing happens. I say we take it to them once and for all," she replied, smacking a fist into her open palm. The impact was loud in the small room and several of them jumped.

"I'm with her," Kempler said in a voice so penetrating he could have been using a megaphone. "We need to get these bastards before they get us."

Clem and Miles had been silent and were staring at each other intently, as if somehow telepathically sharing their intentions. They bobbed their heads in unison, but it was Clem who put words to their thoughts.

"We're in, too," he said, with one eye still trained on Miles. "If it means they're out of our lives. We can't have them hunting us forever. And besides, we need to get even for what they did to Patrice."

Boon saw how determined they were, even though there was no way they could truly grasp the risks involved. He leaned forward again and tried to make eye contact with Sasha, but she ignored his stare.

"If we do this and you get him," Kempler said, "what happens to us then?"

Hollenbeck straightened up and spread his hands out. "If this works, I can personally guarantee nothing will happen to you. Your involvement will be buried so deep in the case files that nobody will know who you are or what you've done. I've got some clout banked within the Bureau. It will take some doing, but you'll all walk." He made a dusting motion with his two hands, as if brushing dirt away.

Rising to his full height, Steve took a menacing step toward the agent. His cheeks flared cherry red, and his hands were balled into tight fists at his sides. He could have been a linebacker about to rush the quarterback. "Let me get this straight, FBI guy. If we help you, we go free. And if we don't, we're screwed? Christ, do I have that right? You're blackmailing us?"

Boon was impressed to see Hollenbeck not backing down from Kempler's looming physical threat. "Not exactly how I'd put it, but yes. Listen, it's a lot easier to call in favors when there's a positive outcome. It wouldn't be the first time I've done something like this, and it won't be the last. This is a messy business sometimes."

Miles laced his fingers together and glowered at the agent. "Pretty convenient how this is all playing out, isn't it? Our lives for this Galo person."

"Even Boon?" Sasha asked, ignoring the tense interchange between the men. She motioned in Dohir's direction, her stare intense enough to punch holes through the agent's skull. "He'd go free, even with what happened to this Marsden guy?"

Hollenbeck shook his head and did something no one expected. He smiled, although the genial expression never made it above his cheeks. Then he pulled out his phone and tapped on it a few times. His gaze flicked back and forth as he read something on the screen. "Before anyone passes judgment on what happened, let me share some fun facts about Phillip Marsden," he began. "This man was no saint, no matter what you may have seen in the news. The Bureau has had its eye on him for a very long time."

Boon shook his head, caught off guard. "What are you talking about? I researched him. He was just an ordinary guy. Successful and financially well off, sure, but otherwise pretty normal."

The FBI agent didn't roll his eyes, but he may as well have. "That's the difference between the research you can do, versus the resources we have at our disposal. Yes, Marsden owned several legitimate transportation and hauling businesses. Mainly trucking. Two of the busiest highways in the country, Interstates 75 and 70, intersect just north of Dayton. This makes central Ohio a very appealing hub for both honest and illegitimate enterprises. Marsden probably started off legit, but we believe his business model changed when he started associating with some very shady characters. Our friend Galo, for example, before he was head of El Grupo Nuevo." He tapped his phone again and continued checking his notes.

"Marsden ended up on our radar five or six years ago when one of his trucks got busted at the southern border trying to smuggle weapons into Mexico. We arrested the driver, but couldn't pin anything on Marsden himself. He's been under surveillance ever since. We suspect he's been transporting contraband around the world for Galo and El Grupo Nuevo, mainly drugs and weapons, and getting paid very handsomely for it, too. We just couldn't catch him."

"This is crazy," Boon said.

"Not as crazy as you might think," Hollenbeck replied. "Most of Marsden's illicit millions were made over the years and subsequently squirreled away at the Ohio Citizens National Bank. But there were some more recent deposits, large ones, likely payments by Galo to transport hundreds of kilos of cocaine and fentanyl into the US. Those shipments, I'm happy to announce, were intercepted at the border, and that was the beginning of the end of their arrangement."

"How does the bank fit into all this?" Sasha asked.

"Good question. Their contact was Leslie Harbaugh, the manager. Together she and Marsden were concealing vast sums of his money right under the noses of their auditors and regulators. And before you ask, yes, doing that is much easier than you would think at a small financial institution. Because of cost and a lack of manpower, they rarely have proper controls in place like the bigger banks. Most cases of fraud and embezzlement happen at small banks and credit unions like this."

Boon couldn't believe his ears. "But why the hell did she transfer $20 million into that account instead of the $200,000 I was asking for? That doesn't make sense."

"She panicked, that's why. Harbaugh rightly thought we were onto her, and she was feeling the heat. She got scared and screwed up. She dumped all of Marsden's money into that account, thinking it really was for him, and the two of them were going to take it and bolt. It was just her bad luck that you were at the receiving end of that."

"Her bad luck? Shit, I think the bad luck was all ours," Miles muttered, absently drumming his fingers on the counter.

Everyone was quiet for a moment while they digested this. "Y'all sure figured out a lot in a short period of time," Clem finally chimed in, running his fingers through his messy hair. His lopsided grin was absent for once.

"We did, although to be fair we've been working on this case for years. Plus, it's pretty easy when you've suddenly got an accomplice like Leslie Harbaugh behind bars, with the threat of decades of jail staring her in the face. She hasn't stopped talking since we picked her up. Although," he emphasized, making eye contact around the room, "she doesn't know anything about you or your involvement. As far as she knows, she transferred the money and Marsden got it. She has no idea why he was kidnapped and then murdered. She's guessing Galo did it because he thought his partner in crime was trying to screw him over somehow. No one has told her otherwise."

"I'll be damned," Kempler muttered, shaking his head. He had calmed down from his earlier blow up, and no longer looked like he was ready to take out the FBI agent.

"But that doesn't explain how Galo got my phone numbers," Boon said, trying to keep his head above water with this tsunami of new information. "If Harbaugh didn't know about me, she would have no reason to have those. Only Chet did."

Hollenbeck consulted his phone again, still tapping away. "Ah, yes, Chester Anderson. Chet, to most people. A very nice young man, although he's scared to death right now. Harbaugh must have told Galo that Chet was working with you. Mr. Anderson got some very threatening calls from an individual with a thick Spanish accent, demanding your personal information, and promising some very bad things would happen to him and his family if he didn't comply. As you can imagine, he did what he was told. I can't say I blame him. We've got him under heavy surveillance now, for his own safety."

Boon exhaled, suddenly feeling lighter, as if a backpack of guilt had been lifted off his shoulders. He'd been certain something horrible had happened to Chet, and was relieved to hear the young man was okay. Well, *"okay"* might be a stretch, but at least he was still alive.

Hollenbeck looked around at the faces staring at him. "What other questions are there?"

"I've got one," Dohir said, and every head in the room swiveled towards him. "You've talked about nailing Galo once and for all, but back in the restaurant last night you told me how slippery this guy has been. You've been close to busting him before, but he always manages to get away. What makes you think this time will be any different?"

The agent's gaze never wavered, and nothing about his posture or expression changed. Even so, his normally soothing voice took on a new and steely edge. Granted, Boon thought, he hadn't known him long, but even so, he had never heard the man sound quite like this before. His tone had a distinct sense of finality to it.

"You leave that to me," Hollenbeck said. "I'll take care of him."

Several people around the room sucked in a collective breath. There was no mistaking what the FBI agent meant by that. Boon had never killed anyone before, had never even considered it, and he didn't think he could under any circumstances. But Hollenbeck, it seemed, would have no problem pulling the trigger. There were many types of people in this world, including those who could easily take a life, and those who couldn't. Boon was glad he was firmly in that second camp.

"Damn, dude. That's pretty rogue cop of you, don't you think? Whatever happened to innocent until proven guilty?" Miles asked.

Kempler frowned at the agent. "No shit, at least you could use a word like 'neutralize' or something. Isn't that the sort of thing an FBI agent would say?"

Hollenbeck turned to him. "Trust me. Galo is one very bad person. He doesn't deserve due process or anyone's mercy. But if a euphemism helps, then sure. Leave him to me and I'll neutralize him."

Dohir glanced around the room at everyone, trying to gauge their reactions to this newest development. Sasha appeared coolly unfazed, not that he would expect anything else from her at this point. Clem and Miles had paled and both looked a little ill. Sir Jim's gaze was locked on his shoes. Kempler, on the other hand, rubbed his hands together and leaned forward in anticipation, as if poised to attack.

Hollenbeck paused for a second, surveying the room. If he was waiting for someone to object to moving ahead, it appeared he might be waiting a long time. The agent had them effectively boxed into a corner; their cooperation in exchange for their freedom. When no one seemed ready to say anything else, he took a few steps forward into the center of the room to make sure he had their undivided attention.

"Here's the problem," the agent began in clear frustration. "We don't know why Galo is here. Despite how elusive he is, he's still taking a terrible chance setting foot in the states. He almost never leaves the safety of his palatial fortress in Mexico."

"Not even to get his $20 million back?" Boon asked.

"No, not even for that. He has people to handle those problems, people like Gonzalez and Luis. But I'm assuming he got involved with you because he was already here for something else. That, and you embarrassed the hell out of him."

Boon winced. "But for $20 million? He wouldn't want to take charge of getting that back?"

"No, probably not. That's a lot of money to you and me, but it's chump change to him. No, he must be here for something else. Maybe to make a deal, or to oversee some big operation. Whatever it is, it must be important or he would never chance it."

"Okay, so how does this go down?" Steve asked, eager as ever to plow ahead. "If we're going to do this, then let's do this. How do we nail this guy?"

"Good point," the agent continued. "Wherever he's holed up, he'll have an army of men protecting him. It would take a major assault to even get close to him. But, like I told you, that's not possible because assembling an assault team means bringing in the Bureau. I can't risk that. I've got to do this myself while he's still here. If he makes it back to Mexico, he'll be home free. This is our only chance."

Clem asked, "What do you want from us? I don't see how we can help."

Hollenbeck spread out his hands. "Like I said, first we need to find him, and then we need to draw him out from wherever he's hiding. Once he's out in the open, it'll be up to me to…neutralize him once and for all. Several of you have interacted with him and his men, and you've shown yourselves to be smart and skilled enough to survive against pretty overwhelming odds. You're a bright bunch. I'm hoping you might have some insight on how we can make this happen."

The entire group stared silently at the agent, then began looking back and forth between themselves with shrugging shoulders and blank expressions. Bright or not, several seconds passed and it was clear no one had any ideas. A few heartbeats later Boon sighed to himself, internally debating whether he should speak up or not. His mind was a maelstrom of conflicted thoughts because a possible plan had begun to coalesce there. But speaking up meant potentially putting all his friends in danger again, something he had been hoping to avoid at all costs.

On the other hand, he also knew that if he didn't, he was essentially condemning them to a lifetime of watching and worrying, of never knowing who might be waiting for them around the next corner. The remainder of their lives would be a paranoid hell. In the end, he concluded, the choice was clear. While he would never do this simply to help himself, he would for the benefit of his friends.

"I know how we can find him," he said reluctantly. "Right now, actually."

"What? How?" Hollenbeck asked, his eyebrows raised. He stood up very straight, and his eyes were alive. It was the most animated Boon had ever seen him. "How do you propose we do that?"

Boon sighed again. "Because we still have the tracker, and I know his phone number. We can pinpoint his location using his own technology against him."

Hollenbeck shook his head in disbelief. "What are you talking about?"

"When we made the exchange in downtown Cincinnati, I tricked Galo into giving me his number so I could make the bank transfer," Boon explained. "We needed it so Sasha could record his keystrokes when he checked his balance at his bank. I still remember it."

The agent's eyebrows arched comically high, and his wide eyes magnified behind the lenses. "Really? I'm impressed."

Boon tapped the side of his head. "Yeah, well, I've got a good memory for phone numbers. I always have." He turned to Sasha, and unbidden she began digging in her backpack. After a few seconds of rummaging around, she pulled out the tracker and handed it to him. Dohir held the black box toward the agent.

"All I have to do is enter the information here, and if his phone is on, then we'll know exactly where he is." He stared mutely at the device in his hand, knowing that by following through with this he was committing them to this operation, whether they were ready for it or not. There was almost no way back after this. Then an idea came to him, and it was all he could do to mask his expression. In that instant, he knew there might be a way.

Hollenbeck stared at the tracker, barely believing what he was seeing. Everyone else was watching with different expressions, a few thick with fear, others brimming with excitement. Boon held the small device with all the care of a live grenade.

"Go ahead," the agent urged him. "Do it."

Dohir turned on the tracker and the word NUMBER? appeared on the tiny screen, just like it had at Kempler's house. With shaking fingers, he carefully entered Galo's cell phone number and hit SEND. The small display instantly went to work, popping up a color map of Ohio, Kentucky, and Indiana. The cursor blinked a few times, then began to flit around until it zeroed in on Cincinnati. The screen zoomed closer until the blinking cursor stopped in the middle of a large, irregularly shaped building on the corner of 5th and Walnut in downtown, a few blocks from the Reds' and Bengals' stadiums. The name superimposed over the outline stated *Renaissance Hotel*.

"We got him," Boon said, passing the tracker over to Hollenbeck.

The agent peered at the screen, almost in disbelief. "I'll be damned. You're sure?"

"Yeah. Well, his phone is there. That's all I can guarantee."

Hollenbeck's lips compressed as he peered at the display. "If this is right, we certainly couldn't mount an assault even if we wanted to. Like I said, Galo's sure to have dozens of men protecting him. There's also hundreds of guests and employees there. There's no telling how many innocents could get hurt or killed if we try anything. No wonder he's holed up there."

"Just like you thought," Miles said.

Hollenbeck stared at the tracker and tapped his finger on it. "Exactly. His men will be armed to the teeth, and wouldn't think twice about doing whatever it takes to protect him. They've probably rented the entire floor. The ones above and below it, too, if I had to guess. No, we can't go after him there. We'll have to figure out some way of drawing him into the open, away from crowds. We can't risk it otherwise."

Once again there was silence while they considered options, although after a minute it was evident everyone was coming up blank. Boon was just as deep in thought as the rest, but contrary to the others, ideas were forming in his mind again. Quite a few, actually. Next steps were lining up and falling into place as he considered and discarded possibilities. The longer he thought, the more these sequences of events began to crystallize, individual puzzle pieces clicking together to form a completed picture.

"The men you arrested last night," he began, as if thinking out loud. "How difficult would it be to let one of them out of jail? At least for a little while? And you'll need his phone, too. Unlocked, so we can use it."

Boon could see Hollenbeck was trying to figure out why he would ask such a thing. "I could make that happen," he eventually said, speaking slowly. "But why?"

"That's just one part of it," Boon explained. "Hold on a minute."

With all eyes on him, he left the kitchen and went outside to Kempler's SUV. He opened the driver's door and reached into the center console. In seconds he was back in the kitchen with a phone in his hand. He held it up for everyone to see.

"This is the burner phone I used when Galo and I swapped Patrice for the money," he began. "Like I said, we shared numbers so he could text me his bank information, which means my number was logged into his phone. If I had to guess, he's been using one of his own trackers to watch for it ever since. All I have to do is turn this on, and I bet he'll come after me. We can use that to draw him out."

Sasha's eyes lit up and she snapped her fingers. "That's right. You know what this guy's like. That bastard won't rest until he's got Boon. He'll come after him for sure."

"But what if he just sends some of his goons instead?" Miles countered, playing devil's advocate. "There's no way to make sure he'll come himself. He could even think it's a trap of some sort."

Despite the potentially fatal consequences hanging over their heads, Boon felt invigorated. His whole life he'd been proficient at almost everything he did, but planning was where he excelled. It had always been this way with him, from the debate club in high school, up to the mock trials later on. In his mind, he could see what was essentially a road map, each step clearly marked toward an ultimate goal. He had to resist the temptation to rub his hands together as the final parts of his plan coalesced. Boon knew precisely what he had to do, although, in the end, everyone was going to hate him for it. But he could live with their hate, as long as they were out of danger.

"Galo has no idea we're working with the FBI," he said, his mind at a full sprint. "In fact, with the lives we've led and the kind of legal consequences hanging over our heads, that's the last thing he'd figure we'd do."

"Granted," Miles admitted. "But that doesn't explain how you're going to draw him out of the hotel."

Boon pointed at Sir Jim, who was still keeping himself busy by staring resolutely at his shoes. "That's where he comes in."

Jim's head jerked up when he realized he was now the center of attention. In his deep baritone, he asked, "I beg your pardon?"

Now Boon did smile. With a slight wince, he stood and walked over to the refrigerator. From inside he grabbed the mustard and ketchup, along with some bottles of hot sauce, pickles, and any other items he could find. He carefully hauled the armload over to the table and set everything down, then picked up the salt and pepper shakers as well.

"Let's say this table is our factory office in Cincinnati," he began, holding up the salt shaker and placing the other objects around the large rectangle. "These bottles and jars represent all of us."

Boon began detailing his plan, laying out the phases one by one. He talked for the next thirty minutes, exuding confidence the entire time. There was a lot of back and forth, especially from Hollenbeck. The seasoned agent corrected some of Boon's assumptions, highlighted a few shortcomings, and offered his own ideas. Based on their talents and temperaments, Dohir relayed to each person what their roles would be, along with the timing of events. As they continued talking, with everyone leaning forward and taking it all in, eventually every person in the room stood up, including Hollenbeck. When Boon finally outlined the last piece, everyone grew silent.

"So, this is it?" Miles asked, intrigued despite himself. "We're really doing this?"

"Looks like it," Dohir answered, his good eye flicking between the FBI agent and Sasha, inwardly pleased he had them hooked.

Hollenbeck stepped back and put his hands on his hips. "You came up with this whole thing in the last few minutes? That is impressive. You sure you weren't a party planner in a prior life?" he added. "I like it, but I've been through more of these situations than I can count, and something is bound to go south. It always does. People never act the way you think they will. When that happens, there's no way we've got enough hands on deck. On top of that, except for Sasha and perhaps Steve, none of you seem like the rough-and-tumble type. We're going to need some more muscle if we're going to make this work."

Boon asked him, "You want to bring someone else in now? You said there's no one else you can trust."

The agent thought for a moment, absently rubbing his jaw. "I got a guy. Well, a few guys, actually."

Miles rolled his eyes. "Damn, Boon. He sounds just like you."

23

Hollenbeck left with Sir Jim in tow shortly afterward. The agent had some electronics shopping to do, he said, but he also wanted to discuss the big man's upcoming role in more detail. The government-issue sedan squatted dangerously low when Jim eased into the passenger seat. After the sound of the car faded away, Boon's team sat and stared quietly.

"This is going to work," he stated, breaking the heavy silence.

Miles' breath exploded through his lips like a man bursting to the surface after too long underwater. "Damn, Boon, I've never doubted you before, but our lives were never on the line, either. Man, are you sure?"

With complete conviction, he said, "Yes, I am."

"Why are we still discussing this?" Sasha asked, edging protectively closer to Boon. "We already told Hollenbeck we were in. Anyway, you heard him; if we don't, we're in jail or dead. I don't care for either of those options, thank you very much."

Clem leaned back and rubbed his hands through his hair. They came away damp with sweat, and he stared at his glistening fingers as if confused. "Damn, this is not the kind of stuff I signed up for."

"I know, Clem," Boon implored. "But we don't have any choice. Please let me help get us out of it. This will work. Trust me."

One by one their heads nodded, some more energetically than others.

"Good," he said, standing and noisily cracking his knuckles. "Go get cleaned up and gather your things. Meet back down here in half an hour. We'll regroup and take off then."

Boon watched them all head upstairs. The second they were out of sight he snatched his burner phone and the keys to Kempler's SUV off the counter. Moving quietly, he slipped outside and behind the wheel of the big vehicle, shutting the door as silently as he could. He started the Suburban. He was just about to put it in reverse and give it some gas when sudden movement in the rearview mirror caught his eye.

Sasha was standing directly behind the SUV and blocking his exit. She had her arms locked across her body, and her head was lowered as she stared daggers at him. "What the hell do you think you're doing?" she yelled.

Cursing, Boon rolled down the window. "Dammit, Sasha, get out of the way!"

"No way, not until you tell me what the hell you're doing."

"I don't have time for this," he snapped at her. "Move!"

She didn't answer, but in the rearview mirror he saw her reach down. There was a beep from the back, and the rear hatch began to raise. Boon frantically tried to locate the button to close it but was too late. She scrambled into the cargo area and started climbing over the rear seats towards him.

Still swearing under his breath, Boon finally found the correct button and shut the rear hatch. By that time, however, Sasha had crawled into the seat behind him, her mouth inches from his ear.

"You mind telling me what you're doing?" she asked in a voice devoid of warmth. "You were just going to leave me here? What the hell?"

Boon smacked the steering wheel in frustration, furious he'd been found out. He'd been so close! All the talk around the table earlier, all the theatrics with the contents from the refrigerator, had been a ploy from the very beginning. He'd had no intention of bringing his friends along. His performance had been nothing but an elaborate con designed to fool Hollenbeck and leave everyone behind.

"Sasha, please get the hell out!"

She glared at him. "You haven't answered my question yet. What the hell are you doing?"

Boon stared at her in the rearview mirror. He wanted her out of the vehicle more than anything, but he also knew what an impossible task that would be on a good day, much less in his current condition. Besides that, the longer he sat out here, the more likely it was that he'd be discovered by others in the house. Before the situation went from bad to worse, Boon punched the gas and the big vehicle roared backward. He slammed the selector into drive and floored it, gravel pinging like automatic gunfire on the undercarriage as he flew down the driveway. Sasha yelped and tumbled backward under the sudden acceleration.

He had gone only a few hundred feet, however, when he spotted a sedan blocking the end of the driveway. Cursing, he briefly considered taking the Suburban off-road and going around, but there were deep ditches flanking the exit that would sideline anything less robust than a tank. He punched the steering wheel in frustration again, then eased off the gas and stopped with his bumper inches from Hollenbeck's car. The agent climbed out and casually walked up to Boon's window, spinning his finger for him to roll it down. When Boon grudgingly complied, Hollenbeck rested his elbows on the windowsill and pursed his lips.

"Going somewhere?" he asked, although his lack of inflection made it less of a question and more of a statement.

"Get out of my way," Boon growled, eyes locked straight ahead. He could see the outline of Sir Jim's head in the passenger seat.

"That's not going to happen, not until you tell me what you're doing. I know all that talk back there was nothing but a show. Admit it. You never planned on involving your people. None of them have the skills or nerve to participate in this, and we both know it." He peered in the backseat at Sasha. "But I must say, I'm curious why she's here."

"Because I figured out what he was up to. He's not as sneaky as he thinks he is," she said, pushing her dark hair from her face and peering around the seat.

"That explains that, I suppose. It still doesn't tell me what your plan is, Boon. You can't do anything alone, you know. Besides, get both of you killed."

Dohir sighed, his hands gripping the steering wheel so hard his knuckles looked ready to pop. He met the agent's steady gaze. "I was still going to do it, but without them. They're in this mess because of me, and I have no intention of involving them any longer. I'll fix this myself."

The agent's eyes narrowed. When he spoke, he sounded like a teacher scolding a student. "Really? And how are you going to do that? You're very good at organizing and planning, so I'd be curious to know what you've come up with."

Boon stewed for a moment, then looked away, his eyes focused on nothing in the distance. "I haven't figured that out yet."

Hollenbeck glanced back towards the house, tapping his fingers on the sill of the door. "That doesn't sound like you at all. You don't strike me as the kind of guy to go into this half-cocked. Wouldn't that violate your planning nature?"

"Fine," Boon snapped. "I was going to go to the factory and turn on the phone. When Galo showed up, I was going to make a deal with him: his money and my life for his promise to leave the others alone forever, okay? Happy?"

Sasha snatched at his arm from the backseat. "What? You can't do that! That's crazy."

He shook her hand off. "I can and I will. I need this to be over with once and for all."

"She's right, you know. Martyring yourself won't do any good. You can't trust Galo, and you know it. He's got the conscience of a shark. He'll take his money, happily kill you, then go after the others in his own good time. They'll be no safer than they are now, and you'll be dead and unable to help."

Boon was so overcome with frustration it was all he could do not to scream at the sky. "Dammit, I need to put an end to this. Tell me how I can do that!"

The agent kept tapping his fingers on the windowsill, thinking. "Honestly, I like what you came up with this morning. Parts of it were good, but to make it work, we're going to need people a little more ruthless than your friends."

Boon threw his hands in the air. "What I came up with this morning? Are you insane? That was total bullshit I made up just to fool everyone. It was never even a real plan."

Hollenbeck tapped his temple. "Don't sell yourself short. It's better than you think, and we're going to use it. We just need a few more pairs of seasoned boots on the ground to help pull it off."

"I thought you said bringing in your FBI buddies wasn't an option," Boon countered, intrigued despite himself.

"You're right, it's not, but we both know people more suited to this sort of operation. People who've had to scratch and fight for everything their entire lives, and who aren't afraid to get their hands dirty for the right price."

Boon twisted in his seat, flinching at the pain in his side. "I don't know who you're talking about."

"You will. Hold on," Hollenbeck told him, pulling out his phone and keying in a number. There was a pause while he waited for someone on the other end to pick up. "Yes, it's me. I've got someone here who wants to talk to you." He handed the phone over.

Boon slowly lifted the receiver to his ear, his face twisted into a question mark. "Hello? Who's this?"

There was a moment of silence, followed by a deep chuckle. "Hey, this Mr. Moneybags? Damn, man, why you hanging out with that fed, anyway?"

It took Boon a second to place the voice, but then it came to him. "Dante? Is that you?"

"Hell yeah, it's me. That Fibbie called and said you got yourself into a mess, and you gonna pay each of us ten grand to help get you out. That true?"

Boon slowly lowered the phone and stared in shock at Hollenbeck. "Really? Dante and those guys? You want to use them?"

"I do. And you're going to pay each of them ten grand for doing so. It may sound like a lot, but it won't even make a dent in that $20 million you've got squirreled away."

"I don't care about the damn money. How can these guys help us?"

Hollenbeck grinned. "I've seen their rap sheets, remember? I have a hunch they can be as ruthless as Galo's men. Maybe even more so." He took the phone from Dohir's limp hand. "Hey, it's me again. You and your friends meet us at the factory at three O'clock. That should give me enough time. Yes, come prepared. And stay out of trouble until then." He hung up and pocketed the phone.

"I can't believe you're involving those guys. What if one of them gets hurt? Or killed?"

"It's up to you and me to make sure that doesn't happen," the agent replied, not unkindly. He tilted his head a little. "If it helps, think of them as another one of your Robin Hood projects. I've dealt with guys like Dante my entire career, and most of them have very little chance of breaking out of the cycle of poverty and violence they were born into. Someone believing in them may be what helps them make it. And the ten grand won't hurt, either." He straightened up and started toward his car.

"Wait a minute! Now what?" Boon yelled at his retreating back.

"Follow your plan. Head down to the factory and wait for me. It's a perfect location for this. I've still got those errands to run. I'll meet you there as soon as I can."

"But that wasn't a real plan!" he screamed at the agent's back. Hollenbeck got into his car and drove off, heading east. Boon sat in the driver's seat with his mouth hanging open, a thousand conflicted thoughts pinballing around in his mind. For someone who was only comfortable when he was in charge of his own well-planned destiny, he was shaken at how out of control his life had become. Boon felt like a sparrow caught in a storm, blown wildly about and helpless to steer himself to safety. He was shaken from his tortured silence when Sasha nudged his shoulder.

"I still can't believe you were going to leave without me," she said, crawling between the seats and sitting next to him.

Boon was too angry and upset to talk, so he threw the selector into drive and pulled away. Just like Kempler had the night before, he kept off the interstate and stuck to the surface streets, the grill of the big SUV pointed south toward Cincinnati. Driving angry and with only one good eye was tricky, he quickly discovered. He had to force himself to keep a good deal of distance between himself and the cars in front of him, but he got the hang of it after a bit.

After his initial anger had ebbed, he turned to Sasha. "Okay, how'd you figure out something was going on? I was sure I had everyone back there fooled."

She leaned toward him and placed a hand on his arm. "You're not all that sneaky, you know. I had a hunch something was up. Besides, you cracked your knuckles. You only do that when you're ready to leave. It's a dead giveaway."

Boon shook his head, briefly annoyed with himself. He hadn't been aware he had a tell like that. On the other hand, he'd had no clue she was paying such close attention to him, either, but it unexpectedly warmed his heart to know that she had been.

They drove in silence, Boon's anger at her still ebbing. In half an hour, when they were near the factory, Boon slowed down and pulled off to the side. After he parked, he noticed he was directly outside of a small Irish pub. Music and laughter leaked out through the green front door. The sight of the place induced a sudden and overpowering urge for a drink, a craving so desperate it felt like a physical force. As he fought the temptation, it hit him again how many days he'd been sober. That realization, in turn, made his hands tremble. Sweat began to trickle down the back of his neck. To mask this sudden anxiety, he kept both hands glued to the steering wheel at ten and two.

"You okay?" Sasha asked him, sensing a problem.

After taking several deep breaths to steady himself, he turned towards her. "Yeah, I'm fine."

"You sure don't look fine."

No, he wasn't. Looking at himself from the outside, he wasn't proud of what he'd become. He knew his addiction was starting to control his life. In fact, most of the time he felt like little more than a passenger on a runaway train, helpless to do anything but watch while the inevitable collision loomed. But even so, even with all the blackouts and almost daily binges, it ate at Boon's basic nature that he wasn't in control of himself. He sat in silence as the irony and weight of that sank in. He must have looked as bad as he felt because when he glanced at Sasha the concern in her eyes was heartfelt. It was time to get his life back on track, he knew. Not just for him, but for her, too.

"You know what? You're right. I'm not fine, and I guess I've been pretty shitty for a long time. But I'm starting to accept that, and I think that's the first step." He took a deep, cleansing breath and tried to manufacture his sincerest smile. "But right now, we've got a stupid, insane job to do, so let's focus on that. Deal?"

She smiled back at him. Hers was much more natural than his. "Deal."

"Now, unless Patrice told them about the factory, Galo and his men shouldn't know anything about it. But just to be sure, I'm going to cruise past it a few times. Be on the lookout for anything suspicious, like black Escalades. Even if they're here, I doubt they'll be stupid enough to be parked out front. They'll be hidden on a side street or in some nearby parking lot."

"What is it with bad guys and black SUVs?" she asked, genuinely curious. "Was there a big sale that day? You know, buy two, get one free? Or maybe I'm way off base and they're just compensating for something?"

The smile he felt was real that time. "I wish I knew," he replied with a laugh.

They both kept their eyes peeled while he navigated around the block and up and down numerous alleys. After several passes around the factory and adjacent streets without any sightings, Boon was reasonably confident their office was safe. Even so, and out of an abundance of caution, he parked a block away and approached the place on foot, instructing Sasha to wait. When he got there, he was relieved to see that the security system was showing green with no indication of forced entry. He tried to calm down, although the way his hands shuddered and his heart hammered made it clear his adrenaline levels were spiking dangerously high. Now that they were in the thick of it, his earlier nervous energy was leeching away, leaving behind nothing but raw nerves. How in the hell did the Hollenbecks of the world do this sort of thing day after day?

He keyed in the code to disarm the alarm. Inside it was as dark and cool as ever, with some tepid light streaming down from rows of filthy windows high up on the walls. The shadowy shapes of machinery loomed all around him like graveyard monuments, and the oil and dust made the air seem heavier than air had any right to be. The scraping of his shoes on the dirty concrete floor was jarring as it echoed around the cavernous space. A few minutes later the door behind him eased open and Sasha stepped in.

"Follow me," Boon told her quietly. There was no rational reason to whisper, but it seemed like the proper thing to do.

Together the pair moved deeper into the factory, then up the steps to the office. Boon keyed in the code. Once the heavy door was closed and locked behind them, the tension in his shoulders eased. He turned on a small desk light, then went to the bank of security monitors. He flipped a few switches and watched as the cameras outside the factory came to life. He turned on others, and more screens revealing the darkened interior of the factory blinked on, the old machines and serpentine conveyor belts illuminated in various shades of gray and black in the low light.

Sasha watched him go through his routine. "What was this place before? We've never really talked about it."

"They made five-gallon steel buckets here," he answered idly, moving around the room. "You know, the heavy-duty kind that paint and chemicals are stored in. Conveyor belts run all through this place, along with steel presses, paint sprayers, and a huge oven that bakes paint onto the cans. Everything is controlled up here from that panel." He pointed behind him at the expansive electrical board filled with heavy-duty switches and dark red lights. The panel was so wide it nearly covered the entire wall, like something out of an old science fiction movie. "The owner passed away several years ago, and none of the family wanted to take it over, so it's been on the market ever since. I'm just renting it for now."

"They're just giving up on it? That's kind of sad."

"Yeah, but someone will buy it, in time," Boon told her. "Hopefully they'll tear it down and turn it into apartments or something, which would be fine. Cincinnati doesn't have enough moderately-priced housing these days, and the suburbs are way too expensive for most people around here."

Sasha snapped her fingers. "That reminds me of something Hollenbeck said. What the hell are these 'Robin Hood' projects of yours he was talking about?"

Boon looked at her, then went back to inspecting the control board. "It was nothing. Forget about it."

"Come on. It can't be nothing. What is it?"

Boon knew she wouldn't give up until he told her. "Fine. For the last few years, I've been secretly funding projects around Dayton and Cincinnati. Rehabbing houses. Building baseball diamonds in low-income areas. Fixing up old playgrounds. Stuff like that. I've got all the money I need, and it's my way of giving back, I suppose."

She smiled warmly at him, and it dawned on him how much he liked it when she did that. "That's nice. I had no idea. You really are Robin Hood, aren't you?"

He stopped what he was doing and grinned shyly at her, a genuine expression that seemed to be gracing his face more and more often when she was around. "Yeah, I guess I am, in a way."

"No, really, it is. I could get on board with that. Stealing from the rich and giving to the poor. That'd be a nice change from the shit the rest of us are used to doing."

"Thanks, that means a lot. And yeah, there's more I'd like to do, too, assuming we get out of this alive."

That last comment sobered both of them up in a hurry. She stayed out of his way while he fiddled with controls on the big board. Down on the shop floor, overhead lights flicked on and off, and the sounds of heavy machinery waking up rumbled through the floor and shook the walls. At one point the entire building vibrated as the conveyor belt began running. It wound around the factory like a tremendous snake constructed of steel wheels and rollers in place of scales. He let it run for a few minutes as he stood at the window peering down at the shop floor, his head moving as he traced its circuitous path around the factory. The volume of noise was so extreme he felt as if the sound waves were pushing through his body. Then, with a nod to himself, he killed the power and it trundled to a stop. After so much racket, the silence was almost as startling as the noise had been.

"It all still works," he said to himself, rubbing his hands together. "Excellent."

She flipped her dark hair out of her face. "You didn't know if they still worked? Isn't that kind of important?"

"Yeah, pretty much. I've tinkered with all this before and I know in theory how it operates, but I've never had to worry about it before. I just wanted the space for our office."

She sat on the edge of one of the desks and her eyes tracked him as he checked out a few more switches on the board. When he had done all that he could, he went and sat next to her, his hands in his lap. It was a rare, peaceful moment, and they leaned into each other, their shoulders touching.

"I'm going to ask you a favor," he said, his tone as serious as at any time that day. "It's important."

Her eyes narrowed. "What?"

"I want you to leave. Hollenbeck and the rest of us will take care of this. But I want you out of here and somewhere safe. This has all been horrible so far, but I wouldn't be able to forgive myself if something happened to you."

"Screw that," she said immediately, a delicate vein in her temple coming to life in indignation. "You need me here. I mean, look at you. You couldn't arm wrestle a toddler right now. I can be an asset in all this, and you know it."

He pulled away from her a little. "No, dammit. I can't do this knowing you'll be in danger, too."

"Sorry, no can do. And before you freak out, just listen to me. You're going to be up here orchestrating everything, right?"

"Yeah. So?"

"So you're going to be busy as hell. Someone's gotta watch your back while all this is going on, just in case."

He looked at her, about to start meticulously laying out sensible reasons why she should leave. But then he saw the set of her jaw and the determined glint in her eyes. He knew her well enough by now that she would be deaf to his arguments once her mind was made up. Just like he had when she crawled into the SUV, he fleetingly thought about forcing her out but knew there wasn't a prayer of that working. In the end, he sighed in surrender, knowing he was helpless to change her mind. Her presence in the factory worried him to no end.

"Fine. I know I can't force you, so just promise me you won't do anything stupid, okay?"

She blinked and placed a hand on her chest. "Me? Of course not. Why would you think such a thing?"

They both grinned at her mock innocence, then resigned themselves to wait. To help mask his unease and pass the time, Boon brewed some coffee. They drank coffee and made small talk as the hands on the wall clock crept towards three O'clock. While Boon was a bag of nerves, Sasha appeared as unruffled as someone waiting their turn at the BMV. Once more he wondered what made some people immune to the pressures of these situations, while he himself was close to losing his mind.

A little before three O'clock, Boon spotted Hollenbeck's sedan pull into view on the outside monitors. The agent slowly drove past the factory and parked down the street. At about the same time, he saw an old, rusty panel van drive up out front, stopping in the lot where Boon would usually park his vehicle. The windows on the beat-up van were tinted so dark they could have been black. Bluish exhaust belched irregularly out of the tailpipe. He watched as Hollenbeck and Sir Jim walked up to the van's driver's side. Hollenbeck had a backpack over his shoulder, and Sir Jim was carrying a shopping bag. The window of the van rolled down, and the group started talking. Sir Jim handed small items of some sort through the window.

"Stay here," Boon told Sasha. "I need to let them in."

He hustled out and down the steps and to the main door, happy to finally be doing something instead of stewing in his own tension. When he stepped out, he was surprised to see that the van had moved and was now backed up almost to the door. Hollenbeck and Sir Jim were standing off to the side. Boon was about to ask what was going on when the back doors of the van popped open. Five Black men in their early twenties began to pile out. Each man carried weapons, from baseball bats to long steel pipes. Most had pistols stuck in the belts of their sagging jeans. They glanced left then right as they hurried into the factory. To a man they also carried a small package about the size of a brick. The white kid with the neck tattoos and permanent sneer was not there. Dante was the last man out, and he smiled at Boon, his gold tooth gleaming.

"Yo, Moneybags, wassup?"

Boon took him by the arm and drew him close. "Dante, you don't have to do this. This is going to be dangerous. I'm serious. You could get killed."

Dante's smile faltered once but burst back larger than life half a second later. He threw his head back and laughed. "Man, you don't know shit. This gonna be fun. Happy hunting to you!" He slammed the double doors shut behind him and pounded on the back of the van. The decrepit vehicle belched blue smoke and merged out into traffic. Dante pushed by Boon and trotted into the factory, shaking his head and chuckling to himself. Hollenbeck walked up and stared after them as the van vanished down the street. He handed one of the boxes to Boon.

"What's this?" Dohir asked.

"A walkie-talkie, complete with an earpiece. Put it in, please. Everyone's got one. Except Sasha, who will be with you. We'll all be able to talk to each other without worrying about anyone tracking our cell phones."

Boon fumbled open the box and inspected the contents. Inside was a small walkie-talkie and an earpiece. The wireless earpiece was small and black and reminded him of the type of hearing aid worn inside the ear canal. He had to twist and turn it a little before it was properly seated. He turned the walkie-talkie on and heard a short burst of static.

Sir Jim stepped up and rested a comforting hand on Boon's shoulder. "How are you holding up, my friend?"

"Me?" Dohir replied. "I'm a nervous fucking wreck. How are you doing?"

Jim's complexion was a red and splotchy mess, looking worse than ever, if that was possible. That made it all the more surprising when he answered with a voice that was steady and composed. "I'm shockingly okay, believe it or not. My part in this scheme is minimal, and I should be far enough away from the action to be safe." He leaned closer to Boon. "To be honest, I'm rather looking forward to it. I've been many voices and people in my day, but this may be my most important role ever. Don't you agree?"

"I do. Just promise me you'll do your part, then get the hell out of here."

His friend smiled and patted Boon on the shoulder again. "No need to worry, my good man. I may be looking forward to this, but I have no intention of being involved beyond that. You may have noticed, but my days of being physically active are somewhat behind me."

Boon gave him an appraising look up and down. "Really? I hadn't noticed."

Jim didn't reply for a few seconds, then he burst out laughing despite the current circumstances. "Look at you! You actually made a joke!"

Hollenbeck had been listening to the exchange patiently, but he glanced at his watch and informed them it was time to go inside. Boon's improved mood vanished, and his nerves began to assert control again. They stepped into the dark factory.

Hollenbeck looked at him and said, "Okay, let's go fill everyone in on your plan."

Boon felt like grabbing the man and shaking him. "Dammit, Hollenbeck, there was never a plan!"

The agent grinned and motioned them forward. They followed the path through the shop, with Boon cursing under his breath as he trailed behind. They went up the stairs to the office where the others were waiting.

24

"I've got one rule for operations like this," Hollenbeck said to everyone gathered around him. "No one dies. Understand?"

Heads all around him slowly moved up and down in agreement. Dante smiled.

"Boon and Sasha will be running the entire show from up here," the agent continued. Sasha, the only female in the room, was leaning against the door with her arms crossed. Sir Jim was seated in a corner well away from everyone. Dante and his crew were perched on the edge of desks as they listened to the FBI agent, baseball bats and steel pipes held loosely in their hands. One or two had pistols out. Their heads were angled down, but their eyes were aimed up at him, very white against their dark skin. Besides Dante, none of them had talked. They were hunter-still as the FBI agent detailed his instructions. The emotional essence of each young man seemed buried deep inside years of hardship and frustration, as if their souls had aged much faster than their bodies.

"We don't know how they'll be coming in, but I assume they'll break down the main door and enter that way," the agent continued.

"There are some loading bays at the back of the building, but those doors are heavy-duty and should hold up to nearly anything shy of a bazooka."

"What about us?" Dante asked a little impatiently. He was holding a large pistol in his hand, and he used it to point as he talked. No one but Boon seemed to care that he was waving a deadly weapon around so casually.

"This is a big place. We're going to make sure they have to split up once they get inside as they look for Boon. When they do that, I want you and your men to cull the herd."

Dante's face screwed up. He moved his mouth around as if he had swallowed a bug. "You want us to do what?"

"Cull the herd. Take out as many as you can. The more of his men you incapacitate, the fewer I have to worry about."

"You want us to kill them?" Dante said so matter-of-factly it made Boon shudder.

"No, not unless you have no choice." Hollenbeck reached into his backpack and withdrew a handful of thick zip ties. He handed them out to the group. "I'd rather you capture them alive so we can interrogate them later. Secure their hands and feet with these, and stand guard over them. Keep them quiet if you can, but it's not a big deal if you can't. Boon has assured me it will be extremely noisy in there, so it shouldn't matter."

"What then?" Sasha asked from her post by the door.

"Once their numbers have been reduced, you can leave the rest to me. I'll be keeping close tabs on Galo as he makes his way towards where I'll be waiting. When the time is right, I'll take care of him."

"How you gonna get him moving to you?" Dante asked, twirling the pistol some more. Boon flinched every time the end of the barrel swung around to him.

"That's where he comes in," the agent said, motioning for Dohir to take over.

Boon cleared his throat and held up the burner phone. "Galo, our target, has a device that can track phones, right down to within a few feet of where they are. Once Sir Jim does his part and I turn this on, I can guarantee he'll be coming for me. I'll put the phone in a steel bucket at the beginning of the assembly line, and when they come in, I'll set the belt in motion. The bucket will travel all through the factory, and they'll think it's me trying to hide from them. We're hoping most will follow it, but that'll be a lot harder than they think."

"That's right," Hollenbeck added. "This place is a maze of machines, dead ends, and conveyor belts. They won't be able to track it easily. It's one of the reasons they'll be forced to split up. We'll position each of you throughout the factory. You'll be able to see them, but they won't be able to see you."

Boon pointed toward the big panel next to him. "I'll control everything from up here. Lights, conveyor belts, machines. Everything. Watch this."

He started flicking switches on the panel. Different overhead lights on the shop floor began flashing on and off like strobes in a funhouse. He turned on several other switches, and the sound of huge machines began vibrating through the office walls with the deep thrumming of an ocean liner's engine room. Dante's eyes widened as he looked down at the factory floor.

"See what you mean," he muttered.

"Exactly. The noise and lights will keep them so disoriented they won't know what's going on. That should give you a huge advantage."

Sasha said, "Why don't you just sit up here and shoot Galo when comes in? That sure sounds a lot easier and cleaner."

"I would," the agent answered. "But I don't want to take a chance on missing him and starting a gunfight. That's the last thing I want to do. I need to be close enough so there's no margin for error. Remember — Galo doesn't know we're here. Plus, we're going to make sure he believes Boon is the only other person here, which should make him careless. I want to keep it that way as long as we can until I can do what I need to do."

Dohir stared at the agent, carefully appraising him again. He recalled comparing Hollenbeck to a Boy Scout the first time he'd met him, and Boon couldn't shake that comparison. No matter how hard he tried, he couldn't reconcile the agent's words with what the man planned on doing.

"All of you have walkie-talkies," Hollenbeck continued, holding up the small radio. "Hold the chatter down, but keep everyone up to date on what's happening. We need to know what's going on and where they all are. If this goes to plan, Galo should follow the bucket with the phone all the way to the big oven. Hopefully by himself. That's when I'll take over. Questions?"

Boon took that opportunity to turn on all the lights in the factory. He walked over to the big window and motioned everyone over. When they were gathered close with their noses against the glass, he pointed down below him.

"See the main door over there where you came in? That's where they should enter, too. To the right of that is the start of the assembly line. That's where the bucket with the phone will be. The conveyor belt moves in a sort of double S through the shop. Sasha and I will be up here watching, and we'll do our best to keep the lights on over them as much as possible." He moved to the right and pointed at a huge square machine the size of a garage at the other end of the building. "That's the oven Hollenbeck was talking about."

"That's where I'll be waiting," the agent interjected.

"Yes, that's where he'll be, and where we want Galo to end up. Right in front of the oven, in that big open space. He'll be out in the open with no place to hide."

Dante massaged his chin for a moment. "What if this all goes balls up? What then?"

The agent shrugged. "If that happens, I'll let you know over the radio. Everyone will clear out and never look back. Get the hell out of here, and you never met me and none of this ever happened. Understand?"

Dante took a second to digest that. "And if it all works out?"

"I'll let you know that, too. And you'll all be ten grand richer."

Dante looked around at his men, seemingly deep in thought. He rubbed his chin. "Yeah, well, this shit sounds a lot more dangerous than we thought. Sounds like this Galo and his posse are crazy as fuck. Our price just went up. Let's call it a cost-of-living increase."

Hollenbeck straightened. "Really? We had a deal, Dante."

"Deals change and shit happens," the young man said, his eyes twinkling.

The agent squinted at him. "How much will it take?"

Dante rubbed his chin again. "Fifty grand. Each."

"Done," Boon answered almost immediately. "Fifty thousand for each man. Cash."

The FBI agent opened his mouth to argue but held his tongue. After a few seconds, he said, "Fine. Are we good to go now?"

The Black youth laughed. "Damn, man, now I'm thinking I should of asked for more! You making this too fucking easy!"

"Really?" Boon asked. "How about a hundred thousand each? How's that sound?"

Dante slapped his thigh and winked at Boon. "Woo, I like the way you work, Moneybags. One hundred Gs it is. And once this is over, you and me need to do business again."

Hollenbeck stood up straight and glared at Dohir, his cheeks flushed. "Enough of that. Are we all set? Now, if there aren't any more questions, let's get ready to go. We can't take the chance that Galo will leave the area."

Dante and his men got to their feet and filed out the door, several of them laughing loudly once they crossed the threshold. Boon knew they thought he was crazy, but he didn't care. He hated putting them in danger, and no amount of money was going to ease his guilt if anything happened to them. To be fair, he would have gladly given them whatever they asked for. One hundred thousand per man was peanuts.

When they were out of earshot, Hollenbeck strode up to Boon. "That was an incredibly stupid move. Do you have any concept of the potential problems you just caused? What happens if they get caught with that amount of cash? There's no way they'll be able to explain where they got it. What if they somehow trace it back to you? There's only so much I can do to protect you, you know."

Boon put a hand on Hollenbeck's shoulder and gave it a gentle squeeze. "Relax, Hal," he said, using the agent's first name. "I'm Robin Hood, remember? I take from the rich and give to the poor. These poor guys need it a lot more than I do."

Hollenbeck glared at him and his lips nearly vanished, his eyes hard behind the gold rim glasses. The normally taciturn agent looked like he was seconds away from losing his temper, but then he took a deep breath. When he spoke again, he was back to his normal self. Boon was impressed at the man's self-control. "Let's just make sure we get Galo, okay? If we do, then I probably won't care about the money. After all, it's technically not ours anyway."

"Works for me. I just want this whole shitshow to be over."

"That makes two of us. Sir Jim, are you ready to go?"

At the sound of his name, the portly man grunted and levered himself up from his chair. "Is it showtime?"

"It is indeed. Let's head back out to my car. You can do your part there where it's safe."

When the four left the darkness of the factory behind, the sudden afternoon sunlight blinded Boon for a moment, like he was stepping outside after an afternoon matinee. They walked down the street towards the agent's car, with Sasha and Sir Jim bringing up the rear.

"You okay, old man?" Boon heard her ask him.

"Quite. Thank you for asking, my dear."

"Don't do anything stupid," she said with unexpected warmth. "I'd miss giving you shit all the time."

"I won't. Honestly, this may be the highlight of my year."

"That's fine, but promise me you'll be careful."

"Of course, dear."

The friendly interchange between the two once again reminded Boon how much he had missed with this group. He had no one but himself to blame for so much time lost with his friends, but that admission did nothing to diminish his regret. Even so, hearing the warm banter between the two of them lifted his spirits. Thinking back, perhaps their back-and-forth barbs had always had an undertone of warmth, and Boon had just missed it.

They reached Hollenbeck's car a few minutes later. The agent took one look at how hot and sweaty Sir Jim was from the short walk, so he started the car and turned on the AC. After it had had a chance to cool down, Jim levered himself into the driver's seat. He had to force his substantial stomach behind the steering wheel, an effort which caused him to break out into a full-body sweat all over again. He squirmed side to side, then blew out an expansive breath and finally proclaimed he was as comfortable as possible.

"You sure you're okay?" Hollenbeck asked. "I'd say you could move the seat back, but I'm pretty sure that's as far as it goes."

"I'm fine, thank you," he replied, adjusting his bulk. "Just don't ask me to drive anywhere. That might prove to be problematic."

Sasha stared at him. "We may need the jaws of life to get you out of there when this is all over."

"No worries," he assured her. "Now, before I have to take a deep breath or sneeze, are we going to do this or not?"

"We are," the agent assured him. He shifted his gaze to Boon. "You're up."

Dohir crouched down until he was at eye level with the portly man, wincing ever so slightly at the ache in his ribs. "Like we discussed back at the house when Sasha and I were with Galo's men in your factory in Dayton, one of the guys with them was named Alan. Most of them were Latino, but not this guy. I heard him talk a few times, and he had a very distinctive voice. It was high-pitched, and he had an accent like he was from northern Wisconsin or Minnesota. He held his Os long and stretched his words out more than we would. You know what I mean?"

"I do. I've been working on this ever since." Sir Jim cleared his throat and shook himself, then said, "We're gonna kick back with a Snowshoe Ale at the Packer's game before we fly back to Minnesota. You comin', too, eh?"

Boon's mouth fell open. Sir Jim had nailed the accent perfectly, with the emphasis right where it needed to be. "Holy hell, that's it. That's spot on. Now raise your voice a few octaves. Make it almost as high as Sasha's."

He cleared his throat again. He repeated the sentence, but this time in a voice so high that Boon couldn't believe it was still Sir Jim talking. He sounded so close to Alan it gave him shivers. He turned to Hollenbeck.

"He's got it. It's almost perfect."

Sasha said, "Fuck me, that's amazing. You sound just like him."

The agent smiled and pulled out a piece of paper and a beat-up cell phone from his backpack. He handed both to Sir Jim. The agent pointed to the slip of paper, which had a short paragraph written in neat script.

"We couldn't take chances using just any phone in case Galo has the number, so here's Alan's. It's unlocked for good, thanks to what he mistakenly thought was going to be a plea deal for early release. And here's the script I want you to follow. Galo's number is written on the top. Dial the number, follow the script, and then hang up right away. Got it?"

"Yes, I do."

"And like we talked about in the car earlier, try to sound nervous as hell. Remember, this is a guy who is out of jail and doesn't understand why, and is scared he might go back. Can you do that?"

Sir Jim raised an eyebrow at him, affronted. "Of course I can. I'm a professional, remember? I can sound like Richard Nixon if I want to."

Hollenbeck raised his hands in apology. "Sorry. If you get voicemail, go ahead and follow the script and leave a message. Hopefully, someone answers, but don't let yourself get drawn into divulging more information than what's here. Stick to the message, then hang up fast. Okay?"

"Understood." Sir Jim took a deep breath. "Are we ready?"

The agent held up a finger. He pulled the small walkie-talkie out of his pocket and pushed a button. Dohir heard a click in his one ear, followed by Hollenbecks' voice both in-person and through the earpiece in a strange sort of stereo. "We're ready at this end. If you're not in position, you need to speak up now," he said.

Boon listened for any responses but heard none. The four of them waited a few more seconds just to be sure, but there was only silence. The agent looked at Sir Jim.

"It's go-time," he said.

Sir Jim inhaled deeply, then dialed the number.

25

Boon didn't realize he was holding his breath until the need to exhale was irresistible. He couldn't take his one good eye from Sir Jim holding the phone in front of him as he dialed the number. The big man put the device to his ear and held the script in front of him against the steering wheel. For a moment, Dohir was afraid no one was going to answer, and then Sir Jim flinched ever so slightly.

"Hey, is this Galo? This is Alan," he said, in a scared voice so hauntingly close to the real thing that Boon had to make sure Alan wasn't lurking over his shoulder. "Remember me? I got busted by the Feds with Luis the other night. Yeah, he gave me your number and told me to call you. I was with him at that creepy factory. Up there in Dayton, eh?" He paused while whoever was on the other end said something. After a few seconds, Sir Jim kept going. "Yeah, I'm out. I don't know why, but I'm not lookin' a gift horse in the mouth, neither. Listen–I was getting processed out when I heard these FBI guys talking about some factory down in Cincinnati where that son of a bitch Boon has been hiding out. They're sure he's there, and they said they're gonna raid the place tonight and bust him. I only got part of the address, but I figured I'd see if I could do you a solid and find it. Know what? I'm down the block from it right now."

Sir Jim glanced up at the three of them and sketched a hasty thumbs up as he listened to whoever was on the other end. Boon could hear some faint chatter coming from the receiver, but not well enough to understand what was being said.

"No shit," Sir Jim said. "I'm pretty sure I saw that girl, too. The one that fucked up Pablo, eh? Yeah, the hot one." Sir Jim had to hold the phone away from his ear while whoever was on the other end started shouting something. He winked at Sasha, who covered her mouth with her hand.

"Yeah, you can't miss it. It's a big yellow building that takes up the whole block. Here's the address," he said, and rattled it off. "Now if it's all the same to you, I'm outta here. What? No, there's no fucking way I'm sticking around. Sorry. I'm out, and I plan to stay that way, thank you very much. I figured I owed you this much, eh? I'm gonna lay low for a very long time and, you know, reassess my career choices. Adios, and good luck."

Sir Jim hit the end button, exhaled, and turned to the group. "That was quite exhilarating if I do say so myself!"

"Give that man a fucking Oscar!" Sasha cried out, reaching in and hugging him.

Hollenbeck gave her a second, then nudged her aside. "Who was on the other end?"

"I'm pretty certain it was Galo," he answered. "Heavy Spanish accent? Mad as a hornet the entire time? Do I have that right?"

"I'd say so," Boon admitted.

"What did he say?" the agent demanded impatiently. "I need details."

Sir Jim said, "From what you've described, it had to be him. He didn't seem to care much about me or how I got out, but he was very interested in where you were, Boon. And from what I can tell, Sasha, he doesn't care for you very much either. He demanded I stay here and wait for them, but as you heard I made it pretty clear that wasn't going to happen."

"What else?" Hollenbeck asked.

"There were other people in the background. Some men talking, and a woman, too. She was shouting something. At one point Galo had to tell everyone to shut up so he could talk. In the end, he was barking orders at people in Spanish, but I don't know what he was saying. If I had to guess, I'd say he was rounding up his men to come over here. Then he hung up without so much as a how-do-you-do."

Hollenbeck clapped his hand on Jim's shoulder in thanks, then he took Alan's phone back and powered it down. He pulled out the walkie-talkie.

"Okay, everyone, we're on. Boon, Sasha, and I are heading back and will get into position. The rest of you be ready. They're coming."

"What do you want from me?" Sir Jim asked.

The agent handed him a slip of paper. "Take this. If this goes south, get the hell out of here. See the name and phone number? Find a payphone and contact Special Agent Rob Warrian at that number. Tell him what happened. He's the closest thing to a friend I have at the Bureau. Then ditch the car somewhere and do your best to vanish off the grid forever. All of you. Understand?"

Sir Jim frowned. "I don't like the sound of any of that."

Neither did Boon, but he didn't say anything.

"Let's hope it doesn't come to that," Hollenbeck assured him. "But we need to be prepared just in case."

With a final goodbye, they closed the door and left Sir Jim by himself with the car running and the AC cranked. The three of them hurried back the way they had come. When they stepped into the darkened interior of the factory, the FBI agent removed his tan jacket and holster, then pulled something from his backpack. He slipped on what Dohir recognized as a bullet-proof vest. After the vest and holster were securely in place, he stuffed the coat into the backpack and handed it to Boon.

"In the front pocket is the same information I gave to Jim," he told them. "If anything happens to me and you get out of here, make that call. Then do the same thing I told him. Vanish forever. Run. Run and don't look back. Got it?"

Boon found he was nodding without realizing it. Sasha just stared at him, her eyes showing significantly more white than usual. The fact that she was worried made it even worse.

"Give me your burner phone," the agent instructed. Boon did, and watched as Hollenbeck turned it on. The FBI agent walked over to the beginning of the conveyor belt and dropped it into the solitary five-gallon bucket that was sitting there. The inside of the bucket glowed for a few seconds, then the light faded and went dark. He stepped up to the two of them.

"You know what to do," he told Boon. "Keep them disoriented and off balance. Dante and his men are counting on that. And stay out of sight. You two are our eyes up there. It's up to you to keep us informed. Got it?"

"Yeah," Boon replied, not in the least bit surprised to hear his voice tremble a little. "Just promise me you'll be careful, too."

"You, too. And happy hunting," the agent said with a smile and trotted off in the direction of the huge oven at the back of the factory. They heard his footfalls receding until there was nothing but the sound of their own breathing. Finally, Sasha touched his arm.

"We need to get upstairs," she urged him.

Boon shook himself once, then locked and bolted the door behind them. Together, they hurried upstairs, where he repeated those same steps with the sturdy office door. He killed the lights inside and then moved to the monitors where the security cameras were dutifully showing all angles of the factory, both inside and out. His hands were shaking as he adjusted some settings, more out of nervous energy than anything else. Sasha stepped up and kissed him on the cheek.

"Good luck," she told him.

"Thanks," he said, unable to take his eyes from the multiple screens in front of him.

She moved closer. "This is going to work," she said. "You know how I know that? Because this is your plan, that's why. If there's one thing you're good at, it's setting up something like this."

His eyes flicked over to her for a second. "God, I hope you're right. Especially since this wasn't really a plan at all."

"I am right. And Hollenbeck wouldn't be doing it if he didn't believe in you, too."

He was about to say something when motion in the parking lot camera caught his attention. Two black SUVs were racing towards the factory, and at the last minute, they hit the brakes and skidded into the parking lot. The big vehicles sat there for a few seconds rocking back and forth, then a dozen men and the blond woman piled out. Several of them were armed with shotguns. One of them, a stocky man with shocking white hair and gold chains around his neck, approached the door. He had a small black device in his hand and kept glancing down at it. Boon recognized him immediately.

He grabbed at his walkie-talkie but was so nervous he nearly dropped it. Holding it in both hands, he blurted out, "They're already here, at the main door. There's, ah, twelve of them. A few of them have shotguns. And Galo's with them."

Hollenbeck's steady voice in his ear asked, "Any sign of our friend Gonzalez?"

Boon shook his head, forgetting for a second that the agent couldn't see him. "No. Not that I can see."

"That's okay. Just keep your eyes peeled," the agent replied. "Here we go, people. Time to earn our keep. And remember rule number one: nobody dies."

Sasha and Boon watched the small screens as the men clustered around the door outside. One of them jiggled the doorknob, then put his shoulder into it and tried to force it open. He bounced back and rubbed his arm, but the sturdy steel door didn't give an inch. One of the other men trotted to the back of the nearest SUV and returned with a crowbar. While the others gathered around to shield his actions from anyone driving past, the man rammed the crowbar between the door and the jam and gave it a mighty shove. After a few seconds of straining, the steel door surrendered and popped open. A light near the monitors by Sasha's head flashed red as the alarm was tripped.

"They're in!" Boon said into the walkie-talkie, a lot louder than he had intended.

"Excellent," came Hollenbeck's voice in his earpiece. "Stay sharp, everyone. Boon, fire it up."

Dohir jumped from the monitors to the control panel and began flipping switches one by one, until they were all on. Immediately, a deep rumbling shook the floor as the conveyor belt began moving and the rest of the machines came to life.

"The bucket is on the move," he barked into the radio. Without waiting to see what was happening, he turned on some of the lights on the shop floor where the intruders were standing. He kept flicking them on and off rapid-fire until the area by the entrance resembled some sort of industrial rave. He chanced a quick glance at Sasha.

"What are they doing?" he asked, his voice just loud enough to be heard over the ambient noise.

"They're standing there, trying to figure out what's going on," she replied, her face glowing from the monitors. "Galo has his tracker out and he's pointing it towards the bucket, but he keeps moving it around like he can't pinpoint it." She put a hand to her mouth and laughed. "Oh, man, he looks pissed."

Boon stepped towards the monitors and could see all the intruders now had guns in their hands. Galo was feverishly pointing in different directions as he kept his eyes on the tracker. He motioned for several of his men to move out in one direction as the others hovered near him. The blond woman stuck close to his side.

Sasha said, "Three men just split away from the main group, heading roughly in the direction of the office. The others are staying close to Galo."

"That's your cue, Dante," the FBI agent said as soon as Dohir passed along the information. "Don't do anything stupid. Just take them out."

Boon turned more lights on and off above the heads of the advancing men, keeping them as blind and off-balance as possible. The bucket containing the burner phone had already made it a third of the way around the conveyor belt, so he pushed another button to pause its advance, keeping it tantalizingly close but far enough away not to be spotted.

"Three more have just moved off in the other direction, away from the office towards the far side of the factory," Sasha reported, excitement driving her voice higher. "That leaves Galo with four men and the blond bimbo. Five total. That group hasn't left their spot by the door." Boon repeated everything she said to the group, word for word.

"Dante," came Hollenbeck's voice in Boon's ear, "you and your men take care of this second bunch that just moved away from the main group, too. Be careful."

"Telling me to be careful ain't gonna make me more careful," Dante admonished him softly. "But don't worry. We got eyes on 'em. Keep flickin' those lights, Moneybags."

Boon did. The inside of the factory could have been the epicenter of an electrical storm. The flashing lights threw crazy shadows of the hulking machinery every which way. Dohir flinched when there were several loud bangs and flashes of light well away from them. He was about to demand to know what happened when Dante's chuckle came through his earpiece.

"Nothin' to worry about," the young man said. "Crazy fuckers are scared shitless and shooting at shadows. We good."

"Okay," came Hollenbeck's voice, his relief clear. "Boon, ask Sasha if she's still got eyes on everyone."

Boon glanced over at her and repeated the question. She was staring at the monitors like they were Vegas slot machines about to hit it big, her eyes dancing this way and that. "Yeah, kind of. The lights going on and off make it hard to follow them. Tell him I think the two groups of three have separated a little bit and are advancing toward his position. Galo's group is still by the entrance, but he looks supremely pissed. He's yelling at everyone around him and stomping his feet like a kid having a tantrum."

"We're on it," Dante said when Dohir relayed the information. "Leave those dudes to us."

It was killing Boon not being able to watch what was happening, but he had to do his part at the control panel. He kept turning the lights on and off over all three groups, making sure their eyes never had time to adjust. Just then there was another loud bang almost underneath them that made him jump.

"What's going on?" he shouted into the walkie-talkie.

Seconds passed while he clenched the small radio in front of his face. He looked at Sasha, but she was still focused on the monitors.

"Don't lose your shit, Moneybags," Dante's voice said, a little breathlessly. "We got 'em. All six. They ain't happy, but they ain't goin' nowhere, neither. A few gonna need medical attention when this is over. We're culling the herd, just like ordered."

Boon exhaled noisily. "Okay, thanks. Good work. That just leaves Galo and the group by the door. Sasha, what are they doing?"

She shook her head. "Nothing. Just standing there while Galo screams at them. I wish I could hear what the hell he's saying."

Boon thought for a moment. Then he said into the walkie-talkie, "Hold on. I'm going to give them a little nudge."

He fiddled with some controls, and carefully peered out the office windows. Down below he could see the conveyor belt as it began running in reverse, taking the phone and the bucket closer to Galo's group.

"Any change?" he asked from his post.

Sasha stared straight ahead. "No, he's just… Wait, that did it. He's on the move!"

Boon hurried back and halted the conveyor, his hand hovering over the controls to set it in forward motion again. He kept his eyes fixed on Sasha. Her face was filled with the glow of the monitors, her eyes wide and unblinking. A strand of dark hair hung straight down from her temple.

"He's getting close!" she warned him.

He waited a few seconds longer, then flicked a switch and the bucket began to move forward again, toward the oven.

"What now?" he asked.

"He's still following it, but I think he's figuring it out. He's staring at the conveyor belt. Wait. He's talking to the woman, and…" She finally tore her gaze away from the screens and looked up at Boon. Her face was pale in the glow of the monitors. "Shit. He's pointing up here, right at us. Blondie and one of the men are coming this way. They're headed for the steps!"

"Boon, talk to me! What's happening?" Hollenbeck barked in his ear.

Boon lifted the radio to his mouth. "Um, Hal, I think we're about to have company," he told him.

26

Boon felt the vibrations through the floor as feet pounded up the metal steps outside the office. He was ninety-nine percent sure he had already locked the door, but he did a quick visual check just to be sure. Then he kicked himself when he realized they should have barricaded themselves in with some of the furniture. He took half a step away from the control panel but knew if he left his station he would leave Dante and the others exposed down below. He couldn't do that to them.

"Sasha!" he yelled, pointing madly. "The desks!"

To her credit, it only took her a second to figure out what he meant. She smacked her forehead with her palm, then dashed towards the nearest desk and heaved. The heavy desk inched across the floor as the muscles in her arms and legs strained. The large computer monitor on top slid to the ground with a crash, but they were past the point of caring about giving away their position now. Kicking the shattered equipment aside, she ran to the next nearest desk and rammed it against the first. She had just grabbed an office chair to augment the pile when the doorknob jiggled. The two of them froze, staring at it. There was a pause, then the door itself began to shake as someone outside slammed into it. Boon, vividly recalling how they got into the room at the factory in Dayton, furiously waved Sasha away.

"Watch out! They're going to shoot the door!" he warned her.

At the same moment she danced aside, there was a boom from the hallway. A bulge popped into life near the doorknob, silvery steel suddenly exposed as the paint was blown away. There were two more shots, and on the third one, the doorknob spun off and landed across the room. Someone outside slammed into the door again, and this time it jerked open a few inches, only stopping when it impacted the barricade. As they watched, a pistol gripped in a man's hand was thrust through the narrow opening.

"Get down!" Boon screamed.

The gun went off with a flash and a bang loud enough to deafen them, but the shot went over their heads and thudded harmlessly into the far wall. Sasha quickly grabbed the monitor from the floor and slammed the edge down on the man's arm as hard as she could. There was a scream from outside as the wounded arm was yanked back.

"Boon!" came Hollenbeck's voice in his ear. "What's happening up there?"

He didn't have time to answer, although he never stopped working the lights in the shop. Sasha was in a crouched position and panting hard. She glanced at him.

"Are they gone?" she asked.

"If they are, it's just to get reinforcements. Pretty sure they figured out we're running the show from up here now. They'll try again. Quick, shove some more desks in the way."

She didn't have to be told twice. Sasha ran around to the next closest desk and jammed it against the first two. She was going back for a fourth when he felt vibrations through his feet again.

"Here they come!" he yelled. "Get away from the door!"

She jumped away just as another boom came from beyond the door, although this one was much louder, like a cannon going off. A hole the size of a cantaloupe was blasted into the wall next to the door. Shards of wood and drywall showered the inside of the office, and the very distinctive stench of gunpowder tainted the air. Boon took half a step toward Sasha when there was a second boom, and another hole appeared below the first. With a start, he guessed what they were doing and ran to her side.

"They're cutting a doorway through the wall!" he screamed, pulling her away.

The two stood there helpless as the shotgun continued blowing away ragged chunks of drywall and two by fours, until there was an opening roughly big enough for a person to crawl through. Sasha jerked out of Boon's grip and pressed herself next to the gaping hole. Just as Boon took a step towards her, the long barrel of the shotgun was thrust through the opening and into the office. He saw what she was going to do, and lunged at her.

"Sasha, no!"

She grabbed the barrel with both hands and with a scream yanked as hard as she could. The rest of the shotgun and the man holding it were pulled into the office. Their attacker's dark, contorted face was a mixture of anger and surprise. She forced the barrel up just as the intruder pulled the trigger again, and several ceiling tiles overhead were obliterated. Dust and chunks of acoustic tiles rained down on them.

"Um, little help here!" she yelled, straining against the intruder.

Boon dodged away from the shotgun and took a swing at their attacker, ignoring the pain lancing into his side. His faulty depth perception threw off his aim, so instead of hitting the man's jaw as he intended, his fist caught the intruder behind the ear. Boon's hand exploded in pain as the attacker's head snapped sideways, and the assailant staggered and went down on one knee. Sasha took that opportunity to let go of the gun, and in the same motion delivered a powerful kick to his head. The heel of her foot caught him just below the temple, and he slammed against the desk. His eyes rolled back in his head and he went limp at their feet. She dove for the shotgun and aimed it at the opening.

"Fuckin' A that was close," she said, panting. "Remind me to thank Duke back at the gym. He taught me that." Her hair and face were covered in white dust as fine as flour. Splinters of wood and drywall littered her shoulders and stuck to her clothes. Sasha took a few steps back until she was next to Boon. She spared a second to glance at him.

"You okay?" she asked, breathlessly.

He nodded yes before he really had time to figure that out. Then he noticed his right hand was throbbing and discovered he couldn't move his fingers without pain shooting up his arm. "Yeah. Maybe. I think I broke my hand."

"Sorry, dear, but we'll have to worry about it later," she told him, ever the pragmatist. "Keep doing your thing with the lights while I guard this new doorway. We're not done yet."

He kicked through the debris on the floor. Once at the control panel, Boon resumed working the lights in the shop below with his one good hand. He was wondering if Sasha could guard the opening and monitor the shop floor at the same time, when movement by the hole caught his attention.

"Watch out!" he shouted.

That was the instant the blond woman stepped into the opening. Sasha saw her, too, and she leveled the shotgun and pulled the trigger. The blast in the small space was truly deafening this time. Sparks and smoke shot from the barrel. Boon stood there in shock, half of him terrified at what Sasha had done, the other half relieved she'd had the guts to do it. A red shell was ejected from the bottom of the shotgun and bounced on the floor at her feet. Smoke trickled from its scorched end.

"Ooh, you're pretty quick, missy, I'll give you that," came a low, syrupy voice from outside the room. "But I'm faster. And what are you going to do now? The gun's empty, you know. I've been counting."

The blond stepped through the opening. In her hand was a baseball bat, which she spun around as comfortably as a professional ball player stepping to the plate. She was smiling, the corners of her big red lips curled up. The blue of her eyes somehow managed to glimmer in the low light. She didn't appear scared, or even nervous. What she looked like, Boon thought, was straight-up crazy.

Sasha pulled the trigger again, but there was a dull click and nothing more. Quick as a snake, the blond woman leaped toward her with the bat coming down in a sweeping arc. Sasha barely managed to lift the shotgun to parry the blow, but the woman's swing was so powerful it almost knocked the weapon out of her hands. The blond spun a full three hundred and sixty degrees and brought the bat down in a two-handed, wood-chopping arc. This time the bat glanced off the raised gun and smacked into Sasha's shoulder, who crashed to the floor with a yelp of pain.

"See? I'm more than just a pretty face, missy," she said in a pleasant, Disney-princess voice, one utterly contrary to her actions. "I'm Galo's right hand, and I can't begin to tell you how happy he's going to be that I've got both of you. I always want to make him happy. A happy Galo is much better than an angry one."

She lifted the bat over her head with both hands again, but Boon launched himself the short distance between them and tackled her before she could complete her swing. The pair stumbled in a drunken pirouette across the room and smashed into the far wall. He tried to hold onto her, but his injured hand was next to useless and she was maniacally strong. She roughly forced him off and wriggled free, then snatched up the bat, her chest heaving. Boon stumbled backward and tripped, going down hard on his back. A twisted look of joy filled her round face.

"That hurt," she said. She strode towards him, smacking the barrel of the bat into her open palm.

Boon crab-walked backward as fast as he could. He made it several feet until his head slammed into the wall on the far side. With a flash of panic, it dawned on him that he had nowhere else to go. The blond woman stood over him. She wiped a hand across her face. The smeared lipstick turned her grinning mouth into a gruesome-looking wound.

"You're in over your head, little man," she told him in her lilting voice, lifting the bat again. "Say goodnight."

Boon flinched and raised his arm to ward off the coming blow. As the bat started to come down, there was a dull thud and the woman's head snapped sideways. She spun completely around and then crashed to the floor. Laying there with her arms and legs spread out like a snow angel, she spasmed violently several times, then seemed to deflate as consciousness left her. The bat rolled out of her limp grip. The entire side of her face was thick with blood, her hair going from blond to red as he watched. Dohir blinked and slowly lowered his arm, clueless to what just happened. Then he looked up. Where the blond had been standing was Dante, a steel pipe in his hands. The young man gazed down at Boon and shook his head in exaggerated sadness.

"Damn, Moneybags. You gots to be more careful," he admonished. "How you gonna pay me if you dead?"

Boon suppressed a laugh that was more manic than amused. He held up his good hand. Dante easily helped him up, then the two of them stepped over the inert form of the blond and hurried to Sasha's side. She was sitting up but was cradling her left arm in her right. Dohir quickly knelt down and reached out to her.

"Oh my god, Sasha," he said, his voice thick with worry. "Are you okay?"

"I think that bitch broke my arm," she hissed. "Give me a hand up."

He hurried behind her and lifted her to her feet. She wobbled for a moment, wincing. Steadying herself by leaning against him, she tried to move her arm and grimaced in pain. Her eyes were screwed shut.

"Okay, I don't know if it's broken or not, but it hurts like hell," she admitted.

Boon wanted to help her, but he didn't know how. He did, however, know one thing: the fight wasn't over yet, and to ensure the safety of the others, he had to act. He'd sworn to himself that he would do anything to save his friends, and he was not going to let them down. He turned to Dante.

"What's going on down there?" he asked. He patted his pockets as he searched for the walkie-talkie, but it was gone. It must have been lost in the scuffle. He gave the room a quick survey, but couldn't spot it in all the debris.

Dante said, "I think all that's left is that Galo dude and one other. Last I saw, they was headed towards the oven. I heard all that shit goin' down up here, and figured you could use some help."

Boon held out his hand. "You figured right. Give me your radio, please."

"Can't. One of those fuckers busted it when I was tying them up."

Shit, he thought. "Okay, stay up here and protect Sasha. I'm going down there."

"You can't!" Sasha protested. "You'll get killed!"

He turned to her, and his face softened. "Maybe. But if we don't stop Galo, this will all be for nothing. I can't let that happen."

She opened her mouth to object but stopped when she saw the determination in his eyes. He leaned in and gave her a kiss. Her dusty lips had a bitter tang from the powder and debris, but he didn't mind. He gifted her a warm smile.

"Remember what we said about waiting five or six weeks?" he asked her, his hand on her cheek.

She grinned then, and her eyes may have been glistening. "You bet I do. It's marked on my calendar with a big smiley face."

"Good. I'm looking forward to it, too," Boon said. He held his hand against her cheek, then hurried out through the makeshift hole in the wall.

"Dammit, Boon," she called after him. "You be careful!"

He ran down the steps. When he got to the bottom, he hugged the wall and hurried towards the oven at the other end of the shop. The lights in the center of the building were on, but even so, he couldn't see anyone. He was moving as quickly as he could in the near-darkness when he almost plowed into some of Dante's men. There were three of them, gathered together with pistols and lengths of pipe in their hands. They were standing guard over some of Galo's thugs, who were on the floor and glaring daggers at him. The men had blood running freely from wounds on their heads. Their hands and feet were securely lashed together with the zip ties.

"Where's Hollenbeck?" Boon whispered, glancing around.

The young man closest to him jerked his head to the side. "Last I saw he was back by that big-ass oven. Waitin' for the white-haired dude."

"Got it. Have you seen him? That white-haired guy?"

"Sorry, man. We been busy with these guys. Dante told us to wait here and guard 'em."

Boon cursed under his breath while he considered his next move. He started to leave, then took a step back and pointed. "Mind if I borrow that?"

The young man shrugged and passed him the steel pipe. With a nod, he moved on toward what he hoped was still Hollenbeck's location. Breathing faster than he should have been considering the level of exertion, he stuck to the shadows as he went, dodging around massive steel presses and other unidentifiable industrial machines. The metal pipe was cool and heavy as he hefted it. It wasn't much of a weapon compared to guns, but it would have to do. He belatedly wished he had taken their walkie-talkie, but it was too late now.

Overhead, the lights began going on and off again, and he knew Sasha and Dante had taken up where he had left off. He whispered thanks to them under his breath and kept his eye trained on the space around him. About thirty yards away he spotted the vast square bulk of the oven. The mouth of the huge contraption was about twenty feet wide and three feet high, big enough to swallow a dozen cans at a time. Deep inside the bowels of the oven, the machine radiated an ominous red glow reminding him of coals at the base of a campfire. Using that as a guide, he pressed forward. He couldn't see Hollenbeck yet but knew the FBI agent had to be close.

When he was almost to the open space in front of the oven, he spotted Galo and one of his goons. The drug lord was holding the tracker in front of him and pointing it at the lone bucket that had nearly completed the entire circuit and was about to enter the oven's maw. The pair moved forward quickly and Galo snatched the bucket off the line. Boon saw him reach inside and pull out the phone. He held it for a moment, then dashed it to the ground in fury. The tracking device in front of him again, he spun around slowly, searching. Even from here, Boon could see how the man shook with rage. It was at that moment that Hollenbeck chose to step out from the shadows, his gun leveled at the two men from only a dozen feet away.

Galo's man began to raise his own pistol the instant the pair saw the agent. A half-second after that, Boon was surprised to find he was sprinting toward them as fast as he could, the metal bar raised high. The two attackers had their backs to him and couldn't see him coming. Ignoring the pain in his side, he covered the short distance in the time it took Galo's thug to aim at Hollenbeck. Boon had been a standout baseball player in his day. Letting muscle memory take over, he swung the steel pipe with all the gusto he could manage, as if he were aiming for the fences. The pipe smashed into the man's head with a crunch that Boon felt up through his arm and into his shoulder, and the gunman went down hard. The pistol clattered away. It all happened so suddenly that neither Galo nor Hollenbeck had been able to react. Boon's forward momentum carried him beyond the downed man, and he ended up next to the agent, panting. Hal lifted an eyebrow at him.

"Good timing," Hollenbeck said, loud enough to be heard over the din.

Boon stared down at the attacker on the ground. Blood was running freely from a nasty, swollen gash above his ear. The man moaned and a hand fluttered up towards the wound, which was already visibly swelling. He was mumbling something inaudible just before he passed out. Dohir was thankful to see that the guy was still alive, although he wasn't sure how. Maybe he was losing his touch.

"You're welcome," he answered, still breathing hard. This close to the oven he could feel the heat pouring from it like an entrance to hell. The back of his neck was slowly being roasted.

Hollenbeck swiveled his gaze back to Galo. The cartel boss was staring at them, his eyes burning bright. His hands were at his sides, but they were balled into tight fists. Sweat coursed freely down his face.

"So, you're Galo," the agent said, nodding at him. "My name is Hal Hollenbeck, special agent for the Federal Bureau of Investigation. I've been trying to meet you for a long time."

The drug lord spit on the floor. His face screwed up in anger and he launched into a tirade of coarse-sounding Spanish that flew completely over Boon's head. The hard consonants and trilled Rs came across in what was likely a long and involved curse. Hollenbeck listened for a moment, then replied to him in Spanish. Dohir stared at him.

"You speak Spanish? That would have been nice to know. What's he saying?"

"It involves our ancestors and what he plans to do to us and our families," Hollenbeck told him, not taking his eyes from the ranting drug lord. "It's very colorful. I just told him to shut up, which he didn't like either. He does not like being told what to do."

As Boon watched, the agent refocused the gun, sighting down the barrel at Galo's chest. The drug lord's diatribe chopped off in mid-sentence, and he stared at the mouth of the pistol without a shred of fear. He crossed his arms and glared at Hollenbeck as if daring him to pull the trigger. The three of them waited, but nothing happened.

"What are you waiting for?" Boon asked, his eyes flicking back and forth between the two men. "This is what you wanted, isn't it?"

Hollenbeck's lips compressed, and his stare never wavered behind the gold-rimmed glasses. But, after a few moments, he exhaled and lowered the weapon a fraction of an inch. His shoulders sagged as if dragged down by insurmountable weight.

"Damn, I can't do it," he said angrily, wincing and dropping the barrel a few more inches. "I've run this scenario through my head a hundred times and in a hundred different ways. I've spent hours rationalizing why this is the optimal resolution. But now that it's here in front of me when I've got this bastard dead to rights, I can't do it. I can't shoot someone in cold blood. Not like this."

Despite the scene playing out in front of him, Boon almost smiled. It turned out his appraisal of the agent had been right along; Hollenbeck wasn't a cold-hearted killer. After everything that had happened to him and his friends, this confirmation of the man's humanity was welcome.

On the other hand, if the agent couldn't follow through with this and Galo got away, then everything they'd gone through would be for nothing. Both options were awful, but he couldn't let this maniac win.

He couldn't!

"Shit, now you're taking the high ground?" Boon demanded of the agent, shaking his finger at the drug lord. "Look at him! He's there, right where you've always wanted him. And now you're not going to take the shot? If you don't, he's going to walk free again, right? You know he will!"

Hal tore his eyes off Galo only long enough to do a double-take at Boon. "Really? After all the grief you guys gave me about this? Now you want me to kill him?"

"Hal, this shit will never end if you don't!" Boon felt a sudden rush of blood to his head, and couldn't believe what he was about to say. He jammed his hand out and was surprised at how steady it was. "Damnit, if you can't, then give me the gun and…and I'll do it myself!"

Before Hollenbeck could reply, a towering form emerged from the shadows and a massive fist slammed down on the agent's arm. The gun crashed to the floor, and a monster-sized hand snatched it up. As the two of them stood there in shock, Gonzalez eased his bulk into the light between them and Galo. The giant's pock-marked face was shrouded in shadows beneath his massive brow, the sight made even more horrible by the dancing lights. He loomed over the two of them, wider than a doorway and just as tall. The pistol was aimed directly at them from three feet away. He couldn't miss from this distance. No one could. The steel pipe in Boon's hand felt utterly useless.

"*Lo siento.* I can't let you do that," the huge man said in clear but accented English.

Wide-eyed, both men took a defensive step backward. Galo began clutching his sides and laughing. A cruel smile filled with yellowing teeth broke out across his face. The gold necklaces glittered in the reddish light. His eyes danced with joy.

"I am lord of El Grupo Nuevo, and I will always win! You are both stupid and weak. Kill them! Kill them both!" he ordered the giant, pointing at Boon and Hollenbeck in glee.

Then Gonzalez turned and shot Galo in the stomach.

27

Galo's white shirt exploded in blood, the bright red rapidly expanding as if it were alive. He stumbled backward. Too stunned and in shock to properly break his fall, he toppled over like a statue pushed off a pedestal. He landed hard, his head cracking on the unyielding floor loud enough to be heard over the noise. Boon stared at Gonzalez and the wounded man, gawking like an idiot. His reeling mind was incapable of shifting gears fast enough to keep up with the pace of the events around him. The giant glanced at the pistol that looked like a toy in his hand, then began methodically wiping away his fingerprints with his sleeve. When he was satisfied with his handiwork, he grunted and tossed the pistol into the shadows.

Boon glanced at Hollenbeck. For the first time since he had met the agent, the man was speechless. In fact, Hal was so shocked he wasn't able to form a coherent sentence. A few seconds passed before he could gather his wits about him enough to speak.

"I don't understand. What the hell did you just do?"

Gonzalez peered down at him from his nearly seven-foot height. He shrugged his shoulders. In accented English, he said, "How do you say it? Now we are even."

The FBI agent stared at him, his eyes incredulous behind his glasses. "What do you mean, 'Now we're even?' Are you talking about that time back in the jungle? Is that it?" Hollenbeck asked.

The huge man stared at him for a moment, then dipped his head once.

Hollenbeck slapped his forehead and pointed at Galo. "What is wrong with you? I needed him alive, so I could question him. Now I've got nothing, plus you'll have the entire cartel after you! They'll never stop until they kill you."

The giant waved that away. "Do not concern yourself with that."

"Don't concern myself?" Hollenbeck snapped. "What are you talking about?."

Gonzalez thought for a moment, his face working as he carefully considered his words. "You and your companions saved my life once, and for that I am thankful. But that is not the only reason," Gonzalez said, nudging Galo with his foot. He swiveled his huge shaggy head back and forth, looking every bit like a lion shooing away flies. "I am tired of taking orders from *pendejos* like this. He is vengeful and stupid and would eventually do great damage or even destroy the cartel. I did all of us a favor by getting rid of him. He will not be missed. Also," he added with a sly grin, holding his hands out and turning to encompass all four corners of the darkened shop, "there are no witnesses. Who can say what happened here? Remember, it was your gun that shot him."

Just then Galo moaned loudly and twitched on the ground. His eyes fluttered open, but they saw nothing except his own life leeching away. Blood was oozing out the sides of his mouth and staining his heavy cheeks. He was not dead yet, but Boon didn't have to be a medical professional to recognize that he probably would be soon.

"Do you know why he was here?" Hollenbeck asked the giant urgently, suddenly remembering his mission. "He wouldn't leave his compound unless it was for something big. What was he doing here? Who was he going to see?"

The giant pointed with his chin at Boon. "Besides wasting time trying to kill him? No, he did not tell me. He did not tell anyone. He kept that information to himself."

Hollenbeck hurriedly got down on one knee next to the dying man. He rapidly dug through Galo's pockets and pulled out his phone. He shook it at Dohir, who dropped the steel pipe long enough to take it.

"Can you get into it?" Hollenbeck asked hurriedly.

Boon shook his head. "No. It's locked, and I have no clue what the code is."

Gonzalez rolled his eyes in exasperation at the two of them. He strode behind Galo and easily picked him up under the armpits. The wounded man let out a bark of pain before promptly passing out. The giant motioned Boon closer, who quickly figured out what he was doing. He shoved the phone up to Galo's face. He held it there until it unlocked.

"What am I looking for?" he asked the FBI agent, his voice rushed.

Hollenbeck clenched his eyes tight in thought. "Um, texts. Recent calls. Voice messages. Anything to help us figure out why he's here."

Boon quickly searched through the phone's contents, then stopped when he came to the list of recent calls. He saw a number near the top, and time seemed to stand still while he stared at it.

"Do you have what you need?" the giant asked.

Boon said, almost in a daze, "Yeah, I think I do."

"Good." With that solitary word, Gonzalez grabbed the unconscious man by the hair and dragged him to the conveyor at the base of the oven. He effortlessly tossed the limp figure onto the belt and watched dispassionately as the body began trundling towards the red-hot maw.

"Holy shit, what are you doing?" Boon shouted. Both he and Hollenbeck rushed forward, but the giant raised his massive arms and held them at bay as easily as a parent would restrain their children from a busy street.

"He is not dead yet," Gonzalez said. "And none of us can take the chance he might survive. Besides, this is a good end for him. Trust me. He did far worse to others more times than you can imagine."

"But he's going to be burned alive in there! You can't do that," Boon shouted, pleading, his hands outstretched. Yes, he wanted Galo dead, but not like this! The heat from the oven on his face was strong enough to be painful, even at this distance. He was straining forward, but Gonzalez didn't budge. Hollenbeck lunged at him, and the towering man batted him away. The agent crashed to the ground.

As they watched in horror, Galo's limp form trundled ever closer to the glowing mouth of the oven. When he was only a few feet away, the ends of his hair began to crinkle and smolder, like tiny wisps of smoke from a burning cigarette. Boon tried to force the giant's arm away again, but it was like pushing aside a parked car. He fleetingly considered running back to the office and reversing the conveyor belt, but there was no time.

The body of the unconscious man inched closer to the oven, and as he did so, his white shirt began to crisp and turn brown. The corners of his collar blackened and curled up. With expressions frozen in horror, they watched as the drug lord's long hair burst into flames. It was at that moment that Galo woke and became intimately aware of what was happening to him. He screamed and struggled to sit up, but then his clothing seemed to explode all around him, engulfing him in yellow and red flames. He fell back down, his body arched in agony. The almost inhuman howl of terror that sliced through the air was cut mercifully short as his body vanished in flames. A second later there was some weak thrashing and another flash of bright light, and whatever was left of the man disappeared from sight forever. The only noise after that was the rumbling of the conveyor belt as it emotionlessly continued inching along. Boon's stomach convulsed as an overwhelming stench of singed hair and burnt meat rolled across them.

Hollenbeck staggered to his feet, his face pale and covered in a sheen of sweat and dirt. The fire from the oven was reflected in his glasses, lending him a sinister look that couldn't have been farther from the truth. Boon's knees wobbled, and he had to grab hold of a nearby railing to keep from falling over. Sweat from a combination of nausea and the intense heat rolled down his temples and stung his eyes.

"Good lord, how could you do that?" the agent muttered.

Gonzalez shrugged nonchalantly as if this sort of thing happened every day. "He deserved this, and more," he repeated, staring for a moment at the oven. Then he turned and began to walk away.

"Wait. Where are you going? You can't just leave!" Hollenbeck protested, charging after him. "Not after all this!"

The huge man grabbed the front of the agent's vest and tossed him backward. Hollenbeck hurtled through the air and landed hard on the floor, sliding a dozen feet before coming to a stop. He stayed down this time, moaning in pain. Boon rushed to his side. Gonzalez stared down at them, seemingly miles tall from that angle.

"And take the men," the giant answered, turning to leave and waving a hand around him. "They are yours. Consider them a parting gift."

"No, goddammit, I can't let you go, not after what you did," Hollenbeck shouted, levering himself up on his elbows. But as the two of them watched from the floor, the behemoth strode away into the darkness. Within seconds, his towering form was consumed by the shadows, becoming simply another massive shape on the shop floor. The pair remained where they were in stunned silence, neither of them able to come to grips with what had just happened. Finally, with Boon's help, the FBI agent managed to get to his feet. He absently rubbed the back of his head where it had impacted the floor.

"Galo's phone," he said, wincing and holding out his other hand.

Boon's heart jumped. "Oh, damn. I forgot about that!" He held the device out, but his shoulders slumped in disappointment. "Ah, shit. It's locked up again."

"And there's certainly no way the facial recognition will work now," Hollenbeck muttered, nodding in the direction the giant had taken. "I wonder if that was part of his plan, too."

Boon felt his stomach flip-flop dangerously again at the mere mention of what they had seen. The back of his throat filled with thick, gooey saliva, and he nearly gagged. "Ah, no, it won't."

"But I saw your face. Earlier. You have something, right?" the agent asked, leaning towards him.

Boon gulped. "Yeah, I think I do. I saw a phone number I recognized. Even more important, I'm pretty sure I figured out what Galo was doing here."

Despite himself, Hollenbeck's dirty face broke into a grin. He wiped away some of the sweat and grime with the back of his hand. "Bless you and that memory of yours, Boon Dohir, but it'll have to wait. We need to round up Galo's men and call for backup. And we need to get Dante and his guys out of here. There's going to be a huge police presence here pretty soon. Are you up to that?"

Boon groaned. "Pretty sure I don't have a choice, do I?"

"Nope. Not really."

28

Up until then, Boon had never truly understood just how much clout an FBI badge carried. It was like the magic wand of law enforcement. The Cincinnati Police were technically not subservient to the Bureau, but when they arrived in force they were so deferential to Hollenbeck and his authority they barely questioned the events of the afternoon. In fact, all the agent had to do was wave his badge and utter the words "national security," and every last cop clammed up and followed orders like it was their own idea. Those of Galo's men who could walk were taken into custody on the spot. The rest, who had been on the unfortunate end of additional attention from Dante's group, had to be stretchered out. No matter their condition, horizontal or vertical, Hollenbeck gave strict orders that no one was to speak to them, not unless they wanted the full weight of the FBI to come crashing down on their careers. Still zip-tied, the men were herded into armored vans or ambulances and taken away to jail or the hospital.

The parking lot was surrounded by lengths of yellow caution tape. Sasha and Boon stood to the side. She leaned her head against him as they watched the surreal scene play out before them. He put his good arm across her shoulder and hugged her close, relishing this novel, peaceful moment. Now that the worst was over, he began to wonder what might become of the two of them. Their relationship had been formed in the crucible of a crisis, and he was worried about how they might move on from here. He truly hoped they would, and not simply because he was tired of living like a hermit. No, he had always been fascinated by her intelligence and awed by her physical capabilities. But now he was seeing her as so much more. She was multifaceted and complex, with a tender side of her that had never been revealed to him before. Boon hoped he would have the chance to learn everything he could about her. He tilted his head down onto hers and the gentle aroma of shampoo tickling his nose made him smile, just like it had when they had first shared a bed. After everything they had been through, that simple bit of normalcy was a wonderful thing.

When the police were done rounding up the remaining attackers, several EMTs pushing a gurney came through the door. On it was strapped the blond woman, her hair and face a mass of blood. Unlike the others, however, she wasn't taking her capture in silence.

"You fuckers are going to pay for this!" she screamed into the sky, her words slurred. A concussion, Boon knew, could do that to a person. "He's going to kill all of you! You have no idea what you're in for. You and everyone you care about are going to regret this for the rest of your short fucking lives!"

Apparently, no one had gotten around to telling her about the demise of her boss. That, or Hollenbeck had intentionally omitted that fact for some reason. Boon had told the agent about her professed relationship to Galo, and how important she might be. Because of that, several police officers joined her as she was lifted into the back of an ambulance. As it pulled away, they could still hear her vitriolic threats even over the howl of the siren.

"Is that it?" Sasha asked quietly, watching it take off down the road. "Is this all over now?"

Boon gave her a light squeeze. "Not quite, but almost. There's one last piece of the puzzle we need to take care of."

Sasha started to ask what he meant, but just then Hollenbeck walked up to them. The expression on his face was neutral, showing neither joy nor concern. Considering what they had just been through, Boon couldn't fathom how he managed to pull that off. He wondered if the agent practiced that specific look in a mirror, and figured he would have to to get it just right.

"Okay, the messy part is done," he told them. He took a deep breath, then addressed Boon directly. "You ready to wrap this up? If you're right, then the end is in sight."

"Yeah, let's do this. You may enjoy this stuff, but I don't. If it's okay with you, I'd like to go back to my boring life now."

Sasha elbowed him gently in the side, just hard enough to make his ribs twitch. "I hope you don't mean that," she warned him. "You and I have some unfinished business to attend to once we're all healed up."

He held her at arm's length and looked down into her eyes. Her words had been lighthearted, but the complex expression on her face was not. Boon wasn't sure he could define it, but it seemed like one of concern mixed with a dash of her signature pugilistic defiance. He could see then that Sasha would not only fight for him but would fight to keep him, too. She would not willingly go back to the way they were before, not now, and he was fine with that. He gave her a genuine smile and hugged her as hard as his battered body would allow.

"I take it back," he amended, finally beginning to understand not only what they meant to each other, but what she truly meant to him, too. "What I meant to say was, we're ready to start a new chapter in *our* lives. Different than before, but hopefully a lot more boring, too."

Hollenbeck permitted a small grin to break through his stoic façade. "Makes sense. By the way, has anyone ever told you two that you make a cute couple?"

"Actually, no," Boon answered. "But I appreciate it."

The agent accepted the thanks, then his mercurial grin vanished as quickly as it had come. Once again all business, he stated, "We need to get going. Sasha, how's your arm?"

She flexed it a few times, wincing a little as she did so. "I won't be kicking ass in the ring anytime soon. The EMT didn't think it was broken but said I should get an X-ray just to make sure. Same with Boon's hand."

The agent said, "That's good, but unfortunately we don't have time. We'll take both of you to get checked out as soon as we can. Right now, I need to drop you and Sir Jim off at the house and get Steve."

"What about Steve's SUV?" Boon asked.

"Give me the keys. I'll have someone take it to his house later. I need to talk to all of you first."

As they were getting ready to leave, the last group of EMTs and plainclothes police came out the door. Between them, they were lugging a large, formless black bag that sagged in the middle. The contents appeared too small to be a person, but there was no doubt what it contained. The trio remained mute as they watched them carry it out to the last ambulance and swing it into the back. There was a distinctive whiff of charred meat.

"Oh, god," Sasha whispered, her nose wrinkled up in distaste. She waved a hand in front of her face and paled a few shades. "Is that what I think it is?"

"I'm afraid so," Hollenbeck grunted.

"Ugh. If I wasn't a vegetarian before, I sure as shit would be now," she said.

Several uniformed policemen were still stationed at the door. Hollenbeck gave them some final orders, then motioned to Sasha and Boon to follow him. Together, the three walked down the block to the agent's car. When they arrived, they found Sir Jim still wedged between the driver's seat and the steering wheel with the AC at full blast. His face was flushed in righteous anger and he was breathing so hard his cheeks puffed out.

"Good lord, it's about time," the big man snapped, waving a meaty fist at them. "It would have been nice to know what the hell was going on. I've been worried sick out here!"

"Sorry," Boon said, not unkindly. "We've been a little busy."

Jim inspected each one of them in turn and was quick to come to a conclusion. "I presume from the expressions on your faces that it's over. Am I correct?" he asked the FBI agent.

Hollenbeck didn't answer but helped tug him out of the car. After both feet were planted on the sidewalk and the big man had a chance to catch his breath, the four quietly piled back in. Boon sat next to the agent up front and eased his seat forward so Sir Jim could fit behind him. Once they pulled into traffic and were underway, the agent's shoulders slumped and he shrunk a little in his seat, as if he had aged decades in seconds. Fresh wrinkles born of stress were etched in the corners of his eyes.

"Yes, it's over," he finally answered, exhaling. "You won't have to worry about Galo ever again. None of us will."

Sir Jim leaned forward and opened his mouth to ask what had happened, but Sasha touched his arm and shook her head. He accurately read the mood of the room and decided not to press the issue. With a nod at her, he settled back in his seat and stared out the window. As they headed north, the inside of the car was eerily quiet except for the humming of the tires on the road and the occasional clicking of the turn signal as they navigated traffic. Hollenbeck drove with such regard for the law that it was slightly annoying, but Boon could see how tight his hands were on the steering wheel, as if that circle of steel and plastic were the only thing keeping him from tumbling into an abyss. Periodically glancing at him in the driver's seat, he realized that, as emotionless as the seasoned agent appeared on the surface, inside he was anything but. The events of the last few hours had to be tearing him up.

"You know what?" Hollenbeck said after they had gone a few more miles. His voice was light and casual, almost as if he were talking to himself or a group of friends at a bar. "I think I'm going to step away from the Bureau for a while. I've been doing this a long time. I could use a break."

Boon agreed. "Can't say I blame you."

Sasha caught the agent's reflection in the rear-view mirror. "Me, neither. Got anything planned?"

"Oh, I don't know. Maybe I'll take a vacation. I haven't done that in a while. I've got a condo on the beach south of Ft. Myers. I could spend some time down there. Open a bait shop or something low-stress like that."

"That sounds nice. You deserve some rest."

The agent seemed pleased with the confirmation. "I do, don't I?"

Twenty minutes later, they pulled into the long driveway of the house in West Chester. They drove slowly up to the back door. Hollenbeck put the car in park and removed his glasses. He took a few seconds to absently polish them on his jacket. After he slid them back on, he turned to Boon.

"I know this may seem like a big ask, but you and Sasha can never discuss what happened back there," he told them, motioning with his thumb towards Cincinnati. "The fewer people that know the details, the better. For them, and for the rest of us. They can't tell what they don't know. It's safer for everyone that way."

Boon's initial reaction was one of disbelief. How could the agent even suggest that? After all, the entire group had been involved in this almost from the beginning, some of them more than others. They deserved to know. No, they had a right to know.

But after he gave more consideration to the potential ramifications, both legal and otherwise, the rational side of him began to have second thoughts. This was Hollenbeck's world, and they were just passing through it. Besides, the vision of Galo's final moments was something he wouldn't wish on anyone, not even in a retelling. That horrific sight was going to be the genesis of night terrors for decades, and sharing it would serve no useful purpose.

"Yeah, I agree," he said, then turned to Sasha for her take.

Her eyes flicked between the two of them as if she couldn't believe the subject was even up for debate. "Fuck, yeah. I couldn't see much of what happened from where I was in the office, but what I saw was gruesome as hell. No one needs to have that image fried into their brains, if you know what I mean. I'm with you. This stays between the three of us."

Just then the back door of the house banged open, and Steve Kempler came barreling towards the car like he planned on tackling it. Never one to keep his emotions in check, his round, expressive face was crimson with outrage. Miles and Clem were hot on his heels. Miles' mouth was drawn down and his eyes were thin slits. In his own way, Boon thought the normally mellow musician may have been more pissed off than Kempler.

"Dohir, you and me gotta have a talk," Steve roared, rushing up to the car with his finger stabbing the air like a knife. "What the fuck were you thinking, ditching us like that? What the hell, man?"

The four passengers got out of the sedan, Sir Jim with some significant help from Miles. Boon could have used a hand as well since he was moving very gingerly now that he'd been sitting for a while and his body had stiffened up. The aches and pains he'd been able to ignore in the factory were back in spades, almost as if he were suffering from a sudden attack of arthritis. The possibility of a hot bath, as unlikely as it was, sounded like a stellar idea. Steve rounded the car until the two were face to face.

"Whoa, there. Take it easy, big guy," Boon implored, his hands up and calling for a truce.

"Don't you tell me to take it easy!" Kempler snapped. "You fucking tricked us this morning and took off. Friends don't do that to friends, Dohir. We're a team. We were supposed to do this together!"

Clem detoured around Steve and planted himself squarely in front of Boon, towering over him by at least six inches. The normally sedate Southerner's face was locked down as if he were struggling to keep unfamiliar emotions in check. His quivering chin was the only indication of how upset he truly was.

"Tell me y'all took care of that son of a bitch," he said quietly, his hands clenched at his sides. "For Patrice. Tell me y'all killed him for what he did to her."

Boon's lips pursed as he considered his words, remembering the warning from Hollenbeck. In the end, he reached out and rested his hand on Clem's arm, who stiffened at the touch. Finally, he simply said, "Yeah, we did."

Clem stared at him a few seconds longer, as if he was about to demand a full recounting of the drug lord's demise, but he stopped short when he noticed the bruised expression stamped across Boon's face. His eyes glistened as he said, "Good. That's what I needed to hear."

Boon's declaration of Galo's demise served to calm Kempler instantly, like water dousing a fire. His big friend's breathing slowed, and his rage and reddish complexion diminished in equal amounts. He studied Hollenbeck and then Sasha as if for confirmation.

"Do I want to know how it all went down?" he asked them, one eyebrow raised.

"No," Boon answered him quietly. "Trust me. You don't."

"Okay, guess I'll take your word for it." Then his face broke into a huge grin, the remainder of his anger turned off like a switch had been flipped. He spread his arms out wide, almost as if he were about to initiate a group hug. "That's it? We can go back to our lives now?"

Hollenbeck walked around the car and faced him. "Not quite. I need you to do one more thing for me. If you're up to it, that is."

Kempler squinted at him, his hackles raised again. "Why don't you tell me what you want before I agree, Mr. FBI guy? I've been conned by you two before, and I'm in no hurry to fall for something again."

The FBI agent pulled his phone from his pocket and held it out. "Simple. It starts with a phone call."

29

It was early evening, and the country club on Dayton's east side was not nearly as crowded as the last time they'd been there. Boon and Kempler were at the first tee already, leaning against their cart and working to appear casual. Each man had a club out, but only Steve held his with any real intent, swinging it back and forth like a pendulum and hacking divots out of the pristine grass. Boon's injured hand was so sore that doing anything more than gripping his was out of the question.

With an impatient grumble, Steve began prowling back and forth around the tee box like a bear on a leash. His choice of outfits this time around, orange pants and a fluorescent yellow shirt, was so bright he could have been spotted from space. Not for the first time, Boon wondered where he found clothing like that.

"Where the fuck are they?" Kempler growled under his breath.

Boon had no answer to that, and was about to say so when he heard his name called. He shot a glance over his shoulder towards the clubhouse and saw Jeff Barton, the federal judge from Dayton, waving at him. The man's white hair was so distinctive he would have been recognizable from anywhere. Boon wondered if he had it colored. A few dozen steps in his wake came his clerk, Larry Block. The young man was struggling with the pair's oversized golf bags. As Boon watched, Larry stumbled and one of the bags crashed to the ground.

"Dammit, Larry, be careful with those!" the judge snapped at him, instantly furious. "Those clubs cost more than your car."

"Sorry, your Honor," Larry replied, the apology sounding very routine. He hefted a bag onto each shoulder again and carefully made his way toward them. The weight of the clubs made him waddle like an oversized duck.

When Judge Barton was less than a dozen yards away, he caught his first good look at Boon. He pulled up short, genuinely shocked. His white eyebrows arched in surprise.

"Jesus, Dohir, what the hell happened to you?" he asked. "You look like hell."

Boon grinned as well as he could, and gestured at his face. "What, this? Just a little car accident a few days ago, that's all. Took an airbag to the face. I'm fine."

"Good lord, man, looks someone beat you with a bag of nickels. Are you certain you're up for a round? I'm not sure you should be driving golf balls, much less a cart. Can you even see with that thing on?" the judge asked, pointing at the eye patch.

"Hey," Kempler interjected with a grin and slap on Boon's back that caused his good eye to water. "What are you complaining about? This might be the only time we're able to beat the son of a bitch!"

Barton didn't seem convinced. "Steve, when you called and asked if we wanted to play another round today, I was happy to oblige. But, Boon, I've seen corpses in better shape."

"Honestly, your honor, some physical activity is just what I need to work out the kinks. I'll be fine," he assured him.

Both newcomers were dubious, but before they could mount any kind of protest, Kempler said, "What do you say we mix up the foursomes? Your honor, I'll pair up with you, and Boon and Larry can share the other cart. Deal? Judge, why don't you tee off first this time."

Still clearly doubting Boon's ability to play, much less stand, the judge accepted his driver from Larry and stepped up to the number one tee. As he was warming up and doing some light stretching, Larry strapped his bag on Boon's cart and the two sat down to wait their turns. Boon carefully placed his phone in the cart's cubby in front of them.

"Wow, you really do look like crap," the young man commented, appraising him up and down. "That must have been one helluva wreck."

"I'll be fine," he reiterated, trying to sound calm even though his pounding heart said otherwise. Larry Block was no longer paying attention to Boon and was busy arranging some balls in the tray by his knees. That done, he clipped the scorecard onto the steering wheel and began to slip on his glove. Boon wondered for the hundredth time how Hollenbeck did this sort of thing day after day. He took a deep breath and, in a voice too low to be heard outside their immediate area, he said to Larry, "Galo still wants to make the deal."

At the mention of the drug lord's name, the clerk jerked so violently that he nearly fell out of the cart. His eyes grew so wide they appeared unnatural, and what little natural color he had in his face drained away until he looked more like an animated cadaver than a living person.

"W-what did you just say?"

Boon never stopped staring at him. He leaned closer, doing his best to project confidence and trust. "Galo. He still wants to make the deal. He's tied up with some other business and wanted me to let you know."

Larry's head whipped from side to side. "How do you know about that? How do you know him?"

"We're business partners, I guess you could say. He's busy right now, but wanted me to close the deal with you today. I'm assuming you want your payment deposited in the Ohio Citizens National Bank like usual, right?"

Larry shot a furtive glance over Boon's shoulder to check out the judge. "Of course, I do. Where else could we do it? But we can't talk about this now, you idiot. What if he hears you?"

"The judge?"

"Yes, of course, the judge!" the young man hissed, visibly shaken. "If anyone finds out about this I'm screwed!"

Boon sat back in the cart. He tapped his pencil on the steering wheel as he considered what to say next. "Okay. I'm authorized to make the payment, and Leslie Harbaugh at the bank will take care of it for you, just like before."

"And don't forget, it's more this time. A shitload more. That's what I negotiated with that son of a bitch. For me and the other clerks. Don't forget about them. We're all in this together."

The moment Larry said that it all clicked into place; Galo had come to the states to negotiate with Larry, to guarantee his mole kept working behind the scenes on the drug lord's behalf. Galo hadn't trusted the reason for his trip to anyone, not even Gonzalez. He must have considered Larry and the other clerks too valuable to leave the negotiations to anyone but himself. That was why the clerk's phone number had been on the top of Galo's recent calls.

"Sure. No problem, I'll take care of them, too," he said in confirmation, not even blinking when he heard Larry's use of the plural, as in "clerks."

"Good. Now can we please stop talking about this? I've been a nervous fucking wreck since this started, and you're not helping. Just make the payment, and I'll keep working behind the scenes for…him." Larry tamped sudden sweat from his forehead with a towel. He held his hands out and saw they were shaking. "Jesus, look at that. I hope I can hit the damn ball now."

At the first tee, the judge finally finished his pregame warmup. He took a measured swing, and his ball soared down the fairway, landing several hundred yards out and just short of several trees. He turned to Kempler with a huge grin.

"Damn, I love it when it works," he said, pleased with himself.

Steve looked over and caught Boon's eye, who gave him a slight nod. His friend stood there for a moment, sighed, then walked to his cart and slid his driver back into the bag. He began taking off his glove.

Judge Barton stared at him, confusion contorting his otherwise handsome face. He pointed to the tee box. "What the hell are you doing? You're up."

Steve tossed his glove into the cubby of their cart. "Sorry, your honor. The game's over."

Barton opened his mouth, but clamped it shut as he noticed four men in dark suits walking toward them, one pair coming from the parking lot, and the other from the clubhouse. One of them was Hal Hollenbeck, his gold-rim glasses glinting in the late afternoon sunshine. The four bypassed the judge and zeroed in on Larry Block, who, by the look of dawning terror on his face, was beginning to comprehend what was happening. They surrounded the cart before the young clerk could make a move. Boon picked up the cell phone out of the drink cubby. The screen showed a call in progress. As he stood, he hung up and held it out to Hollenbeck.

"You got all that, right?" he asked, handing the device to the agent.

Hollenbeck held up his own phone. "I did. All recorded right here for posterity and evidence."

"Good. Because I really didn't want to go through that again."

Hal patted him on the shoulder as Boon walked past him, and then the agent turned to the young clerk. "Larry Block, you're under arrest," he said, flashing his FBI credentials at him.

The clerk's eyes flicked wildly around as if he were trying to manufacture an escape. For half a second Boon thought he was going to make a run for it, but the men spotted this and boxed him in. There was nowhere to go.

Judge Barton stormed up to them, his club gripped in his hand. He shook it at Hollenbeck fiercely. "This is an outrage! What is the meaning of this?" he shouted, his voice overflowing with anger and privilege. "Don't you know who I am?"

"As a matter of fact, I do, your Honor," Hollenbeck said.

"Then you know this is my clerk. How dare you try to arrest him. What's this all about? What are the charges?"

Hollenbeck put his wallet away. "Money laundering. Aiding and abetting. Receiving stolen property. Conspiracy. That's just for starters. Sir, Larry Block has been working on behalf of the head of El Grupo Nuevo, one of the most ruthless drug lords in Mexico," he began. "His name's Galo. You may have heard of him. We've been after him for years, but every time we tried to arrest him, he managed to elude us. We thought he had somehow managed to get actual judges or agents within the FBI on his payroll, but he was smarter than that." He turned to Larry, who appeared close to puking on the spot.

"No, he went a few levels down," he continued. "He bribed Larry and other clerks like him to feed him inside information. You know how the system works, your Honor: every time we file a search or arrest warrant, it has to go through the clerks before you and your fellow judges sign off on it. Armed with that knowledge, these clerks were able to warn our target ahead of time, giving him a chance to escape. It's a failing in the overall system that we'll need to address. Honestly, I'm rather upset with myself for not figuring it out sooner."

One of the agents handcuffed Larry behind his back, the metallic ratcheting the same as on any cop show. One second later, perhaps with the sudden ramifications of his arrest truly sinking in, the clerk did vomit. His last meal splattered on the floor of the cart. To their credit, none of the FBI agents even flinched, although one may have sneered when a glob of something landed on his shoe.

"I'm not cleaning that up," Kempler stated with distaste, pointing.

Judge Barton stepped up to Larry. The pained look on his face was clear for everyone to see. "Is this true? Did you really do this?"

The clerk's eyes were screwed shut, and his head was down. He was shaking all over, tremors that traveled from head to toe. "I'm not saying anything. I want a lawyer."

"My god, man, I trusted you," the judge continued, his anger on the rise. "You had tremendous potential. Why would you do this?"

Larry Block wouldn't answer, but Boon did. "Money, your Honor. Take it from me, undergrad and law school wracks up huge bills. Hundreds of thousands of dollars. My guess is they saw this as a way to get out of debt quickly and kickstart their careers. Right, Larry?"

The clerk still wouldn't look up. "I want my lawyer," he repeated, now close to tears.

"And it's not just him. We'll find a whole network of clerks on the take," Boon continued. "I thought it was just Larry at first, but now I'm positive that's not the case."

Wide-eyed, the judge took a step back. In that disappointed tone a parent would reserve for a troubled child, he shook his head. "My god, man, I can't believe you would do this to me. If this is true and the press finds out, it could be the end of my career. I could be kicked off the bench! Did you ever think about what this could do to me?"

Block lifted his head, and his eyes were suddenly fierce. "No, you pompous asshole, I didn't. You've treated me like shit ever since I got here. No, I wasn't thinking about you! All I ever wanted was to get the hell away from you and start my own life, but I couldn't. I'm up to my ass in debt and thought I'd never get out. But you didn't care, did you? No, you only care about yourself." He barked out a laugh. "I hope they do kick you off the bench, you pretentious prick!"

Hollenbeck motioned to the other three FBI agents, and they began dragging Larry away towards the parking lot. As they pulled the shocked clerk along, he could hear one of them begin reading him his Miranda Rights. His emotional outburst over, the young man stumbled and nearly fell, but the agents grasping his arms held him up. The sounds of his sobs slowly faded as they grew distant.

"Your honor," Hal said, sidling up to the judge. "We'll do our best to keep this out of the papers, but I can't make any assurances. Right now, I suggest you go home and get some rest. Agents from the Bureau will come to your office in the morning to ask you some questions. I suspect it will be a long day. I recommend you contact your lawyer."

Judge Barton stood there in stunned silence, his mouth working soundlessly like a goldfish in a bowl. It was just beginning to dawn on him, Boon thought, how much hell he was about to go through. He himself had done no wrong, not legally, but his proximity to the crime would forever haunt him. He might not be removed from the bench, but his career as he knew it was likely over. The club the judge was holding slipped from his fingers and fell to the ground, forgotten, and he walked in a daze towards the clubhouse. He weaved when he went, as if he were slightly drunk.

"Hey, he forgot his clubs," Kempler said.

Hollenbeck turned to Boon, and his face softened. His eyes behind the gold-rim glasses crinkled in a smile. "You did great. Thank you. We never would have gotten this far without you."

Boon dipped his head, guilt overriding any sense of accomplishment. "Yeah, well, I'm glad I could do this much. Especially after everything else, you know?"

Kempler's belly laugh was loud on the quiet course. "Hell, yeah, we all know! But what a fucking adventure, right? I mean, what a great tale to tell when we're old and gray."

Hollenbeck cocked an eyebrow at him. "When you're old and gray? Sure, that should be long enough. But until then, not a word about this to anyone. Understand? You can't say anything to anybody outside your group about this."

Steve rolled his eyes. "Yeah, okay, I get it. But you're killing me, man. What a great story!"

"Sorry, but that's the way it has to be. But for now," he added, indicating the parking lot, "let's get you guys back to the house with the others."

Kempler picked up his clubs. "No, if you don't mind I'm going to call a cab and get home. I've got some damage to my house I need to work on. Plus, I need to check on my son. I haven't talked to him in days, and I miss the hell out of him. If that's okay with you, Mr. FBI guy."

"That's fine. And, after the US Government repairs the back end of your SUV, I'll make sure it's delivered to your house. And I may be in touch before then. You never know."

Kempler laughed. "Hey, no worries. Call anytime. This cloak and dagger shit's in my blood now!"

The agent smiled and started walking, purposefully giving Steve and Boon a moment to themselves. Kempler's jovial manner waned, replaced by one filled with a combination of warmth and concern. "You let me know if you need anything, you got that? I'm serious."

Boon's smile may have been minimal, but it was heartfelt. Whatever friendship they had shared before all this began paled compared to what it had become. Shared experiences, especially traumatic ones, tended to do that. "I can't thank you enough. We never could have done this without you, you know."

"Hell no you couldn't have!" Kempler laughed loudly, his head back. "But I wouldn't have missed it for the world. Don't be a stranger, Boon. Or Robin Hood. Or whatever the hell your real name is."

Dohir extended his hand for a handshake, but Steve knocked it aside and enveloped him in a bear hug. He squeezed so hard Boon may have re-cracked several ribs, but he was in no hurry to break the embrace. When the two pulled apart, Kempler gave him a final shake and began heading towards the clubhouse, whistling. Dohir watched his broad backside until he rounded a corner and was gone. They had spent so much time together the last few weeks that, without his boisterous friend by his side, the world suddenly seemed a little smaller and not nearly as bright.

He sighed, then hurried after the FBI agent. When he caught up with him, the two climbed into the sedan. Once they were buckled in and driving south, Boon turned to Hollenbeck.

"That's it then, right?" he said, the question sounding almost like a statement. "Galo is gone and you've got your leak. Or leaks, to be precise."

"Yes, that's it for you. I've got interrogations and more arrests ahead of me, followed by several weeks of paperwork. But I'm used to that."

Boon's tone turned sober. "We did what you asked," he told him. "Now you need to keep your end of the bargain. My friends all go free. Right?"

Hal's eyes never wavered from the road. "Of course. You have my word. I'll do my best to bury their names so far in the case files no one will ever know they were involved. A deal is a deal."

Boon stared straight ahead as the agent drove. He wondered if Hollenbeck was being totally honest. After all, Luis and the blond woman were still alive, and he had no idea what they might say to others - which meant there was always the chance their identities and involvement could be spilled. He realized he should be more concerned with that, but he also knew there was nothing he could do about it now. That was a problem for future Boon to worry about.

"I do have some questions I'd like answers to," the agent continued. "Starting with Larry Block's involvement with Galo. How'd you piece that together? We never could."

"Pure dumb luck, that's how," Boon admitted. "I'd like to say it was brilliant sleuthing on my part, but I'd be lying. When I had Galo's phone and scrolled through his recent calls, Larry's number at the top of the list jumped out at me. There was no reason those two should be connected, and yet here it was, right in front of me. Then I remembered that Larry was Judge Barton's clerk, and it sort of fell into place."

Hal's head shook back and forth. "No, I get the part about you recognizing his phone number. That's not what I was talking about. What I mean is, what made you connect Larry's job as Barton's clerk with how Galo was getting his backdoor information? Clerking and what it entails is not something the average Joe knows about. Not unless you've got a background in law, that is."

Boon was silent for a moment, his finger tapping on the armrest of the car. He and Hollenbeck had been through hell and back together. He owed the agent so much, including his newfound relationship with Sasha. In fact, he doubted he'd even be alive now without him. He looked out the side window and started talking.

"To answer that, we're going to have to go back in time a little, so bear with me," he began. "Let's say there was this young guy, we'll call him William. Will was a solid high school student and a very good athlete. A three-sport athlete, as a matter of fact. Was top of his class, too. Graduated with honors from college, and went on to a pretty prestigious law school. But during his first year, his parents both died in a freak boating accident. One of those stupid things that just seem to happen and makes the local news for a day or two. Will had no siblings, his grandparents were long gone, and his parents were both only children, so he was alone after that. No family at all." Boon paused, his mind turned inward.

"Go on," Hal urged him gently.

Boon sighed. "Will went on to graduate from law school and was studying for the bar when he went out with some friends one night. No drinking, just taking a break from the books. It was storming like hell when he left, and the roads were awful. On the drive home, he clipped the rear bumper of an SUV that had almost stopped because of the storm. It spun into a flooded ditch on the side of the road and flipped over. Will did the right thing and went back to help whoever was in the vehicle. There was just one person inside, a young girl, but she was trapped and he couldn't get her out fast enough. She was underwater too long. In the end, the girl survived, but she suffered brain damage. And ever since she's been in a persistent vegetative state." Boon took a deep breath, as if to steady himself.

"Turns out," he finally continued, "the girl was alone, too, just like Will. Parents had passed away already. No siblings. She was struggling to put herself through college by working two jobs. In fact, she was coming home from her gig as a waitress when the accident happened. She had no real money, no savings, and no one to take care of her.

"Will knew right then he had a choice to make," Boon went on. "Without someone to watch out for her, she'd become a ward of the state and would end up in some crappy state-run facility for the rest of her life. He couldn't live with that."

"So, he did something about it," Hal said.

"He did. He knew he needed money, a lot of it, if he was going to take care of her properly. With a bright future as an attorney, he had no doubt he'd be doing well later in life, but that wasn't going to be soon enough. Instead, Will dropped out of sight completely and began a different career, one where he could generate significant income right away.

And guess what? Just like everything else he tried, he was pretty damn good at that, too. He made more than he thought possible, all under the table and tax-free. Ends up he made so much he was able to bring on more people to help. He had an entire team making money. After that, the cash came in so fast he was able to spread it around and do good things for the community. Baseball diamonds in underprivileged areas. Flipping houses for people who needed places to live. Starting homeless shelters. But," Boon continued, "he couldn't get the memory of her out of his mind. No matter what he did. That's…that's when the drinking started. But even so, no matter how many times he got hammered, no matter how blackout drunk he got, the image of her forever on that hospital bed haunted him. And trust me, boy did he get hammered. All the time. He achieved pro-level status doing everything he could to keep from thinking about her. But nothing he did worked."

Hal kept his eyes on the road while traffic moved all around them. "This girl. Is she still in a coma?"

"She is, and probably will be forever. But he's going to make sure she's as comfortable and well-taken care of as possible, for as long as she lives."

Hollenbeck turned towards Boon. "Are you still drinking like that?" he asked, the pretense of the third person gone. "Are you going to be okay?"

"Honestly, I don't know. It's been really bad for a long time. But I haven't had a drink in more than a week. And you know what? I barely miss it. I thought I would, but I don't. I was drinking to forget, you know, to keep my mind in a constant fog when I wasn't busy. I always tried to keep myself occupied with work or working out, but you can't do that all the time no matter how hard you try. It was during the down times when the memories of what I'd done would come flooding back. I couldn't deal with it. So, I'd get hammered, and for a short while, I wouldn't think about it. It's amazing how well a bottle of booze can bless you with temporary amnesia. At least, until you're sober again."

"And now? Things are different?"

Boon almost permitted himself the beginnings of a smile. "They are. Or, at least I think they are. I've got Sasha and my friends now, people I care about and who care about me. You know," he said, almost sounding surprised. "I've been alone ever since the accident, living like a recluse in the middle of a million people. It's like I've been asleep all this time. But that's changed now. I'm finally awake. Does that make sense?"

"Sure. I get it."

"That isolation was the worst thing I could have done to myself. I don't want that anymore. I'm done with being alone. I want more."

Hal came up to the West Chester exit and followed the gradual curve of the road off the highway. Neither spoke as they neared the house where they'd been staying.

"Listen," Hal finally said. "I'll do all I can to keep you and your friends out of this, just like I promised. You've proven yourself to be very useful. Don't be surprised if I call on you for help again in the future."

Boon barked out a single laugh. "You're kidding, right? I hated every minute of that shit. I'll never understand how you do it."

Hollenbeck grinned as he turned into the driveway. "I'm not saying it'll ever happen, but it might. Like I told you, I'm going to take a break for a while, but probably not forever. You never know when I might need to help outside of normal channels again. You guys are very good at this, whether you know it or not. And to show how serious I am, go ahead and keep the Marsden money. If I turn it in, it'll just go to waste in some government account to pay off a microsecond of the national debt." He paused, considering. "Well, we have to pay Dante and his friends, but the rest is yours. Keep doing your Robin Hood gig. Or split it up between your friends. They deserve it, too."

Boon stared at him, certain the agent must have been concussed by Gonzalez. Truth be told, in all the commotion he had almost forgotten about the money. He also understood he was now in Hal's debt, and he had little doubt the agent would come to collect down the road. But that was okay, too, especially as he began to consider how much good he could do with a bankroll of this magnitude. It was then that Boon recalled the conversation he and Sasha had shared regarding the fate of the yellow factory. Hadn't he told her it would be a great place for a low-income apartment building? Damn if that didn't sound like a project right in Robin Hood's wheelhouse.

Meanwhile, Hal parked and killed the engine. As the two men got out of the car, the back door of the house burst open and Sasha rushed toward him, a rare look of joyous relief filling her face. She ran to Boon and hugged him tight, her head buried in his shoulder. The two of them clung together for a long time. Miles and Clem followed close behind and hurried towards the couple. Sir Jim was last, a vast smile visible through his beard. To a man, he could see how relieved they were to see their friend back safe and sound.

The agent looked at him over the roof of the car. "Hey, Boon. Or is it Will?"

He lifted his head from Sasha's shoulder. "Yeah?"

"You sure you're going to be okay?"

Boon smiled, then intertwined his fingers and noisily cracked his knuckles. "Yeah, Hal, I think I'm going to be just fine."